Th_____es
int_____an
ele_____to
the_____lo.
Leia O_____ry
figures _____xt
month, vete_____nor Kathy
Tyers continues the epic struggle between
good and evil, as the New Republic, led by
the battered but still unbroken Jedi, braces
for the next onslaught of its merciless alien
foe . . .

*In the aftermath of one tragedy,
will a young Jedi's search for
redemption lead to yet another?*

BALANCE POINT
by Kathy Tyers

**Coming to bookstores in
November 2000!**

Also by James Luceno:

The *Robotech* Series (as Jack McKinney, with Brian Daley)

The Black Hole Travel Agency Series (as Jack McKinney, with Brian Daley)

A Fearful Symmetry

Illegal Alien

The Big Empty

Kaduna Memories

The Young Indiana Jones Chronicles:
   The Mata Hari Affair

The Shadow

The Mask of Zorro

Río Pasión

Rainchaser

Rock Bottom

STAR WARS

THE NEW JEDI ORDER

Agents of Chaos II

JEDI ECLIPSE

James Luceno

A Del Rey® Book
THE BALLANTINE PUBLISHING GROUP • NEW YORK

A Del Rey® Book
Published by The Ballantine Publishing Group

www.starwars.com
www.starwarskids.com
www.randomhouse.com/delrey/

Library of Congress Card Number: 00-191290

ISBN 0-345-42859-5

Manufactured in the United States of America

First Edition: October 2000

10 9 8 7 6 5 4 3 2 1

For Carmen, Carlos,
and Dimitri—
13 years after.

ACKNOWLEDGMENTS

For looking over my shoulder and enriching this book, heartfelt thanks to Shelly Shapiro, Sue Rostoni, Dan Wallace, and Alex Newborn.

UNKNOWN REGIONS
SSI-RUUK STAR CLUSTER
ORD MANTELL
ANOBIS
VORTEX
BILBRINGI
REECEE
CORUSCANT
KOORNACHT CLUSTER
DEEP CORE
ALDERAAN
KUAT
COMMENOR
CORE WORLDS
CORELLIA
FONDOR
DURO
GYNDINE
INNER
COLONIES
RHOMMAMOOL
OSARIAN
BAKURA
ENDOR
CORELLIAN TRADE SPINE
RIM
YAG'DHUL
TYNNA
EXPANSION REGION
MID RIM
VAIRONAT
BESPIN
HOTH
ISON
SENEX-JUVEX SECTORS
RIMMA TRADE ROUTE
BOTHAN SPACE
RODIA
BOTHAWUI
UMGUL
NABOO
SULLUST
ERIADU
CORELLIAN RUN
ROON
OUTER
CLAK'DOR VII
SLUIS VAN
DAGOBAH
TATOOINE
RYLOTH
ELROOD SECTOR
ZHAR
AIZOC III
KATHOL SECTOR
MINOS CLUSTER
WILD SPACE

STAR WARS: THE NOVELS

44 YEARS BEFORE
STAR WARS: A New Hope

Jedi Apprentice #1–2

32 YEARS BEFORE
STAR WARS: A New Hope

Star Wars:
Episode I
The Phantom Menace

22 YEARS BEFORE
STAR WARS: A New Hope

Star Wars:
Episode II

20 YEARS BEFORE
STAR WARS: A New Hope

Star Wars:
Episode III

3 YEARS AFTER
STAR WARS: A New Hope

Star Wars:
Episode V The Empire
Strikes Back
Tales of the Bounty
Hunters

3.5 YEARS AFTER
STAR WARS: A New Hope

Shadows of the Empire

4 YEARS AFTER
STAR WARS: A New Hope

Star Wars: Episode VI
Return of the Jedi
Tales from Jabba's Palace
THE BOUNTY HUNTER WARS:
The Mandalorian Armor
Slave Ship
Hard Merchandise
The Truce at Bakura

6.5–7.5 YEARS AFTER
STAR WARS: A New Hope

X-Wing: Rogue Squadron
X-Wing: Wedge's Gamble
X-Wing: The Krytos Trap
X-Wing: The Bacta War
X-Wing: Wraith Squadron
X-Wing: Iron Fist
X-Wing: Solo Command

14 YEARS AFTER
STAR WARS: A New Hope

The Crystal Star

16–17 YEARS AFTER
STAR WARS: A New Hope

THE BLACK FLEET CRISIS
TRILOGY:
Before the Storm
Shield of Lies
Tyrant's Test

17 YEARS AFTER
STAR WARS: A New Hope

The New Rebellion

18 YEARS AFTER
STAR WARS: A New Hope

THE CORELLIAN TRILOGY:
Ambush at Corellia
Assault at Selonia
Showdown at Centerpoint

— What Happened When?

10–0 YEARS BEFORE
STAR WARS: A New Hope

THE HAN SOLO TRILOGY:
The Paradise Snare
The Hutt Gambit
Rebel Dawn

APPROX. 5–2 YRS. BEFORE
STAR WARS: A New Hope

THE ADVENTURES OF LANDO CALRISSIAN:
Lando Calrissian and the Mind-harp of Sharu
Lando Calrissian and the Flamewind of Oseon
Lando Calrissian and the Star-cave of Thonboka

THE HAN SOLO ADVENTURES:
Han Solo at Stars' End
Han Solo's Revenge
Han Solo and the Lost Legacy

STAR WARS:
Episode IV
A New Hope

0–3 YEARS AFTER
STAR WARS: A New Hope

Tales from the
Mos Eisley Cantina
Splinter of the Mind's Eye

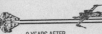

8 YEARS AFTER
STAR WARS: A New Hope

The Courtship of Princess Leia

9 YEARS AFTER
STAR WARS: A New Hope

THE THRAWN TRILOGY:
Heir to the Empire
Dark Force Rising
The Last Command
X-Wing: Isard's Revenge

11 YEARS AFTER
STAR WARS: A New Hope

THE JEDI ACADEMY TRILOGY:
Jedi Search
Dark Apprentice
Champions of the Force
I, Jedi

12–13 YEARS AFTER
STAR WARS: A New Hope

Children of the Jedi
Darksaber
Planet of Twilight
X-Wing: Starfighters of Adumar

---

19 YEARS AFTER
STAR WARS: A New Hope

THE HAND OF THRAWN DUOLOGY:
Specter of the Past
Vision of the Future

22 YEARS AFTER
STAR WARS: A New Hope

JUNIOR JEDI KNIGHTS:
The Golden Globe
Lyric's World
Promises
Anakin's Quest
Vader's Fortress
Kenobi's Blade

23–24 YEARS AFTER
STAR WARS: A New Hope

YOUNG JEDI KNIGHTS:
Heirs of the Force
Shadow Academy
The Lost Ones
Lightsabers
The Darkest Knight
Jedi Under Siege
Shards of Alderaan
Diversity Alliance
Delusions of Grandeur
Jedi Bounty
The Emperor's Plague
Return to Ord Mantell
Trouble on Cloud City
Crisis at Crystal Reef

25 YEARS AFTER
STAR WARS: A New Hope

THE NEW JEDI ORDER:
Vector Prime
Dark Tide I: Onslaught
Dark Tide II: Ruin
Agents of Chaos I:
Hero's Trial
Agents of Chaos II:
Jedi Eclipse

DRAMATIS PERSONAE

Anakin Solo; Jedi Knight (male human)
Beed Thane; archon of Vergill (male human)
Borga Besadii Diori; Hutt ruler (female Hutt)
Brand; New Republic commodore (male human)
Chine-kal; commander, *Crèche* (male Yuuzhan Vong)
Droma; spacer (male Ryn)
Gaph; refugee (male Ryn)
Han Solo; captain, *Millennium Falcon* (male human)
Jacen Solo; Jedi Knight (male human)
Kyp Durron; Jedi Master (male human)
Leia Organa Solo; New Republic ambassador (female human)
Luke Skywalker; Jedi Master (male human)
Malik Carr; commander (male Yuuzhan Vong)
Melisma; refugee (female Ryn)
Nas Choka; supreme commander (male Yuuzhan Vong)
Nom Anor; executor (male Yuuzhan Vong)
Prince Isolder; Royal House of Hapes (male human)
Randa Besadii Diori (male Hutt)
Roa; prisoner (male human)
Sapha; prisoner (female Ryn)
Talon Karrde; liaison (male human)
Viqi Shesh; senator (female human)
Wurth Skidder; Jedi Knight (male human)

ONE

It was morning in Gyndine's capital city, though that fact was scarcely evident to anyone on the surface. The rising sun, when glimpsed at all, was a blanched disk behind roiling smoke belched from flaming forests and buildings. Sounds of battle reverberated thunderously from the surrounding foothills, and a hot scouring wind swept down across the landscape. A crepuscular darkness, ripped ragged by flashes of blinding light, ruled the day.

The artificial light was supplied by warriors and war machines, coursing over scorched ground, streaking through the racked sky, in orbit above the madness. Through leaden clouds allied and enemy fighter craft pursued one another doggedly, adding sonic claps to the strident score of combat. East of the beleaguered capital, beams of energy stabbed mercilessly at the surface from on high, fanning out like shafts of profuse sunlight or concentrated into dazzling curtains that set the horizon glowing red as a frozen dawn.

Loosed by advancing enemy contingents, missiles of superheated rock assailed what remained of the city, holing surviving towers and toppling those already gutted by fire. Hunks of shattered ferrocrete and twisted plasteel tumbled onto cratered streets and clogged alleyways. A few civilians dashed desperately for shelter while others

1

huddled, paralyzed with fear, in gaping, fire-blackened maws that were once entryways and storefronts. In some quarters, ion cannons and nearly depleted turbolaser batteries answered the missile barrage with darts of cyan light. But only in the environs of the New Republic embassy were the enemy projectiles deflected, turned by a hastily installed containment shield.

Dangerously close to the shield's shimmering perimeter, a thousands-strong mixed-species throng, massed behind stun fencing, pressed to be admitted. At the edges of the crowd droids perambulated in a daze, keenly aware of the fate awaiting them should the invaders overrun the city.

Were the stun fence the sole obstacle to safe haven, the crowd might have panicked and stormed the embassy grounds. But the perimeter was reinforced by heavily armed New Republic soldiers, and there was also the force field itself to consider. An umbrella of energy, the lambent shield had to be deactivated before it could be safely breached, and that occurred only when an evacuation ship launched for rendezvous with one of the transports anchored in local space.

Ashen faces masked with cloth against the mephitic air, Gyndine's would-be evacuees did all they could to ensure their survival. With arms extended protectively around the shoulders of terrified children or clasped tightly to tattered bundles of personal belongings, they pleaded with the soldiers, tendered bribes, inveigled and threatened. Ordered to remain silent, the grim-faced troops offered neither comforting looks nor words of encouragement. Only their eyes belied the seeming dispassion, racing about like taurill or angling imploringly toward the one person who could accede to the entreaties and demands.

Leia Organa Solo caught one such glance now, aimed

her way by a human soldier posted close to what had become the communications bunker. With her face smudged and her long hair captured under a brimmed cap, it was unlikely that anyone in the crowd recognized her as onetime hero of the Rebel Alliance and former chief of state, but the sky-blue combat overalls—bloused sleeves emblazoned with the emblem of SELCORE, the Senate Select Committee for Refugees—identified her as everyone's best chance for rescue, their purveyor of deliverance. As it was, she couldn't venture within five meters of the stun fence without having wailing infants, necklaces of prayer beads, or rushed missives to offworld loved ones extended to her in dire urgency.

She didn't dare make eye contact with anyone, lest in her gaze someone read hope or evidence of her anguish. To provide some measure of equipoise, she drew deeply on the Force. But more often than not she paced unswervingly between the bunker and the leading edge of the shield, eager for word that another evacuation ship had landed and was waiting to be filled.

Ever in her wake moved faithful Olmahk, whose native gray ferocity made him appear more stalker than bodyguard. But at least the diminutive Noghri looked at home among the chaos, whereas C-3PO—his normally auric gleam dulled by soot and ash—was positively dismayed. Lately, though, the protocol droid's apprehension had less to do with his own safety than with the larger threat the Yuuzhan Vong posed to all machine life, often the first to suffer when a world fell.

A forceful explosion rocked the permacrete under Leia's feet, and a swirling globe of orange fire mushroomed from the heart of the city. A searing wind laced with droplets of even hotter rain tugged at Leia's cap and jumpsuit. Created by the energy exchanges and conflagrations, microclimatic storms had been washing across the plateau all night long. Hail mixed with cinders lifted from Gyndine's ruined surface pelted everyone, blistering exposed flesh like acid. Even through the insulated soles of knee-high boots, Leia could feel the ground's aberrant heat.

A loud sizzling sound made her swing toward the shield in time to see it evanesce in undulating waves of distortion.

"Evac ship away," a soldier reported from the communications bunker, both hands pressed to the outsize earmuffs of his comm helmet. "Two more headed down the well."

Leia raised her eyes to the tenebrous sky. Defined by running lights as oblate in shape, the departing ship raised itself on repulsor power, then shot upward on a column of blue fire, escorted by half a dozen X-wings. Lying in ambush, a cataract of coralskippers vectored in from the foothills to give chase.

Leia whirled to the soldiers posted at the stun fence. "Admit the next group!"

Crushed shoulder to shoulder, cheek to jowl, folks at the forward edge of the crowd—humans, Sullustans, Bimms, and others—were funneled through the embassy gates. With the shield lowered, enemy projectiles that would have been deflected plummeted like fiery meteors, one of them striking the east wing of the Imperial-era embassy and setting it ablaze.

Leia clapped the evacuees on the back as they streamed toward a shuttle craft idling on the landing zone. "Hurry!" she urged. "Hurry!"

"Shield repowering," the same comm officer relayed from the bunker. "Everyone back."

Leia gritted her teeth. These were the worst moments, she told herself.

Soldiers at the gate resealed the cordon and scanned

the vicinity for evidence of field disruptors. In response the crowd surged forward, railing against what had to seem the inequity, the arbitrariness of it all. Folks closest to the front, fearing they would miss their chance at salvation by one or two persons, tried to worm or force their way past the soldiers, while those in the rear shoved and scrambled, determined to fight their way forward. Leia saw that it was futile, and yet the crowd refused to disperse, hoping against hope that New Republic forces could keep the invaders at bay until every civilian and noncombatant was evacuated.

"Mistress Leia," C-3PO said, approaching in haste with his hands raised and his photoreceptors glowing, "the deflector shield is weakening! If we don't leave soon, we're sure to perish!"

As many would that day, Leia thought.

"We'll leave on the last ship," she told C-3PO, "not before. Until then, make yourself useful by cataloging names and species."

C-3PO lifted his arms higher and skittered through an abrupt about-face. "What's to become of us?"

Leia exhaled wearily, wondering, as well.

The bombardment had commenced two days earlier, when a Yuuzhan Vong flotilla had arrived unexpectedly in the nearby Circarpous system from enemy positions in Hutt space. A slapdash attempt had been made to fortify the sector capital, but with fleets and task forces already committed to safeguarding major systems in the Colonies and the Core, the New Republic had little to offer worlds of secondary importance like Gyndine, despite its modest orbital shipyard.

By the same token, there was no rhyme or reason for the Yuuzhan Vong attack—beyond continuing to sow confusion. With the recent fall of several Mid Rim worlds, Gyndine, because of its relative remoteness, had been thought ideal for use as a transit point for refugees, and indeed many of those outside the fence had been shipped in from Ithor, Obroa-skai, Ord Mantell, and a host of enemy-occupied planets. It was becoming clear that the Yuuzhan Vong delighted in pursuing displaced populations almost as much as they delighted in sacrificing captives and immolating droids. Even the ground assault on Gyndine seemed to be their way of proving themselves as adept at seizing worlds as they were at poisoning them.

The voice of the comm officer put a quick end to Leia's musings. "Ambassador, we've got a live surveillance probe feed from the field."

Leia hesitated, then ducked into the bunker, where a reduced-scale hologram, dazzled by noise, had the attention of the several men and women gathered there. It took her a moment to make sense of what she was seeing, and even then part of her refused to accept the truth.

"What in the name of—"

"Fire breathers," someone said, as if anticipating her amazement. "Rumor has it the Yuuzhan Vong stopped off at Mimban so the things could fill up on swamp gas."

Leia's quivering legs urged her to sit, and as she did she brought a hand to her mouth. Parading out of sunrise like the harbingers of a new and dreadful dawn, came a legion of enormous bladderlike creatures, supported on six stubby legs and equipped with arrays of flexible proboscises from which gushed streams of gelatinous flame.

"The methane and hydrogen sulfide have to be mixing with something they carry in their guts to produce that liquid fire," a woman at the controls of the holoprojector commented, more intrigued than horrified. "They're also exhaling antilaser aerosols."

Yet another example of the enemy's genetically engineered monstrosities, the thirty-meter-tall fire breathers didn't so much march as loll over the terrain, like loosely tethered lighter-than-air balloons, incinerating everyone and everything in their path.

Leia could almost smell the nidor of the carnage.

"Whatever they are, they've got thick hides," the comm officer said. "Can't be taken out by anything less than a turbolaser beam."

Unable to slow the advance of the deadly blimps, Gyndine units were abandoning entrenched positions and falling back in droves toward the city. Strewn about were fire-blackened war machines of all variety—tank droids, aged Loronar mobile turbolasers, even a couple of AT-AT walkers, tipped over, headless, collapsed on the ground with legs splayed.

"They're withdrawing!" Leia said harshly. "Who issued the retreat order?"

Even as the words left her mouth, she was sorry she had uttered them. Those officers who weren't scrutinizing her were suddenly studying their hands in unease. Could she blame the troops for retreating when that was precisely what the New Republic had been forced to do almost from the start of the invasion—withdrawing toward the Core, as if the density of the star systems there afforded protection? Who could say any longer which actions were just, and which were dishonorable?

Exiting the bunker without a word, Leia found a shaken C-3PO waiting for her.

"Mistress Leia, the most distressing news has reached me!"

Leia could barely hear him. In the few moments she had spent in the bunker, the battle had advanced to the outskirts of the capital. The crowd was more agitated than before, surging forward and from side to side.

Through a gap in the city's skyline, Leia thought she could discern the bobbing form of a Yuuzhan Vong fire breather.

"It seems," C-3PO was saying, "that Gyndine's citizens are laboring under the impression that you are deliberately discriminating against folks of former Imperial persuasion."

Leia's jaw dropped and her brown eyes flashed. "That's absurd. Do they think I can pick out a former Imperial on sight? And even if I could—"

C-3PO lowered his voice conspiratorially. "In fact, there is some statistical justification for the claim, Mistress. Of the five thousand thus far evacuated, an overwhelming percentage have been inhabitants of worlds whose early loyalty to the Rebel Alliance is well documented. However, I'm certain that owes to nothing more than—"

C-3PO's explanation was swallowed by a deafening explosion. Electricity danced wildly along the periphery of the energy dome, and the shield disappeared. At once, the telltales that lined the stun fence flickered and went out. A frightened gasp rose from the crowd.

"The field generator has been hit!" C-3PO said. "We're done for!"

The crowd surged again, and the soldiers closed ranks. Weapons powered up with an ominous whine.

C-3PO began to back toward the embassy gates. "We'll be crushed!"

With lethal efficiency, Olmahk moved to Leia's side. She was about to caution him to remain calm when one of the soldiers panicked and fired a sonic weapon at point-blank range into the crowd, dropping dozens and sending the rest rushing in all directions.

Without thinking, Leia ran to the dazed soldier and

yanked the weapon from his lax hands. "We're supposed to be rescuing these people, not injuring them!"

She threw the weapon aside. Drawing her hand across her forehead, she inadvertently dislodged the brimmed cap, spilling her hair to her shoulders. Wending her way back to the bunker, she grabbed the nearest comlink and demanded to be put through to the task force commander.

"Ambassador Organa Solo, this is Commander Ilanka," a basso voice responded shortly.

"We need every available ship, Commander—immediately. Yuuzhan Vong forces are entering the city."

Ilanka took a moment to reply. "I'm sorry, Ambassador, but we've got our hands full out here. Three more enemy warships have exited hyperspace on the far side of the moon. Whatever craft are on the surface will have to suffice. I urge you to load and launch. And, Ambassador, I strongly suggest you get yourself aboard one of them."

Leia thumbed the comlink off and scanned the crowd in alarm. *How can I choose?* she asked herself. *How?*

A storm of blazing yorik coral meteors battered the embassy and neighboring buildings, setting fire to all they touched. The inferno triggered an explosion at a fuel dump near the landing zone, fountaining shrapnel far and wide. The right side of Leia's face screamed in pain as something opened a furrow in her cheek. Instinctively she brought her fingertips to the wound, expecting to find blood, but the airborne fragment had cauterized the wound in its white-hot passing.

"Mistress Leia, you're injured!" C-3PO said, but she waved him back before he could reach her. Peripherally she saw that a tall sinewy human was being ushered forward, his arms vised in the grip of two soldiers. Beneath a soft cap he wore low on his forehead, the man's face was bruised and swollen.

"Now what?" Leia asked his custodians.

"An agitator," the shorter soldier reported. "We overheard him telling people in the crowd that we're only extracting New Republic loyals. That anyone with an Imperial past might as well kiss his—"

"I understand, Sergeant," Leia said, cutting him off. She assessed the captive briefly, wondering what he could possibly have to gain by spreading lies. She had her mouth open to ask him when a meaningful sniff from Olmahk put her on alert.

Leia stepped closer to the man and peered intently into his eyes. As she raised her right forefinger, a low growl escaped Olmahk. The captive recoiled when he realized Leia's intent, but his reaction only firmed the soldiers' resolve to hold on to him. Leia's eyes narrowed in certainty. She thrust her finger into the man's face, striking him just where his right nostril curved into his cheek.

To the soldiers' utter astonishment, the man's flesh seemed to recede, taking with it his expression, to reveal a look that combined pain and pride on a face incised with brilliantly colored designs and flourishes. The flesh-like mask that had taken flight at Leia's touch disappeared down the throat of the man's loose-fitting jacket, bunching somewhat as it flayed itself from his torso, only to pour from the cuffs of his trousers like flesh-colored syrup and puddle on the ground at his feet.

The soldiers leapt back in shock, the sergeant drawing his blaster and putting repeated bolts into the living puddle. Free of their grip, the Yuuzhan Vong also took a step back, tearing open the front of his jacket to expose a body vest every bit as alive as the ooglith masquer had been. With his lashless eyes fixed on Leia, he lifted his face and howled a bloodcurdling war cry.

"Do-ro'ik vong pratte!" And woe to our enemies!

"Down! Down!" Leia screamed to everyone nearby.

Olmahk drove her to the ground even as the first of the thud bugs were bursting outward from the Yuuzhan Vong's chest. The sound was not unlike that of corks being popped from bottles of effervescent wine, but accompanying the lively explosions were the pained exclamations of soldiers and hapless civilians who hadn't heard or heeded Leia's counsel. For ten meters in all directions, men and women fell like trees.

Leia felt Olmahk's weight lift from her. By the time she looked up, the Noghri had ripped out the Yuuzhan Vong's throat with his teeth. Left and right, people lay on the ground groaning in pain. Others staggered about with hands pressed to ruptured bellies, compound fractures, broken ribs, or smashed faces.

"Get these people to the battle dressing station!" Leia ordered.

Yorik coral missiles were continuing to rain down on the embassy and the landing zone, where a dozen soldiers were overseeing the loading of the final evacuation craft.

The crowd had long since pushed through the gates, but stun batons and sonics were keeping many from reaching the waiting craft. Groggily, and with Olmahk falling in behind her, Leia began to move that way herself. She spied C-3PO, whose chest plastron had been deeply dented by one of the thud bugs, just above his circular power-recharge coupler.

"Are you all right?" she asked.

He might have blinked if he could. "Thank the maker I lack a heart!"

As the three of them were closing on the evacuation ship a vintage AT-ST limped into view, blackened along one side and leaking hydraulic fluid, its grenade launcher blown away. A lightly armored box perched on reverse-articulated legs, the All Terrain Scout Transport wheezed and clanked to a halt, then collapsed chin first to the permacrete landing apron. In a moment the aft hatch lifted, loosing a cloud of smoke, and a young man crawled coughing but otherwise unharmed from the cockpit.

"Wurth Skidder," Leia intoned, folding her arms across her chest. "I should have known it was you from the brilliance of your entrance."

Blond and sharp-featured, Skidder jumped agilely to his feet and threw off his smoldering Jedi Knight cloak. "The Yuuzhan Vong have overrun our defenses, Ambassador. The fight's lost." He grinned smugly. "I wanted you to be the first to know."

Leia had heard from Luke that Skidder was on Gyndine, but this was her first contact with him. She had had trouble with him during the Rhommamoolian crisis eight months earlier, when he had downed a couple of Rodian-piloted Osarian starfighters intent on interfering with her then-diplomatic duties. At the time she had found him to be reckless, insolent, and overconfident in his abilities, but Luke insisted that the Battle of Ithor, and the injury Skidder had sustained there, had changed him for the better. No doubt because he reveled in being able to put a lightsaber to constant use, Leia thought.

"You're a little late with your update, Wurth," she told him now, "but you're in time for the final flight out of here." She nodded in the direction of the landing zone. "My brother would never forgive me if I didn't see you safely back to Coruscant."

Skidder returned an elaborately chivalrous bow, extending his right arm toward her. "A Jedi avoids argument at all costs." He held her gaze briefly. "Nothing in the Jedi Code about having to answer to civilians, but I'll comply out of respect for your celebrated sibling."

"Fine," Leia said sarcastically. "Just see to it that you

get aboard." Someone tapped her on the shoulder, and she twisted around.

"Ambassador, we're holding space for you, your bodyguard, and droid," a male flight officer reported. "But you'll have to come now, ma'am. The New Republic envoy is already aboard, and we've received orders to lift off."

Leia nodded that she understood, then swung back to Skidder, only to see him running toward the embassy gates. "Skidder!" she yelled, making a megaphone of her hands.

He stopped, turned to her, and waved a hand in what at least appeared to be genuine acknowledgment. "Just one small task to perform," he shouted back.

Leia frowned angrily and turned to the flight officer once more, cutting her eyes back and forth between him and the sizable crowd gathering at the foot of the ship's boarding ramp. "Surely the ship can accommodate a few more."

The officer's lips became a thin line. "We're already at maximum payload, Ambassador." He followed her gaze to the crowd, then blew out his breath. "But we can probably cram in four more."

Leia touched his forearm in indebtedness, and the two of them hastened for the ramp. Behind a barricade of soldiers, at the head of the line of evacuees, stood a group of tailed, spike-haired, and velvet-furred aliens attired in colorful if threadbare vests and wraparound skirts.

Ryn, Leia realized in surprise—the species to which Han's new friend Droma belonged.

"Four," the flight officer reminded, even as Leia was doing a head count of the Ryn. "Some of them will have to be left behind."

Six Ryn, to be exact, she told herself. Even so, four was better than none. She edged between two broad-shouldered soldiers closest to the ramp and beckoned to the aliens in line. "You four," she said, pointing to each in turn. "Hurry!"

Expressions of relief and joy appeared. The chosen four turned to exchange embraces with those who would be abandoned. A swaddled infant was passed from the rear to one of the females up front. Leia heard someone say, "Melisma, should you find Droma, tell him we're here."

Leia gave a start and glanced about for the one who had said the name, but there wasn't time to seek out the Ryn. Already the soldiers were backing their way up the ramp, taking her with them.

"Hold on!" she said, coming to a sudden stop and refusing to be moved. "Skidder. Where's Skidder? Is he already aboard?"

She leaned forward to gaze across the devastated landing zone and spotted him dashing for the ship, dragging a human female behind him and cradling a long-haired infant in his left arm. The sight gave Leia pause. Maybe Skidder had changed, after all.

"Make certain they get aboard," Leia instructed the officer in charge, pausing when a coralskipper-delivered projectile impacted the permacrete only meters from the ramp. "And I don't care if you have to use a shoehorn to do it."

TWO

Death pursued the shuttle to the edge of space, spitting fire from below, needling with fighter-launched missiles, clutching with dovin basals housed in warships anchored just inside Gyndine's envelope. The X-wing escort had to blaze a route through swarms of coralskippers and take on a frigate analog, five pilots sacrificing themselves in the attempt to see the evacuees to safety.

Leia sat in the cramped cockpit watching the battle rage, wondering whether they would reach the transport in time. A ship that had launched before dawn hadn't been so lucky. Hull perforated in several places, the oval craft drifted lazily in golden sunlight, venting atmosphere and debris into space.

Wherever Leia's eye roamed, New Republic and Yuuzhan Vong vessels assailed one another with lasers and missiles, while enemy drop ships fell obliquely into the well, winglike projections extended and ablative coral blushed crimson red. Farther from the planet were the new arrivals Commander Ilanka had mentioned. Two of the ships had tentlike hulls fashioned from some sort of diaphanous material, from which protruded a dozen or more lightning-forked arms, as if dendrites from an insect-spun nest. The third resembled nothing so much as a cluster of conjoined bubbles, or egg sacks waiting to hatch.

In the shuttle's passenger cabin, Gyndine's refugees conversed in hushed tones or prayed boldly to sundry gods. Fear rose off the group in waves that stung Leia's nostrils. She was circulating among them when a familiar shudder passed through the ship, and she recognized with relief that a tractor beam had possession of them.

Moments later the shuttle was pulled gently, almost lovingly into the docking bay of the transport.

But even there death reached for them.

During the deboarding process, a pair of coralskippers that had somehow duped the transport's energy shield came streaking into the hold on a suicide run, skidding across the deck and exploding against a blast shield raised in the nick of time. Several refugees and crew members were killed, and a score more were injured.

Two of Leia's female aides who had remained aboard the transport hurried to her as she was picking herself up off the coral-littered deck. She made plain what she thought of their attempts to comb her hair back from her face.

"You're worried about my hairstyle," she fulminated, "when people here need immediate medical attention?"

"But your cheek," one of the women said, chagrined.

Leia had forgotten all about the shrapnel. Of its own accord her hand reenacted the movement it had made earlier, fingertips tracing the raised edges of the furrow that had been opened. She exhaled wearily and dropped cross-legged to the deck.

"I'm sorry."

Silently she allowed the wound to be ministered to, suddenly aware of just how exhausted she was. When C-3PO and Olmahk came within earshot, she said, "I can't remember when I last slept."

"That would be fifty-seven hours, six minutes ago,

Mistress," C-3PO supplied. "Standard time, of course. If you'd prefer, I could express the duration by other time parts, in which case—"

"Not now, Threepio," Leia said weakly. "In fact, maybe you should immerse yourself in an oil bath before your moving parts freeze up."

C-3PO cocked his head to one side, arms nearly akimbo. "Why, thank you, Mistress Leia. I was beginning to fear I would never again hear those words spoken."

"And you," Leia said, glancing at Olmahk. "See to washing that Yuuzhan Vong's blood off your chin."

The Noghri muttered truculently, then nodded curtly and moved off with C-3PO.

Fifty-seven hours, Leia thought.

Truth be told, she hadn't slept soundly since Han had left Coruscant almost a month earlier. A day didn't pass when she didn't wonder what he was up to, although ostensibly he was searching for Roa, his onetime mentor, who had been captured by the Yuuzhan Vong during a raid on Ord Mantell's orbital facility, the *Jubilee Wheel*, as well as for members of his new Ryn comrade's scattered clan. Was it possible, Leia wondered, that the Droma mentioned on Gyndine was the same one Han was suddenly running with?

Reports would occasionally reach her that the *Millennium Falcon* had been spotted in this system or that one, but Han had yet to contact her personally.

He hadn't been the same since Chewbacca's death not that anyone or anything had, especially occurring when it did, at the start of the Yuuzhan Vong invasion, and largely at their hands. It was natural that Han should mourn Chewie's passing more than anyone, but even Leia had been surprised by the direction he had taken—or the one his unabashed grief had driven him to take. Where Han had always been cheerfully roguish, there was an angry gravity to him now. Anakin had been the first target of his father's outrage; then everyone close to Han had gradually fallen victim to it.

Experts spoke of stages of grief, as if people could be expected to move through them routinely. But in Han the stages were jumbled together—anger, denial, despair—without a hint of resignation, let alone acceptance. Han's stasis was what worried Leia more than anything. Though he would be the first to deny it—vociferously, at that—his grief had fueled a kind of recidivism, a return to the Han of old: the lone Solo, who guarded his sensitivity by keeping himself at arm's length, who claimed not to care about anyone but himself, who allowed thrill to substitute for feeling.

When Droma—another adventurer—had first entered Han's orbit, Leia had feared the worst. But in getting to know the Ryn, even slightly, she had taken heart. While not a replacement for Chewie—for how could anyone replace him?—Droma at least presented Han with the option of forging a new relationship, and if Han could manage that, he just might be able to see his way to reembracing his tried-and-true relationships. Time would tell—about Han, about their marriage, about the Yuuzhan Vong and the fate of the New Republic.

With her cheek sporting a strip of itchy synthflesh, Leia took leave of her aides to wander forward into the passenger hold, where many of the refugees were already claiming areas of deck space. Despite the battle swirling around the transport, an atmosphere of chatty relief prevailed. Leia spotted the New Republic envoy to Gyndine and went over to him. A man of distinguished handsomeness, he sat with his head in his hands.

"I promised I would get everyone offworld," he told

Leia sullenly. "I failed them." He shook his head. "I failed them."

Leia caressed his shoulder in a comforting way. "Awarded the Medal of Honor at the Battle of Kashyyyk, cited for exemplary service during the Yevethan crisis, former member of the Senate Advisory Council to the chief of state . . ." Leia stopped and smiled. "Save your recriminations for the Yuuzhan Vong, Envoy. You did more than anyone thought possible."

She moved on, listening in on scraps of conversation, mostly devoted to the uncertain future, rumors about the horrors of the refugee camps, or criticisms of the New Republic government and military. She was happy to see that the Ryn had found space for themselves, until she realized that they had been banished to a dark corner of the hold, and that no one, of any species, had deigned to sit within a meter of them.

Leia was forced to take a meandering route to them, in and through and sometimes over family groups and others. She addressed the female Ryn who held the child.

"When you were boarding, I heard someone mention the name Droma. Is that a common name among your species? I ask only because I happen to know a Ryn named Droma—slightly, at any rate."

"My nephew," the only male among them answered. "We haven't seen him since the Yuuzhan Vong attacked Ord Mantell. Droma's sister was one of those you . . . who chose to remain behind on Gyndine." He gestured to the infant. "The child is hers."

"Oh, no," Leia said, more to herself. She took a breath and straightened. "I know where your nephew is."

"He's safe then?"

"After a fashion. He's with my husband. They're searching for all of you."

"Ah, sweet irony," the male said. "And now we're further divided."

"As soon as we reach Ralltiir, I'll try to reach my husband."

"Thank you, Princess Leia," the one named Melisma said, catching her completely by surprise.

"Ambassador," she corrected.

They all smiled. "To the Ryn," the male said, "you will forever remain a princess."

The comment warmed and chilled her at once. The Ryn wouldn't have been on Gyndine in the first place if Leia had not relocated them there from Bilbringi. And what of the six she had been forced to leave behind to face imprisonment or death? Was she princess or deserter in the eyes of Droma's sister? The flattering comment had sounded sincere, but it might have been more sweet irony.

Leia was heading for the bridge when the transport sounded general quarters. By the time she reached the command center, the ship was already being jarred by concussive explosions that tested the mettle of the shields.

"Ambassador Organa Solo," Commander Ilanka said from his swivel-mounted chair, as violent light flashed outside the curved viewport. "Glad to have you aboard. It's my understanding that you were last to board the evacuation ship."

"How much trouble are we in?" she asked, ignoring the sarcasm.

"I'd classify our situation as desperate verging on hopeless. Other than that, we're in fine shape."

"Do we have jump capability?"

"Navicomputer's working on coordinates," the navigator said from her console.

"Coralskippers in pursuit," an enlisted-rating added.

Leia glanced at the target-assessment screen, which displayed twenty or more arrowhead shapes, closing fast on the ship. She turned to look out on Gyndine, and again she thought about the thousands she had been forced to abandon to fate. Then it suddenly occurred to her that she hadn't seen Wurth Skidder aboard the shuttle or during her passage through the transport. She was about to page him over the comm when the evac craft's flight officer stepped onto the bridge. He remembered Skidder, along with Leia's orders.

"But when you told me to make sure they got aboard, I thought you were referring to the mother and child, not their rescuer." He showed Leia a docile look. "I apologize, Ambassador, but he didn't have the slightest interest in coming aboard. Who is he?"

"Someone who thinks he can save the galaxy single-handedly," Leia mumbled.

On Gyndine, explosions began to blossom along the transitor and deep into the planet's dark side. A fiery speck in the night, the planet's orbital shipyard slowly disintegrated. Leia became dizzy at the sight and had to steady herself against a bulkhead. The explosions didn't so much stir memories as prompt a troubling vision of some event yet to come.

A tone sounded from the navicomputer. "Hyperspace coordinates received and locked in," the navigator announced.

The ship shuddered. Starlight elongated, as if the past were making a desperate bid to forestall the future, and the transport jumped.

Crouched in the shadows of the smoldering embassy building, Wurth Skidder watched the last of the troop carriers take to the scudded sky. Thousands of Gyndine's indigenous forces had fallen back to the gated compound on the off chance of being evacuated with New Republic effectives. Few had been taken, however, and many of those who had were officers with political ties to Coruscant or other Core worlds.

There was still some furious fighting going on in the city, but the majority of ground troops, realizing that their hopes for salvation had left with the last ship out, had tossed aside their repeating blasters and stripped off their uniforms in the belief that the Yuuzhan Vong would go easier on noncombatants.

Which just went to show how slowly news traveled to remote worlds, Skidder thought ruefully.

When it came to sacrificing captives to their gods, the enemy drew no such distinctions. In fact, in some cases a uniform—or at least evidence of a fighting spirit—could mean the difference between the mercifully quick death the Yuuzhan Vong offered those who measured up to their warlike ideals and the lingering death they reserved for those taken into captivity. He had heard rumors about captives undergoing dismemberment and vivisection; others about shiploads of captives being launched into the heart of stars to ensure victory for the Yuuzhan Vong.

As if the invaders needed a helping hand.

The gasbag, fire-breathing abominations that had torched Gyndine's forests and turned lakes into boiling cauldrons were gathered on the eastern outskirts of the capital. Flame-carpet warheads couldn't have done as much damage. Yuuzhan Vong infantry units—reptilian–humanoid Chazrack warriors—had followed the fire breathers in to clean out pockets of resistance and generally mop up. The sky had actually brightened slightly, but what light filtered in through smoke and scudding clouds was blotted out by descending drop ships.

One of them—a mesh tent pierced by crooked sticks—

was hovering over the embassy grounds now. Skidder had just changed positions to get a better vantage on the ship when its tentlike hull suddenly burst open, releasing a dozen or more huge, rod-shaped and bristled bundles that fell straight to the ground. Skidder didn't understand that they were living creatures until he saw the bioluminescent eyespots, twitching antennae, and the hundred pairs of sucker-equipped legs that sprouted down the length of the segmented bodies.

He observed the creatures in undisguised awe. They had the capacity not only to ambulate forward and backward, but also to skitter sideways—which they commenced doing at once, creating a living perimeter around the embassy grounds and moving slowly inward, as a means of forcing everyone toward the center.

The sight of the creatures was enough to strike fear in the heart of the most valiant, but Skidder had the Force on his side and was undaunted. Large as the creatures were, he was not without his own grab bag of abilities, and he could easily vault his way to freedom if he wished. After that it would be a simple matter to conceal himself from the Yuuzhan Vong. He could set off into the countryside, away from the devastation, and live off the land, as many of Gyndine's residents had opted to do when word of the imminent attack had spread. But Wurth Skidder wasn't a forager, and he certainly wasn't a deserter.

The fact that so few had lived to speak of their experiences as captives made it imperative that someone elect to be taken—someone with more interest in winning the war than in understanding the enemy, as Caamasi Senator Elegos A'Kla had attempted to do, and been butchered for his efforts.

Danni Quee, an ExGal scientist who had been captured shortly after the Yuuzhan Vong's arrival at the ice world Helska 4, had told Skidder of the final days of another captive, Skidder's fellow Jedi and close friend Miko Reglia. Quee had recounted the psychological tortures the Yuuzhan Vong and their tentacled yammosk—their so-called war coordinator—had inflicted on quiet and unassuming Miko in an attempt to break him, and of Miko's death during his and Quee's escape.

Vengeance went against the Jedi Code—as the code was taught by Master Skywalker, at any rate. Vengeance, according to Skywalker, was a path to the dark side. But there were other Jedi Knights, as powerful as Skywalker in Skidder's estimation, who took issue with some of the Master's teachings. Jedi Master Kyp Durron, for one. It was whispered, even on Yavin 4 in the wake of the Yuuzhan Vong invasion, that there were times when darkness had to be fought with darkness. And the Yuuzhan Vong were nothing if not the blackest evil since Emperor Palpatine.

Skidder was astute enough to recognize that he was motivated in part by a desire to show Skywalker and the rest that he was not some brash kid but a Jedi Knight of old, willing to put his life on the line—to sacrifice himself, if necessary—for a greater cause.

He rose from the shadows.

The outsize, insectile creatures loosed from the drop ship had succeeded in herding everyone to the center. Some of the creatures were beginning to curl themselves into rings, corralling their captives and employing their numerous sucker-equipped legs to prevent anyone from making over-the-top escapes.

Skidder tossed aside the lightsaber he had fashioned to replace the one he'd lost at Ithor, along with everything else that might identify him as a Jedi Knight. Then he chose his moment. As one of the creatures approached, pushing a score of beings in front of it, Skidder rushed forward, infiltrating the fleeing group before the creature had made a complete circle of itself—and much to the bafflement of a group of Ryn in whose midst he landed.

As the bioengineered creature joined its head to its tail parts, Skidder found himself pressed face-to-face with a Ryn female, whose oblique eyes mirrored her terror. He reached down and took her long-fingered hand.

"Take heart," he said in Basic, "help has arrived."

THREE

"Handles just as well as she always did," Han announced confidently, as the newly matte-black *Millennium Falcon* left behind a lush little world of green and purple forest.

"A simple coat of paint and you're feeling invulnerable," Droma said, frowning. "Who would have guessed?"

Han made adjustments to the *Falcon*'s drives. "Next stop, Sriluur. Somebody once described it as the source of every foul wind that blows through the galaxy, but—"

"You figure they were just being kind," Droma completed.

Han glanced at the Ryn, absurdly small in the oversize chair that had been Chewbacca's. "Haven't I warned you about doing that? Anyway, quit your worrying. I've been to Sriluur more times than I can count. And let me tell you, dodging Imperial bulk cruisers was a lot harder than dodging Yuuzhan Vong battleships."

"*Han Solo* has been to Sriluur," Droma pointed out, growing more agitated. "Unless you plan on revealing your true identity, you're just another scruffy spacer with a freshly painted ship and a death wish."

Han scowled, stroking the mostly gray growth on his chin as he tried to catch a glimpse of his reflection in the closest of the cockpit's transparisteel panes.

"Quit your worrying," Droma mimicked him, "the beard looks fine. But it's not going to keep us from arousing suspicion when we start asking questions about Yuuzhan Vong prisoner ships."

"Maybe not, but Sriluur's worth the risk. The Weequays might not be the most attractive folks in the galaxy, but they're real good at keeping an ear to the ground. And if anyone can tell us where to start looking for Roa or your clanmates, it'll be them."

Droma tugged nervously at his mustache. "Let's just hope your pheromone levels are up to it."

Han waved a hand in dismissal. "They only communicate like that among their own kind. I always managed to get by with Basic." He smirked. "I'd like to see you second-guess what a Weequay's about to say."

"Scent."

"Huh?"

"What a Weequay is about to scent."

Han put his tongue in his cheek, nodded slowly, and threw switches on the navicomputer. "Maybe we'll get lucky at Sriluur and have to put down in a sandstorm," he said in a casual way.

"Extra concealment for the ship?"

Han snarled at him. "No, so I can see how much sand it takes to plug that perpetual motion machine you call a mouth."

Droma grimaced, then sighed with purpose. "I guess I just don't like the idea of venturing so close to Hutt space—with or without Yuuzhan Vong in the area. There's no love lost between Hutts and Ryn. Many of us were enslaved by them to provide entertainment in one court or another. Some of my ancestors were required to prognosticate for a Desilijic Hutt. When predicted events didn't come to pass, the Hutt would have a Ryn killed by his henchmen or fed to a court beast."

"True to form," Han said. "But you've got my word, no Hutt'll stop us from locating your clanmates. We'll have your family back together soon enough."

"Then we can make a start on yours," Droma mumbled.

Han threw him an angry glance. "You want to explain that?"

Droma turned to him. "You and Leia to begin with. If it weren't for me, you'd be with her now. I only hope she can find it in her heart to forgive me."

Han compressed his lips. "You've got nothing to do with what's come between us. Heck, it's not even between me and Leia. It's between me and"—he flicked his hand at the starfield beyond the viewpoint—"this."

Droma didn't speak for a moment, then said, "Even friends can't be protected from fate, Han."

"Don't talk to me about fate," Han snapped. "Nothing's fixed—not these stars and definitely not what happens to us in life." He clenched his hands. "These are what determine my fate."

"And yet even you end up in situations that are not of your making."

"Like my being with you, for instance."

Droma frowned. "I've lost friends and loved ones to tragedy, and I've tried to do exactly what you're doing."

Han looked up at him. "What I'm doing?"

"Trying to beat tragedy by outracing it. Filling your life to the brim, even when it puts you in danger. Burying your heartache under as much anger as you can muster, without realizing that you've shoveled love and compassion into the same grave. We live for love, Han. Without it we might as well jettison everything."

Despite himself, Han thought about Leia on Gyndine, Jaina flying with Rogue Squadron, Anakin and Jacen off to who knew where with the Jedi. When he considered, even for a split second, where he might be without them, the angry words and recriminations that had spewed from him since Chewie's death pierced him like rapid fire. *If something should happen to them,* he started to think, only to feel a great black maw opening beneath him, undermining everything he believed in. Protectively, he tugged himself from dark imaginings.

"I got along just fine without love for a lot of years, Droma. Love is what starts things rolling downhill. It's like being sucked into a gravity well or being caught by a tractor beam. You get too close, there's no escape."

Droma nodded, as if in understanding. "So your mistake was in befriending Chewbacca to begin with. You would have been better off keeping your distance. Then you wouldn't be grieving now."

"Befriending him wasn't a mistake," Han said.

"But if you'd kept your guard raised all those years, you would never have grown as close to him as you did."

"Okay, that was a risk I took. But that was then."

"Let me suggest an alternative error. You didn't see his death coming and you're angry that you let your guard down."

"You're right about that. I should've been more vigilant."

"So let's suppose you did everything you could and still failed. Would you be grieving now, or would doing everything have satisfied you enough so that you wouldn't miss him?"

"Of course I'd still miss him."

"Then who are you angry at—yourself for the things you didn't do, or fate for having snuck up on you?"

Han swallowed hard. "All I know is I won't make that mistake again. I'll be ready for anything *fate* dishes out."

"And if you fail again?"

Han glared at him. "I won't."

Deep in one of the fathomless canyons formed by Coruscant's soaring superstructures, Sullustan Admiral Sien Sovv switched off his private comlink and relayed the tragic news to the twelve officers seated in the recently readied New Republic Defense Force war room.

"Gyndine is lost."

The uncomfortable silence that greeted the announcement came as no surprise. The planet's fall had been a foregone conclusion from the moment it had been identified as a target. Filling the silence, machines whirred and hummed as they received and processed intelligence updates from all sectors of New Republic space. In projected light, virtual battle groups of starships moved lazily among virtual worlds.

"For allowing this to happen, we are all diminished," Brigadier General Etahn A'baht remarked at last, voicing what many in the room were thinking. And yet the silence lingered.

"While I number myself among those who in the end voted against dispatching a force of suitable might to safeguard Gyndine," the aubergine-skinned Dornean went on, "I wish to reiterate the remarks I made during the arguments preceding that regrettable decision. By all but surrendering worlds like Gyndine, we reinforce widespread conviction that the New Republic is interested only in protecting the Core, and in doing so we play into the enemy's hand by weakening ourselves from within."

A scornful muttering rose from across the oblong table, and all heads turned to Commodore Brand. "Perhaps it would have been wiser to send an entire fleet to Gyndine and thus deprive Kuat or Fondor of any defense."

A'baht stood his ground, meeting the dour human's gaze. "Will that be your justification for allowing the Yuuzhan Vong to occupy the entire Inner Rim? Is the Inner Rim the price we're willing to pay to protect the Core?" He paused for effect. "A wise action, Commodore, would be to cease this exercise in selective defense and begin sending forces where needed."

A'baht glanced around the table. "Doesn't it disturb any of you that threatened worlds have begun to surrender without a fight? That former allies have refused to allow us to use their systems as staging areas out of fear of reprisals by the Yuuzhan Vong?"

He continued before anyone could respond. "Even a cursory look at the situation reveals that those populations who, at our urging, mounted a resistance have seen their worlds poisoned or devastated, while those like the Hutts, who have struck deals with the Yuuzhan Vong, have escaped bloodshed entirely."

"You disgrace all of us by bringing the Hutts into this," Brand said angrily. "Was their capitulation ever in doubt?"

A'baht made a placating gesture. "I offer them only as an example, Commodore. But the fact remains that Nal Hutta has been spared the ruination visited on Dantooine, Ithor, Obroa-skai, and countless other worlds. My point is that populations throughout the Mid Rim and the Expansion Region are fast losing faith in our ability to put an end to this war—and I use the word intentionally, since few of you seem to realize, even at this late stage, the great peril we face. Events are reaching a point where it's every system for itself."

A'baht gestured broadly to the holoprojectors and screens. "Even this space reflects our denial to embrace the depths of our peril. Instead of meeting openly for all of Coruscant to see, we wind up down here, as if in hiding from the truth."

"No one is hiding," Brand objected. "Thanks to the ineptitude of the Intelligence division, we came close to escorting two saboteurs into our midst—or doesn't it matter to you that our security has been compromised?"

"The saboteurs were after the Jedi, not us," Director of Fleet Intelligence Addar Nylykerka interjected.

A'baht swung to him. "And why? Because, until Ithor, the Jedi were the ones who were leading the campaign. Now either we assume that role, or we allow the New Republic to splinter beyond repair. We must demonstrate our commitment to stopping the Yuuzhan Vong, and we must do so before additional worlds fall."

He adopted a more affable tone. "I'm not saying that security isn't an issue; only that we set a proper example. By relocating to Dometown we have encouraged everyone to think in terms of concealment."

A kilometer-wide cavern of homes and buildings, Dometown had originally been financed by a consortium of investors, including former general Lando Calrissian. But the hundreds of thousands expected to abandon the frenetic surface for underground tranquillity had never arrived, and the enterprise had gone bankrupt. Repossessed by banks and various credit unions, the would-be community had ultimately become the property of the New Republic military.

"Already there are new hotels and restaurants being opened on the lowest levels," A'baht was saying, "in anticipation that those currently fortunate enough to live in Coruscant's lofty towers will have nowhere to go but down should the Yuuzhan Vong attack. And mark my words, there'll be no survival, even here. For if what is occurring at Sernpidal and Obroa-skai is any indication, the Yuuzhan Vong will remake Coruscant in their own image, entombing any who have fled to the depths."

"Has thought been given to just where we will go should Coruscant fall?" Ixidro Legorburu asked while most of the officers were mulling over A'baht's dire prediction. A native of M'haeli, Legorburu was director of the New Republic's Battle Assessment Division.

"That will never happen," Sien Sovv assured, then lowered his voice to add, "Nevertheless, we're exploring options for relocating key government and military personnel to the Koornacht Cluster or, should worse come to worst, the Empress Teta system in the Deep Core."

"Key personnel," someone said leadingly.

The Sullustan admiral frowned. "It's a moot point, in any case, since most of the proposals have met with opposition by certain members of the senate."

Knowing glances were traded around the table.

"General A'baht's point about honoring our commitment to secondary worlds is well taken," Sovv said, "but I'm certain that even he would be willing to concede that sending a flotilla to Gyndine wouldn't have slowed the enemy's advance."

When everyone looked at A'baht for confirmation, he nodded, though with obvious reluctance.

"The attack on Gyndine indicates a change in the enemy's battle campaign. Clearly they are probing for weaknesses, perhaps routes into the Core. At the same time, there has been a marked increase in their mining of select hyperspace routes, which has narrowed our access to several outlying sectors."

"In other words, they're attempting to contain us," Brand said.

The diminutive Sovv stood and directed everyone's attention to a holomap that projected from the table's center, showing the current disposition of Yuuzhan Vong forces. "This is what we have been able to piece together from direct observation, in addition to stasis probe reconnaissance and hyperspace orbiting scanners.

"As you can see, their fleets are concentrated between Ord Mantell and Obroa-skai, and now between Hutt space and Gyndine. Should they move Coreward from Obroa-skai, Bilbringi, Borleias, Venjagga, and Ord Mirit are imperiled. From Gyndine, Commenor, Kuat, and Corellia are vulnerable. Analysis suggests that the conquest of Gyndine was effected to ready the way for a two-pronged attack. Logic dictates that—"

"You err in believing that they strategize as we do," A'baht interrupted, "when, in fact, they are waging a psychological war. The destruction of natural beauty and repositories of learning, the pursuit of refugees—such tactics are meant to confound and dishearten us. The Yuuzhan Vong are as much as saying that the civilization we have fashioned means nothing to them. All that we hold sacred is imperiled."

Impatience coaxed Brand out of his seat. "Spare us the rhetoric, General, and come to the point. With such keen insight into the Yuuzhan Vong, you no doubt have some foreknowledge of where they will strike next."

A'baht squared his shoulders. "The next targets will be Bothawui and Kothlis."

Everyone regarded the Dornean for a long moment. "You have evidence to support this?" Sovv asked.

"No more than what you present to support your belief that they will push for the Core. With their forces in Hutt space, they are practically at Bothawui's door."

"So this is what he's been getting at," Brand muttered. "He's finally gone over to Borsk Fey'lya's side. Fey'lya the warrior, the hero of Ithor."

A'baht refused to speak to the remark. "I propose that elements of the Third and Fourth Fleets be relocated to

Bothan space as soon as possible. Bothawui is where we should draw the line and launch our counteroffensive."

Brand snorted derisively. "And if you're wrong? If the Yuuzhan Vong should decide to assault Bilbringi, Kuat, or Mon Calamari instead?"

A'baht glowered. "Are you suggesting that those worlds are more important than Bothawui?"

"I'm saying precisely that. If any of our shipyards fall, the New Republic will topple."

"And if Bothawui falls?"

"We will mourn the loss, but the New Republic will survive."

A'baht shook his head in dismay. "Times like this make me wish that Ackbar could be persuaded to come out of retirement."

Sovv held up his hands to silence half a dozen separate conversations. "Contrary to General A'baht's assertions, no scenarios have been ruled out. Based on current intelligence, Bothawui is just as likely to be targeted as Bilbringi. But more important, we are not simply standing by, waiting for the Yuuzhan Vong to strike. Two plans have already been put into action." He looked at Brand. "Commodore, if you would be so kind."

A'baht leaned forward in interest.

"The first plan involves inducing the Hapes Consortium to join the fight," Brand said. "The Hapans are not only well armed but well positioned to outflank the enemy. Indeed, the Yuuzhan Vong may have skirted the Hapes Cluster in order to avoid having to engage them."

"Then why should the Consortium worlds elect to get involved now?" A'baht asked. "Why wouldn't they secure their own space as the Imperial Remnant has, or cut a deal, as the Hutts appear to have done?"

"Because the Consortium has allied with us in the past," Sovv explained calmly. "Following the Battle of

Endor, they captured several Imperial Star Destroyers, but instead of holding on to those ships, they donated them to the New Republic. Additionally, the Hapan queen mother's homeworld of Dathomir is threatened."

"More to the point," Brand interjected, "the Jedi recently did the royal family a favor by foiling a coup directed against the queen mother. It is hoped that Ambassador Organa Solo can persuade the rulers of the noble houses to repay us in kind."

A'baht feigned a look of confusion. "The Jedi did them a favor, and yet you've asked Organa Solo to intercede. To the best of my knowledge, she is not a true member of that order. Or is it perhaps that she was once courted by Prince Isolder?"

Brand fielded the question. "I won't deny that that didn't influence our decision to approach her."

"And she has agreed?"

"For a price. We had to promise to back her in seeking added funds for SELCORE—refugee relief. But, yes, she has agreed. She will leave for Hapes immediately on her return from Gyndine."

A'baht allowed an uncertain nod. "And this other plan?"

Brand adjusted the fit of his collar. "We're hoping to lure the Yuuzhan Vong into attacking the Corellian system."

For a moment, even A'baht was too surprised to speak; then he said, "Corellia isn't Gyndine, Commodore. If it's your aim to make that system a battlefield to avoid fouling Coruscant's space lanes, you will never have my vote. Wasn't it enough that we stripped the Corellians of the ability to defend themselves after the Centerpoint Station crisis?"

Sovv put his small hands on the table and leaned

toward A'baht. "Centerpoint Station is the very reason we hope to lure the Yuuzhan Vong there."

Larger than the Death Star, the artifact had been discovered to be a hyperspace repulsor, used in the dim past and by an unknown race, to capture and transport planets to the Corellian system. The station was also a weapon of unparalleled power, both starbuster and interdiction field generator, and eight years earlier had been employed as such by a group known as the Sacorrian Triad, in an unsuccessful attempt to achieve independence from the New Republic.

"Are you telling me that Centerpoint is operational?" A'baht asked in disbelief. "The last I heard, it had been shut down."

"It shut itself down," Brand snapped. "But as we speak several hundred scientists are attempting to return it to operational status. If the Yuuzhan Vong can be encouraged to attack Corellia, we will use a Centerpoint-generated interdiction field to prevent their ships from going to hyperspace while our fleets attack from the rear."

"Much to the dismay of the species of the Corellian sector, I would imagine," A'baht said. "After all, we didn't win many friends by interceding in the system's attempts at self-governance. If memory serves, the blowback from that interference is what prompted Organa Solo to resign as chief of state."

Sovv nodded. "But Governor-General Marcha is a New Republic appointee, and she has given her conditional approval. As a Corellian citizen, her word carries a lot of weight, not only on her native Drall but on Selonia, Corellia, and the Double Worlds. What's more, we haven't made the full extent of our plans known."

A'baht stared at him for a moment, then looked at Brand.

"As far as the Corellians know, we're readying Centerpoint as a defensive weapon, in lieu of stationing a flotilla there."

"How very noble of us," A'baht said in obvious disgust. "Here they've been supplying us with *Strident*-class Star Defenders, and we withhold the fact that we're planning to use their system as a battleground. Just how do you plan to lure the Yuuzhan Vong into attacking?"

"By making Corellia appear too attractive a target to pass up," Brand said. "By leaving the system essentially unprotected."

A'baht stroked his jaw in thought. "It's bold, I'll grant that much. But have Fey'lya and the Advisory Council members been apprised of this plan?"

"They know only what Corellia knows," Brand barked, then softened his tone to add, "Fey'lya would never sanction the rearming of Centerpoint—if only to prevent Corellia from reaping such power." He laughed shortly. "Even in the remote chance he did support us, how then could we ensure that word of the plan wouldn't leak? Once that occurred, every world in the Corellian system would rise up in revolt."

A'baht snorted in displeasure. "Fey'lya's isn't the only voice on the council. He can be overridden by a majority vote."

Brand and Sovv traded looks. "From what we have been able to determine," the admiral said, "three of the council members would certainly follow Fey'lya's lead. Four of the others could very well support us."

A'baht considered it. In response to the clamor from far-flung sectors for increased representation, two additional senators had been appointed to the council since the poisoning of Ithor. "That's four against, four in favor. Who is the unknown quantity?"

"The council's newest member," Brand said, "Senator Viqi Shesh."

"Has anyone approached her?" A'baht asked. "Unofficially, of course?"

Brand shook his head. "Not yet."

Sovv pressed his hands together. "Then I suggest we do so, Commodore. Before our window closes."

Ixidro Legorburu spoke up. "Is there any hope that the Hutts can be persuaded to join us, actively or indirectly?"

"Intelligence agents on Nal Hutta and Nar Shaddaa have reported that the Hutts' decision to ally themselves with the Yuuzhan Vong is a ruse," Sovv said. "They apparently wish to serve as conduits of information for the New Republic."

"You accept that?" A'baht asked.

"Given their history of alliances, they wouldn't align themselves with anyone without having a contingency plan in place." Sovv ran his hand down his prominently jowled face. "Even the Hutts can't risk being caught on the wrong side when the Yuuzhan Vong are defeated."

"When, not if," Commodore Brand said around an arrogant grin. "I find such optimism refreshing."

A'baht frowned. "I find it wishful thinking."

FOUR

From the waiting room of the great spired and onion-domed palace of Nal Hutta's ruling Hutt, Nom Anor gazed out on a despoiled landscape of feculent swamps, mold-covered stunted trees, and parcels of wan vermin-riddled marsh grass. Stained by a mélange of industrial pollutants and spotted with flocks of ungainly birds, the sky was a brooding ceiling, frequently lamenting its wretched state with lackluster showers of grimy rain. The stilted, destitute precincts so abundant in the vicinity of the spaceport were nowhere to be seen, but the terrain itself reeked of impoverishment and decay.

"What a vile world this is," Commander Malik Carr commented as he joined Nom Anor at the bay window.

"The Hutts know it as 'Glorious Jewel,' " the executor replied nonchalantly. "But it's not without potential. The moon, Nar Shaddaa, is far worse—completely encased by buildings and technology."

Malik Carr grunted. "I see no potential. But perhaps your one true eye sees more clearly than my pair."

Nom Anor quirked a smile. "I have been in this galaxy for some time, Commander, and have learned to look beyond appearances." He turned slightly in Malik Carr's direction. "Imagine Nal Hutta as, say, a laboratory for genetic experimentation."

Malik Carr smiled slowly. "Yes, yes, even I can envision that."

Taller than Nom Anor, the commander was displayed in all his glory, without ooglith masquer or cloaker. Malik Carr's incised face and bare upper torso told of an illustrious military career. Cinched around his backward-sloping forehead was a vibrant head cloth whose tassels were braided into lustrous black hair, forming a tail that hung nearly to his waist. Recently arrived from the galactic edge, where argosies waited eagerly for the warrior caste to complete the invasion, the commander had been charged by Supreme Commander Nas Choka with overseeing the next phase of the conquest.

To keep his own identity concealed—even from the Hutts—as well as in deference to Malik Carr, Nom Anor wore an ooglith masquer that obscured the scars, augmentations, and like evidence of his sacrifices to the gods, along with a prosthesis in the empty eye socket that normally housed a venom-spitting plaeryin bol.

Malik Carr swung from the window and planted his fists on his hips in anger. "How dare this creature keep us waiting. Is he completely unaware of what he risks for himself and his pathetic world?"

"*She*, Commander," Nom Anor corrected. "Currently, at any rate. Hutts are said to be hermaphroditic. That is to say, male and female characteristics are combined in each."

Malik Carr looked at him askance. "And just now this one is female?"

"Fully female, as you will see. As for the prolonged wait, it's nothing more than tradition."

"But the precedent—"

"Don't concern yourself with precedent. I have a plan for dealing with this outmoded formality."

As the two Yuuzhan Vong walked toward the center

of the antechamber, an entourage of ten honor guards and as many attendants snapped to attention. The guards wore vonduun crab armor and carried living amphistaffs and doubled-edge coufee knives. The female attendants were attired in veils, tunics, and cloaks that left visible only the sinuous markings that adorned their bared arms.

Malik Carr acknowledged the guards' brisk salutes and sat down on a cushioned bench. Nom Anor remained standing. The waiting room's high ceiling was supported by a dozen stately if moldy pillars. The floor was made of cut stone polished to a dazzling sheen, and woven textiles of intricate design graced the walls.

A bright-green, orb-eyed biped of medium size entered the antechamber. The creature's lumpy head featured twin hornlike appendages, pointed ears, and a narrow crest of yellow spines. Its long, tapered fingers appeared to be equipped with suction cups.

"A Rodian," Nom Anor supplied quietly. "A bellicose species given to warfare and bounty hunting. This one is the Hutt's majordomo, Leenik."

Leenik approached his master's guests, his stubby snout twitching. "Borga the Almighty is prepared to grant you audience now," he said in Basic.

Malik Carr shot Nom Anor a vexed glance. The entire Yuuzhan Vong entourage stood and began to trail the Rodian through an enormous doorway flanked by thick-set churlish guards, whose pointed lower teeth and forehead tusks were perfectly matched.

"I suggest you take a deep breath before we enter," Nom Anor advised the commander.

"Is the Hutt odor so unbearable?"

"Picture bathing in a reopened grave."

Malik Carr grimaced and sucked in his breath.

The vaulted ceiling of the opulent court was even

higher than that of the antechamber, and floating midway to the ceiling on a bolstered antigravity couch was an outsize, bulbous-headed slug whose disproportionately short arms might have been vestigial were the small hands they ended in not beckoning imperiously to Malik Carr and Nom Anor.

Atmosphere exchangers were working overtime, but there was enough residual rankness in the air to make the commander's eyes water. Sybaritic toadies sprawled about on couches and carpets—musicians, gunsels, and scantily attired dancers, all of diverse species. Chained to one wall, though obviously a pet, was a ferocious-looking beast Nom Anor knew to be a Kintan strider.

Borga favored Nom Anor with a look. "How pleasant to see you again," her deep voice boomed. "Come and sit beneath me."

Nom Anor—whom Borga knew as Pedric Cuf, and who claimed to be nothing more than an intercessor between the Yuuzhan Vong and the Hutts—smiled without showing his teeth and remained where he was, a good distance from the repulsor platform. At his hand signal the attendants conveyed to the center of the room several ornate boxes of the sort that might contain tribute. Nom Anor went to the closest box and opened the lid. Almost immediately the levitated couch gave a shudder and crashed loudly to the stone floor, nearly spilling Borga the Almighty into her coterie of shocked sycophants.

"I'm terribly sorry," Nom Anor said, as the chagrined Hutt struggled to regain her former composure. "I didn't realize that the Yuuzhan Vong had brought along a finely tuned dovin basal for your amusement. The creature was apparently offended by your couch's attempt to outwit gravity and decided to rectify the imbalance by catching hold of it."

Nom Anor was proficient at mimicking the subharmonics that furnished the Hutt language with nuance. Even so, Borga had difficulty establishing the sincerity of the apology. Her oblique, heavy-lidded eyes blinked in confusion, then she quickly propped herself up, putting a curl in her muscular purple-patched tail, and gestured for two of her attendants to bring chairs for her guests.

The commander and the executor seated themselves with decorum, careful not to demonstrate too much smugness over their small victory, though a fleeting smile did escape Malik Carr.

"The Yuuzhan Vong have brought other wonders, as well," Nom Anor said finally.

Once more at his signal two attendants placed an aquarium well within Borga's limited reach, its murky waters hosting a variety of fist-sized life-forms, the likes of which the Hutt had never seen. Borga whispered something to Leenik, and the majordomo fished one of the creatures from the tank, sniffed at it, and took a cautious bite.

At the Rodian's mildly enthusiastic nod, Borga snatched the thing from Leenik's long-fingered hands, swallowed it whole, and loosed a resonant and lengthy belch of satisfaction.

"Another," she ordered.

This time Borga opened her jaws so wide that Nom Anor could almost hear the living morsel plop into her enormous stomach cavity. She belched again and ran her powerful tongue over her lips and nostrils.

"A bit like a Carnovian eel-pup, but with just a hint of the resistance one expects from the finest nala-tree frogs supplied by Fhnark and Company," she said, as only a gourmand could. "All in all, on a par with some of the classic droch appetizers fashioned by Zubindi Ebsuk." She turned her gaze on Nom Anor. "How did you come by these, Pedric Cuf? On which world can they be found?"

"None in this galaxy." Nom Anor smiled pleasantly. "They are bioengineered."

The Hutt glanced at Malik Carr. "He created them?"

"Not personally. A Yuuzhan Vong shaper did so."

"And this . . . this shaper could replicate the product?"

"I'm certain he could." Nom Anor stood and gestured respectfully to Malik Carr. "Borga, permit me to introduce Commander Malik Carr, who will be overseeing this sector of space."

The Hutt blinked. "Overseeing?"

Head canted slightly to one side, Malik Carr regarded her for what seemed an eternity. "You speak for all of your kind?" he asked in passable Huttese.

Borga's blubbery body stiffened proudly. "I do. And I have been vested with the power to negotiate with your species."

"By whom have you been vested?"

"By the leaders of the voting kajidics, as well as the Grand Council."

"Kajidics?" Malik Carr said to Nom Anor.

"Criminal syndicates," Nom Anor told him in their own tongue.

Malik Carr continued to appraise Borga openly. "Yours is the ruling kajidic, then?"

"I am Borga Besadii Diori, cousin of Durga Besadii Tai, son of Aruk the Great, brother of Zavval. Wealthiest and most powerful of the Besadii kajidic, I lord over the Desilijic, the Trinivii, the Ramesh, Shell, and all other clans. All the three billion of this world pay obei—"

"You are male or female?" Malik Carr cut her off.

Borga blinked. "Just now I am with child." She indicated a pouch, low in her bulging abdomen.

"You birth live offspring?" Malik Carr said in obvious astonishment. When Borga nodded, the commander's jaw dropped ever so slightly. "Like one of our lowliest caste women," he remarked to Nom Anor.

Borga's broad forehead wrinkled in uncertainty.

"Let us talk business," Malik Carr said abruptly. "As . . . Pedric Cuf has undoubtedly apprised you, the Yuuzhan Vong have need of some of your worlds—for purposes of resource gathering. To effect this, we may be required to remove entire populations, and in some cases remake those worlds we select."

"Yes, so Pedric Cuf has explained," Borga said after a long moment. "In fact, we Hutts know a good deal about remaking worlds. When we arrived here from Varl, for example, Glorious Jewel was not the paradise you see now, but a primitive world of dense forests and untamed seas. There was even an indigenous species called the Evocii, who we were obliged to relocate on Glorious Jewel's moon, where the pitiful creatures gradually died out. By then, of course, we had replaced all Evocii structures with proper palaces and shrines . . ."

Malik Carr glanced at Nom Anor while Borga prattled on. "She looks like something our shapers might have cooked up."

Nom Anor laughed shortly. "It's true. I thought the same thing when I first laid eyes on her."

Borga had stopped talking and was eyeing Malik Carr with misgiving. "I'm afraid you have me at a disadvantage, Commander," she said, with cheerful servility. "While I've made some progress in the tutorials Pedric Cuf supplied, I'm not yet fully conversant with your language."

Nom Anor cleared his throat. "The commander was just saying that he loves what you've done with the place."

Borga managed a dubious smile. "In that case, let us return to talking business, as you say."

Malik Carr nodded politely.

"In exchange for granting you the use of certain worlds—one of which we have already provided, as a demonstration of good faith—we Hutts are obliged to ask the Yuuzhan Vong to keep clear of Rimward Hutt space in general, as well as to avoid the worlds Rodia, Ryloth, Tatooine, Kessel, and certain planets in the Si'klaata Cluster and Kathol sector."

Borga raised her voice in anticipation of objections. "I'm well aware that you have a fleet of ships anchored at the edge of the Y'Toub system, but we Hutts are not without our resources and weapons, and a war against us would only sidetrack you from your principal goal of defeating the New Republic." She stopped herself. "That is your goal, is it not?"

Malik Carr and Nom Anor exchanged brief looks of bemusement before the commander replied. "Our goals should not concern you at this point. Furthermore, it would be premature to decide which of us has rights to which worlds when we have yet to see whether our partnership will succeed. That decision, in any event, will ultimately be made by Supreme Overlord Shimrra. In the meantime, I suggest you broach the matter with my direct superior, Supreme Commander Nas Choka, who will certainly wish to meet with you when he arrives in Hutt space, some days from now."

Borga nodded. "I will gladly grant him audience, and I will do as you suggest and discuss terms with him. I do, however, wish to propose something for your immediate consideration. In addition to other enterprises, we Hutts have both a fondness for and a long history of slave trading. With our expertise and our well-established network of space lanes and hyperspace routes, it occurs to me that we might best serve the interests of the partnership, as you say, by overseeing the transportation of captives, laborers, servants, and fodder for sacrifices—a task for which we are uniquely suited. That way, the Yuuzhan Vong needn't employ their own ships for the lowly purpose of conveying inferior beings to their well-deserved castigation, enslavement, or immolation."

"In return for what?" Malik Carr asked mildly.

"Your promise not to interfere with the movement of spice and other proscribed goods."

"Spice?" Malik Carr asked Nom Anor.

"Recreational euphoriants—some of which are arachnid by-products."

Borga followed the exchange, then clapped her hands. Human servants appeared bearing trays mounded with crystalline powders, varying in both composition and color.

"Here you see examples of glitterstim and the kor grade of the mineral ryll," Borga said, indicating one mound after the next. "And there you see carsunum, lumni-spice, gree spice, and andris." She paused to regard Malik Carr. "If you would care to sample any one of them . . ."

Malik Carr lifted his hand in a negative gesture.

"Some other time perhaps," Borga said graciously. "But what of my proposal?"

Nom Anor turned to Malik Carr with purposeful excitement. "It does suit Supreme Commander Nas Choka's plan to gather resistant populations onto a few select worlds for indoctrination and security, Commander."

Malik Carr nodded noncommittally, then looked at Borga. "You have no qualms about betraying the sundry species who embrace the tenets of the New Republic?"

Borga loosed a sinister guffaw. "Certainly no more than Pedric Cuf has. After all, Commander, business is business, and if anyone is to profit from the galaxy's new circumstances, it may as well be the Hutts."

"So be it," Malik Carr said with finality.

Borga grinned broadly. "One more small item, Commander. Since it would be to our mutual advantage that Hutt supply ships refrain from unintentionally bumbling into your operations, is it too much to ask that we be advised of any imminent, uh, activities?"

Malik Carr cut his eyes to Nom Anor. "Exactly as you predicted."

Nom Anor returned a barely perceptible nod. "Negotiation is also part of their tradition."

"You do have a keen eye, Executor."

"A practiced one, Commander."

Borga watched them without comprehending.

"We were just discussing the terms," Nom Anor explained.

"Consider our request an accommodation," Borga said offhandedly. "A show of confidence."

"What you ask seems harmless enough," Malik Carr allowed. "As you say, Borga, we certainly wouldn't want your spice vessels inadvertently disrupting our activities."

"As I say, Commander."

"Until further notice, then, you may want to consider avoiding the Tynnani, Bothan, and Corellian systems. Tynna, especially so."

Borga's broad grin returned with interest. "Tynna, Bothawui, and Corellia . . . As it happens, Commander, we do limited business in all of those systems."

Malik Carr sniffed arrogantly. " I suggest you reduce your business to zero."

No sooner had the Yuuzhan Vong entourage left the palace than three Hutts hurried into Borga's court. A young Hutt, uniformly tan in color, slithered in on his own power; an older one, with a stripe of green pigmentation running down his spine and tapered tail, was borne in on a litter supported by a dozen leathery-skinned Weequays; and an even more aged one, sporting a wispy gray beard, made use of a hoversled.

The latter Hutt, Pazda Desilijic Tiure—uncle of the celebrated Jabba Desilijic Tiure—was the first to voice his outrage.

"Who do they think they are, making demands of the Hutts, as though we were some trifling species concerned only with escaping bloodshed? That Malik Carr, he reminded me of the worst of Palpatine's Imperial moffs. And the one who calls himself Pedric Cuf was equally treacherous—speaking out of both sides of his mouth."

Pazda showed Borga his most austere expression. "The Desilijic would never have permitted such indignities to take place in their court. Jabba would have fed Malik Carr and Pedric Cuf to a rancor and taken his chances with the Yuuzhan Vong fleet."

"Like he took his chances with Jedi Master Skywalker?" the young Hutt, Randa Besadii Diori, remarked. "Personally, I always felt that Tatooine's aridity wreaked havoc with Jabba's judgment." Elevating himself on his powerful tail, he nodded at his parent, Borga. "You handled them expertly."

"Impertinent pup," Pazda wheezed. "What do you know of judgment or strategy, growing up as you have in wealth and privilege?"

"One thing I know, old Hutt, is that I will never lose my wealth and privilege," Randa told him now.

"Enough of this," the littered Hutt, Gardulla the Younger, chimed in, impaling Randa with his gaze. "Respect your elders—even when you don't agree with them." He ordered his muscular bearers to steer him closer to Borga, nodding in regard as he neared the chief Besadii's levitated couch. "To deceive an enemy, pretend to fear him."

The grin Borga had worn for Malik Carr and Nom Anor had been replaced by a look of narrow-eyed fury. "Better to have the Yuuzhan Vong overestimate our subservience than our shrewdness."

Gardulla laughed without mirth. "You succeeded in tricking them into revealing their next targets."

"As I promised you I would."

"Such intelligence is potentially invaluable. Do we now inform the New Republic of the invaders' designs?"

Borga shook her head. "New Republic Intelligence operatives have already been making overtures. Let us wait and see what they bring to the bargaining table."

"It had better be an offer of great worth," Randa said.

Gardulla ignored the comment. "No doubt the Yuuzhan Vong will expect us to reveal their plan."

"No doubt," Borga agreed. "That's why we will make no move. The New Republic will have to come to us."

She lowered the couch to the floor. "When Xim the Despot and his droid legions attempted to invade Hutt space, the great Kossak defeated them at Vontor and sent them fleeing for the Tion Hegemony. And when Moff Sarn Shild attempted to blockade Nal Hutta and destroy our moon, the great clans set aside their differences to manipulate weak Imperials and send their forces fleeing, as well."

She paused to glance in turn at Pazda, Randa, and Gardulla the Younger. "We have weathered many storms, and we will weather this one, as well. With care, we can play the New Republic against the invaders for the betterment of the Hutts."

"And we won't need a bungled Death Star to do it,"

Pazda muttered, in reference to Durga's failed Darksaber Project.

Borga glowered at him. "Insult my family again, and this court will no longer be available to you."

Pazda mustered a chastised look. "Excuse the grumbling that comes with advanced age, Your Highness."

Gardulla shook with sinister laughter. "As my parent used to say, 'There's always enough to divide—enough to keep, enough to spread around, enough to be stolen—as long as you're first to get to it.' "

Borga laughed with him. "For the time being, let the word go out to our subcontractors to exercise caution in their transactions and deliveries." She glanced at Leenik. "Who manages our affairs in the targeted systems?"

The Rodian dipped his head in a curt bow. "Boss Bunji oversees shipments to Corellia; Crev Bombaasa to Tynna and Bothawui."

Borga licked her lips. "Inform them to suspend all business to the threatened systems—and to double their efforts elsewhere." She clapped her hands loudly, awakening those sycophants who had dozed off. "Let us have music and dancing in celebration of this day!"

FIVE

Leia paced from bulkhead to bulkhead in her cramped cabin space aboard the New Republic transport. Head moving back and forth, servos whining and whirring, C-3PO tracked her movements, while Olmahk and Leia's second bodyguard, Basbakhan, stood vigilantly to either side of the curved hatch. An illuminated planetary crescent of blue and brown dominated the view from the cabin's transparisteel observation bay.

A tone sounded from the communications suite, bringing Leia to a sudden halt.

"Ambassador," a raspy voice said, "we have the Ralltiiri minister on channel one."

C-3PO pressed a lighted tile on the console, and the head and shoulders of a gray-haired man resolved in life-size holo. "Madam Ambassador," the man said as Leia positioned herself for the visual pickup. "To what do I owe this honor?"

Leia frowned in anger. "Don't trifle with me, Minister Shirka. Why have we been refused landing privileges at Grallia Spaceport?"

Shirka's deeply lined face twitched. "I'm sorry, Ambassador, I thought you'd already been informed."

"Informed of what?"

"The Ralltiiri Secretariat has vetoed the proposal that would have allowed us to accept any displaced peoples."

"I thought so," Leia fumed. "And just what am I supposed to do with the six thousand refugees who were promised temporary shelter on Ralltiir?"

"I'm afraid that's not for me to decide."

"But the Secretariat agreed to this last week. What could have changed since then?"

Shirka looked uncomfortable. "It's rather complicated. But to be concise, the idea of accepting refugees didn't sit well with several of our more influential offworld investors. That, of course, led the central banks to pressure the Ministry of Finance, and—"

"I assured you that the New Republic Senate had approved the allocation of funds for Ralltiir."

"So you did, Ambassador, but the promised funds have not arrived, and to be frank there is rampant talk that they never will. As it is, investor confidence has been shaken. And as I'm sure you're aware, what happens on Ralltiir affects market response all along the Perlemian Trade Route."

Leia folded her arms. "This isn't some stock issue, Minister. This is about everyone pulling together to help. What's happening in the Mid Rim might not seem of pressing importance here in the Core, but you're fooling yourself if you think you can hide from this. Have you already forgotten what the Emperor did when Ralltiir lent its support to the Alliance?"

Shirka bristled. "Is that meant to be a threat, Ambassador?"

"You misunderstand. I'm only suggesting that you consider the heinous actions of Lord Tion and Governor Dennix Graeber as prelude to what the Yuuzhan Vong are capable of doing—and without provocation. Remember what it was like to be denied relief, Minister? Remember what Alderaan risked for Ralltiir?"

Shirka worked his jaw. "Your mission of mercy at that time has not been forgotten. But, then, the Alliance did receive something in return . . ."

Shirka's allusion was clear. A wounded Imperial soldier Leia rescued had been the first to tell of Palpatine's superweapon, the Death Star.

"Regardless of who gained what," she said after a moment, "is it Ralltiir's intention to remain neutral in the coming storm to avoid disturbing the privileged lives of its wealthy residents and investors?"

Anger mottled Shirka's face. "This conversation is over, Ambassador," he said, and terminated the connection.

Leia glanced at C-3PO and blew out her breath. "Of all the—"

"Ambassador," the same raspy voice interrupted. "Governor-General Amer Tariq of Rhinnal on channel four."

C-3PO pressed another tile, and a miniature image of Tariq rose from the holoprojector.

"Leia," the elder statesman and noted physician began, "I'm so glad to see you safe and sound." Tariq wore an impeccably tailored suit, whose mix of colors was too vivid for the holo.

"Thank you, Amer. Did you receive my message?"

"I did, Leia. But I'm sorry to report that I don't have encouraging news. Rhinnal cannot possibly accept additional refugees at this time, even on a temporary basis."

Leia was confounded. "Amer, if this is about funds—"

He gave his head a firm shake. "Don't confuse Rhinnal with Ralltiir, my dear. It's simply that the ten thousand refugees we received from Ord Mantell have strained our resources to the breaking point. Just yesterday we were forced to reroute more than two thousand to the Ruan system."

Leia's eyebrows went up. "Ruan is still accepting exiles?"

"More than accepting; Ruan is actually soliciting. In fact, I'm certain that Ruan would be willing and able to accommodate everyone you evacuated from Gyndine."

One of a host of agricultural worlds managed by Salliche Ag Corporation, Ruan, on the edge of the Deep Core between Coruscant and the Empress Teta system, was by galactic standards only a short jump away.

"Let's hope so, Amer," Leia said.

"My humblest apologies, my dear."

The transmission ended abruptly, and Leia collapsed into a chair. She brought her hand to her mouth to stifle a yawn. "Maybe I'll get some rest after Ruan," she started to tell C-3PO when the comm tone sounded again.

"Yes?" she directed to the audio pickup.

"A transmission of unknown origin, relayed from Bilbringi."

Leia sighed wearily. "What now?"

"I believe it's your husband, Ambassador."

A snowy image appeared on the communication console's display screen. Leia recognized the forward cargo hold of the *Millennium Falcon*, though it took her a moment to recognize Han behind the beard.

"How do you like my new look?" he asked, stroking the salt-and-pepper growth.

"Han, where are you?"

He swiveled the navicomputer chair. "I'd rather not say just now."

She nodded in a galled but knowing way. "How did you know where to find me?"

"I heard about Gyndine. Wasn't too difficult after that. You're still well known, whether you like it or not."

"So are you, Han. And for all anyone knows, the Yuuzhan Vong could be hunting for you or the *Falcon*."

Han's brows beetled and his mouth formed a puckered O. "I'm not a complete blockhead, you know. That's why I grew the beard and had the *Falcon* painted."

Leia's eyes widened. "Painted?"

"Anodized, actually. A lovely shade of matte black. She looks like a mortician's delight."

"What system are you planning to sneak into this time?"

"Sneak?"

"You heard me."

"Oh, I get it. You mean maybe instead of frolicking around out here, I should be devoting my time to saving planets."

Leia huffed. "I'm not interested in saving planets, Han. I'm interested in saving lives."

"Well, what'd you think I'm trying to do? This is all about finding Droma's relatives and Roa, Leia. It has nothing to do with Ord Mantell or Gyndine or anywhere else. Besides, a man's good for only one promise at a time, and I gave mine to Droma."

Leia exhaled slowly. "I'm sorry, Han. I understand what you're doing." She smiled thinly. "At least we still have something in common."

Han averted his gaze momentarily. "Speaking of which, was it you who arranged for Ord Mantell's refugees to be transferred to Gyndine?"

"Yes—regretfully."

Han gave her a lopsided smile. "You're complicating my search, sweetheart."

Leia's frustration returned. "Am I? And who created such a muddle on Vortex that the local governor decided to renege on his promise to accept any refugees whatsoever?"

"I was only trying to—" Han's image suddenly tilted to one side, as if the *Falcon* had been stood on end. "Hey,

Droma, watch what you're doing up there!" He turned back to the cam, jerking a thumb in the direction of the *Falcon*'s outrigger cockpit. "Guy claims to be a pilot, but you'd never know it by the way he handles a ship."

Leia took her lower lip between her teeth in disquiet. "How are you two getting along?"

He snorted. "If I didn't owe him my life, I'd probably jettison him right here."

"I'm sure," Leia said quietly.

"By the way, you might want to pass along to the fleet office that a flotilla of Yuuzhan Vong ships was spotted near Osarian. Couple of destroyer analogs and—"

"Han," she said, cutting him off. "Droma's sister is on Gyndine."

He sat bolt upright. "What? How do you know that?"

"Because some of his clanmates are among the group evacuated from Gyndine. There wasn't time to take everyone, and his sister was one of at least six Ryn I was forced to leave behind. I didn't know until we'd already transferred everyone to the transports."

"Why didn't you say so in the first place?" Han demanded.

"Because there's nothing either of us can do about it. Gyndine's occupied."

"There are ways around that," Han mumbled distractedly.

Leia compressed her lips. "You are infuriatingly predictable."

"And you worry too much."

"Someone has to."

"Leia, will you be there for a while—on Ralltiir?"

She shook her head. "We'll be leaving for Ruan, if I have any say in the matter. Then I'm going to Hapes."

"Hapes?" Han said in incredulity. "And you accuse

me of putting myself in the thick of things? Why there of all places?"

"With any luck, to enlist the Consortium's help. The New Republic fleets are spread too thinly to defend the Colonies, let alone the Core. And now with Bilbringi, Corellia, perhaps even Bothawui endangered, we need all the support we can rally. Which reminds me, Han, Admiral Sovv has asked Anakin to go to Corellia to help in reenabling Centerpoint Station."

He snorted. "It's about time the New Republic started considering Corellia's defense."

"Then you're all right with his going—without either of us?"

"How old were you when you agreed to carry the technical readouts of the Death Star? Which of us is watching over Jaina when she flies with Rogue Squadron?"

"But—"

"Besides, Anakin's a Jedi."

"I suppose you're right," Leia said, clearly unconvinced.

Han smiled ambiguously. "Be sure to say hello to Prince Isolder for me."

"Why don't you come with me to Hapes and tell him in person?"

He laughed at the idea. "What, and spoil your fun?"

"What's that supposed to mean?"

He started to reply but bit back whatever he had in mind to say, and began again. "Is there any hope for the folks you couldn't extract from Gyndine?"

Leia shut her eyes and shook her head. "I'm not sure any of them even survived."

"I am Chine-kal, commander of the vessel you find yourselves aboard," the Yuuzhan Vong officer announced in expert Basic as he meandered slowly among the immobilized and shackled beings captured on Gyndine.

Slender and of towering height, he wore a turban in which a winged creature was nested, its round black eyes mere centimeters above Chine-kal's own and identical to them. His command cloak, too, had a mind of its own, not so much trailing along the hold's pliant deck as in tow. The designs that twined around his forearms were of a decidedly beastly motif, though of a menagerie unknown to any of the captives, and the fingers of his elongated hands sported curving talons.

"This vessel, which answers to the name *Crèche* in your traders' tongue, is to be your world for the foreseeable future. In time, the purpose of its sphere cluster design will be made clear to you. But even while you grapple with its mysteries, I want you to think of it as your home, and of myself and my crew as your parents and teachers. For you, all of you, have been selected from Ord Mantell's and Gyndine's defeated multitudes to execute a singular service."

Chine-kal stopped in front of Wurth Skidder, perhaps by chance, though Skidder preferred to think that some of his true nature, a touch of the Force, bled through the mental blanket he'd thrown over his identity. Behind the commander walked the tunic-wearing priest who had supervised prisoner selection on Gyndine's surface, as well as the immolation of thousands of droids.

Skidder and the hundreds of unclothed others in the ship's cavernous, organic hold were literally fixed in place by dollops of binding blorash jelly and fettered by the pincers of living creatures. To his right stood an elderly man—clearly a captive of some earlier campaign—made to appear younger than his years by cosmetic treatments; to his left, two of the half-dozen Ryn who had also been selected for "singular service" aboard the

Yuuzhan Vong ship, which, from space, had resembled a bunch of grapes. Elsewhere were other veteran captives, some left haggard, some strengthened by whatever ordeals they had been put through.

"You have no doubt heard rumors of what occurred on the worlds you know as Dantooine, Ithor, and Obroa-skai," Chine-kal said, back in motion, "and you have no doubt heard rumors about how the Yuuzhan Vong treat their prisoners. I can assure you that all you have heard are lies and exaggerations.

"We are only trying to bring you a truth you sadly overlooked in your climb from the primal muck. Met with resistance, we have been left with no option but to force that truth on you; met with acceptance, we have been far more charitable than your New Republic overseers would have been to us.

"Because of political affiliations and other alliances, worlds don't often have a choice in whether to accept or decline our offer of enlightenment; the voice of a few decide the destiny of the many. But on this vessel you are individuals first, and each of you has an opportunity to decide for yourself whether to resist or to accept. You have a hand in determining your destiny—in governing your fate."

Flanked by well-armed guards and still trailed by the priest, Chine-kal came to a halt alongside a tall statue of a creature that could only have sprung from some Yuuzhan Vong bestiary. Its convoluted body might have been modeled on a human brain, and yet the body possessed two large eyes and what appeared to be a mouth or wrinkled maw. Arms or tentacles extended from its base, some stumpy, others gracile.

"I don't want you to think of yourselves as captives or slaves, but rather as collaborators in a grand enterprise," the commander continued. "Serve me well, put your hearts into your work, and you will be rewarded with your lives. Fail me out of weakness, and I may be willing to forgive; but fail me with design, and punishment will be meted out swiftly and without mercy. In either case, I will be rewarded by the gods, though I'll be forced to look elsewhere for collaborators."

Skidder cut his eyes to the man beside him. "How long have you been aboard?" he asked out of the corner of his mouth.

"Losing track," the captive answered in a low voice. "A couple of standard months." With subtle movement of his chin he indicated the emaciated man to his right. "My friend and I were captured on the *Jubilee Wheel* at Ord Mantell. Got sucked out of the facility by some kind of space worm. First we were taken aboard a slave galley. Thought for a while we were going to be launched into a star and sacrificed. Then we were transferred to this vessel." The man shot Skidder a glance. "You?"

"Captured on Gyndine."

"Soldier?"

"Indigenous ground force."

The man turned ever so slightly in Skidder's direction. "But you're not native to Gyndine. From the Core, I'd say."

"On what basis?"

"Hairstyle, for one thing. The way you carry yourself. Intrusion specialist? Intelligence officer?"

"Neither."

The man glanced downward. "Those aren't the feet of an infantry soldier."

"I didn't say I was. Operated an AT-ST scout."

The man nodded. "Okay, have it your way."

"What's your name?" Skidder asked.

"Roa. My friend is Fasgo. You?"

"Keyn. Any idea where we're headed, Roa?"

"None."

"What about this 'singular service'?"

Roa snorted softly. "You'll see soon enough, Keyn."

Chine-kal's preamble had resumed. "It's time you had a look at the centerpiece of our endeavor," he was saying. "Think of it for the moment as a work in progress, but one that all of you will help to complete."

Behind the commander rose a membranous partition, beyond which—Skidder was certain—lay the nucleus of the ship. When Chine-kal turned, the membrane parted like a stage curtain.

Though Skidder had never seen one in the flesh, he knew immediately that he was gazing at the living model for the statue that adorned the hold: a maturing war coordinator—the grotesque biogenetic creature the Yuuzhan Vong called a yammosk.

SIX

A cool mist obscured the flowering crowns of Yavin 4's tallest trees. The steep stairways of the ancient temples the Rebel Alliance had claimed so many years before and that had since become a training ground for the Jedi Knights climbed into the mist and vanished. Chucklucks and chitterwebs, ordinarily raucous at that time of the morning, perched on the low branches of Massassi trees, waiting for the sky to clear. Stinger lizards and stintaril rodents sat motionless as statues. Even the gas giant Yavin was not to be seen, though it backlighted the mist a deep orange color.

Stopped in a pathway that meandered to the Great Temple, Luke Skywalker drank in the stillness. The Force, ordinarily lucid, seemed blanketed by the mist, as well, and could manage little more than a whisper.

Somewhere in the ghostly, virid surroundings a bellybird cooed. But Luke knew that what struck his ear as melodic was only the bird proclaiming its territory, warning others away. He listened more intently, catching the sounds of creatures foraging or on the hunt for food. It was the way of the Force that some should survive and others perish. Death without malicious intent, for nature didn't have a dark side. One couldn't compare the crystal snake's search for prey with what the Emperor had done during his cruel reign and what the Yuuzhan Vong were doing now. But Luke had been asking himself, almost since the start of the invasion, how did life reveal itself to Yuuzhan Vong eyes and ears?

He stared into the mist. It was as if someone had thrown a gauzy veil over his eyes. Images came to him of insects disguising themselves as leaves, twigs, and flower blossoms, and of small animals mimicking the variegated litter of the forest floor. Camouflage, Luke thought.

Deception, stealth, misdirection . . .

The Yuuzhan Vong had swept into the galaxy like one of the unpredictable storms that blew across Yavin 4. Their faith in their gods was like Palpatine's faith in the dark side of the Force. And yet, for all the evil they embodied, they were not Sith; they were not emissaries of the dark side. Blind obedience provided justification for even their most hideous actions. What made them servants of evil was not their faith but their need to force that faith on others and to destroy wantonly any who stood in their path. They failed to recognize light or dark because in some sense they saw existence as an illusion. Lacking any intrinsic value, life was to be lived in service to the gods, and the reward for that service waited in a life beyond.

When Luke or other Jedi had tried to peer into them, the Yuuzhan Vong had been found to be voids in the Force, absent the animated luminosity that embraced all living things. But if the Force did not flow through them, was it possible that the Force was likewise nonexistent in the galaxy in which they had evolved? Could the Force be specific to one place and not another, as if the result of an evolutionary occurrence unique in the universe? Or was it rather that the Force was lacking only in the Yuuzhan Vong—and in their living weapons, of course, which were little more than extensions of themselves?

In all likelihood Mara had fallen victim to one of those weapons—an illness the Yuuzhan Vong had introduced—and while her strength in the Force had held the illness in check where it had overwhelmed others, Luke wasn't absolutely certain that the Force would have been the ultimate victor in Mara's battle. Not when her recent return to better health owed to an antidote introduced indirectly by the Yuuzhan Vong.

Deception, stealth, misdirection . . .

For all his intense curiosity, Luke understood that it was imperative that the invaders be defeated. If defeat could be accomplished short of exterminating the Yuuzhan Vong, so much the better, for then some of his questions might one day be answered. But until such time the Jedi were obligated to aid and abet in the war that had been thrust upon the galaxy. How best to execute the Jedi obligation to peace and justice was an issue he was still grappling with.

The cryptic murmuring of the Force returned him to the moment. He recognized that his visitor had ceased talking some time ago, and he swung to face him now.

"I'm sorry, Talon, you were saying?"

Talon Karrde smiled faintly. But instead of picking up where he'd left off, he smoothed the ends of his dark mustache and continued to observe the Jedi Master with candid interest.

"You know, Luke, I can't tell you how often I've wondered what the universe looks like through the eyes of a Jedi. I used to tell myself that you weren't all that different from an H'kig priest or an Ithorian who had heard the call, only instead of revering H'kig or nature you looked to the Force. But the comparisons never held up. You see things the rest of us don't see—or can't see—and those things aren't just the products of a mind-set the

Jedi have cultivated as a separate reality. You see into the heart of reality, and that ability informs your actions."

Karrde's blue eyes sparkled. "I've seen you make decisions I couldn't fathom at the time, but later turned out to be the right decisions. I used to watch Mara do the same thing. And as someone who has always prided himself on making use of privileged information, I had to ask myself whether those decisions were based solely on data I didn't have access to, or if the Force gave you the ability to tug reality this way or that as needed—as required by your visions.

"I sense the latter's true with you, but I'm not sure if it applies to Mara." Karrde uttered a short laugh. "I'm sorry I never knew you when you were fresh off Tatooine—before you turned into a deep thinker. I'm not saying that Mara isn't a deep thinker, but the Force seems to compel her to act more on intuition than deliberation."

Ceremoniously, Luke lowered the cowl of his Jedi robe. "Mara and I are different but complementary—in the same way Anakin and Jacen are. There are different aspects to the Force, and not all Jedi focus on the same one. My Masters admonished me for always looking toward the future without really seeing it."

"Could your father see the future?" Talon asked carefully.

"My father was not the seer but the lens." Luke grew introspective for a moment, then smiled enigmatically. "By the way, if Mara had known you were coming to Yavin 4, she would have postponed her visit to Coruscant."

"Another evaluation?"

"On the contrary. She refuses to be scanned, examined, or evaluated by anyone."

"Then it actually cured her—this magic elixir Solo was given?"

"Not an elixir—tears. And no one will use the word *cure*, even Mara. I urged her to hold off on taking the antidote until we could be sure it wasn't potentially dangerous, but she refused. She insisted on taking the risk."

Talon nodded. "Her intuition. But you're not convinced?"

Luke gazed at the jungle. "The Yuuzhan Vong priestess who claimed she wanted political asylum was a weapon sent to assassinate as many Jedi as she could gather. The being who traveled with her, Vergere, was not Yuuzhan Vong, but that doesn't mean she wasn't serving their interests."

"The elixir could have been part of the plot," Talon said. "The Yuuzhan Vong could have wanted to make it appear this Vergere was on our side, to erase doubts about the substance she gave Han."

Luke said nothing.

"But Mara's better."

"Healthier than she's been in almost a year," Luke admitted. "Joyous—as I am."

"If she does slide, if the effect turns out to be temporary . . ."

"Whatever is contained in Vergere's tears can't be replicated. The chemical action is as puzzling as anything we've seen from the Yuuzhan Vong. We can only hope the effect is permanent."

Karrde considered it. "You know I'd do anything to help Mara. I'll track down Vergere. I'll wring more tears out of her if I have to."

Luke smiled. "I appreciate that, Talon. I'll tell Mara you said so, though I suspect she already knows."

They resumed their walk to the Great Temple. Off to

one side of the path a dozen young Jedi, varying in age from four to twelve, were watching Tionne and Kam Solusar demonstrate a Force technique. Luke paused to observe one of the older children, Tahiri, attempt to mimic one of Kam's manipulations.

"Yavin 4 has remained undetected, but with the Yuuzhan Vong as close as Obroa-skai, we may be forced to remove everyone to safer surroundings."

"I'm surprised they haven't targeted Yavin already."

Luke turned to him. "We're projecting an illusion. Something I learned from the Fallanassi."

Talon's eyes narrowed in revelation. "So that's why you insisted on guiding me into the Yavin system."

"Your eyes would have contradicted what your ship's instruments were telling you."

Talon put his tongue in his cheek and laughed. "If I'd had a line on that technique, I wouldn't have had to base out of Myrkr, where the trees had a way of tricking scanners." He grinned broadly. "But of course you remember that . . ."

"Yes," Luke said flatly. "And even then, Grand Admiral Thrawn found you out. As Jedi commitment to the conflict increases, there won't be enough of us here to maintain the illusion. The children will have to be sent elsewhere."

Talon glanced at the kids. "Let me know if you ever need help with that."

"I will."

They hadn't gone another ten paces when Karrde asked, "Is it true a Jedi died on Gyndine?"

"You're referring to Wurth Skidder," Luke said. "But we don't know for certain that he's dead. Leia was there to the end. She insists that Wurth deliberately remained behind."

"To allow himself to be captured?"

"Perhaps to go undercover on Gyndine."

Karrde shook his head. "I don't know Skidder, but I've heard rumors. Is he the person for the job?"

"He's skillful."

"Skill's good, but is he lucky?"

Luke didn't answer the question. "Just now, like so many of us who have lost friends and family, he's driven by vengeance. He was close friends with both Miko Reglia and Daeshara'cor."

"Well, there's nothing wrong with being motivated by vengeance if it gets you results."

Luke's expression said otherwise.

"Wrong?"

"Let's just say that we don't see the world in precisely the same way."

They continued walking. Over the cascading sounds of the river that flowed past the Great Temple came voices raised in impassioned debate or argument.

"Sounds like there's some division in the ranks," Talon remarked as they neared the temple's common room.

"That would be Jacen and Anakin."

"Complementing one another, no doubt."

Jaina, with arms outstretched, was positioned between her brothers when Luke and Karrde entered the dimly lighted space. A handful of other Jedi, including Kyp Durron, Ganner Rhysode, Streen, Lowbacca, Kenth Hamner, and Cilghal, looked on. Sensing Luke, R2-D2 began to bounce from foot to foot, chirring and warbling.

"They were just . . . discussing Anakin's invitation to visit Centerpoint Station," Jaina explained.

Luke glanced from Jacen to Anakin and back again. "Finish the discussion."

Jacen scowled at his younger brother. "I'll say it once more, then I'm done with it: Centerpoint is this"—he grasped the hilt of the lightsaber that hung from his belt—"on a gargantuan scale. Assuming the station can even be made operational, it should be used only for defense."

Anakin exhaled wearily. "And I'll say this one last time: I completely agree."

"Then keep away from Corellia," Jacen said. "Don't have anything to do with enabling Centerpoint or any of the hyperspace repulsors. You were a kid the first time—we all were. You didn't know any better."

Anakin snorted. "You're leaving out that my ignorant actions ended up foiling the Triad's plans to detonate another star and annihilate every ship the Bakurans sent against them."

"That was defensive! Your tinkering with the repulsor on Drall prevented Centerpoint from firing!"

"Tinkering," Anakin repeated, snickering. "Let me ask you something: Are you against Jaina flying with Rogue Squadron?"

Jacen glanced at his twin sister, who was on temporary leave from the squadron she had joined only four months earlier. "Not in theory."

"Are you against Mom and Tenel Ka going to Hapes?"

"Not in principle."

"Not in principle? The New Republic is hoping to bring the Consortium into the war. If you think of Rogue Squadron or the Hapans as weapons—an extension of *that*," Anakin said, gesturing to Jacen's lightsaber, "then what's the difference between what Jaina or Mom are being asked to do and what I've been asked to do at Corellia? I said I'd help enable the station. I didn't say anything about firing it."

Jacen made an exasperated sound and swung to Luke. "Where do you stand on this, Uncle Luke?"

Luke folded his arms. "As I told the Defense Force command staff, I'm opposed to reenabling Centerpoint on the grounds that its power is too unmanageable. And you all know that I was against Daeshara'cor's attempts to resurrect another *Eye of Palpatine*. But if there's even a chance that Centerpoint Station can be used to defend Corellia and spare the fleets for service elsewhere, we're obliged to do what we can to help make it operational."

Jacen pressed his lips together and swung back to his brother. "All right, Anakin, have it your way. But I'm going with you."

Anakin shrugged. "Glad to have you along."

The debate decided for the moment, the teens settled down and everyone gradually formed a loose circle around Luke and Karrde.

"Talon has a proposition for us," Luke said. "I haven't heard it yet, but knowing him as I do, I'm sure it will be interesting."

"Or at least entertaining," Kyp Durron mumbled, drawing laughs.

Karrde took the jesting in stride. "As I'm sure you know, the Hutts have struck some sort of bargain with the Yuuzhan Vong. By bargain, I mean just that, since the Hutts would sooner go to war than roll over for an enemy, no matter how commanding. So it stands to reason that in exchange for allowing the Yuuzhan Vong into their space, the Hutts asked for and got something in return. To figure out what that is, all anyone needs to do is follow the spice."

Karrde paused briefly. "I've been doing just that, and I haven't noticed any signs of interruption in the flow of spice—except in three systems: Tynna, Bothawui, and Corellia."

He waited until the murmuring died down before continuing. "The Hutts wouldn't suddenly cease deliveries to three profitable sectors unless there was good reason to avoid them. I'm willing to bet that the reason has to do with intelligence the Yuuzhan Vong provided as their part of the deal. Namely, that those systems have been targeted for invasion.

"The fact that no one has moved in to pick up the slack suggests that the Hutts have advised all their partners and subcontractors to steer a wide berth around Tynna, Bothawui, and Corellia. But even this doesn't add up to a case good enough to present to the New Republic. To do that would require proof positive that avoiding those worlds isn't just the result of the Hutts *speculating* about where the Yuuzhan Vong will strike."

"Why not approach the Hutts and ask them directly?" Kenth Hamner asked. Tall and wellborn, Hamner had been a Defense Force colonel before resigning from military life to follow the Jedi way.

"Easier said than done," Karrde said, "and in fact, the New Republic is trying to do just that. But if someone outside the military could furnish corroborating evidence, the Defense Force would have what they need to catch the Yuuzhan Vong completely by surprise."

"Why do you come to us with this?" Streen asked. "You've been liaison between the Imperial Remnant and the New Republic since the peace accord. You certainly don't need us to get the attention of Admiral Sovv."

"I know why he's come to us," Kyp Durron said, keeping his eyes on Karrde. "Because the New Republic left him out of the loop when they asked Leia to approach the Imperial Remnant about joining the fight."

Karrde snorted. "It wasn't my place to approach the Remnant assembly. I'm a broker, Kyp, not an ambassador."

"Then what makes you think it's your place to approach us?" Kyp retorted.

"The fact is, I don't know who else to trust with this. Judging by the way New Republic Intelligence handled that bogus Yuuzhan Vong defector, I'd venture to say that the Intelligence division, maybe even the Advisory Council itself, has been infiltrated. What's more, the Defense Force can't act without the approval of the senate, and the Security and Intelligence Council isn't likely to back Admiral Sovv on the word of an ex-smuggler."

"You still haven't clarified why you need us," Ulaha said. A Bith, she was delicate-looking and musically gifted. "After Ithor, we're hardly in good stead with the senate ourselves."

"That's the point: you need to get them listening to you again. You'd think they would have learned their lesson from Ithor, but old habits die hard and they're still reluctant to trust you. They don't want to be perceived as indebted to the Jedi. It smacks of Old Republic thinking."

Ganner grimaced, wrinkling the facial scar he had incurred at Garqi. "It warms my heart to see that you're thinking about us, Karrde, but the Jedi don't need a public relations person."

"You're wrong, Ganner. You're too trusting. Anti-Jedi sentiment is spreading. Some folks think you're holding back, others think you're incompetent. A lot of people wish that Emperor Palpatine was still around, because they feel he'd know how to deal with the Yuuzhan Vong. If you want to go back to being monks, that's your choice. But if you want to serve peace and justice, you need to smarten your image, and one way to do that would be to provide intelligence that ends up giving the New Republic a major victory. The best defense against treachery is treachery."

"What role could we play in this?" Jacen asked impatiently.

Talon looked at him. "I can facilitate a meeting with one of the Hutts' spice smugglers. We can find out for ourselves why no one is willing to deliver to Tynna and the rest."

Jacen rolled his eyes. "This is Centerpoint all over again." He glanced at Luke. "The Jedi shouldn't have any part in this. It demeans us."

"It doesn't demean anyone," Anakin argued. "We can help without having to raise a hand—or a lightsaber. You, if anybody, should be in favor of that."

Everyone looked to Luke.

Images came to him of insects disguising themselves as leaves, twigs, and flower blossoms, and of small animals mimicking the variegated litter of the forest floor. The Force whispered to him once more: *Deception, stealth, misdirection . . .*

He realized that he needed to tread carefully, for fear of dividing the Jedi further. Where many lauded Corran Horn's individual actions at Ithor, others favored Kyp Durron's stance that aggression should be answered by aggression. What's more, at Ithor Luke had renounced responsibility for spearheading the Jedi Knights.

"I'm not interested in repairing our tarnished image," he said at last. "The New Republic isn't eager to sanction our actions, in any case. But if we can help provide information that will prevent the fall of another world, the choice is clear."

"I'm willing to go with Talon," Jaina said.

Kyp made a face. "A seventeen-year-old spice buyer? I doubt the Hutts' people will buy it." He looked back at Karrde. "I'll go. You'll need someone to sort the truth from the lies."

"Unlikely," Karrde said, "but I appreciate the offer."

"Then count me in, as well," Ganner said. He glanced at Kyp. "Just to be certain we're getting the full truth."

Karrde glanced around him. "It's settled then?"

Only Jacen remained unconvinced. "Centerpoint, enlistment, espionage . . . I never thought we'd come to this."

Kyp Durron grinned and clapped him hard on the shoulder. "Cheer up, kid. Things are bad all over."

SEVEN

The sign hovering between formidable guard towers read WELCOME TO RUAN REFUGEE FACILITY 17. But just below the greeting someone had scrawled, in a tiny almost undetectable hand, LAST CHANCE TO TURN BACK.

Crushed in among the rerouted mixed-species thousands off-loaded from the transport ships, and still wet and possibly poisoned from Ruan's cursory decontamination process, Melisma read the sign aloud and aimed a worried glance at Gaph, who had Droma's nephew balanced atop one of his shoulders.

" 'Last chance to turn back'?"

"Someone's idea of a joke," Gaph said in dismissal. "Come, child, how bad can it be? We have pleasing countryside all around, fresh air in place of scrubbed oxygen, the promise of food and drink, ten thousand melancholy sentients for company." He grinned and lowered his voice to add, "And where there are melancholy sentients, there are opportunities galore for the Ryn."

Melisma smiled uncertainly, though what Gaph said about the surroundings was undeniably true, for Ruan was nothing if not one of the Core's beauty marks.

One of eighteen agricultural worlds administered by Salliche Ag, Ruan—or at least that part of the planet the refugees had been delivered to—had the manicured look

of a park. The undeviating road that linked the planet's
bustling spaceport to Refugee Facility 17 was bordered
by tall, topiary hedges, and beyond those hedges, as far
as the eye could see, stretched scrupulously maintained
fields of crops, in varying states of maturation. Unlike
Orron III, Ukio, Taanab, and most of the other bread-
basket worlds on which the Ryn had sought employment from time to time, Ruan did not merely rely on
axial tilt and fertile soil, but was climate controlled
and agriformed to maximize output. Also there were far
fewer harvester droids, agribots, and work droids than
Melisma had expected to see, which meant more occupa-
tional opportunities for sentients.

She breathed deeply of the sweet air. Gaph was right.
Arriving on Ruan, especially after spending more than a
standard week in the cramped and fetid living conditions
aboard the transport, was like being delivered to paradise itself. But vague concerns continued to rankle her.
How long would they be required to remain on Ruan,
and where would they end up afterwards? Princess Leia
had made it clear that their stay on Ruan would be temporary, but with the Yuuzhan Vong already in the Expansion Region, how long before they carried their
invasion into the Core? And what then?

Processing the newly arrived exiles was a painfully te-
dious business. With everyone pressed so tightly together
there was nowhere to sit much less recline, and no escape
from the potent sunshine that climate supervision had
apparently ordered for the day. The crowd seemed to extend endlessly to the front and rear. But at last the five of
them—Gaph, Melisma, her two female clancousins, and
the infant—reached a processing checkpoint attended by
armed security guards sporting Salliche Ag arm badges.

A human male with a scarred jaw appraised them

from the window of the checkpoint booth. "What in the galaxy are these?" he asked someone out of view.

Instantly, a no-less-sinister-looking uniformed female appeared at the window and aimed a spherically shaped optical scanner directly at Melisma. "Could take the system a moment to recognize them," she told the first guard. When the scanner emitted a single tone, she glanced at its display screen. "Ryn."

"Ryn? What rock are they from?"

The woman shook her head. "Planet of origin unknown. But what's the difference, they arrived from Gyndine. See if we've got any more like them."

Melisma's misgivings returned. SELCORE advocates and Ruan officials at the spaceport had been cordial and accommodating, but these guards, both in their bearing and manner of dress, brought to mind the Espos who, years back, had policed many of the Corporate Sector worlds.

"Yeah, we actually do have some others," the first guard was saying. "Thirty-two, at last count." He sneered down at Gaph. "Sec 465, Ryn. Behind the communal refreshers."

Gaph heard Melisma's sharp intake of breath and turned to her. "All right, so forget what I said about fresh air. We'll still have food and drink to slack our appetites and a roof over our heads."

"We could have all that in jail," Melisma groused.

Gaph wagged his forefinger. "Trust me, child, jail is no place for the Ryn. Here, at least, we'll be able to sing and dance and revel in our good fortune."

"Follow the droid," the guard barked. "And no lingering or wandering off, or you'll have me to answer to."

"Ah, good fortune," Melisma said sarcastically. "Let's just hope for a roof, Gaph."

The droid, a squeaking, limping protocol model, ushered them into a warren of ramshackle dwellings slapped together from aged harvester and spaceship parts—bulkhead hatchways, harvester blades, foils, and the like. Elsewhere were prefabricated duraplast huts anchored to slabs of ferrocrete, tents and A-frames, primitive lean-tos, self-standing blister shelters, elliptical huts sided with animal hide, and conical ones wrapped in lubricant-stained tarpaulins.

"Facility 17 was built on the site of a former junkyard," the droid said proudly. "Everyone has been very inventive in the use of obsolete equipment."

In unlighted interiors or on muddy ground or patches of lifeless trampled grass sat species native to sectors as remote as the Imperial Remnant and as close as the Koornacht Cluster, all uprooted from the worlds they had called home, some of which the Yuuzhan Vong had rendered uninhabitable or destroyed outright. In a half-circle scan, Melisma's eye fell on Ruurians, Gands, Saheelindeeli, Bimms, Weequays, Myneyrshi, Tammarians, Gotals, and Wookiees. Absent, though, was any indication of fellowship; in its place a sense of impending riot tainted the air. Beings glowered at one another or stood sullenly with jaws clenched and hands balled into fists.

As if reading her concerns, the protocol droid provided commentary, in Basic.

"With everyone crammed together without regard to differences and distinctions, some suppressed prejudices and hostilities have on occasion boiled to the fore, resulting in contentious seizures of territory or sustenance, or melees that have spread throughout the facility. But, of course, those incidents were quickly quelled by Salliche Ag's well-trained staff, who employ physical force only when absolutely necessary."

As had happened on the transport, the Ryn met with looks of suspicion and repugnance from all sides. Fathers safeguarded family valuables, and mothers gathered children within arm's reach. Some made religious gestures of self-protection, and others voiced outrage that Ryn had even been allowed into the camp.

Melisma stared straight ahead. She was accustomed to such treatment, and she understood that the Ryn's penchant for wanderlust and secrecy was at least partly responsible for the fictions that had grown up around them. Ostracized by many societies, the Ryn had grown only more transient, secretive, and self-sufficient over time, and as outsiders they had become keen observers of the behaviors of other species—second-guessers of what many beings, humans especially, often had in mind to say. And so their fondness for song, dance, and spicy foods, and their adeptness at forgery and fortune-telling—lacking any true psychic abilities. The gambling game that had come to be known as sabacc had its roots in a deck of cards the Ryn had invented as a means of disguising their mystical doctrines.

"We're now approaching the distribution center," the droid announced.

"I wondered what that smell was," Melisma said to Gaph, who chided her for being overly critical, only to change his tune when they got a good look at the situation.

Queued sinuously at makeshift stalls, hundreds of beings were waiting to receive squirts of an off-color, pastelike synthfood squeezed by droids from enormous, pliant containers. Other lines snaked to the patched-up hulls of vintage riverboats filled to the gunnels with foam-covered water.

"For paltry sums," the droid remarked, "many of

Salliche Ag's well-trained staff will gladly provide food-stuffs to please the most discriminating palates. Superior housing can also be secured for reasonable fees, as evidenced atop Noob Hill."

Melisma followed the droid's metal finger to a parcel of high ground surrounded by stun fencing. Isolated from the rest of the facility, twenty or so Ithorians could be seen going about their business in open-sided, thatch-roofed pavilions. To one side deep drainage ditches separated them from a waddle of Gamorreans, who were living in bungalows made of sun-baked bricks. To the other side, beyond a wall of thorned shrubs, a rumpus of Wookiees had constructed a log tree house.

Deeper in the camp things were even worse. The mud that had been a nuisance earlier on became ankle-deep for long stretches, and the shelters—a ghetto of unroofed sheds and slat-sided shanties—clustered at the base of a hill that saw scant sunlight and funneled runoff rain-water directly into the food distribution area. In place of prefab tents and blister huts stood hovels more suitable for livestock than sentients. Here a trove of resourceful hollow-boned Vors had made use of starship maneuvering vanes to construct a kind of stilted bower for themselves; and there a nest of batrachian Rybet had fashioned a spacious hutch from empty cargo crates and support pylons off Y-wing engine nacelles.

Nearly everyone else was living in filth.

A new stench in the air told Melisma that they were nearing the communal refreshers. "Maybe it's only when there's no wind," Gaph remarked.

"Then maybe we should petition climate supervision to whip up a hurricane," Melisma said from behind the hand she'd clamped over her mouth.

As promised, just past the refreshers was Section 465,

announced by a sign, to which someone had added the words *Ryn City*.

More than half the thirty-two were on hand to greet Gaph and Melisma's quintet as they trudged into a courtyard that might have struck some as uncommonly sanitary but was in fact normal for the Ryn, who were by nature almost ritualistic about order and cleanliness.

The leader among the ensconced group, a tall male named R'vanna, welcomed them with bowls of tasty Ryn food and a slew of questions about the circumstances that had brought them to Ruan. Gaph started at the very beginning, explaining how they had just fled the Corporate Sector when their caravan of ships had been set upon by a Yuuzhan Vong patrol. Scattered far and wide as a result of emergency hyperspace jumps, many had ended up at Ord Mantell's *Jubilee Wheel*, where they had been caught up in another Yuuzhan Vong attack. Refugees by then, some had found transport to Bilbringi, others to Rhinnal, and still others to Gyndine.

Then R'vanna told his story, which, while it began in the Tion Hegemony, had much in common with Gaph's tale of woe.

One of the women showed Melisma and her cousins to a dormitory. Leaving the infant in the care of her cousins, Melisma rejoined Gaph and R'vanna, who was in the midst of painting a vivid picture of life in Facility 17.

"Though water is rarely a problem—our overseers simply create rainstorms as needed—food shortages have begun to occur on a regular basis and disease is rampant. The diseases could easily be eradicated, of course, and Ruan is capable of supplying all the food needed just from what the labor droids allow to rot in or on the ground, but it's to Salliche Ag's advantage that everyone in camp remain as miserable as possible."

"How is that to Salliche's advantage?" Melisma asked. "And why would Princess Leia praise the company for its unconditional generosity if we're a burden to everyone?"

"Salliche is desirous of refugees, child, but not for the camps. They want us in the fields."

"As workers?"

"Of a sort." R'vanna paused to tap a wad of charred t'bac from the bowl of a hand-carved pipe. "The New Republic is genuinely committed to relocating everyone to populous worlds, but with the war and all, the chances of relocation are slim—even though you won't hear mention of this in the familiarization classes."

"Familiarization?" Melisma said. "For what?"

"Why, to prepare us for our new lives among the civilized peoples of the Core. You'll soon see for yourself. But as I say, chances are slim. Some of those living on Noob Hill can afford to purchase forward passage with private transport companies, but not everyone is so fortunate. In any event, no one wants to be here any longer than necessary, so many have accepted offers by Salliche Ag to work their way off Ruan."

"In the fields," Gaph said.

R'vanna nodded. "Except that very few manage to earn enough to purchase onward passage. Most of the camp's earliest arrivals have been forced into indentured servitude, here on Ruan or on other Salliche-administered worlds, and rumors persist that those who refuse Salliche's benevolence often disappear."

"But it makes no sense," Melisma said. "Sentients will never replace droids as workers. Sentients need more than the occasional oil bath and data upgrades. Not to mention that production would be drastically reduced."

R'vanna showed her a patient smile. "I said as much to a Salliche representative who visited Ryn City only last week. And do you know what he told me? That the hiring of sentients not only eases the refugee problem but allows the company to advertise its products as retaining 'handpicked freshness.' "

Gaph mulled it over for a moment. "So our options, for the moment, are either to go to work for Salliche Ag or remain mired here."

Melisma glanced around the courtyard, and at the masterfully built dormitories and kitchens. "How have you managed to do so well? Walking through the camp, I was afraid we were going to be attacked and killed. If folks could find a way, I'm sure they'd hold us account-able for the Yuuzhan Vong invasion."

R'vanna smiled sadly. "Life has always been thus for the Ryn. But not everyone fears or distrusts us. It's thanks to those few that we've done so well."

"Charity?"

"Bite your tongue, child," Gaph said theatrically. "The Ryn do not accept charity. We work for all we get."

Melisma looked at R'vanna. "What sort of work can we do here?"

"The sort we're best at: apprising people of their op-tions, allowing them to see the error of their ways, pro-viding them with helpful tips to see them through the complexities of daily life."

"Telling fortunes," Melisma said, mildly disdainful. "Reading sabacc cards."

Gaph was grinning broadly. "Singing, dancing, the re-wards that come to those who dispense good advice . . . Life could be worse, child. Life could be much worse."

"Aren't you the one who said that help had arrived?" the red-maned Ryn named Sapha asked Wurth Skidder aboard the slave ship *Crèche*.

"I might have said something to that effect," the Jedi

was willing to concede. "Heat of the moment, and all that."

Roa regarded Skidder with interest, then glanced past him at Sapha. "When was this?"

"On Gyndine," she told him, "when he rushed to be captured by the multilegged creature that was herding us together. He said, 'Take heart, help has arrived.' "

Roa looked at Skidder once more. "He rushed?"

Sapha shrugged. "It looked that way from where I stood."

Side by side, the three of them were standing to their waists in the viscous sorrel-colored nutrient in which the young yammosk marinated, like an excised brain in an autopsy pan. The cloying odor—like garlic roses bathed in nlora perfume—had taken some getting used to, but by now almost all the captives were beyond the retching stage, though a male Sullustan had fainted moments earlier and had had to be carried out.

One of the more gracile of the creature's manifold tentacles floated in front of Skidder and his comrades, and their hands were busy massaging and caressing it, the way the Bimms did with certain breeds of nerf to assure steaks of extraordinary tenderness. Roa's worrisomely wan pal, Fasgo, and two Ryn were doing the same to the other side of the tentacle. The arrangement of six to a tentacle was repeated throughout the circular basin, except at the yammosk's shorter, thicker members, where two or three captives sufficed.

"He rushed," Roa said, more to himself this time; then he fixed Skidder with a gimlet stare. "Sapha almost makes it sound like you wanted to be captured, Keyn."

"To wind up here?" Skidder said. "A guy would have to be either deranged or dauntless."

Smile lines formed at the corners of Roa's eyes. "I've

known a few in my day who were both. I can't put my finger on it, but something tells me you fit the bill."

Two hose-thick, pulsating ducts projected from the yammosk's bulbous head to disappear into the arching, membranous ceiling of the hold. Skidder assumed that at least one of them furnished the creature with a required mix of respiratory gases, though Chine-kal assured that yammosks became oxygen breathers as they matured into actual war coordinators.

At the moment the clustership's commander was completing a circle on the grated walkway that ran around the lip of the yorik-coral basin. Concentric to the basin stood a company of lightly armed guards.

"For all the revulsion it seems to invoke in some of you, the yammosk is an extremely sensitive creature," he was saying. "One effect of its powerful desire to bond is empathy of a high order, which later culminates as telepathy, of a sort. As part of its early training, the yammosk is conditioned to regard select dovin basals as its children, its brood—the same dovin basals that provide thrust for our starships and the single-pilot craft the New Republic military refers to as coralskippers. When, then, we enter into engagements with the forces of your worlds, the yammosk sees its children as threatened and attempts to coordinate their activities to minimize loss."

Chine-kal came to a halt close to where Skidder and the others stood, and gestured to the ceiling. "The darker blue of the throbbing arteries that enter the yammosk just above the eyes is linked even now to the drive of this ship, because the yammosk is still in the process of familiarizing itself with the dovin basal. The kinder you are to the yammosk, the more affection you show for it, the better you make it feel, the better its link with the dovin basal, and the better the ship performs."

The commander pivoted to face one of the membranous walls. In a blister visible to all the captives sat a pulsing, heart-shaped organism.

"Here you see a small dovin basal, approximate in size to the ones housed in the noses of the coralskippers. Its color indicates how well you are succeeding at your task, and its current pale red tells me that you are doing reasonably well, but not as well as you might. So what we're going to do is increase the pace of our strokings in time with the count provided by the dovin basal. If we're successful, the ship will respond in turn. So let us begin . . ."

Skidder braced himself. It wasn't so much that the handwork itself was fatiguing, but intense and constant tactile contact with the tentacles quickly left everyone exhausted, almost as if the yammosk was feeding off the captives' expended energy to somehow enhance itself. It was easy enough to refuse participation, but holding back led only to someone being singled out and punished.

As the dovin basal began to pulse more rapidly, the captives increased the speed and force of the strokings and kneadings, struggling to find a rhythm. The pulses grew even more rapid; the manipulations grew more urgent and frantic. The count quickened once more. Many of the captives were breathing hard, some of them wheezing. Rills of sweat coursed down faces and arms. Those who couldn't sustain the pace collapsed, doubled over atop their assigned tentacles, or slid down into the gluey nutrient. But the rest had found a collective beat the yammosk responded to by sending ripples down its tentacles.

Skidder could almost feel the clustership surge.

Then the dovin basal slowed and gradually returned to a gentle pulsing.

"Good," Commander Chine-kal said at last. "Very good."

Skidder swallowed hard and calmed himself. Sapha and Roa were panting, and Fasgo looked delirious.

Chine-kal began another circuit on the organic walkway. "As some of you have already learned, battle coordination is only one of the yammosk's talents. When I told you earlier that its empathy bordered on telepathy, I was not overstating things. Also as part of its training, the young yammosk is conditioned to establish a cognitive rapport with the commander in whose custody the yammosk will serve. In fact, this yammosk and myself are already on familiar terms. But we're going to attempt something that has never been done—the truly 'extraordinary' part of this joint endeavor. We wish the yammosk to become familiar with you—with all of you—so that we might bring this invasion to a speedy and relatively painless conclusion."

Skidder glanced at Roa. "Did you know about this?"

The old man returned a grim nod.

"As the yammosk becomes more accustomed to your touch," Chine-kal was saying, "it may wish to touch you back, especially on the chest, upper back, neck, and face. You will allow it to do so. It may take no interest in some of you; with others it may find a deep affinity. In either case, I caution you not to resist its telepathic probes, for you risk injuring yourself as much as the yammosk. Resistance could very well result in madness or death. Laugh, cry, scream if you must, but do not resist."

"He's not kidding," Roa said with sudden solemnity. He looked intently at Sapha, then Skidder. "Try to keep your mind blank, otherwise it will pursue your thoughts like a predator chasing the first meal of the day. That's where you can lose your way. Believe me, I've seen it happen more than once."

Skidder had been doing his best to hide his Jediness, his strength in the Force, the events that had motivated him to be captured, his wish to avenge his fallen comrades. Faced with Chine-kal's revelation, however, he suddenly couldn't help but recall what Danni Quee had told him of the way the Yuuzhan Vong had used a yammosk to break Miko. Nor could he suppress his urgency to make contact with his fellow Jedi and apprise them of the enemy's latest plan.

He turned slightly to gaze at the yammosk's eyes, and those ink-black organs seemed to gaze back at him. The tentacle beneath his hands rippled, and its blunt tip rose from the nutrient to wrap around Skidder's shoulders.

Roa, Sapha, and the others fell back in surprise.

"Why, Keyn, you fortunate soul," Roa said after a moment, "I do believe the yammosk has taken a liking to you."

EIGHT

From the rear of Lorell Hall on Hapes, Leia was a bright white speck against the blue-black of the night sky, visible through the towering panoramic windows at her back. Rising at a sharp angle from the ramparts of the sandstone bluff that dominated the capital city, the assembly hall enjoyed a breathtaking view of the Transitory Mists and, just now, four of the planet's seven moons. So seamless was the illusion, that people seated in the lower-tier seats might have easily imagined themselves aboard a space vessel, advancing on the star that was Ambassador Organa Solo.

"Esteemed representatives of the Hapes Consortium of worlds," she began in a voice that surrendered none of its resolve even in the farthest reaches of the hall. "Eighteen years ago, following the New Republic's conquest of Imperial Center, I came before you to solicit financial support for a fledgling government bankrupted by war and plagued by an insidious virus that was killing thousands of nonhumans with each passing day.

"That visit unlocked a gateway between our respective regions of space that had been sealed for the previous three thousand years but has remained open ever since. In fact, not long after my initial visit, the Consortium graced Coruscant with a stay, during which you bestowed upon us treasures we had scarcely dreamed existed—rainbow gems, thought puzzles, and trees of wisdom, along with a dozen Star Destroyers you had captured from Imperial warlords who had sought to intrude on your domain.

"It was thought then that the New Republic and the Consortium might enter into an alliance through matrimony—though destiny had other unions in store for the would-be partners in that marriage."

Gracious laughter and hushed exchanges swept through the audience, and scattered clapping modulated to extended applause.

Leia took the opportunity to glance behind and to the right, where Prince Isolder was leaning forward in expectation of just such an acknowledgment. Beside him, also smiling and elegantly attired, sat his wife, Queen Mother Teneniel Djo of Dathomir, her fingers sparkling with lava node rings and her auburn hair bound by a dazzling tiara of rainbow gems, dawnstars, and ice moons.

Alongside Teneniel sat her mother-in-law, Ta'a Chume, her gray hair elaborately coiffed and only her eyes visible above a scarlet veil. Behind them sat several dignitaries and officials, including the Consortium's ambassador to the New Republic.

Coruscant's ambassador to Hapes was seated to the left of the podium, also among sundry dignitaries and officials, though beside her sat the Jedi daughter of Isolder and Teneniel, Tenel Ka. The biceps of her truncated left arm—severed above the elbow years earlier in a lightsaber training match with Jacen—was adorned with bands of electrum, and a lightsaber dangled from the narrow belt that cinched her robe.

In the wings stood C-3PO, newly polished, and Olmahk, incensed at having been made to wear piped leggings, a dress tunic, and a tight-fitting cap.

"My friends," Leia continued as the applause was dying down, "the New Republic and the Consortium have never been anything but allies. But I come before you tonight with a request that is sure to test the bonds of that alliance. And in place of gifts I bring only an urgent warning."

A guarded silence fell over the gathering.

"Speaking for the New Republic, I respect the high value you have long placed on isolation." Without looking, she gestured broadly at the panoramic window behind her. "Were Coruscant blessed with a heavenly phenomenon as majestic as the Transitory Mists, the New Republic, too, might have chosen a more introspective, self-nurturing course. But sadly that is not the case.

"A great shadow has been cast on the galaxy, eclipsing many New Republic member worlds, and a call to arms has been issued far and wide. Though Hapes, Charubah, Maires, Gallinore, Arabanth, and the other worlds that make up the Consortium have yet to be thrown into darkness, that circumstance is unlikely to endure. For so grim is this shadow, so monstrous and far-reaching, it may well have the power to extinguish all light."

Leia paused and remained silent until the agitated murmuring quieted. "The source of this shadow lies outside the confines of our galaxy, but the intention of those who cast it is clear: conquest—unequivocal and thorough. They are called Yuuzhan Vong, and as I speak they are poised to invade the Colonies and the Core."

Again, Leia waited for the murmuring to exhaust itself.

"Peaceful coexistence is not an option, for the Yuuzhan Vong seek nothing less than to remake the galaxy in their own image—to have all of us swear allegiance to the gods they worship and in whose name they launched their campaign. To avoid conflict, some worlds have already surrendered. And given what the Yuuzhan Vong have done to worlds that resisted, one can hardly fault anyone for capitulating. But the New Republic will neither bargain nor surrender. The invasion must be halted, and that can be effected only through a unified effort on the part of those worlds that choose freedom over enslavement."

Leia planted her hands flat on the podium and let her gaze roam the audience.

"I won't mince words. New Republic Senator Elegos A'Kla tried to sue for peace and was brutally murdered. The New Republic Defense Force tried and failed to save Ithor, Obroa-skai, and scores of other worlds. The Hutts have apparently struck a deal with the Yuuzhan Vong that allows the invaders to occupy and utilize Hutt worlds for resources essential to the invasion.

"Now I ask the Consortium to decide which course it will pursue.

"I do not make this request lightly, for there's a chance, however remote, that the Yuuzhan Vong will leave the Hapes Cluster undisturbed, in which case you will be fighting for a cause rather than survival. If forced, the New Republic will wage this battle alone, but the odds of victory will be greatly enhanced by military support from the Consortium."

She took a breath and showed the palms of her hands. "I can promise nothing in return for such support, for the future is uncertain. But I urge all of you to consider carefully whom you wish to have as galactic neighbors, and as well to recall what Emperor Palpatine was able to achieve by dimming the light of so many worlds with his own shadow.

"I thank you all for attending to one forced to resort to words to express what her heart contains."

The hall couldn't have been more silent if it had been catapulted into deep space.

"Delegate Miilarta," Ta'a Chume said, "Ambassador Organa Solo. Ambassador Solo, Lol Miilarta of Terephon."

Leia extended her right hand with practiced graciousness, and Miilarta shook it. "Charmed, Ambassador," she said, then lowered her voice to add, "I can assure you that Terephon will vote to render aid."

Leia smiled with her eyes. "The New Republic thanks you."

Miilarta bowed smartly and moved down the reception line. In the formal way that typified such functions, Leia introduced her to the New Republic's ambassador to the Consortium, then turned back to Ta'a Chume, who introduced the equally beautiful female delegate from Ut, the world that had sent a song on the occasion of the Consortium's visit to Coruscant.

Standing behind Leia, C-3PO whispered into her right ear, "Delegate Miilarta brings the count to thirty-one worlds, Mistress. You are effectively halfway to completion."

Leia glanced down the reception line, which—with husbands, wives, mistresses, and children—wound nearly to the grand entrance of the Fountain Palace, home to the Hapes royal family.

"Tiring of the formalities, Ambassador?" Ta'a Chume asked from behind her veil.

Leia turned slightly to regard her. "Not at all."

"You mean to say that you don't find the process somewhat—how shall I put it?—antiquated?"

"Actually, it makes me think of Alderaan."

"Alderaan? You surprise me, Leia. Equating a former cynosure of democracy to a matriarchy founded by pirates. What can you be thinking?"

Leia smiled to herself. "In the interest of getting things done, the New Republic had dispensed with ceremony. But I sometimes miss the pomp and circumstance of the Old Republic, and Hapes feels like a fond memory frozen in time."

The scarlet half-veil kept secret Ta'a Chume's expression, but her tone of voice belied a bemused grin. "Why, how sweet of you to reduce our way of life to mere nostalgia."

"You mistake my meaning, Ta'a Chume—with purpose, I think." Leia swept her eyes over the reception room. "This might have been my life, if not for the Empire. The grandeur, the propriety . . . the intrigues."

Ta'a Chume's eyes narrowed. "Ah, but it could easily have been yours, my dear. It was you who chose Han Solo over my son."

Leia looked at Chume'da Isolder, who stood tall, impeccably dressed, and incurably handsome at the head of the reception line. *Yes,* she told herself, *I chose a two-fisted rogue without a credit to his name over a scion of pirates with pockets deep enough to finance his own war. And thank the stars for that.* Childhood memories were one thing, but examined in the light of middle age they surrendered some of their charm. Leia could no more imagine herself a proper princess than she could an actress or an entrepreneur. She glanced over at Teneniel Djo—hands folded in front of her and chin lifted in regal deportment— and shuddered at the thought of standing in Teneniel's thousand-credit slippers.

And yet even while she was thinking it, apprehension

nibbled at her contentment. With Han off on his own, distant in more ways than one, the future they forged had grown formless and clouded. She hated having to worry about him, but in fact, she missed him terribly, and the trappings of royalty, the glance down a path not taken, left her feeling cold and alienated.

"Archon Thane," Ta'a Chume was saying, "Ambassador Organa Solo. Ambassador Solo, Archon Beed Thane of Vergill."

Robust, fully bearded, head and shoulders taller than Leia, Thane was one of the Consortium's few male delegates. He glowered as he stepped in front of her. "Ambassador Solo," he said, slurring his words. "The infamous Jedi."

Ta'a Chume stiffened. "I would caution you to keep a civil tongue, Archon. Or have you perhaps sipped too freely of the drink we provided?"

Thane nodded in a bow. "Your pardon, Most Revered Ereneda," he said, using the title reserved for Hapan queen mothers, past or present. "Your generosity has certainly undone me."

Leia reached out with her feelings. Thane wasn't drunk; he was merely acting drunk. "I am not a Jedi, Archon," she told him. "As to my infamy—it is certainly your prerogative to think what you will."

He swung to her. "Spoken like a Jedi: calmly, in full possession. A statement weaker minds might be inclined to embrace as the full truth."

"Careful, Archon," Ta'a Chume seethed under her breath. "I'm certain you don't wish to cause a scene."

Leia folded her arms across her chest. "A scene is precisely his wish, Ta'a Chume. Why deny him his fun?"

Thane vouchsafed a thin smile. "I happened to be on Coruscant when you went before the senate to deliver the same speech you made us sit through tonight. How it must have vexed your Jedi nature to be ignored."

"Perhaps you didn't hear me the first time, Archon—"

"If he has a problem with the Jedi, he can address his concerns to me."

Tenel Ka was suddenly standing alongside Leia, her hand resting lightly on the rancor-tooth-inlaid grip of her lightsaber. Querulous and stubborn by nature, Tenel Ka had always been quick to take on a fight, and just now her gray eyes were boring into Thane's.

But the archon stood his ground, smiling nastily. "Why, it's the Dathomiri who rejects her Hapan heritage, yet deigned to save the royal family from the machinations of Ambassador Yfra." His gaze moved up and down the reception line. "Isn't this the happy group."

A crowd had begun to form around Thane, and conversations throughout the vast room began to subside. Out of the corner of her eye Leia saw Prince Isolder making a direct line for the center of the commotion.

"We have only the ambassador's word that the Yuuzhan Vong can't be dealt with," Thane was telling everyone within earshot. "And if what she says about forming a united front is true, why is the New Republic divided about where to deploy its fleets and to which systems it should render aid?" He turned through a circle as he spoke. "Is this what we want for the Consortium—a factioned leadership? As archon of Vergill I say we remain neutral until such time as the invaders make certain their plans for the Consortium, either by word or force of arms."

He gestured toward Leia. "She comes to us, asking a favor and bringing only the gift of a warning. Why not the gift of the quick-recharge turbolaser technology the New Republic has withheld for so many years?"

"That'll be enough, Thane," Isolder said angrily. "This isn't the time or place for a political debate. If you can't abide by the rules of decorum—"

"You'll toss me out of your palace?" Thane cut him off. "You'd sooner host the descendants of those Jedi who killed your ancestors than someone who dares speak the truth in your presence?"

"Enough," Isolder snapped.

But Thane was far from finished; he played to the crowd once more. "He prefers the company of a daughter who has denounced her Hapan heritage . . ."

Tenel Ka took a forward step, only to be blocked by her father.

". . . and a speaker of half-truths like Ambassador Solo—"

Demonstrating uncanny speed and precision, Isolder backhanded Thane across the face, knocking him into the crowd and drawing blood from his lower lip. Instantly Isolder's longtime friend and former bodyguard Captain Astarta was at his side, flinging a thick braid of red hair over her shoulder and positioning her hands to parry or strike, as need be.

Two of Thane's supporters had rushed to take him by the arms and stand him on his feet, but now he threw them aside, wiped his hand across his mouth, and snorted a laugh at Isolder.

"The spurned suitor to the rescue."

Leia's heart sank. She could feel Isolder battling to control his rage. As angry as she was at him for allowing himself to be provoked, she couldn't help but dread Thane's next move.

"My seconds will call on you in the morning, Chume'da Isolder," the archon of Vergill said with complete sobriety.

Isolder returned a formal nod of assent. "My seconds will be waiting to greet them."

"Thus begins the schism," Ta'a Chume said in a sad, quiet voice as Thane and his supporters headed for the door.

NINE

"Punch it, Droma!" Han yelled as he veered the *Falcon* into an abrupt bank.

Muttering nervously to himself, Droma boosted power to the sublight drives and maxed the throttle. "We'll be fine venturing into Hutt space, you said. You used to do a lot of contract work up and down the Sisar Run, and Sriluur was like a second home, you said. Nothing to worry about, you—"

"Quit griping and give me an update on those ships!"

Droma swung to the display screen of the ship's friend-or-foe authenticator, which showed seven bezel-shaped icons closing fast on the *Falcon*'s aft. "Yuuzhan Vong, all right."

Han glanced at the display. The scanners limned images of what might have been asteroids save for the distinctive bulges that were cockpits and the pitted noses characteristic of weapons emplacements and dovin basal housings. "Coralskippers."

"Coordinates for the jump to Nar Shaddaa coming in."

"Belay that," Han countered, throwing switches on the console. "There's no shaking those skips. Route power to the rear deflector shields and lock in a course back to Sriluur. I'd rather deal with them in atmosphere than out here."

Droma quickly applied himself to the task. "At least we won't have as far to fall."

"Thanks for the encouragement."

The *Falcon* whipped through a half-twisting loop, and the curve of the dun-and-ecru-colored world ballooned into view. Terrain-following data said they were traveling northward, looking out at a slice of the northern hemisphere just east of the planetary date line.

"Skips don't perform well in gravity," Han assured. "Have to rely on the antigrav capabilities of the dovin basals."

As if they had heard him, the enemy pilots began firing at extreme range, molten-gold comets streaming from the projectile and plasma launchers in the bows of their small craft. Two of the missiles connected and, even though weakened by distance, were powerful enough to rock the larger ship. The *Falcon*'s sensor suite began screaming.

"Rear shields holding," Droma reported while he activated countermeasures and distortion systems. "For now."

Han took a steadying breath, vised his right hand on the throttle lever, and rammed it home. The light freighter surged into Sriluur's upper atmosphere, trembling as it continued its oblique dive. With arrant scorn for the planet's protective wrapping, the Yuuzhan Vong crafts plunged after.

"See what I told you?" Han exclaimed. "They stick like epoxy!"

The ship's indicators railed in protest as the *Falcon* plummeted into denser air, rolling and corkscrewing to evade the deadly fire that sought her. All caution forgotten, Han sharpened the angle of descent, sloughing control in exchange for added speed.

"You've got the bridge!" he told Droma.

Droma threw him a panicked glance. "What?"

Unfastening the straps that secured him to the pilot's chair, Han stood, spun on his heel, and started for the main ladderwell. He didn't make it past the cockpit hatch when ship-rattling impacts aft threw him to the deck and forced him to rethink the idea of getting to one of the gun turrets.

"Enable autotracking for the quad lasers," he said in a rush as he was scrambling to his feet. Buckling back into the chair, he donned a headset and began to call up targeting data on the weapons control display screen. "Let's see if we can't even up the odds."

Droma reached for the joystick that controlled the *Falcon*'s belly gun while Han took hold of the controls for the dorsal gun. Data began scrolling across the respective screens. Han bracketed a coralskipper in the targeting reticle and squeezed the trigger on the control grip.

The enemy craft swallowed the bolt whole.

He pounded his fist on the console. "We've gotta give them more to worry about than laserfire!"

Abruptly he rolled the *Falcon* onto its back while Droma was still firing the belly gun. In an effort to keep up, the lead coralskipper drew deeply on the capabilities of its dovin basal and accelerated.

Again, Han brought the reticle over his target, but the coralskipper sped out of his sights in a flash.

He left the firing to Droma momentarily and peeled the ship away in a sweeping descending bank. Projectiles slammed against the rear shields, and plasma streaked between the ship's mandibles. Han rerouted power to the forward deflector and again increased the angle of their descent.

They ripped through a filmy blanket of high-altitude clouds and went spiraling downward. Far below them ocean and desert lay side by side. Storm systems shrouded Sriluur's western horizon, and to the north an expansive brown haze smudged the terrain.

Droma glanced at the meteorological sensors. "That's a sandstorm!"

"How about that," Han said. "Some wishes do come true."

The words had barely left his mouth when the lead coralskipper dropped with mind-boggling velocity and was suddenly beneath the *Falcon* and firing up at her, plasma geysering from its gun emplacements.

Han pulled out of the spiral, yanked the throttle, and threw the ship up and over the coralskipper directly on his tail. A molten bolt from the craft below caught its squadron mate full on. The coralskipper shuddered as hunks of yorik coral flew in all directions. Then an interior explosion burst from the crystalline cockpit, and the crippled ship went into a helpless free fall, condemned to death by gravity.

The destroyed coralskipper's wingmate veered and glued himself to the *Falcon*'s tail, battering it with projectiles and refusing to be unseated, despite a slew of daring turns and evasions Han took them through.

Han went for a pushover, but not in time. Something hit the *Falcon* like a hard clap on the back. Fighting with the controls, he succeeded in righting her, only to emerge from an end-over-end roll to find three more coralskippers attached to the ship as she entered the sandstorm.

The bristles on Droma's back stood up. "Another hit like that and you may as well plow us into the sand and let the *Falcon* be our gravestone!"

Projectiles raced past the outrigger cockpit. With the *Falcon*'s Quadex power core roaring, Han pushed the ship to its limits, jinking and juking as the coralskippers continued to rake fire at them. He dropped the *Falcon* away in a power dive, leaving Droma struggling to adjust thrust bias and avert disaster as enemy missiles ranged closer.

All at once a mountain loomed before them. Han torqued the ship to starboard so forcefully that both he and Droma nearly sailed from their seats. The lead coralskipper pilot pursued them ferociously, obviously unable to hold the *Falcon* in his sights but firing anyway, perhaps in the hope of shaking Han's concentration.

Without warning, a plasma bolt sizzled through the overtaxed rear shields. A muffled explosion sounded from aft, followed by the sibilant hiss of the ship's fire-suppression system. An acrid smell drifted forward on exhaust fan currents.

Han sniffed and shot Droma a wide-eyed glance. "What was that?"

Droma's eyes roamed over the console telltales. "Power converter."

Han winced. "Of all the rotten luck!"

He utilized more of the ship's amazing speed to improve their lead and leapt deeper into the swirling haze. The three coralskippers decreased velocity, waiting for the *Falcon* to come across their vector, but instead Han poured on all power, climbed, looped, and came around behind the trio.

Droma fired instinctively with the belly gun. With the dovin basal of the trailing ship too stressed to handle defense as well as guidance, the laser bolts sneaked through. The widespread burst caught the craft right on the nose, blowing it to nuggets.

Han hooted triumphantly as he sheered off and settled calmly into kill position behind the second craft. The coralskipper pilot, realizing the position he was suddenly in, climbed slightly, unintentionally placing himself in the overlapping field of fire between the *Falcon*'s upper and lower batteries.

"Money Lane!" Han shouted. "One hundred credits to whoever nails him!"

"You're on!" Droma said.

Simultaneously, the two of them tightened their fingers on the trigger. The quad lasers loosed storms of red darts that peppered the rear of the enemy craft and perforated the cockpit, disintegrating the ship.

Han and Droma howled their joy as Han steered through a corkscrewing dive, zipping through the far-flung remains of the exploded ship. Swooping past the lead craft, Han inverted the *Falcon* and took her back into the storm.

Where it could be glimpsed at all, the land was dark red and studded with monolithic rock towers that were the sandblasted and wind-eroded remains of volcanic upthrusts. And yet despite their size, the swirling sand made the tors almost impossible to see.

Eyes on the terrain-following display and making the most of the *Falcon*'s maneuverability, Han aimed deliberately for the closest obelisk. Faking a climb, he stood the ship on its side and swerved to starboard while Droma triggered bursts from the belly gun. Unsecured items throughout the ship flew from their perches, crashed into bulkheads, or were sent rolling along the deck plates of the ring corridor. But two well-placed laser bolts caught the coralskipper at the cockpit seam, splitting it in two, as if struck by a chisel in the hands of a master stonemason.

Still, the three remaining coralskippers clung doggedly, chomping at the *Falcon*'s tail. Nap of the ground, Han weaved through a forest of storm-obscured spires and wind-sculpted stelae. The engines moaned and the ship vibrated as if on the verge of flying apart. Hiking power to the rear shields, he snap-rolled, then stood the *Falcon* on its side once more to narrow her profile as plasma streaked past them to both sides.

Droma lashed his tail around the seat to keep from being strangled by the seat harness. "At least warn me when you're going to do that!"

Han leveled out and maneuvered through a ludicrously tight turn, feathering the engines until the *Falcon* was at a near stall, then shunting power to the thrusters and throwing the ship into a vertical reversement. Swerving to evade Droma's fire, the trailing coralskipper flipped out of control and careened straight into an outcropping, shattering to bits.

The *Falcon*'s thrusters flaring, Han pulled up sharply, climbing out of the storm at high boost.

Neither of the surviving pair of fighters followed them back up the well.

They collapsed into their chairs as the stars lost their twinkle and swarmed around them as pinpoints of light.

"Nice shooting," Han said after checking in with the threat assessor one final time.

Droma returned the grin. "Nice driving."

The *Falcon* bucked. Indicators flashed and the console came alive with warning tones. Han and Droma fell silent once more and turned to the painful chore of assessing just how much damage the ship had sustained.

"The hyperdrive is viable but responding erratically," Droma said a long moment later.

Han nodded glumly. "Must have suffered collateral damage when the power converter got hit."

Droma tugged at one end of his drooping mustache.

"We might be able to make Nar Shaddaa. It's difficult to tell."

"No," Han said. "We can't chance it."

"Do we return to Sriluur?"

Han shook his head. "I doubt we'll find the replacement parts we need. Besides, I don't want to risk running into those coralskippers again."

Droma called up star charts. "Kashyyyk, then. Two quick jumps and we're there."

Han ran his hand over his mouth. "Not a good idea." When Droma didn't respond, he said, "It's not what you think. I can handle the memories. It's just that Chewbacca's family still consider themselves responsible for my well-being, and I can't face that right now."

"So where to?"

Han studied the displayed star charts and grinned, more to himself. "A little out-of-the-way place I know, where they'll have everything we need."

"Everything *Han Solo* needs," Droma thought to point out.

"Maybe you're right," Han said. He turned slightly to regard Droma. "Think you can handle playing captain for a while?"

On Coruscant, in the new office that had come with her unexpected appointment to the Advisory Council, Senator Viqi Shesh supervised the two labor droids she had tasked with rearranging the furniture.

"Turn the desk catercorner to the window," she instructed them as she moved about the room.

The identical humaniform droids manipulated the hoversled on which the desk sat. When the desk was in place, they turned to her, seemingly eager to see her pleased by the results. But she wasn't.

"No, no, all wrong," Shesh said, shaking her head, then running a hand through her lustrous mane of ink-black hair. "Put the desk back where it was and move the conform chair beneath the window."

The pair of droids looked crestfallen. "At once, Senator," they responded in unison.

Shesh lowered herself into an antique armchair from her native Kuat and glanced around the office, smiling slowly as she took in the spacious room. Well-appointed without being ostentatious, the room enjoyed a breathtaking view of Commerce Way and the New Republic Obelisk. With a bit of work, it would become the most elegant chamber in the building, one that would make a lasting impression on all who entered.

Not bad for someone who had entered the political arena only six short years ago, Shesh told herself. But she had expected no less than this from the start, and she anticipated a great deal more in the coming years, despite the fact that her appointment to the Advisory Council had failed to meet with unanimous endorsement.

Several would-be political pundits had accused Chief of State Borsk Fey'lya of attempting to win the support of wealthy Kuat. Others had denounced Shesh for allowing herself to be seduced by power, and accused her of turning her back on the very things that had fueled her rapid rise. Under Fey'lya's thumb—so the fretting went—what would become of her impassioned concern for the needy, her economic patronage of disenfranchised worlds, her outspoken praise for the Jedi Knights and all they stood for?

Shesh's smile broadened as she considered the questions. In the end, they showed how mistaken everyone was about her, and how successful she had been in fostering illusions.

The office comm sounded. "Senator Shesh," her secretary said, "Commodore Brand has arrived."

Shesh glanced at her watch. "Admit him," she answered.

She rose from the chair, smoothed the black skirt that sheathed her long legs, and ordered the labor droids out of the room. By the time Brand entered she was settled behind the desk.

"Commodore Brand," she began, smiling and extending her hand across the desk. "How delightful to see you."

A rigid, gloomy functionary, with the inward-turning gaze of one who sees only his own truth, Brand took off his cap, shook her hand as decorously as he could, and tried to make himself comfortable in the tight confines of the armchair.

Shesh gestured broadly to the office. "Excuse the mess. I've only just moved in."

Brand's eyes raced about. "Congratulations on being named to the council, Senator."

Shesh feigned solemnity. "I only hope I can measure up to everyone's expectations."

Brand leaned forward. "War speeds the promotion of those best equipped to lead. I'm certain you will *surpass* everyone's expectations."

"Why, thank you, Commodore." Shesh paused briefly. "To what do I owe the honor of your visit?"

Brand cleared his throat meaningfully. "The Corellian situation, Senator."

Shesh nodded. "The reenabling of Centerpoint Station. In my opinion, a judicious decision."

"Then you're not concerned about possible . . . repercussions?"

"An armed and dangerous Corellia, for example? Of

course not. A well-defended Corellia benefits the entire Core."

Brand regarded her for a long moment. "Yes. But what if I were to tell you that even more might be gained by inducing the Yuuzhan Vong to attack Corellia?"

Shesh raised an eyebrow. "Are you in fact telling me that, Commodore? Because if you are—and notwithstanding that I sit on the Security and Intelligence Council—I would be obliged to bring this matter to the attention of the Advisory Council immediately."

"The Defense Force intends to do just that, Senator," Brand said in a rush. "Unfortunately, however, we find ourselves in something of a dilemma."

"A dilemma," Shesh repeated.

"Assuming first that we could succeed in luring the Yuuzhan Vong to Corellia, we must ensure that we can defeat them—soundly. And while we wouldn't want to tip our hand by massing ships at Corellia, we would need to pull from Bothawui and a host of similarly defended worlds to amass the required armada."

Shesh took a moment to respond. "You're concerned that the Advisory Council would refuse to sanction any actions that would imperil Bothawui and the others. And yet, to accomplish your goal, it would have to appear as if Bothawui were being defended to the disadvantage of Corellia."

Brand almost grinned.

She appraised him openly. "I see that I've read you correctly. Though I still wonder why you think it necessary to bring this to my attention."

Brand held her gaze. "Should the matter go to a vote, the Defense Force would want to make certain that Bothawui wins out."

Shesh grinned. "But, Commodore, if the Yuuzhan

Vong are routed at Corellia, wouldn't those who voted in favor of Bothawui be seen in disfavor?"

"Perhaps. But any vote tendered in the interest of the greater good would be seen as enlightened."

Shesh fell silent for a long moment. "A moment ago you said that this entire plan rests on the assumption that you can entice the Yuuzhan Vong to attack Corellia. As I understand it, you hope to accomplish this by leaving Corellia essentially undefended, in the hope that the enemy takes note of that fact. But wouldn't it be more profitable if word got out about what you're doing? For its technological powers alone, Centerpoint Station would be an irresistible target for destruction."

Brand tugged at his earlobe. "This isn't something we can simply announce over the HoloNet, Senator."

Shesh laughed shortly. "There are better lines to the Yuuzhan Vong than the HoloNet." She gave it a moment, then added, "The Hutts. If they had even an inkling of your plan, they would certainly apprise the Yuuzhan Vong, if only in the interest of safeguarding their future."

"But the New Republic has broken off diplomatic relations with the Hutts. To communicate with them at this point—"

"The Hutt consul general is still on Coruscant. I could pay him a visit and let slip a few things."

Brand stared at her. "You would do that?"

"I would. But in return—in the event the true purpose of my visit ever came to light—I would want it known that the Defense Force asked me to intercede."

"You want deniability," Brand said.

"Irrefutable deniability, Commodore."

He took a moment, then nodded. "I think that can be

arranged. We could say that we were merely feeling the Hutts out."

"Just so."

Brand smiled. "You should have gone into the military, Senator. You would have made a brilliant tactician."

"The military?" Shesh snorted in derision. "I don't mean any disrespect, Commodore, but why would I want to be the one who fires the weapon when I can be the one who decides at whom the weapon is pointed?"

TEN

The size of a *Victory*-class Star Destroyer, the bulk freighter *Starmaster* hung above the inert Twi'lek homeworld, Ryloth. Pods of vessels surrounded it—tenders, gunboats, and shuttles—some as smooth as marine creatures, others as boxy and graceless as the freighter itself. Anchored in the umbra of the great ship floated a Ubrikkian luxury yacht. Also in shadow, and closing steadily on a rectangular docking bay, moved a lunette-shaped craft launched from Ryloth's miserly zone of inhabitable twilight.

In a lower-deck compartment forward in the freighter, two Rodians monitored the approaching crescent on a display screen, switching to an interior view of the docking bay as the small craft disappeared from sight.

"Is that his ship?" the Twi'lek pacing behind them asked when the craft had penetrated the bay's magnetic containment field and landed. Like almost everyone else aboard the *Starmaster*, the trio were wearing jumpsuits inflated by large pouch pockets.

"His ship," one of the Rodians scoffed. "He has dozens of ships. Let's wait and see who disembarks."

Three human males and a female appeared on the craft's extensible boarding ramp. Moving with lithe economy, the first two men might have been brothers, though the taller one's face was hideously scarred where the other's was slim and angular. Dark-haired and willowy, the woman also moved with care, but there was a coiled wariness to her step and a vigilant gleam in her eyes. The last man out had an air of confident nonchalance. In one of inherited entitlement, the elevated chin and pocketed hands might have been perceived as arrogance, but he wore refinement well, as only one who had earned it could. In contrast to the shin-high spacer's boots and long cloaks affected by his confederates, he was dressed in silk and leather.

"That's him," the other Rodian said, indicating the latter male with the tap of a long, sucker-equipped finger against the display screen. "That's Karrde."

The Twi'lek positioned his thick tattooed head-tails over his shoulders and leaned between the Rodians for a closer look. "You're certain?"

The one who had made the identification twitched his short snout. "If not, it's either his twin or a clone."

The Twi'lek straightened. "I'll alert the boss."

Hurrying through the compartment hatchway, he entered a large hold, clamorous with activity. Stacked high throughout the space were alloy shipping crates recently ferried up Ryloth's well from Kala'uun Spaceport. Two-legged binary loadlifters supervised by masked Twi'lek foremen were arranging the crates for further shipping and off-loading, while utilitarian-looking asp droids stenciled the crates with port-of-call information and applied laser-readable labels. Despite the forceful draw of overhead exhaust fans, dark motes danced and swirled in the recycled air.

One hand clamped to his mouth, the Twi'lek threaded his way through the maze of stacks, arriving ultimately at a laboratory isolated from the hold by tall permaplas window walls. Inside, two humans wearing goggles, rebreathers, and environment suits were assessing the quality of a fine black powder sampled from an opened shipping crate bearing the corporate logo of Galactic Exotics, alleged to contain edible fungi. The stockier of the pair removed his mask and goggles to reveal bulging eyes in an otherwise bland face.

"He just arrived," the Twi'lek reported. "Docking Bay 6738. Two men and a woman accompany him. They are clearing contamination and control now."

"You're certain it's him."

"Certain. But we'll run an identity scan just in case."

The man peeled off elbow-length gloves, slipped out of the environment suit, and settled himself at a display console. "Keep the cam and scanner feeds open so I can see and hear for myself."

"Will you be informing Borga?"

The man considered it. "We'll see."

The Twi'lek took the same route back to the compartment. By the time he arrived and was peering over the shoulder of the Rodian closest to the screen, Karrde and his companions were literally at the door.

"Positive identification on Karrde," the Rodian said after studying the scanner readouts. "No information on the other men, but neither one is armed with blasters. The scanner matches the woman to Shada D'ukal, a known associate of Karrde's." The Rodian looked at the Twi'lek. "Lethal, even without weapons."

The second Rodian lifted a blaster from his hip holster, checked the charge, and primed the weapon.

"Unnecessary," the Twi'lek told him. "They'd be fools to try anything."

The Rodian's round black eyes fixed on him. "You pay me to be prepared."

The Twi'lek nodded, grinning slightly to show filed teeth. "I stand corrected."

"Look," the Rodian's partner interrupted. "He's on to us."

The Twi'lek glanced at the display screen in time to see Karrde waving at the optical scanner concealed in the bulkhead above the hatchway.

"I still don't understand why Karrde would be interested in dealing with us," the armed Rodian remarked. "He trafficks in information, not spice."

The Twi'lek caressed his bulged forehead and moved to the hatchway. "This isn't about spice. But we're expected to hear him out, so that's what we're going to do."

He aimed a remote at the hatchway sensor, and the hatch pocketed itself into the bulkhead. Karrde and the others entered, his two male companions hanging back and Shada D'ukal sidestepping into a corner where she could keep a watchful eye on the proceedings.

"Welcome, Talon Karrde," the Twi'lek said in Basic. "I'm Rol'Waran."

Karrde nodded. "A pleasure." He didn't bother to introduce anyone else.

"Your chair," Rol'Waran barked at one of the Rodians, who immediately stood and stepped aside. He waited for Karrde to make himself comfortable. "I'm told that you're interested in procuring product."

"Eight blocks."

Rol'Waran's normally narrow eyes widened. "A substantial quantity. However, since your past and recent activities are not unknown to me, would you mind explaining why you're suddenly interested in product?"

Karrde laughed innocently. "If you're concerned about entrapment or anything of that nature—"

"Nothing of the sort," Rol'Waran was quick to assure. "After all, we are only subordinate players in the grand game. But I was given to understand that you had abandoned illegality for activity of a more . . . diplomatic nature."

Karrde crossed his legs, resting his ankle on his knee. "The Yuuzhan Vong invasion has rendered obsolete my position as liaison between Bastion and Coruscant."

"Meaning, he's unemployed," the shorter of the two men behind him said.

"Yes," Rol'Waran said, stroking his left lekku pensively. "The Yuuzhan Vong have heaped changes on us, as well."

"Not the way I hear it," the same man remarked.

"Just what have you heard?" Rol'Waran asked.

The man's upper lip curled. "That spice remains a safe bet."

Karrde cleared his throat. "What he means is that product has always been a prized commodity, and now, what with more mouths to feed—"

"Hard times bring about a need for escape," Karrde's comrade cut him off. "We're all for letting everyone bury their heads in the sand."

Rol'Waran cut his pink eyes to Karrde. "So you're interested in going into business."

"Assuming that shipment can be arranged."

Rol'Waran smiled tightly. "That would, of course, add to the price. Where did you have in mind?"

"To begin with, Tynna."

An awkward silence fell over the compartment, while Rol'Waran and the Rodians traded covert glances. "Tynna is extremely problematic at the moment," Rol'Waran said at last. "I could arrange shipment to Rodia, perhaps even Kalarba, but you'd have to take it from there."

"What about Kothlis or Bothawui?" Karrde said.

Rol'Waran shook his head. "Not at present."

Karrde loosed an annoyed exhale. "If you can ship to

Rodia, can I at least get you to bring it up the run to Corellia? That's the actual destination."

Rol'Waran tilted his head to one side. "Again, I'm afraid we have a problem."

"What's the problem?" Karrde's scar-faced accomplice asked harshly. "We were told you could move spice with impunity under the new terms."

Rol'Waran's tiny eyes darted. "New terms?"

He was about to say more when the hatch opened to reveal the stout laboratory technician filling the portal. Karrde's accomplices reacted swiftly, but Karrde was just as quick to interpose himself between them and the grinning intruder.

"Crev Bombaasa," he said in genuine surprise. "You're a long way from home."

"As are you, Talon." Bombaasa looked at Shada. "And the always enchanting Shada D'ukal. As for my being far from home, even life in the Pembric system can grow boring."

With an explicit nod, Bombaasa dismissed Rol'Waran and the Rodians, then lowered himself into a chair at the console and deactivated the room's security systems.

"If I recall correctly," he said to Karrde, "the last time we crossed paths was in the ThrusterBurn tapcaf in Erwithat. In search of Jorj Car'das, you and Shada required safe passage through the Kathol sector, which I provided to offset an earlier debt I owed to your former partner, Mara Jade. I mention all this by way of stating at the onset that if you're expecting favors—such as product delivery into the star systems you mentioned—be forewarned that I figure we're already even."

He glanced at Kyp Durron and Ganner Rhysode, then smiled at Karrde. "So why have you come, Talon? And don't tell me you're serious about going into the spice trade."

Karrde looked him in the eye. "I appreciate your frankness, Crev. The fact is the Yuuzhan Vong have changed the way everyone is doing business. Many of the players remain the same, but the field has been rearranged. In the Rim, former Imperials are fighting alongside New Republic forces. Adversaries of long standing are putting aside their differences for a common cause. Even the Hutts have been forced to relinquish part of their space as a means of avoiding all-out war."

Again, Bombaasa glanced at the Jedi. "Yes, the only good thing to come of the war is that it gave Kyp Durron something else to do besides prey on smugglers." He paused briefly to glance knowingly at Karrde's confederates, then sighed. "I thought for certain that would draw a reaction, but I can see that this clearly isn't a moment for levity."

"Laugh all you want," Kyp told him.

"I can laugh all I want," Bombaasa repeated in monotone, then touched his head theatrically. "Did someone here make me say that?"

Ganner placed a calming hand on Kyp's arm.

Bombaasa watched the two Jedi, then nodded at Karrde. "You're right, Talon, the lines have certainly been redrawn. Just where that leaves people like you and me has yet to be determined."

"Speak for yourself, Crev. I know where I stand."

Bombaasa took a breath. "I'm a practical man, Talon. I wish only to survive—and under the best possible circumstances I can arrange for myself. You say your stance is decided. Then suppose you tell me what's on your mind."

Karrde's eyes narrowed. "You won't ship to Tynna, Bothawui, or Corellia."

Bombaasa linked his hands and rested them atop his prominent belly. "That much is true. And I commend you on your acuity in picking just those systems where we have temporarily suspended operations."

"The Yuuzhan Vong are in Hutt space," Karrde continued. "They've already hit Gyndine. So one might reasonably assume that you're merely trying to avoid areas of potential conflict."

"Once more I commend you. Why risk shipments by sending them into contested space? Transgression might even prove dangerous to the bearers of those shipments."

"Then either you're merely being careful, or you're heeding orders that came down from the Hutts."

Bombaasa glanced at the ceiling. "Let's just say that the Hutts, at this juncture, are in a better position to ascertain which areas are dangerous."

Karrde nodded. "I thought so. And how will you justify this conversation to Borga?"

Bombaasa's shoulders heaved in a shrug. "I will relate just what happened here. Talon Karrde wanted product delivered into denied areas, so we failed to come to terms." Irony wrinkled his jowled face. "Borga has been expecting just such an encounter, in any case."

"Playing both sides, is she?"

"Looking out for number one."

Karrde could not restrain a smile. "I won't forget this, Crev."

Bombaasa steepled his thick fingers and brought them to his double chin. "Then you might mention me to your friends—as affirmation of just whose side I'm on."

"Count on it," Karrde said. "Someday we might all be called to work together—smugglers, information brokers, pirates, and mercenaries—and this strikes me as a good start."

The yammosk vessel *Crèche* hung in stationary orbit above the planet Ando. In the ship's grottolike docking bay, Commander Chine-kal and the priest, Moorsh, welcomed Randa Besadii Diori aboard. First to exit the loathsome slipper-shaped Ubrikkian space yacht that had arrived from Ando were the young Hutt's Twi'lek and Rodian retainers, followed by the tusked humanoid Aqualish who comprised his limited detail of bodyguards. Then, propelled by his muscular tail, the Hutt himself emerged, smiling broadly and instantly at home in the cavernous, dimly lighted space.

"I see that you are as fond of gloom as we Hutts are," Randa told Chine-kal after he had been announced and introductions had been made.

The commander smiled pleasantly. "We favor obscurity when it suits our purpose."

Randa attributed the ambiguity of Chine-kal's remark to the inexperience of the Yuuzhan Vong translator. "You must come to Nal Hutta, Commander, and visit my parent's palace. I'm certain you would find it to your liking."

Chine-kal's politic smile held. "We've heard much about it, young Hutt. Commander Malik Carr was very impressed."

"As Borga was with Commander Malik Carr," Randa replied with courtly poise. "I am eager to learn as much as I can of your operations, so that we Hutts may expedite your needs." His protruding black eyes disappeared briefly behind the membranes that kept them moist. "With so many worlds falling to your superior might, the task of ferrying captives about must be growing tiresome."

"The task distracts us from our principal objective," Chine-kal allowed. "Which is precisely why we are as eager to instruct as you are to learn."

"Then the sooner we begin, the better," Randa said.

"But perhaps you could first show me to my quarters so that I might refresh from the journey."

"We have prepared a place for you, Randa Besadii Diori," the priest answered. "On the way, we thought we might introduce you to the ship's most prestigious passenger."

Randa pressed his hands together in a gesture of respect. "I would be honored."

Chine-kal voiced a brusque command to his guards, who snapped their fists to their opposite shoulders and arranged themselves in an escort formation, some advancing through an iris portal in the hold's biotic bulkhead while others fell in behind Randa and his retinue.

They moved deeper into the ship, passing from one module to the next, on occasion lifted by decks that bulged under them like a tongue being raised to the roof of a mouth. Illumination varied, but the bioluminescence of the bulkheads rarely provided more than a faint glow. What did increase was a certain tang in the air, which while not unpleasant tended to irritate the nasal passages and promote the flow of mucus and tears. Lubricious by design, Randa found the conditions most agreeable.

Chine-kal brought the procession to a halt in the rank belly of the ship and directed Randa's attention to an aperture in the membranous bulkhead that provided a vantage into an adjacent hold. Below, centered in a circular tank of syrupy liquid, floated a tentacled life-form that could only have been created by the Yuuzhan Vong. Sharing the tank with the creature—and plainly attending to it—stood several dozen captives, anywhere from knee- to shoulder-deep in the liquid. Tended to in kind, a few of the captives were being stroked by the tentacles. In one case a human male was entirely entwined by two of the slender appendages.

Randa found himself thinking about certain members

of the Desilijic clan who were fond of chaining dancers or servants to themselves. Again his eyes were drawn to the fully embraced human. In the midst of regarding the several beings in close proximity to the human, Randa turned excitedly to his Twi'lek majordomo.

"Are those Ryn?" he asked, indicating them with one of his stubby arms.

The Twi'lek regarded them and nodded. "I believe they are Ryn, Excellency."

Chine-kal followed the exchange and asked for a translation. "Something has caught your eye, young Hutt?"

"Indeed, Commander," Randa said. "You have succeeded in capturing a somewhat rare specimen."

"To which do you refer?"

"You see the human your creature takes such an interest in?"

Chine-kal gazed down at the yammosk and its captive attendants. "Keyn, that one is called."

"The sharp-nosed bipeds next to and opposite him," Randa elaborated. "And there, at the adjacent tentacle. They are Ryn—an entertaining species, highly prized by the Hutts, though often disparaged by others."

"Prized for what?"

"They are celebrated for their skill at dancing and singing, but their real talent is prognostication."

Chine-kal waited for the translation, then turned to Moorsh. "Did you know of this?"

"I did not, Commander," the priest said.

Chine-kal cut his eyes to Randa. "They divine, you say?"

"Rather astutely."

"By what technique?"

"Manifold means. I have heard that they can read the future in the creases of the hands, the bumps on the head, the color of the eyes. They sometimes employ a deck of playing cards that are said to have been fashioned by them."

"You have heard," Chine-kal said. "Then you have had no direct experience with them?"

"Sadly, I have not." Randa smiled. "But perhaps you would be willing to relieve them temporarily of their peculiar duties and judge for yourself? Your creation appears to take little interest in them, in any case."

"I confess to being curious about them," Moorsh said in reply to Chine-kal's glance.

The commander nodded and turned to a subaltern of the guards. "Have the six Ryn brought to the young Hutt's compartment."

ELEVEN

To three sides the sea stretched to the horizon—an expanse of surging teal, frosted with whitecaps and dazzled by daybreak sunlight—and at Leia's back climbed the rocky spires and imposing parapets of Reef Fortress, the Hapan royal family's summer home and stronghold in times of crisis.

Against a cool offshore breeze, she hugged herself within the dark-blue wrap of her long cloak and turned through another circle, taking in the island's surf-slapped black-rock shoreline, the majestic fortress, a droid picking wild dewberries, and closer at hand, Olmahk, along with a score of visitors who'd arrived at dawn by dragon yacht to witness the duel between Isolder and Beed Thane.

The archon of Vergill and his seconds were gathered on the square of lush lawn that was to serve as an arena for the contest. As the offended one, publicly dishonored by Isolder's reckless backhand, Thane had been entitled to choose the weapons from a wide assortment that included everything from vibroblades to sporting blasters. The location, however, had been selected by Isolder, who had passed the previous night in Reef Fortress, along with Teneniel Djo, Tenel Ka, Ta'a Chume, Leia, and a minimal staff of advisers and retainers.

Though the designated hour was drawing near, Isolder

and his second, retired Captain Astarta, had yet to show themselves. Plainly disquieted by the lapse in etiquette, Tenel Ka was unable to remain still for more than a moment.

Leia could feel the young Jedi's agitation clear across the lawn. It was here at the fortress that she, Jacen, Jaina, and Chewie's nephew Lowbacca had braved carnivorous seaweed and Bartokk assassins to foil Ambassador Yfra's plot to overthrow the monarchy. Here, too, Tenel Ka had finally come to accept the mutilation she had accidentally suffered at Jacen's hand, preferring to make do with her stump rather than employ a prosthesis—even for a swimming race.

As the memories of what Jacen had told her of those events were supplanted by concerns for the present, Leia saw Tenel Ka gaze up one of the hedge-bordered paths that climbed to the fortress and quickly walk away from the lawn. A moment later Ta'a Chume appeared where the natural path debouched into the lawn, her graying auburn hair falling from beneath a tall conical cap, to which was affixed a triangle of gauzy white fabric that veiled her lower face. Notwithstanding Tenel Ka's efforts on behalf on the Hapan monarchy, the former matriarch refused to condone her granddaughter's decision to embrace the life of a Jedi over that of a future queen mother.

Ta'a Chume tracked Tenel Ka's deliberate departure, then she turned and, spying Leia, gathered her long gown in one hand and headed directly for her.

"I trust you slept well, Ambassador," she said as she approached.

"I'd like to report that I did, but in fact, I didn't sleep a wink."

"This business with the duel," Ta'a Chume said in dismissal. "Don't worry."

Leia stared into her green eyes. "You're that confident of your son?"

"You're not?"

"I've seen the best bested, Ta'a Chume."

The former queen mother studied her. "I have to wonder to whom you're referring. Your father, perhaps, bested by your brother; or my son, bested by the smuggler you helped make a hero."

Leia refused to take the bait. "Isolder shouldn't have allowed himself to be provoked."

"But, my dear, what other course of action was open to him after Thane insulted you?"

"He could have allowed me to respond."

Creases formed at the corners of Ta'a Chume's eyes. "My dear Leia, here on Hapes noblewomen are expected to comport themselves as something other than warriors. It has been thus since the founding days of the Consortium. Blame the Lorell Raiders for placing us on pedestals."

"I'm not a Hapan noble, Ta'a Chume. And I've been called far worse than a liar."

"I'm sure you have."

Leia bristled, then regained her composure. "I'm more concerned about unity among the Consortium worlds than I am about defending my honor."

Ta'a Chume forced a world-weary sigh. "There can be no unity without honor, Leia. And speaking of honor and dishonor, I've been meaning to inquire about your charming rogue of a husband. Why isn't he here with you?"

Leia held Ta'a Chume's piercing gaze. "Han is contributing in his own way to the war effort."

"What a curious answer." Ta'a Chume lowered her voice in feigned intimacy. "I trust there are no troubles at home."

"There are troubles everywhere. That's why I'm here."

"Indeed." Ta'a Chume fell silent for a moment, then said, "Since your arrival on Hapes I've been meaning to tell you how wrong I was about you."

Leia waited.

"Unlike the Dathomiri witch's daughter"—she glanced in the direction of Tenel Ka—"you chose against becoming a Jedi."

Leia had to remind herself that she was talking with a woman who had not only ordered the murders of her elder son and Isolder's first love, but whose own mother had despised the Jedi almost as passionately as Palpatine had. Isolder's grandmother had wanted to see the Jedi extinguished, if only to prevent the resurrection of what she had deemed an oligarchy ruled by sorcerers and readers of auras.

"Tenel Ka chose wisely," Leia said at last, "as did your son. Teneniel Djo is perfect for Isolder."

Ta'a Chume shook her head. "No, my dear. Their marriage is beset by difficulties. There is talk of Teneniel Djo's returning to Dathomir."

"I'm sorry. I didn't realize—"

"*You* would have been perfect for my son. He undertakes this duel as much to demonstrate to me that a man is capable of taking initiative, as to demonstrate to you his continuing affection. That's why, regardless of the outcome of today's contest, you can rely on having my full support in the matter of the Consortium allying itself with the New Republic against the Yuuzhan Vong."

Leia was still recovering from the unexpectedness of the disclosure when Isolder, Teneniel Djo, and Astarta strode into view.

"With mere moments to spare he arrives," Ta'a Chume remarked on seeing them. "How like him."

Trailing the prince and queen mother came staffers and other witnesses, including C-3PO, who hurried to Leia's side.

"Mistress Leia," the droid began in a fret, "I had hoped you would decide to spare yourself the torment of having to watch Prince Isolder engage in such an anti-quated and obviously vain exercise, in what can only be considered pecking-order politics."

Leia frowned at him, thinking of Corran Horn's con-test with the Yuuzhan Vong commander Shedao Shai at Ithor. "As the insulted party, I could hardly absent my-self, Threepio."

"But, Mistress," C-3PO pressed, "do you have any idea of what Prince Isolder and Archon Thane are about to do?"

Leia glanced at the lawn where Thane's seconds and Astarta were establishing the ground rules, and the ar-chon and the prince were already donning the sensor- and electrode-studded headgear, power gloves, boots, and body armor that were integral to the contest.

"I have some idea," Leia said.

The droid tilted his head to one side and flapped his stiff arms. "Then you shouldn't permit yourself to watch. This form of hand-to-hand combat has its origin in a martial art developed by the Lorell Raiders when their chief preoccupation was the capture and distribu-tion of female prisoners. While perhaps not as deadly or as mystical in nature as teräs käsi—the 'steel hands' tech-nique taught by the Followers of Palawa in the Pacanth Reach star cluster in the Outer Rim—it is nonetheless—"

Leia shushed him. "Isolder spent two years as a priva-teer," she said quietly. "I'm sure he knows a few moves."

"But, Mistress," C-3PO said hopelessly.

She silenced him again in order to hear what Isolder

was telling Thane as they faced off in the center of the lawn.

"Should you win, you will not only have redeemed your honor but earned the right to brag of having defeated the prince of Hapes. Should I win, I gain nothing more than the right to demand that you solicit the pardon of my daughter and of Ambassador Organa Solo for your remarks."

Thane sneered at him. "If you'd like to sweeten the pot, Prince Isolder, you need only say so."

Isolder slipped his right hand into the power glove and flexed his fingers. "Should I win, I want your pledge that Vergill will support the New Republic."

The witnesses gasped. "This cannot be permitted!" someone shouted.

"Neither of you has the right!" another voice added.

Thane considered it while the arguments continued. "You have my pledge," the archon said at last. "Providing that Hapes will withhold support if you lose."

"You bring disgrace on all our Houses!" a witness remarked.

Isolder nodded. "You have my pledge."

Leia's heart raced.

Beside her, Ta'a Chume said, "This has been Thane's goal all along. As Hapes goes, so goes half the Consortium of worlds." She looked at Leia. "You see what my son undertakes for you?"

On the lawn, the principal referee raised a red scarf high overhead and let it flutter to the ground. It had scarcely touched the tallest blade of grass when the fight commenced.

Hapan tradition dictated that honor duels commence with little fanfare and even less preamble. Leia quickly grasped that it was largely a matter of making sure that everyone had their wagers in place. From what she could gather by eavesdropping on nearby conversations—and Ta'a Chume's avowals to the contrary—Thane was favored to win.

Despite his agitation, or perhaps as a response to it, C-3PO insisted on providing commentary, even after the fight had begun. Olmahk, by contrast, was clearly entranced, down on his haunches at the edge of the manicured lawn, his bulging eyes riveted on Isolder and Thane as they circled, feeling each other out with tentative kicks and punches.

Like Isolder, Thane was tall and muscular, but his thick legs and broad shoulders made Isolder look positively wiry by comparison. His moves, as he loosened up, suggested both great power and dexterity, and he wasn't timid about showing right away that he was good. He came at Isolder with double- and triple-kick combinations, fired by the same leg, recocking and letting fly without bringing his foot down in between.

And he had fast hands, as well.

Isolder parried the attack skillfully, but refrained from counterpunching, as if undecided about which offense to employ. Even so, it was obvious to Leia that they were both essentially footfighters, with Thane's style drawing on traditional techniques and Isolder's on straightforward boxing.

The rules of the honor duel were known to everyone present, save for her and Olmahk, but Leia understood that the body armor and headgear served a dual purpose. In addition to dampening the bone-breaking and electroshock capabilities of the gloves and boots, the sensor-studded padding indicated when a contestant landed a scoring blow, by way of a remote receiver.

"What an appalling display," C-3PO remarked worriedly. "And I fear it will only get worse, Mistress. Where most opponents agree beforehand to refrain from inflicting serious injury, the prince and the archon waived the usual restrictions!"

Leia tried to ignore him. At the same time, she repressed an urge to think aloud, *Don't do this, Isolder,* for fear that he might hear her through the Force and come undone. Corran Horn's actions at Ithor had been noble, and yet they had failed to preserve the planet.

Isolder and Thane worked each other around for several long minutes without scoring, though the punishing blows they rained on each other sounded like the muffled reports of ancient firearms. Exposed flesh reddened and swelled. A punch from Isolder drove Thane clear across the lawn; a front kick by the archon lifted the prince completely off his feet. Then both of them scored in rapid succession when Isolder left himself open to a blow to the head in order to land a powerful twisting punch to Thane's ribs.

The rooting of the onlookers was enthusiastic, but nothing like the bloodthirsty tumult professional gamblers would have raised. Inaudibly, Teneniel Djo, Tenel Ka, and some of the advisers intoned calming chants.

Leia kept her concern in check by telling herself that what she was witnessing was no different from so many of the lightsaber practice duels she'd seen and engaged in over the years.

Isolder and Thane went at each other again, this time at Isolder's lead, with a set-piece attack of left fist, right fist. Thane confidently went for the block and counter against an expected right roundhouse kick, only to realize too late that it was a feint. Isolder cocked his leg back like lightning and again struck him in the ribs. Falling back, Thane grimaced in pain, but managed nonetheless to slip in an off-balance counterkick that caught Isolder unprepared.

The primary referee glanced at the remote receiver and

declared points for each fighter. With the match a two-two tie and both of them panting, he called for a sudden-death round.

"Sudden death?" C-3PO moaned in alarm. "Sudden death?"

It was plain that Thane understood how Isolder had set a trap for him. Once more he moved tentatively, though seemingly less out of respect for Isolder's prowess than out of wariness for his talent to deceive.

Isolder kept his distance, as well, ultimately forcing Thane to bore in on him. The archon faked a punch, twirled, and cycloned his right foot at Isolder's thigh. Isolder twisted to avoid the full force of the impact, but an agonized yelp escaped him, and everyone realized that he had nearly been incapacitated.

The injured leg collapsed under him, and he dropped to one knee, aiming a stiff-armed punch to Thane's mid-section on the way down. Thane anticipated the blow and stopped short, just out of range, then brought one foot around and down in a crescent kick meant to shatter Isolder's extended forearm and open him up for a frontal attack. But Isolder withdrew his arm in time and shoulder-rolled out of harm's way. Shooting to a crouch, he launched himself at Thane.

Thane backed away, windmilling his arms to parry punches and kicks, then stepping to one side and executing a fast one-handed forward flip, right foot extended to smash Isolder in the face.

Isolder stooped, catching Thane's lower calf in the crook of the X he formed with raised forearms, then called on his thigh muscles to spring him upright. Thane's planted foot slipped on the grass, and he slammed supine to the ground.

Isolder went after him, whirling for a back kick going

in. But Thane spun on his shoulders and neatly swept Isolder's feet out from under him. Springing themselves upright, they exchanged lightning volleys of kicks and body punches. Plosive sounds cut the salt air as they alternated in having the wind knocked out of them.

Thane's right foot caught Isolder's left forearm just above the edge of the power glove, and Leia was certain she heard bone fracture. It struck her all at once that sudden death could mean just that.

Surprised that neither of them had scored, the crowd grew louder, urging each man on. Leia heard Captain Astarta's voice cut through the din, commanding Isolder to regain focus. Only Leia and Ta'a Chume stood silently now, wrapped in concern.

With a deft hop, Isolder reversed his stance to keep his maimed forearm out of the line of fire and launched another counteroffensive. Thane's huge fist tagged him a glancing blow on the side of the head, but the archon received a toe kick to the knee in return.

Thane apparently wasn't accustomed to fighting someone his own size, and Isolder made the most of it. Time and again he caught Thane's foot in his upper arm or shoulder or managed to duck his head out of the way. But Isolder appeared to be tiring. With little left to pitch that he hadn't already tried, he again advanced with left fist, right fist, as windup for a right roundhouse kick.

Leia's breath caught in her throat. It was the most elementary and binary kind of gamble. Thane had to decide whether Isolder was setting the move up as a feint, or was going to commit to it this time. It came down to whether or not Thane believed Isolder was fool enough to stake everything—his reputation, Thane's promise to side with Hapes with regard to the Yuuzhan Vong, perhaps even the respect of the royal family and Leia—on trying the same trick after it had been compromised the first go-round.

Thane set himself for a feint and counter. Isolder let him believe he had chosen correctly by using broken timing—appearing for an instant to be faking—then let fly the intended roundhouse.

From the sound of the impact, it was clear that Isolder had planned the kick to connect with enough force to end the match. Even so, he exercised more restraint than Thane probably would have shown. The slap of the boot on the headguard echoed off the black rocks that graced the shore, and the primary referee had one hand up to signal the winning point before Thane had hit the ground.

Betting stakes were changing hands even as the two opponents were bowing to each other. Given the added wager, many of the witnesses were beside themselves with outrage, and arguments began to erupt on all sides of the lawn.

One to whom success came often, Isolder didn't flaunt his victory. Even the customary embraces he received from his wife and daughter failed to elicit so much as a smile. Archon Thane appeared grudgingly congratulatory, but Leia could see that there would be no lasting peace between House Thane and House Isolder.

At the moment, however, that didn't matter. Thane's loss meant at least one more vote on the side of supporting the New Republic.

Thane and his seconds began to storm away from the lawn, but before he reached the path that led to the dock, Thane changed direction and angled for Leia.

She braced herself.

"Ambassador, I will make my formal apology when the Consortium representatives convene to vote on the issue of rendering aid to the New Republic," he began.

"Rest assured that I will honor my pledge to stand with Prince Isolder." He scowled, despite himself. "For now I wish only to applaud you for moving the Consortium one step closer to what will no doubt prove to be a catastrophic campaign."

TWELVE

Melisma, Gaph, and a dozen other Ryn slogged through the shin-deep mud that had formed in the wake of Ruan's most recent on-command downpour. Conditions in Facility 17 were deteriorating rapidly and no one was smiling, not even Gaph, who was usually unflappingly sanguine in the worst of situations.

The camp's overseers had requested that the Ryn report to the familiarization sector, for purposes yet to be disclosed. A facsimile of civilization as defined by any number of Core worlds, the sector functioned as a training and indoctrination ground for those refugees bound for the heart of the New Republic.

Despite Salliche Ag's attempt to maroon on Ruan as many refugees as possible, a host of worlds and corporations had similar employment scenarios in mind for the displaced peoples of the Outer and Mid Rims. Optical concerns were seeking species with innate visual acuity, and acoustical concerns sought species with expanded ranges of hearing. Some companies were desirous of nothing more than folks of size and brute strength. Still, most of the refugees had never resided in the Colonies, let alone on Core worlds, and so the need for indoctrination classes meant to bring the culturally deprived up to speed for their new lives.

Melisma and the rest trudged past crude buildings and

pavilions where Basic was being taught to Ruurians and Dugs. Other structures were devoted to instructive sessions in interfacing with droids, computers, and virtual life-forms; riding turbolifts, drop shafts, and beltways; dealing with bacta treatments, durasheet, and flimsiplast; the use of comlinks, holoprojectors, and conform loungers; proper behavior in restaurants, theaters, and other public places; and comportment in the presence of the wealthy, the politically connected, or the influential.

The Ryn contingent had been directed to structure 58, which was empty when they entered, save for a grouping of rickety tables and chairs and a human female whose eyes bugged out of her head on seeing them. She glanced at the display of a datapad she wore around her neck, quickly composed herself, and asked everyone to be seated.

The fact that Melisma and the others opted to sit on the floor undermined the woman's aplomb, which was obviously as flimsy as the furniture, and once again she looked to the datapad for advice of some sort.

"You've been asked to report here," she began in Basic, "because an opportunity has arisen that could provide you with transport to Esseles, as well as employment once you arrive."

In pure surprise, Melisma turned to Gaph, whose optimism made a sudden comeback.

"The job is somewhat peculiar, but as it is the only job offer targeted specifically for your species, I'm certain you'll want to consider it."

She cleared her throat in a meaningful way. "Essentially you would be residing in a kind of living museum, where diverse folks coexist, displaying to the intellectually inquisitive or the merely curious the various and sundry elements unique to their species."

No one spoke for a long moment; then Gaph asked, "What, exactly, would we be required to do?"

"Why, simply to be yourselves," the woman said in an unintentionally high-pitched voice.

His former grin abandoned, Gaph glanced at Melisma, then looked back at the woman. "You're suggesting that it would be just like being here—except that we'd have thousands of visitors gawking at us day and night."

"Observing," the woman clarified. "Not gawking."

Melisma shook her head in dismay. "I'm sorry, but we'll have to decline the offer," she said, speaking for everyone.

The woman spent a moment gnawing at her lower lip, then moved to the door to ascertain that no one was about. When she swung around to the Ryn her eyes twinkled in a way they hadn't earlier, and her tone of voice was conspiratorial.

"I shouldn't really be telling you this, but Salliche Ag is prepared to furnish you with employment right here on Ruan." She paused to allow her words time to sink in. "I'm certain that some of you have had past experience on agricultural worlds, and that you would adapt easily to both the work and the environment. In return, Salliche Ag would expect you only to sign a contract stating that you will remain onworld for at least the next three standard years."

"What does the work pay?" Gaph asked with elaborate enthusiasm.

"Salliche Ag will furnish everything you need in the way of shelter and food, and deduct the costs from your wages. The rest is, of course, yours to do with as you please—although the company discourages its employees from actually accepting credits, for fear they might be spent . . . frivolously or gambled away. The last thing Salliche Ag wants is employees who have overspent and have no recourse but to work off the debts they incurred."

Gaph slapped his thigh in fabricated delight. "What a sweet deal!"

When everyone had stopped laughing, Melisma said, "We're not interested."

The woman folded her arms across her chest. "Won't you at least consider the offer? I'm sure you don't want to remain in this camp any longer than you have to."

The scarcely veiled threat was still ringing in Melisma's ears when the Ryn filed out of the building some moments later. She didn't know whether to be angry, anxious, or both. Fortune-telling had been earning the Ryn enough credits to purchase decent foodstuffs, but business was already beginning to fall off. Without credits the camp would rapidly become the prison it was meant to be, and in the end she and the others would be forced to accept Salliche Ag's offer.

She didn't think she could feel more disheartened, until they arrived back at the Ryn encampment to find two human males waiting for them, no doubt to drive home the hopeless nature of their predicament and to sell them again on the wisdom of signing on with Salliche Ag.

And yet there was something about the pair that gave her pause. For starters, they were too seedy even for representatives of Salliche Ag. The taller one was gangly and bearded, and his long fingers were t'bac stained. He wore utility coveralls that were a size too small, and his boots were more suited to spaceport work than a desk job. The other man was equally unkempt, with grease under his fingernails and grime on his forehead. Black hair curtained his pale pointed face and fell lanky and unwashed to his shoulders.

"Lush as it is, Ruan's a rock like any other when you'd rather be elsewhere," the tall one said to Gaph as he approached.

"But every rock has its secret exits," the other chimed in, "even Ruan."

Gaph smiled pleasantly. "Yes, and every one of those clandestine egresses requires a toll we can't afford to pay."

Tall seemed to take the reply as a good sign. "Then maybe you'd like to earn the toll."

Gaph waved the men to a couple of chairs R'vanna had cobbled together. At the same time, he asked someone to bring tea and food.

"We represent a concern that provides private transportation to other worlds," Tall explained.

"For thousands of credits per passenger," Gaph said.

The man nodded. "But believe it or not, there are folks here with more than that to spend."

"The problem is," the short man took over, "they lack official permits to travel. Now normally their credits would buy them documentation, as well, but Salliche Ag is making it difficult because they have their own reasons for wanting to keep everyone onworld."

R'vanna sighed. "We're aware of those reasons."

"Well, then, here's the thing," the first man said. "The business concern we represent has official authority to transport a shipload of paying clients to Abregado-rae, which is accepting exiles."

"Abregado-rae," R'vanna said in delight. "A much happier alternative than any of the Core worlds. Positively flush with opportunities."

Tall nodded. "No camps, no labor contracts, no fine print. Everyone gets off to a fresh start. But unless we can show our clients' names on official permits of transit, all the credits in the universe won't get any of them off Ruan."

Gaph mulled it over. "Then you need a good slicer to enter those names in the database."

Short shook his head. "Salliche Ag is on the lookout for slicers. Everything has to be done by durasheet and official seal."

Gaph and R'vanna traded knowing looks. "Go on," Gaph said.

The humans also traded looks. "It's no secret that you people are good at forging permits and such," Tall said.

"Yeah, like the ones you forged allowing you to emigrate to the Corporate Sector way back when."

"Unsubstantiated rumors," R'vanna said.

Tall smiled. "Even so . . ."

Gaph cut him off. "Do you have an example of the seal you want copied?"

Short opened a case and handed Gaph a square of durasheet bearing an elaborate official seal. "This comes straight from Coruscant. Each letter of transit can list up to one hundred names, so we'd need five of them."

Gaph and R'vanna conferred for a moment. "This seal and the calligraphy are intentionally antiquated," Gaph said at last. "We'd need the proper tools, along with the inks and such."

Tall shrugged. "Whatever you need."

"What's in this for us?" Melisma asked before anyone else could.

The same man shrugged. "That's entirely up to you. Clothing, food, furniture, you name it."

She gazed at him. "How about transport off Ruan?"

Again, the two men traded glances. "How many are you?" the first asked.

"Thirty-seven—including an infant."

Tall deliberated, nodding his head slowly. "We just might be able to arrange that."

"Only to Abregado-rae, you understand," his partner added. "No alternative destinations."

Gaph glanced at Melisma, R'vanna, and some of the others. "Abregado-rae would suit us fine."

Tall folded his arms. "Then here's how it's going to work: We'll provide everything you need to forge the permits. If we're satisfied that they'll pass muster with Salliche Ag and the spaceport authorities here on Ruan, you've got yourselves a deal."

"I am Plaan," Tholatin's Weequay security chief said as he joined Droma and Han in the *Falcon*'s forward hold.

Plaan had the thumbs of his big hands hooked into the broad gunbelt that gathered a quilted, knee-length garment the color of Sriluur's desert wastes. His broad-nosed, desiccated face was deeply creased, and dark age spots showed on the almond-shaped bony plate that reinforced his skull from brow ridge to spine. His deep-set eyes gave him a haunted, fearsome aspect. Behind him stood two mean-spirited humans in camouflage combat suits, one cradling a new-generation blaster rifle, the other a twenty-year-old BlasTech E-11, which had been the weapon of choice among Imperial stormtroopers. Half a dozen other humans and aliens were inspecting various parts of the ship. Han couldn't make out their muffled comments, but the mere thought of them pawing through his property filled him with rage. It took all the control he could summon to keep from going ballistic.

"My first mate, Miek," Droma said, gesturing off-handedly toward Han.

Plaan nodded. "Sorry about having to search ship, Captain Droma. Furnished passcodes checked out. But as things are now, even we must take precautions." A being more apt to communicate by pheromones than words, Plaan spoke in a clipped and heavy accent.

With the hyperdrive behaving erratically, it had been a long, slow trip to Tholatin, an uninhabited world, save for a deep, almost undetectable rift legions of smugglers had used over the years. The *Falcon*—going under the name *Sunlight Franchise*—had been directed to a landing zone on the floor of the forested cleft, but berthing spaces and maintenance areas were located under a ceiling of cantilevered rock at the base of a sheer cliff. Although he had taken heart that the old passcodes had worked, Han was troubled by the motley nature of some of the berthed ships.

"You have been to Esau's Ridge before?" Plaan asked suddenly, studying Han with interest.

"Not in a lot of years."

"Back then, who running things?"

Han stroked his beard, as if in hazy recollection. "Let's see, there was Bracha e'Naso. And an information broker named Formyaj—a Yao, as I remember."

Plaan nodded. "Long gone, with almost everyone from those days. Left when the Yuuzhan Vong pushed through on way to Hutt space." He glanced at Droma. "Where acquired, those passcodes, Captain?"

"From a friend on Nar Shaddaa," Droma said, as Han had instructed. "A human by the name of Shug Ninx."

Plaan nodded again. "Ninx is known to us. So you are coming from Nar Shaddaa?"

Droma had his mouth open to affirm that they'd arrived from Hutt space when a baritone voice rang out from the starboard ring corridor.

"Plaan, get a look at this."

Han and Droma followed the security chief into the corridor. Just where the outrigger cockpit branched off, two human members of the search team had discovered the removable panels that covered the secret compartments Han had used for smuggling, in what felt to him like another lifetime. Like Plaan, the two snoops had the rawboned look of mercenaries or pirates rather than smugglers, which jibed with the mix-and-match ships— the uglies—Han had observed in the berthing spaces.

Plaan was grinning bemusedly. "Smugglers?"

"Now and again," Droma said.

"Freelance or for Hutts?"

"We're independent contractors."

Plaan snorted. "Better ways of earning credits these days. Even Hutts have to take care. With Boss Bunji forced off *Jubilee Wheel*, not enough glitterstim on Ord Mantell to fill bantha's horn."

As he was saying it, a short man wearing mechanic's utilities entered the corridor from the extended landing ramp. "Looks like your ship has seen some recent action," he told Droma. "Whoever you were running from ruined your new anodizing."

Droma replied to Plaan's inquisitive look. "We encountered a Yuuzhan Vong patrol. Fortunately, we escaped with nothing more than a damaged power converter and hyperdrive."

The mechanic pursed his lips, glanced around, and nodded. "Vintage ship, but I think we can fix you up with the parts you need."

Plaan seemed to relax somewhat. "Would not have to worry about Yuuzhan Vong patrols if you knew the right people," he said as he followed Droma and Han back to the forward compartment.

Droma glanced at Han before saying, "Knowing the right people is something we've never been especially good at."

The security chief uttered a dour laugh. "Perhaps luck is about to change." He walked to the entrance to the port ring corridor, then into the adjacent circuitry bay. "How many passengers this crate carry?" he asked without turning around.

"She's smaller than she looks," Han answered, taking a few steps toward Plaan. "Belowdecks she's nothing but crawl space, and even if we packed passengers in like fingerfins, the air scrubbers and oxygen supply couldn't handle more than fifty or so—and then only for a few hours."

"Why do you ask?" Droma said.

Plaan turned and walked back into the hold. "Many here at Esau's Ridge do contract work for employer who has a direct line to Yuuzhan Vong."

Han watched Plaan. "Yeah, a couple of friends of ours were working for a guy who claimed to have a direct line to the Yuuzhan Vong, but when it came down to cases the guy was no help at all. Ever hear of the Peace Brigade?"

Plaan nodded slowly. "Outfit of Reck Desh."

"Same employer?"

"Same," Plaan confirmed. "But in kinds of activities Peace Brigade handled, we steer clear. Many risks. Relocation runs our specialty."

"Relocation runs," Han said.

"Private transport for refugees eager to escape New Republic camps."

Han's eyes narrowed with suspicion. "Depending on what you charge for services, you're either a philanthropist or a predator."

Plaan laughed. "Because we receive large bonuses on back end, passengers pay only modest amounts."

"So this nameless contractor is the philanthropist?" Droma said.

"To earn bonuses, contractor requires that we deliver refugees to specific worlds—worlds that end up Yuuzhan Vong targets."

Han had to force his mouth to work. "You're recycling them. Refugees pay to leave one camp, find themselves caught up in an invasion, and end up in another camp." He fought down an urge to tear Plaan limb from limb. "And, of course, the Yuuzhan Vong are happy because you're making things all the more complicated for the New Republic relief workers."

Plaan shrugged. "Added burden for New Republic. But steady employment for us. Interested?"

"We might be," Droma said. "Do you have anything going at the moment?"

Plaan made a regretful sound as he cocked his head to one side. "Too bad you not arrive sooner. Some of our people moving a bunch off Ruan very soon."

Droma sat unsteadily at the engineering station, determined not to look at Han. "Ruan?"

Han glanced briefly at him and began to pace. "Maybe we're not too late to join in," he said, only partially successful at keeping alarm and apprehension from his voice. He turned to Plaan. "How soon can we get the parts we need?"

THIRTEEN

In the dank and underlighted hold that served as both mess hall and dormitory for the privileged captives aboard the yammosk carrier, Wurth Skidder placed his bowl beneath the spout of the nutrient dispenser, waited while his allotted share drizzled out, then carried the bowl to his usual spot of deck space, where he lowered himself into a cross-legged posture and forced himself to eat.

Like all things Yuuzhan Vong, the container had surely been fashioned from some creature—perhaps from the egg of an outsize oviparous animal—and the spoon, though made of an exotic hardwood, bore no traces of carving or machining and appeared to have been grown with handle and bowl provided. Even the thick, tapered spout of the nutrient dispenser gave all evidence of being attached to some living thing that resided unseen on the far side of the hold's curved and membranous bulkhead.

Shortly, Roa and Fasgo joined him on the floor, as had become their habit. Both of them, along with almost everyone else in the hold, looked bedraggled and water-logged from having had to endure long sessions in the tank with the yammosk. Four captives had died as a consequence of the creature's attempts at mind probing, and more than twice that number had been rendered catatonic. Skidder had survived only by drawing gently on the Force, just deeply enough to maintain sanity without revealing his Jedihood.

He was down to his last spoonful of nutrient when Roa said, "Well, look who's returned."

Following Roa's delighted gaze, Skidder turned and saw Sapha and her five fellow Ryn entering the hold. Instantly he got to his feet and waved them over, appraising them as they approached. None of the six had been seen since Commander Chine-kal had ordered them away—what must have been standard days earlier. Everyone had wondered about their mysterious disappearance, and Skidder was eager to learn where they had been taken.

"To the Hutt," Sapha said in reply to his question as she lowered herself to the floor.

Roa's mouth fell open. "A Hutt? On board this ship?"

Sapha nodded. "Randa Besadii Diori. The son of a Hutt named Borga."

Skidder waited to speak until three of Sapha's companions had moved off to join the food line. "Why is Randa here?" he asked quietly but forcefully.

Sapha regarded him for a moment. "It seemed to us that the Yuuzhan Vong are grooming him to take charge of transporting prisoners of war. For sacrifices, perhaps, or some other purposes."

"So that's the deal they cut for themselves," Skidder said through locked teeth. "But why were you brought to Randa?"

She laughed without mirth. "To tell his fortune. Using Ryn as diviners was once a pastime of the Hutts—amusing to them, frequently fatal to us. When forecasts failed to come true, the diviners were killed in various but always gruesome ways. I grew up hearing tales of such things."

Skidder considered it. "So Randa asked you to predict his future," he said at last. "What did you tell him?"

Sapha shrugged. "Innocuous things, open to interpretation."

"For instance?" Roa asked.

"The near future will be a sometimes puzzling mix of pleasures and challenges. He has much on his mind as a result of monumental events that have recently come to pass. The future hinges on his ability to think clearly and see all sides . . ."

Fasgo laughed with his mouth full. "I've been told the same things by you people."

"And Randa accepted that?" Skidder said.

"He seemed to." Sapha gestured broadly to the hold. "We're here, and not to the best of my knowledge slated for imminent execution."

Skidder's eyes narrowed with intent. "Did he ask to see you again?"

Sapha nodded. "After his beauty sleep. Probably to evaluate our accuracy."

"Was Chine-kal present?"

"The first time. The commander took some interest in our reading of Randa's body markings and palm lines. On the second occasion, he grew bored. I doubt he'll be there next time."

"He's just accommodating the Hutt," Roa suggested. "I suspect that the Yuuzhan Vong consider themselves shapers of the future, not destined for one outcome or another."

Skidder was deep in thought.

One of the Ryn returned with a bowl of nutrient for Sapha, but she pushed it away in disgust.

"The same stuff for every meal, for every species."

Fasgo nodded. "One gruel fits all." He eyed the

untouched bowl Sapha had set aside. "You going to eat that?" he asked finally.

"Help yourself," she told him.

He did, ravenously, only ceasing his spooning to remark, "You'll learn to tolerate it. Besides, it's the only way to keep up your strength."

"Answer me this," Sapha said. "The Yuuzhan Vong employ organic technology where we use machines, correct?"

"Thus far," Roa said.

"Then they don't use machines or droids to prepare this stuff."

"I wouldn't think so."

"And yet I haven't seen any chefs, or any kitchen staff. So who prepares it?"

Fasgo stopped eating, his spoon in midair, to exchange glances with Roa. "Critters," he said to Sapha. "Creatures."

Sapha gazed at the thin gray gruel. "Creatures cook this?"

Again, Roa and Fasgo swapped glances. "In a manner of speaking," Roa said delicately.

Sapha frowned. "In what manner of speaking?"

Fasgo set the bowl down. "Look, you don't care for the stuff as is. Maybe you shouldn't be wondering where it comes from or how it's cooked."

Sapha was about to ask regardless, but Skidder abruptly surfaced from his pensive trance.

"Randa has an entourage with him? Bodyguards?"

"Some Rodians, Aqualish, and Twi'leks," Sapha said. "The usual mix."

"How many bodyguards?"

Sapha looked to one of her clanmates, who said, "Ten."

"Roughly the same number of guards in the yammosk

tank hold," Skidder muttered. He fell silent, then looked hard at Sapha and the other Ryn.

"Listen carefully: The next time you're summoned, you're going to tell Randa that he's going to be betrayed. He's been lured aboard only so that Commander Chine-kal can sacrifice him." He cut his eyes to Sapha. "You understand?"

She and the other Ryn regarded one another in bafflement. "And when that doesn't come to pass? You'll have us all sucking vacuum."

Skidder shook his head. "It will come to pass, because I'm going to plant an idea in the yammosk that Randa is going to betray Chine-kal, and that he only agreed to come aboard to free us. The yammosk is sure to alert Chine-kal, and Chine-kal might even want the yammosk to take a peek at what's in the Hutt's head."

Sapha shook her head as if to clear it. "People have found unusual purposes for the Ryn, but this . . ."

Roa frowned at Skidder. "Look, Keyn, just because the creature has taken a liking to you, that doesn't mean you can actually talk to it, much less plant an idea in its brain."

Skidder sneered. "You're wrong. I've already been conversing with it."

Fasgo choked on his food and made a comical gesture to indicate madness. "Someone's been in the tank too long," he fairly hummed.

Roa continued to stare at Skidder. "You say you've been conversing with the yammosk?"

"By using the Force."

Fasgo broke the protracted silence by saying, with patent disbelief, "The Force?"

"I'm a Jedi Knight," Skidder announced, in a way that managed to combine modesty and pride. "My real name is Worth Skidder."

"Well, well," Roa huffed, "that certainly answers a lot of my questions about you."

"Then I was right," Sapha said. "You deliberately allowed yourself to be captured."

Skidder nodded. "At the time I didn't know they had a war coordinator aboard this ship. But one thing is clear: they're conveying it to a world they plan to invade and utilize as a forward base of operations. We need to learn that destination, and find some way to get the information to the Jedi or the New Republic military."

Roa was the first to respond. "Let's say you do manage to turn Chine-kal and the Hutt against one another. How's that going to help you get what you want?"

Skidder was one step ahead of him. "Once I've gained the yammosk's trust, it's going to tell me where we're headed."

"Okay," Roa said tentatively.

"I'll make use of the yammosk to control the dovin basal that drives the ship."

Roa and Sapha traded glances. "And then?" the old man asked.

Skidder fixed him with a look. "We mutiny."

The Hutt consulate on Coruscant was chaotic. Servants and dozens of hired workers were busy emptying the place of the vast amount of antiques, keepsakes, and collectibles Golga had amassed in his too-brief reign as consul general. Reclining on the couch that occupied the center of the courtyard chamber he had come to think of as home, he could only hope that the galaxy would return to normal in the near future, and that Borga the Almighty might deem him fit to continue serving as Nal Hutta's envoy to the New Republic. Until such time, he would simply have to accept whatever posting Borga assigned him, though it chilled him even to imagine being sent to somewhere like Sriluur, Kessel, or—perish the thought—Tatooine.

"Careful with those hookahs!" he said to the three Gamorreans who were crating his waterpipes. "Some of those once belonged to Jabba himself!"

He lowered his stubby arms, cursing himself for not having had the good sense to order the Rodians on his staff to see to the hookahs. But they were in the sleep chamber packing away even more personal belongings, and everyone else was too occupied destroying documents, making round trips to the launch platform, or keeping the demonstrators from storming the consulate, as one group had attempted to do only the previous evening.

Turmoil had been the order of the day since the Holo-Net had broken the story that Nal Hutta had made a separate peace with the Yuuzhan Vong, and that the Hutts were severing diplomatic relations with the New Republic. Had Borga notified Golga in advance, the consulate could have been quietly closed. Instead the penthouse of the Old Republic–style Valorum Tower had become a target for every Outer Rim refugee on Coruscant, and thus a precarious place to reside.

Servants, attachés, and staffers had decamped, including Golga's chargé d'affaires. Suppliers had refused to deliver food and other needed supplies. Coruscant Energy had engineered power failures, and Coruscant Water had so reduced the flow that daily bathing in the penthouse's converted fountain had become impossible. The number of bomb threats exceeded one hundred, though no devices had been discovered, and on the HoloNet rumors flew fast and furious, accusing the Hutts of everything from treason to sabotage, with many calling for the arrest of all Hutts, and some advocating a declaration of war.

Even now a mixed-species crowd was assembled on the observation balcony of the tower across the city canyon, chanting for retribution, throwing fists in the air, and appealing to the ceaseless flow of air traffic with huge and multicolored Hutt-condemning holoplacards. Early on, Golga had tolerated the strident gatherings, but he had since ordered the transparisteel windows curtained so he wouldn't have to be greeted by the sight of demonstrators each time he entered the chamber.

Soon, in any case, the angry crowds would be nothing more than an unpleasant memory. He would be on his way to Nal Hutta, and to diplomatic duties elsewhere in the galaxy. Once more, worries of a posting on Tatooine assailed him, but they were interrupted by the arrival of his Twi'lek secretary.

"Highness, New Republic Senator Shesh requests audience."

"Now?" Golga said incredulously. "Doesn't Senator Shesh realize that I'm preparing to depart?"

"She does, Highness. But she asserts that it is vital that she speak with you beforehand. She asserts further that you will be passing up a unique opportunity should you elect not to grant her audience."

"A unique opportunity, indeed. Is this Senator Viqi Shesh of Kuat?"

"Yes, Highness."

Golga grimaced in derision. "A member of the Advisory Council and the Security and Intelligence Council. Shall I tell you beforehand about this unique opportunity? She is going to ask me to serve as an agent for New Republic Intelligence. She will promise generous compensation for my keeping her committee apprised of what goes on in Borga's court—of who comes and goes, and of what matters are spoken. She will avouch in the strongest terms that the Hutts will ultimately be betrayed by the Yuuzhan Vong, and that Borga will be brought down. She will be quick to assure that the New Republic will one day prevail against the Yuuzhan Vong, and at that time my contributions to their defeat will become public knowledge and I will reap the benefits of my treachery by being awarded a position suitable to my new station in life. Perhaps a palace here on Coruscant, or a political appointment to the world of my choice."

The Twi'lek waited until he was certain that Golga was finished. "I should inform her, then, that Your Highness is not interested in speaking with her?"

Golga blinked and wet his lips with his fat, pointed tongue. Lending voice to what heretofore had been most private musings had accorded them a sudden credibility. Under the guise of sufferance, he motioned with his tiny hands.

"No. Show her in. But make sure she understands that I have a flight to catch."

The Twi'lek bowed graciously and left the chambers. When he returned a moment later he was accompanied by a comely, dark-haired human female, on whom even normally drab senatorial garb looked like evening wear. Golga was a Besadii, but he had more than a touch of Desilijic in his veins, which accounted for a certain partiality to human females. Watching Viqi Shesh, he envisioned her dancing for him, or fetching him succulent morsels of living food. Of greater surprise than her beauty was the fact that she had apparently come alone, without so much as an interpreter.

Golga arranged himself on the couch and motioned Shesh to the closest of several comfortable chairs. "Never let it be said," he began in Basic when his secretary had exited, "that Golga Besadii Fir is one to allow unique opportunities to pass him by."

Shesh smiled with purpose. "I'm glad to hear that, Consul Golga. It simplifies matters."

Golga licked his lips.

"As you may or may not know, recent information has come to light, indicating that the Yuuzhan Vong intend to attack Tynna."

"Tynna? I know nothing of this."

"Certain parties thought it odd that no spice was being delivered to Tynna, and they brought this matter to the attention of New Republic Intelligence. Given the Hutts' alliance with the enemy, members of the Intelligence community had to ask themselves whether the suspension of deliveries was perhaps a cloaked message from Borga—a way for her to reveal the intentions of the Yuuzhan Vong without actually saying as much."

Golga grappled with what he was hearing. "Clearly you know more about these matters than I do, Senator. In any event, you certainly can't expect me to speak for Borga."

"You are her envoy, are you not?"

"Yes, but—"

"Then don't concern yourself with speaking for Borga. Simply listen as she might."

Insulted, Golga had an impulse to have Shesh escorted from the chambers, but then thought better of it. "I'm listening, Senator—as Borga would."

Shesh flashed a warmer smile. "Should the intelligence about Tynna prove reliable, one has to wonder if the suspension of spice deliveries to Bothawui and Corellia might signal threats to those systems, as well. Or"—she held up a meticulously manicured forefinger—"whether this is merely what the Yuuzhan Vong would like us to think, while they devise an entirely different attack."

She gave Golga a moment to ponder it, then continued. "You see, the senate and the Defense Force are very divided on just this issue. With New Republic fleets widely dispersed to protect the Core Worlds, a decision has to be reached on whether additional ships should be deployed at Bothawui or Corellia."

Golga laughed. "Senator, I haven't the slightest idea what the Yuuzhan Vong plan to do next. Furthermore, it is ludicrous to assume that Borga has been made privy to their plans."

Shesh crossed her legs and leaned forward. "You can assure me of that?"

"I can. Everyone has attached too much import to this so-called alliance. Borga and the clan leaders of the Grand Council wished to avoid a war at all costs. To do so required that we allow the Yuuzhan Vong access to certain worlds in our space—worlds of little consequence— which they intend to mine for resources or remake in some way. Granted, this is a form of aiding and abetting the enemy, but the end result would have been the same had we opted to go to war. We are powerful, but not as powerful as the enemy."

"The Hutts managed to hold the Empire at bay," Shesh pointed out. "Delaying the Yuuzhan Vong would have helped."

"I won't deny it. But our society would have been destroyed. We have always believed in keeping to ourselves, Senator. We have never attempted to intrude on New Republic space—well, there was that one regrettable episode involving Durga. But other than that, we Hutts have been content to move spice, indulge ourselves with food, drink, music, and dance. We are not warriors, Senator, much less warlords."

Shesh's eyes narrowed in thought. "So you are only trying to preserve what you have. You're not actually siding with the Yuuzhan Vong."

"We are not."

"And should they defeat the New Republic?"

"If I may speak plainly, we'll go on as we always have—poorer, perhaps, for not selling spice, or wealthier from selling even more than we do now."

"To the miserable, defeated masses," Shesh said, loosing a short laugh.

As the statement didn't beg a response, Golga didn't offer one.

"I want you to deliver a message to Borga, Consul. Tell her that while the fleets are deployed elsewhere, the New Republic would like nothing more than to see the Yuuzhan Vong attack Corellia. They have a surprise in store—including a big shiny toy that could spell trouble for your new overlords. But tell her also that this information is offered as a means of redressing an earlier wrong. Borga won't understand, but there are those who will."

Golga stared at her. "If I didn't know better," he said at last, "I would be tempted to surmise that you are supplying me with intelligence that would be of great value to the Yuuzhan Vong."

Shesh shrugged. "Think what you will."

"Nevertheless, how do I know that this isn't simply disinformation, designed to make the Hutts look like fools?"

Shesh said nothing.

"Whichever the case, Senator, this is most unexpected."

Shesh's smile was enigmatic. "Who knows, Consul, someday we might be working together. To that possible end, I think we're off to a good start."

FOURTEEN

In Ryn City's dormitory, with all thirty-seven Ryn gathered around them and waiting breathlessly, the two humans—Tall and Short—appraised the completed letters of transit. The forgeries had required almost four Ruan days of clandestine work, with almost everyone contributing in one way or another. Where Gaph was skilled at line drawing, R'vanna excelled at calligraphy. Many of the females had seen to mixing and applying the colors, and even Melisma had lent a hand by proofreading the passenger names and scrutinizing the letters for imperfections.

She stood between Gaph and R'vanna now, Sapha's infant—quiet as a skimp for a change—balanced on her hip. The stuffy air of the dormitory was so tense that when Tall finally pronounced the letters "perfect," it was as if fireworks had gone off.

Everyone exhaled in relief and grinned broadly. Melisma handed the infant to one of the other females and gave Gaph and R'vanna tight hugs of joy.

The humans waited for the Ryn to calm down. Displaying one of the sheets of durasheet, Tall showed Gaph an appreciative look.

"I see you've already listed yourselves."

Gaph puffed out his chest in theatrical pride. "That's because we knew you would find them impeccable."

Tall nodded and handed all the letters to Short, who placed them inside a beat-up alloy case.

"We'll submit everything to Salliche Ag later this morning. They'll drag the process out for a day or so. But assuming everything goes as planned, you should be prepared to leave on the day after tomorrow. How's that sound?"

Instead of answering, Gaph raised his hands over his head, made a clicking rhythm with his tongue, and began to dance, cross-stepping and turning slowly as he moved about the room. In a moment, everyone was clapping and clicking in time and joining him in celebration.

Melisma could hardly believe their good fortune. In two days they would be headed clear around the Core to Abregado-rae!

Apparently in dire need of beauty sleep, Randa hadn't asked for the Ryn as expected. By Skidder's reckoning, two standard days had passed before the Hutt summoned them. Later that same day, however, Skidder was delighted to find the six Ryn already in the yammosk tank when he and the other captives were led into the hold.

Slipping into the gelatinous liquid and taking his assigned place at one of the tentacles, he gave Sapha a meaningful look but said nothing.

The session began as usual, with the captives striving to induce the yammosk—by lulling the creature into a state of tactile elation through caresses and massage—to urge the dovin basal to drive the ship to greater speeds. While those sessions had become less demanding psychologically, they were still physically exhausting, and by the time Chine-kal returned the count to normal many of the captives were bent double over the tentacles, straining for breath and trying to rub the soreness from their hands, arms, shoulders, and chests.

The important thing was that Chine-kal was pleased with their efforts, which meant that there would be no more speed work for the remainder of the session.

When the commander's circuit on the tank rim had taken him 180 degrees from Skidder, the Jedi threw Sapha a quick glance and spoke under his breath.

"You met with Randa?"

She gave him the faintest of nods. "We just finished with him."

"You did as I asked?"

"Against our better judgment. But, yes, we did as you asked."

"How did he react?"

"With palpable concern. He dismissed us almost immediately, probably to confer with his bodyguards and advisers."

Skidder's eyes narrowed in covert pleasure.

The moment had come to talk to the yammosk. In previous sessions, Skidder had drawn on the Force only enough to grant the creature access to his surface thoughts and emotions. The ease of the bond had brought the yammosk back time and again, and on each occasion Skidder had given the creature a bit more of himself, as reinforcement. Now he had to reverse the flow and speak directly to the yammosk, as it obviously believed it had been doing with him.

He had been practicing the necessary Force technique since the Ryn had first told him of their meetings with the Hutt. With no more effort than it had taken to slip into the nutrient fluid in which the yammosk floated, Skidder went into a light trance.

The goal was to convey through images that Randa

Besadii Diori was plotting against Commander Chine-kal. Skidder had run through the deceit so often in the past two days that the images unreeled before him like some HoloNet drama. Immediately the tentacle draped almost tenderly across his shoulders began to twitch, then tremble.

Then all at once the appendage tightened its hold on him. At the same time, and throughout the tank, the tentacles fastened to other captives dropped away, slapping the fluid with enough force to send nutrient slopping over the rim and onto the floor of the hold.

Several captives screamed in alarm as the yammosk's convoluted body stiffened. Skidder instantly broke mental contact and ducked out from under the tentacle's grip. But that only prompted the creature to twist toward him, as if to fix him in its gaze. Skidder, Roa, Sapha, and some of the others had the foresight to submerge themselves in the nutrient, but a dozen others were hurled clear out of the tank by the yammosk's counterclockwise whirl. Fasgo was among the latter group, and he was hurled farther than the rest, his already weakened body slammed with bone-breaking force into the yorik coral bulkhead, where it stuck fast for a moment, then began a slow tumble down the scabrous surface to the floor.

Some of the longer tentacles made a sudden grab for Skidder as he resurfaced, but he back-somersaulted out of the liquid and onto the rim walkway. Frustrated, the yammosk reared up, then flattened itself, extending its reach to the edge of the tank. The tentacles flailed and slapped against the coral grating, but Skidder deftly avoided them by hopping from foot to foot and executing flips that sent him over their slimy top sides.

Elsewhere in the hold, Chine-kal and the guards had been thrown into utter confusion. They raced around the tank, making futile attempts to calm the creature, convinced for the moment that Skidder was the victim rather than the instigator.

The Jedi front-flipped to the deck, landing on his feet, but the guards weren't about to cut him too much slack. He could have avoided or defeated the ones who rushed him from all sides, but with nowhere to run he quickly decided that his purposes would best be served by playing the panicked captive, fearful for his life.

He pretended to struggle, throwing some of the guards aside with the strength that panic affords. Ultimately, though, he let them get the better of him, and sank to the deck under their hold, shrieking, wailing, and gesticulating to the yammosk.

"It tried to kill me! It wants to kill me!"

Having lost its fury, the war coordinator was bobbing on the waves its own actions had stirred. Many captives were pressed to the rim of the tank. Most of those flung outside by the creature's abrupt spin were picking themselves up from the deck, dazed but not seriously hurt. Except for Fasgo, who was sprawled lifelessly in an expanding pool of blood.

Even Chine-kal seemed wary as he approached the yammosk. Skidder had to believe that not all the creatures developed as planned, and that despite the bioengineering that went into them, some could be flawed, as was sometimes the case with skips and other examples of Yuuzhan Vong organic technology.

Seeing or perhaps sensing the commander's approach, the yammosk extended two tentacles to him, then a third, which the yammosk curled around Chine-kal's neck. The commander's eyes rolled up in his head, and he might have collapsed except for the support of the tentacles. Then, blinking back to consciousness, he turned and stared wide-eyed at Skidder.

Skidder couldn't begin to guess what the yammosk

had related about Randa, or about Skidder himself. But the words that flew from Chine-kal were the last thing he expected to hear.

"A Jedi!" The commander eased out of the yammosk's embrace and approached Skidder. "A Jedi!"

Out of the corner of his eye, Skidder saw Roa and Sapha hang their heads in defeat.

Chine-kal stood before Skidder, shaking his head in both disbelief and wonderment. "A valiant effort, Jedi. Truly inspired. But what you failed to realize is that yammosks are not grown but *spawned*. Each passes the sum total of its learning on to the next." He glanced at the creature. "This one's progenitors have had experience with Jedi."

Chine-kal turned back to Skidder and rested his hands on Skidder's shoulders. "But be proud, Jedi, for you have pleased me greatly. In fact, you will be my gift to Warmaster Tsavong Lah, who will one day arrive to govern Coruscant."

FIFTEEN

The tempo of the rousing march that welcomed Supreme Commander Nas Choka aboard the Yuuzhan Vong warship *Yammka* was kept by warriors with drums, but the theme itself was supplied by a menagerie of bioengineered insects and avians, droning, trumpeting, and whistling from within cages and atop perches situated throughout the great hold.

Enormous villip-choir transparencies broke the obsidian monotony of the starboard bulkhead, providing a star-strewn panorama of the anchored fleet, as well as a distant view of the Hutt space world known as Runaway Prince, remade for the sowing of yorik coral, villip shrubs, and other necessities of war. To the ships that resembled asteroids, marine behemoths, and tumbled and faceted cabochons had been added an even more massive and sinister specimen: a flattened lapidary orb of glossy black, from the dense center of which spiraled half a dozen arms, as if in dark imitation of the galaxy the Yuuzhan Vong were determined to conquer.

Supreme Commander Choka, along with his commanders and foremost subalterns, moved on levitated dovin basal cushions in tiered heights above the deck. In advance of them floated four smaller cushions, their diminutive riders screened by flutters—living creatures that resembled squares of patterned cloth. Arrayed on either side of the arriving group stood five thousand warriors dressed in battle tunics and armed with amphistaffs and coufees.

Confined to a small space among the starboard-side group cowered two hundred prisoners taken from Gyndine and already purified for sacrifice. Bony growths affixed to voice boxes and jaws prevented them from giving voice to their fear.

Behind Choka marched troops of his own command, their precision footfalls crushing an ankle-deep carpet of maroon flowers, whose aroma—wafted about by the rhythmic beating of wings—had aroused the insects to song. Their stridulations intensifying and diminishing, the insects sustained notes lifted from an otherworldly scale. One moment the march was fiery and inspiring; the next it was a somber dirge.

Opposite the arrival bay, at the far end of the cloyingly perfumed parade corridor, waited Commander Malik Carr and his chief subalterns, a coven of priests, and off to one side, Executor Nom Anor, all revealed in tattooed and modified splendor.

As the train of elite warriors neared the dais, the drumbeats and insect voices ceased and Malik Carr stepped to the lip of the raised platform.

"Welcome, Supreme Commander Choka," he crowed, his augmented voice resounding from the arching ceiling and tympanic bulkheads. "The *Yammka* and all here gathered are yours to command."

A wrathful droning filled the hold. Simultaneously, ten thousand fists snapped crisply to their opposite shoulders in salute.

Supreme Commander Choka, military commander of the recently arrived spiral-arm worldship, transferred himself from the dovin basal cushion to an elevated seat at the center of the dais. While the four trailing hover cushions lined up behind him, priests, shapers, and others arranged themselves on the floor to both sides. Only when they were seated did Malik Carr and his contingent follow suit. On the deck the warriors bade their amphistaffs to coil around their bare right arms and dropped ceremoniously to one knee, heads bowed in deference.

The drumming and stridulations resumed, playing to the body as well as the ear. With five loud fanfares, some of the insects rested; but heroic bursts were immediately loosed by other insects, as if in reply. The counterpoint continued for some moments. Then, as Choka raised an ophidiform baton of command, the hold fell preternaturally silent.

"I bring salutations from Warmaster Tsavong Lah," he intoned. "He commends you on the work you have done in preparing the way, and he looks forward to the time when he may join you in battle."

Choka's modest stature did not lessen his power. Narrow-hipped but braced by thick, muscular legs, he sat rigidly on the provided chair of carved and polished coral like a statue himself, while black-feathered avians cooled the air around him with their great wings. Facial tattoos, flattened nose, and decurved eyes—above large bluish sacs—afforded him a regal demeanor. His unadorned tunic was offset by a bloodred command cloak that fell from the tops of his shoulders, and rings of gaudy variety grew from his fingers and banded his wrists and upper arms. Black throughout, his long, fine hair was combed straight back from a sloping forehead and reached nearly to his waist.

"I, too, congratulate you on your successful harvest," he went on after a moment. "You have acquitted yourselves well. Your captives from Obroa-skai, Ord Mantell, and Gyndine will bloody your nomination. But before we enact the sacrifice of the captives or learn from Commander Malik Carr the status of the invasion, we will use this moment to reward some of you for the measure of your commitment."

The high priest who accompanied Choka rose to his feet and spoke.

"We thank the gods for delivering us into this promised domain. May the blood you shed purify and cleanse it for the coming of Supreme Overlord Shimrra. We honor the gods with the nurturing sap that flows within us, so that they might thrive and grant that we might continue to caretake their creations. All we do, we do in emulation and in veneration of them."

The priest turned to the cushions that hovered behind Choka and motioned with his hand. The flutters lifted off, exposing four meter-high religious statues. The first represented Yun-Yuuzhan, the Cosmic Lord, absent those parts of himself he had sacrificed to create the lesser gods and the Yuuzhan Vong. The second and third statues represented Yun-Yammka, the Slayer, and Yun-Harla, the Cloaked Goddess. The fourth, and undeniably the most grotesque, was Yun-Shuno, the many-eyed patron deity of the "shamed ones"—those whose bodies had rejected the living implants, due either to a lack of preparation or to ambitious overreaching on the part of the candidate.

Choka's subordinate commander now rose.

"Subaltern Doshao," he began, "for his actions at the world called Dantooine. Subaltern Sata'ak, for his actions at the world called Ithor. Subaltern Harmae, for his actions at the world called Obroa-skai. And Subaltern Tugorn, both for his work in sowing the world called Belkadan and his actions at the world called Gyndine." He paused briefly, then added, "Step forward and be escalated."

As the four lesser-grade officers were ascending the dais, a quartet of implanters scuttled from recesses in the throne. When the candidates had arranged themselves in a line facing the supreme commander, the implanters took up positions behind each of them.

A variation on the creature responsible for outfitting captives with crippling growths, the implanters were small, gray, and six-legged. Like their cousins they were equipped with botryoidal optical organs and a quartet of appendages efficient for slicing through flesh and tucking surge-coral into open wounds. But where the calcificator made use of bits of itself, the implanter carried whatever enhancements were necessary for the ritual escalation. Each of the four that began slow climbs up the naked backs of the subalterns bore two finger-length horns of coral, whose pointed tips were slightly hooked.

The implanters didn't begin their work until they had secured themselves to the back of the subalterns' necks, from where they could reach to both shoulders. Employing the sharper of their appendages, they made deep cuts through the tops of the shoulder muscles, clear down to the bones that formed part of the ball-and-socket joints. When the incisions were complete and acolytes had collected the flowing blood in bowls, the implanters inserted the hooked horns into the cut, employing a resinous exudate they produced to weld the horns to the shoulder bones and to seal the wounds around them. At the same time, a sluglike ngdin wove a helix trail through the candidates' feet, sopping up whatever blood the acolytes failed to capture.

Though perspiration ran freely and legs trembled, not one of the junior officers cried out in pain or so much as grimaced. Pleased with their sangfroid, Choka gestured to four of his aides, who hurried forward with neatly folded and differently colored command cloaks.

By then the acolytes had conveyed the blood-filled bowls to the high priest, and while he dribbled the contents of the bowls over the idols, Choka's aides unfolded the cloaks and hung them from the newly implanted hooked protrusions.

The drummers beat out a short tattoo, then stopped.

"You are escalated and remade," Choka pronounced. "And now that you wear the cloak of command, you will be given your own ships, made sector chiefs, and tasked with overseeing and reeducating the populace of those worlds that constitute your domain."

"For the glory of the gods!" warriors and officers alike shouted.

Choka watched the promoted warriors step down from the dais, then turned slightly in the direction of Malik Carr. "One more matter before we proceed, Commander." He looked past Malik Carr to where Nom Anor was seated. "Come forward, Executor."

More flamboyantly attired than anyone in the hold, Nom Anor rose and walked slowly across the platform. Opposite Nas Choka he inclined his head in a nod. As a member of the intendant caste—though of the lowest rank—he was not obliged to offer salute.

"Since you and I do not hail from the same order, I am not entitled to escalate you. But know this, Executor: Were I so entitled, I would be more inclined to demote than promote you."

Clearly surprised, Nom Anor did not respond, though his mouth twitched several times in rapid succession.

"Your actions, Executor, have been closely monitored and widely discussed, and it is the opinion of many in Shimrra's court that you have strayed from your assigned course. First you chose to ally yourself with the Praetorite Vong, who believed they could spearhead an invasion of this magnitude without suffering tragic consequences."

"I was not allied with them," Nom Anor said when he could. "My assignment was to destabilize the New Republic in ways I saw fit. That is what I did among the Imperial Moffs, as well as in the Osarian system, and have since done—under different guises—in a half-dozen other systems."

Choka shot him a gimlet stare. "Who helped the Praetorite Vong obtain a yammosk—and an imperfect one at that?"

Nom Anor swallowed hard. "I may have mentioned something—"

"You facilitated them."

"Only from a certain point of view."

"Don't try your doublespeak on me, Executor. You may have managed to distance yourself from Prefect Da'Gara and the rest by escaping the price they paid for their miscalculation, but you cannot deny engineering the plan that ended in the death of the priestess Elan, daughter of high priest Jakan—who, I might add, is most displeased with you."

"There is no proof that Elan or her mascot Vergere are dead. Even so, I can scarcely be held accountable for what happened to them."

"You take no blame for employing agents who act without orders from their handler?"

Nom Anor added force to his voice. "My agents were endeavoring to please me—*us*—by returning Elan. I had no knowledge of their designs until it was too late."

"Is it true that Elan was to have assassinated a number of *Jeedai* Knights?"

"It is."

Choka tempered his voice with curiosity. "Why this

fascination with the *Jeedai*, Executor? I, for one, am not convinced they pose a serious threat to our conquest."

"It is not the Jedi who pose a threat, so much as the Force—the mystical power they embody."

"The Force is nothing more than an idea," Choka said loudly, "and the best way to extinguish an idea is by replacing it with a better one, such as we bring."

Nom Anor risked a patronizing sniff. "As you say, Supreme Commander."

Choka glowered. "Now I learn from Commander Malik Carr that *you* were instrumental in gaining the allegiance of the creatures that occupy this space—these Hutts."

Nom Anor's genuine eye narrowed. "The Hutts are critical to a plan devised by Commander Malik Carr and myself to force a significant defeat on the New Republic. In fact"—he tilted his head to one side—"you arrive at an auspicious moment, because part of that plan is shortly to be put into effect. If you would care to accompany us into battle, you could observe firsthand our strategy for conquering the Core Worlds in advance of the arrival of Warmaster Tsavong Lah."

Choka took a moment to weigh the consequences of such an action, then grunted an affirmative. "I will go. But let me caution you, Executor, about the perils of ambition. It's obvious that you are hungry for escalation, but there are no shortcuts to the rank of consul, to say nothing of prefect." He gestured over his shoulder. "Look to Yun-Shuno for counsel, Executor. Escalation is awarded only to those who have discharged their obligations in service to the gods. You appear to act in your own behalf, as if possessed of a personal stake in the results." He leaned slightly forward. "Or is it this galaxy, Executor, and the heathen beliefs of those who populate it that have corrupted you?"

Nom Anor held his gaze, wishing he had filled his empty eye socket with a venom-spitting plaeryin bol. "I care only for what this galaxy is capable of providing the Yuuzhan Vong." He cast a glance at Malik Carr. "With all due respect, Commander, our target awaits."

Malik Carr nodded to Choka. "He speaks the truth."

The supreme commander folded his arms. "Let us enact the sacrifices and see what Commander Malik Carr and Executor Nom Anor have masterminded." He pointed to the knot of prisoners. "Bring the captives forward. In sacrificing them, perhaps we can help ensure Executor Nom Anor a much-needed victory."

SIXTEEN

On a purely objective level, battles in space had a savage beauty, an incendiary splendor. Any veteran warship commander or fighter jock ordered to speak the truth would have said so. The more candid among them might even have confessed to moments of exhilaration or, at the very least, moments of hypnotic fascination, when ranging laser bursts or the stroboscopic dazzle of short-lived explosions were enough to carry a pilot completely out of him- or herself. Add distance to the view and the enchantment increased a hundredfold, for along with fiery and coherent light there was the black velvet tableau of stars, planets, moons . . . and ships—thrusters flaring, burnished by starlight, reduced to fleeting comets, twirling and pirouetting in a slow, pyrotechnic ballet of death.

The Battle of Tynna was no exception.

Being seven hundred thousand kilometers removed from the cloud-wreathed, cool-blue and dark-green gem was like having an upper-tier balcony seat at the Coruscant Opera, but the lofty vantage compensated for the lack of details. And as at the opera, technological assists were available for any who wished to bring the action into extreme close-up.

Major Showolter might have expressed as much to fellow intelligence officer Belindi Kalenda, but he feared being misunderstood. Consequently, he kept his thoughts to himself as the two women at the helm of the KDY LightStealth-18 reconnaissance leaned to either side to afford him and Kalenda an unobstructed view of Tynna's ruination.

A carbon-black six-passenger craft with a needlelike body and disproportionate, downsloping stabilizers, the LightStealth recon was the closest anyone had come to producing a starship capable of hiding itself even while it scanned. Unlike the wide assortment of vessels designed by Raith Sienar, Imperial Section 19, or Warthan's Wizards during the days of the Empire, the LSR wasn't cloaked, but was instead built for silent running and remarkable speed. Bristling with low-profile rectennae and packed with signal-augmented sensor jammers, blind-band hypercomm transmitters, crystal gravfield trap scanners, and a power core more suitable to a ship of the line, the LSR could all but see around the universe to its own aft and could outrun nearly anything that got wind of it.

The craft's pilots, on temporary duty from the Intelligence division's own Black Force Squadron, had assured Showolter that the LSR could be moved to within visual range of the Yuuzhan Vong flotilla and still evade detection. But Showolter had no desire to be any closer to the rout than necessary. They were only there as observers, in any case.

"It's horrible," Kalenda said abjectly, turning away from the narrow viewports. "I can't stand just sitting here, doing nothing."

"Showing ourselves will allow the Yuuzhan Vong to know we've found a flaw in their strategy," Showolter pointed out. Even so, the realization that they really could do nothing brought an end to his ruminations about the beauty of battle and pulled down the corners of his mouth. "But I agree: it's horrible."

Kalenda was slight, dark-skinned, and a touch glassy-eyed, where Showolter was thickset, pale, and a bit more conspicuous than Intelligence liked its officers to be. Recently they had worked closely together in overseeing the Yuuzhan Vong defector case, which had not only turned into a political debacle of major proportions, but had also landed both of them in bacta tanks.

In private moments Showolter still chided himself for having been so easily manipulated by Elan—the Yuuzhan Vong priestess and faux defector who had very nearly done in Han Solo, as well. Showolter had never trusted her, and yet despite his suspicions he had relaxed his guard and ultimately failed to deliver her to Coruscant. He often wondered what might have happened had he succeeded. Would he have been a victim of her poison breath, as Solo had come close to being? Would she have accomplished her goal of assassinating Luke Skywalker and other Jedi Knights? He wondered, too, about the fate of the strange being that had accompanied Elan, the one called Vergere, who had fled in one of the *Millennium Falcon*'s escape pods, perhaps back into enemy hands, perhaps not.

Kalenda had also borne the brunt of the fallout from the affair, as it was thought that she had unwittingly divulged vital details to an informer who sat—even now—in the senate or on the Security and Intelligence Council.

Showolter's and Kalenda's tarnished reputations were clearly what had prompted Talon Karrde to seek them out. Karrde, and the Jedi apparently, had uncovered evidence linking the spice trade to New Republic worlds in imminent danger of attack by the Yuuzhan Vong. The nature of that link was so tenuous, however, that few would have paid it any heed—save for two defamed officers intent on clearing their names at any cost.

Knowing that high-ranking members of the military would be disinclined to hear them out, Showolter and Kalenda had shared Karrde's data only with select members of the intelligence community. One such member had kept them apprised of Yuuzhan Vong fleet movements in Hutt space, and another of HoloNet S-thread disturbances in the hyperspace routes linking Hutt space to the Tynnani system. The jump of several warships from Hutt space had been enough to prompt Showolter and Kalenda to take a gamble on the flotilla's destination. Already en route to Tynna when confirmation of the HoloNet disruptions had been received, they had arrived almost simultaneously with the Yuuzhan Vong ships.

Arms wrapped tightly around herself, Kalenda was staring as if mesmerized by the distant flashes of light. "What were we thinking, Showolter? We should have at least tried to bring the Defense Force into this."

"We've been through that," he reflected sourly. "They wouldn't have listened. And even if they had, they would have dismissed the evidence as unsubstantiated or at best coincidental—especially considering the source." He glanced over his shoulder at the LSR's fifth and only civilian passenger. "No offense, Karrde."

"None taken," Karrde assured from one of the seats. He glanced at Kalenda, then added, "Remind her, Major, of the most important reason for not going to the military."

Showolter snorted ruefully. "On the off chance Admiral Sovv actually listened to us and dispatched a battle group to Tynna."

Kalenda pondered the fact dully. "If the Yuuzhan Vong had found New Republic ships waiting for them, they'd know we're on to them." She gazed out the viewport. "Tynna has to fall to save Corellia and Bothawui."

Showolter shrugged meaningfully. "And maybe dozens more have to fall."

Kalenda sighed with purpose. "I've been to Tynna. It's one of the most beautiful worlds in the Expansion Region. And the Tynnans are probably one of the most well-informed and well-intentioned species anywhere." She turned to Karrde. "I just can't accept that there wasn't some other way of corroborating the intelligence you brought us."

"If nothing else, it'll be over quickly," one of the pilots remarked. "Tynna's space defense didn't number more than two hundred fighters to begin with, and by our count they're already down to less than thirty."

Kalenda squinted, as if to hold the battle at bay. "Why don't they surrender? It's suicide." She compressed her lips in bitterness. "If only they understood what they're dying for . . ."

"Telling them wouldn't have changed anything," Karrde said, joining her at the viewport. "If your choice was to fight with your last breath or allow yourself to be captured and sacrificed, what would you do?"

While Kalenda brooded, Showolter studied the LSR's authenticator screen. "Do the scanners recognize any of the Yuuzhan Vong ships?"

The pilot called up data. "Vessel types, more than anything else. But we have verification on three of them. Two were at Obroa-skai. One—the heavy cruiser analog—was at Gyndine."

"Enemy fighters and drop ships penetrating the envelope," the copilot announced. "Bearing on a course for Tanallay Surge complex."

"Can we access the satellite feed?" Showolter asked.

The copilot threw several switches. "Onscreen. What we're seeing is going live to every city on Tynna."

The screen showed the sprawling, multilevel structure that was Surge complex, with its surrounding pools, fountains, and chutes. On the broad steps that fronted the complex and disappeared under water stood several hundred dark and glossy-pelted bipeds, all with pointed ears and tapering tails erect, and whiskered, quivering snouts lifted to the sky.

Abruptly the screen shifted to a reverse point-of-view shot of Yuuzhan Vong vessels dropping through the atmosphere like slow-motion meteors. Cams tracked the descent of those closest to the Surge complex and held on them as they landed on the far side of bridges that spanned the picturesque lagoon above which the Tynnans had assembled.

"No indication of weapons among the Tynnan contingent," Showolter said when the screen had returned to a midrange shot of the web-fingered, bucktoothed aliens. "Must be a welcoming party."

"Has to be," Kalenda mused. "Cunning and quickwittedness have always been the Tynnans' best weapons, but it'll take time before they deploy those."

"Meanwhile," Showolter said, "it looks like they're ready to hand over the codes to the city."

Karrde smoothed his mustache. "I still can't figure what the Yuuzhan Vong want with Tynna. Sure, it's rich in natural resources, but nothing that can't be found in Hutt space."

"Tynna's a step closer to the Core," the pilot suggested.

Showolter shook his head. "Karrde's right. Has to be something peculiar to Tynna."

The point of view shifted again, this time to Yuuzhan Vong warriors and officers filing from one of the larger drop ships. The cam closed on two officers perched atop levitation seats. The seemingly higher ranked of the pair was black-haired and relatively short for a Yuuzhan Vong. The other was rail thin and elaborately tattooed.

"I don't think I'll ever get used to the look of these butchers," Kalenda said.

Karrde snorted and made a toasting gesture. "Here's to hoping you never have to."

Showolter's eyes were glued to the display screen. He touched the copilot's shoulder. "I want all of this recorded and backed up in triplicate."

"Already on it," she told him.

Whoever was operating the cam obviously thought that the Yuuzhan Vong were going to continue across the bridges to the gathered Tynnans, because the cam momentarily raced ahead of its subjects when the enemy suddenly stopped short of the lagoon.

"They want the Tynnans to come to them," Showolter surmised.

"I don't know about that," Karrde said skeptically. "They're up to something else."

As he was saying it, the cam closed on the black-haired officer and watched as he motioned back to the drop ships. Then it quickly panned across the landscape, focusing on one of the ships in time to see compartments open in its pitted base and a swarm of minuscule red spheres spill onto the ground and rush for the lagoon as if self-propelled.

"What the . . . ," the pilot said.

Instinctively and with patent apprehension, Kalenda reached for the nearest arm, found Karrde's right, and vised on to it.

The leading edge of the spill had reached the shore of the lagoon, and the first of the red spherettes were already plunging into the cold blue waters. On the steps the Tynnans were crowding forward, snouts snuffling in agitated curiosity.

Showolter, Karrde, and Kalenda huddled around the monitor display.

Abruptly, the lagoon lost color.

Showolter's first thought was that something had happened to the satellite feed signal. But when he raised his head to glance out the LSR's viewport, he could see even at great remove from the planet, the sparkling blue of Tynna's northern waters was rapidly changing to a sickly pale yellow.

In the absence of Supreme Commander Choka and Malik Carr—and assured of victory at Tynna—the priests had performed the rituals necessary for removing from its crèche aboard the *Yammka* an enormous, dedicated villip Choka had brought with him from the outer rim of the galaxy. The rituals had involved the intonation of countless prayers, the use of much sacrificial blood, and ceaseless stroking of the bony ridge that was the helmet-shaped villip's most prominent feature.

By the time the commanders returned from their brief visit to Tynna, the villip had been relocated to ceremonial surroundings in a hold cleared of everyone but the most exalted of the priests. Below their far-larger companion sat the transmitting villips consciousness-joined to Nas Choka and Malik Carr, who genuflected reverently before the towering communicator, bare heads lowered, wrists crossed atop the elevated knee, and command cloaks falling around them like shrouds.

Nearby the priests sat cross-legged, chanting the invocations that would put the villip in sequential contact with scores of signal villips that had been positioned in space along the invasion path.

With loud sucking noises, a cavity resembling an

eye socket puckered to life in the center of the villip's ridge; then along that line the villip everted, turning completely inside out and assuming the features of Warmaster Tsavong Lah.

As elect protector of Supreme Overlord Shimrra, and well on his way to a kind of apotheosis, Tsavong Lah, through an endless series of escalations, had come to resemble the incarnation of Yun-Yammka, the god of war. Tsavong Lah's head sloped back from his face, with dark hair both upswept and trailing like tassels from the blunt end. The blue sacks under eyes that were all pupil drooped like deep pockets to the corners of a voracious-looking mouth, and a deep notch bisected his skull from ear to ear. His full lips were ridged by myriad scars, and his ears protruded from his skull like little wings, with the lobes of each descending almost to his shoulders like elongated teardrops of molten wax. Below the neck, overlapping scales the color of rust grew like armor plates from breastbone and collarbones.

"Behold your leader," Tsavong Lah's villip told the commanders in a voice garbled by space and time.

"Warmaster," the two said as they lifted their eyes.

Each had learned of the warmaster's role in the poisoning of Ithor and the downfall of Shedao Domain Shai. To dishonor Tsavong Lah was to court an untimely death.

The eyes of the facsimile fixed on Nas Choka. "Inform me of recent events, Supreme Commander."

"We occupy the world called Tynna, Potent One, which fell to us with so meager a fight we might have deemed it unworthy were it not so well suited to our needs and our campaign."

The eyes moved to Malik Carr. "I would hear more of this."

"Tynna's clement waters will one day furnish dovin

basals of the size needed to remove the shields that guard Coruscant and other worlds of the Core. It is our conviction that the indigenous species—furred bipeds of diminutive size—can be reeducated and trained, and will make for able and affable tenders of our creations."

"And as to Tynna's importance to the conquest?"

"Potent One, the world will also serve as a staging area for eventual incursions into the Corellian and Bothan sectors."

"Eventual, you say."

"Tynna is but the first stage of a strategy that will speed us to the Core. To guarantee this, we entered into an agreement with the Hutts, the terms of which require that we apprise them of planetary systems to avoid in their dispersal of a ludicrous product called spice. We did so in complete expectation that they would either alert the New Republic, or that New Republic analysts would discover that spice was moving freely in some sectors and not at all in others, and leap to the conclusion that the latter provided a glimpse of our battle plan. Tynna was one of the worlds we cautioned the Hutts to avoid, along with Corellia and Bothawui. Tynna was deliberately *won* as a means of fortifying the disinformation."

The villip was silent for a long moment. "The meager battle you waged suggests that the New Republic failed to behave as predicted. Otherwise, their fleet would have been lying in wait."

"Testimony to the New Republic's notion of cleverness, Warmaster," Nas Choka answered. "Through the whole of the battle and its aftermath we observed spies observing us from a stealthy craft I'm certain they believe went undetected. To have met us in force might have saved the day for Tynna, but the New Republic is well aware that we have targets of greater significance in mind, so they purposely gave Tynna away.

"With tribute to Commander Malik Carr," Choka continued, "I am now convinced that the same tactic will work for the planned assault. Many coralskipper pilots are readying themselves for the sacrifice the attack will require. And we will soon begin positioning autonomous dovin basals along the routes New Republic ships will use in jumping to the target once they learn the truth."

"Then these Hutts alerted the New Republic?"

"I deem it of little consequence either way, Potent One. As a bonus, the Hutts will make for bountiful sacrifices when we're finished with them."

The facsimile's eyes closed for a moment. "I am not fully swayed. Even if your assumption is correct—that the New Republic is now convinced that we mean to assail either Corellia or Bothawui—surely they have sufficient ships to safeguard both worlds."

"They do, Warmaster," Malik Carr said, "although Corellia remains relatively unprotected, while Bothawui enjoys the protection of a large flotilla."

"The New Republic cares so little for Corellia?"

Nas Choka smiled faintly. "They wish us to think so, Potent One."

"It has been our hope all along to maneuver them into fortifying only one of those worlds," Malik Carr explained, "and the gods have favored us by providing help from an unexpected quarter. A New Republic senator informed the Hutts that Corellia conceals a trap of some sort."

"A deceit."

"Your pardon, Warmaster, but we have some reason to trust this human being. She may well be the same person who thought she was helping us by apprising our agents that the priestess Elan had defected."

"Then you already know the identity of this betrayer."

"Her name is Viqi Shesh, Potent One."

"This bodes well," Tsavong Lah's villip allowed. "But delay any contact with her until your strategy is successfully executed. She may be of greater use to us once we are closer to the Core." The villip began to close. "I leave the rest to you."

"Your will be done, Potent One," the commanders said in unison.

SEVENTEEN

Commodore Brand tried not to be distracted by the traffic that gushed horizontally and vertically past the transparisteel wall of the Advisory Council chambers, or by the cityscape itself, ignited to flickering splendor as that part of Coruscant turned away from the sun. Seated with their backs to the window wall, Chief of State Borsk Fey'lya and the now eight members that made up his council had nothing to focus on but Brand, who stood rigidly at a podium opposite them, reading from a screenful of notes prepared in haste by his staffers after an intelligence briefing on the fall of Tynna.

"What is significant," Brand continued, "is that the assault was foreseen, and that alone affords provisional corroboration of the Intelligence division's belief that the Hutts have been supplying us with data. In those systems where the Hutts have curtailed spice operations, the enemy has set its sights on a world. Whether the Hutts were aware of what they were doing in asking for fore-warning regarding their smuggling enterprise is presently unknown—though we are looking into the matter—but the fact remains that Tynna, a transshipment point as opposed to an actual market, has not seen a spice vessel since the Hutts forged their pact with the Yuuzhan Vong."

Fey'lya interjected a transparent snort of ridicule into Brand's brief pause, then had the gall to offer a pretense of apology.

"I'm sorry, Commodore, but something seems to have become lodged in my throat. Please, carry on with your . . . report. I know that I speak for everyone in saying that I can scarcely wait to hear the rest."

Brand refused to be rattled by the sarcasm. "At the moment, the only other systems where spice operations have been suspended are Corellia and Bothawui. It has yet to be ascertained in which order the Yuuzhan Vong mean to strike. But we do expect an attack sooner rather than later. For that reason it is the opinion of Admiral Sovv and the Defense Force that a decision is critical on the matter of the redisposition of New Republic warships."

Brand activated the holoprojector table adjacent to the podium. Depressing a tile on the console built into the lectern's sloping desk, he displayed a galactic map, faintly blue in the cone created by the projector's modulasers.

"The Yuuzhan Vong have established and fortified what amounts to a resupply corridor that stretches from the Outer Rim to Hutt space. Since the battle at Obroa-skai they have been receiving a steady influx of warships and matériel, clearly in anticipation of launching a major offensive—their first since Ithor. Against such a formidable fleet, and without weakening our security in the Core or at Bilbringi, where harassment continues despite holding actions by the Imperial Remnant, we can mobilize and deploy a task force of vessels borrowed from battle groups currently in service at Commenor, Kuat, Ralltiir, and a score of other worlds. Should the Hapes Consortium vote to support New Republic efforts, some of their ships would also be allocated to the task force, which would be led by the heavy cruiser *Yald*, under my command."

Brand paused again and planted his large hands on the podium. "Councilors, we have not discounted that the assembled intelligence could be a ploy to keep us from identifying a different target entirely, but at the same time we cannot afford to ignore the evidence."

"Evidence," Fey'lya grumbled. "Inferences, suggestions, remote possibilities, but certainly not evidence." His violet eyes mocked Brand openly. "What has the command staff decided, with regard to this redisposition of naval power?"

Brand motioned to the holograph. "As you know, we have been triaging in all sectors, allowing worlds like Gyndine and now Tynna to fall in order to safeguard others like Kuat, Bilbringi, and Commenor. Our actions—or shall I say inactions—have hardly endeared us to worlds that consider themselves to be in the path of invasion. Regardless, even if we can manage to amass a sizable task force, it will not be of sufficient size to provide adequate protection to both Bothawui and Corellia."

He straightened to his full height. "After analyzing all available data, it is the conclusion of the command staff that Corellia is the target. Therefore, Admiral Sovv is recommending that all available ships and resources be moved to the Corellian sector as soon as possible."

Fey'lya's cream-colored fur bristled. "I thought as much," he said in a flat, menacing voice. "You would, as you say, 'triage' Bothawui for the sake of saving Corellia. But I won't have it." He shook his head angrily. "I'm sorry, Commodore, but I refuse to authorize such action at this time. Your 'evidence' is too scanty."

"No one said anything about abandoning Bothawui,"

Brand rejoined. "The flotilla already there will remain in place. We are only trying to protect Corellia."

"Protect the sacred Core, you mean." The Bothan stood to regard his eight peers. "I wish the council to consider closely the source of this *spicy* intelligence. Commodore Brand would have you believe that it was gathered by the Intelligence division or gleaned through hours of painstaking investigation and analysis. But, in fact, it was brought to the attention of two officers of questionable standing in the intelligence community by a person of even more dubious reputation, who claims to be serving as a kind of ombudsman for the Jedi Knights—Talon Karrde."

"I fail to see the pertinence of that," Cal Omas said. "Talon Karrde is well known to this council."

Fey'lya glared at him. "Well, of course you wouldn't see the pertinence, Councilor Omas, because you fail to grasp that the Jedi would sooner rid the galaxy of Bothans than do anything to protect them."

"The Jedi had nothing to do with our decision," Brand argued.

Fey'lya made a gesture of dismissal. "We all know that the Jedi have been holding back, downplaying their role until such time as they might truly show their hand. With Bothawui defeated, they will do just that."

"In what way have they been holding back?" Cal Omas interrupted. "They've done nothing less than lead this fight from the start, making a stand on Dantooine and Ithor while the senate insisted on thinking of the Yuuzhan Vong as a 'local problem.'"

Fey'lya wasn't unprepared to defend his accusations. "Consider what the Jedi are said to have accomplished when their little retreat on Yavin 4 was threatened by Imperial admirals Pellaeon and Daala, and how Luke Skywalker all but single-handedly turned the tide against the

Yevetha with *illusions*. Then talk to me about their current contributions."

He wagged his clawed forefinger at Omas. "Never underestimate what they are capable of, Councilor. Skywalker's Jedi are not the Jedi Knights of old, but a surreptitious, ambitious new breed. With Bothawui occupied, they would be ready to make their move and take control of the senate."

Chelch Dravvad of Corellia took on the fight. "The chief of state should learn to keep his private fears to himself. It is against the Jedi Code to spearhead an offensive, on the battlefield or in any other arena. In this the new Jedi are no different from the old. Skywalker and the rest are attempting to do what the Jedi have always done: uphold peace and justice without turning themselves into full-fledged warriors. If there is a growing misunderstanding of them, it owes to a lack of information. Perhaps by isolating themselves on Yavin 4 they are to blame for some of that. Perhaps their time would have been better spent demonstrating what they stand for. Even so, they have all our best interests at heart, and they certainly haven't singled out the Bothans as their enemy."

Fey'lya's voice became higher pitched. "You're wrong, Councilor. And I say again that, based on Commodore Brand's data, I will not grant the command staff's request that Corellia be reinforced."

"Then I demand that the issue be put to a vote," Omas said.

Fey'lya held up his hand to silence debate and looked pointedly at Brand. "What do your actual field agents tell you, Commodore? What do your analysts say? What are you hearing from the costly hyperspace probes you've sent out? Instead of relying on conjecture, we should be looking to hard data. We'd do just as well to seek the counsel of a fortune-teller as accept as truth what you've told us this afternoon."

"Our findings are based on neither prophesy nor conjecture," Brand said firmly. "The data supporting our decision are of a highly sensitive nature, but they are available for your perusal whenever you wish."

Fey'lya sneered. "Oh, I'm certain you've concocted an airtight case, Commodore." He scanned the eight councilors. "For the record, then, who will begin the vote?"

"I stand with the chief of state," Fyor Rodan of Commenor declared. "I don't trust Karrde or the Jedi. With enough popular support Skywalker knows the senate will be constrained to yield to his demands. Then it will only be a matter of time before the Jedi are overseeing all decisions. I warn you, allow Bothawui to fall and we'll soon be headed for malevolent times—an empire disguised as a theocracy." He stopped to take a breath. "Commenor will be threatened should Corellia fall, but I am compelled to vote against the Jedi, and for Bothawui."

"Thank you, Councilor," Fey'lya said.

"Why not take the battle to the Yuuzhan Vong before they completely outflank us?" Councilor Triebakk asked Brand through his droid translator.

Brand turned to the towering Wookiee. "That isn't possible without leaving the entire Core unprotected. If we could put the Imperial Remnant and the Hutts at their back, or have the Hapan Consortium open a new front in the Mid Rim, a counteroffensive could be considered. But now is not the time."

"I agree that we can't afford to leave Coruscant or any of the Core Worlds open to attack," Dravvad said, "but do you actually expect us to sit here and debate which world—Bothawui or Corellia—is more important to the New Republic?"

"Not more important, Councilor, more imperiled."

"Stop wasting time," Fey'lya snapped. "Your vote will go to Corellia and we all know it."

Dravvad nodded his head once. "Just as yours must go to Bothawui."

Fey'lya swung to Cal Omas. "Your vote."

"Corellia—but not for the reasons you imagine. It simply makes no sense for the Yuuzhan Vong to have struck at Gyndine and Tynna if Bothawui has been their goal all along. Furthermore, Corellia is essentially defenseless, where Bothawui is already sufficiently defended. How would we appear to our constituents if we allowed a helpless system to fall—a system we made helpless, no less? We might as well convince Corellia to surrender."

"Spoken like a true Alderaanian," Fey'lya muttered. "Also, Councilor, you falsely assume that surrender to the Yuuzhan Vong guarantees survival. But that is another matter." He turned to the Sullustan, Niuk Niuv.

"The Corellians have long wanted independence," Niuv began. "We nearly went to war with them in recent memory over that very issue—a war that only strained relations to the breaking point. The New Republic is under no constraint to defend Corellia. But the fact of the matter is that Corellia's lack of defenses will be its salvation. The Yuuzhan Vong will strike against Bothawui."

"Your sense of direction is astute, Councilor," Fey'lya remarked, "and I further applaud you for breaking ranks with Admiral Sovv." He turned 180 degrees. "Councilor Triebakk. Do I even need ask?"

"I accept Commodore Brand's data, and defer to the expertise of the command staff," the Wookiee said through the translator. "The Yuuzhan Vong plan to use Corellia as a staging area to penetrate the Core—"

"There's no need to belabor the point," Fey'lya cut

him off. He narrowed his eyes at Councilor Pwoe. "And you?"

The Quarren's mask tentacles quivered and his baggy eyes narrowed in anger. "Corellia. As Councilor Omas said, Bothawui is adequately defended by some of the very Bothan Assault Cruisers it convinced the New Republic to finance some time ago."

"And I can promise you that we will make use of *all* those cruisers, even if we have to withdraw them from the Core," Fey'lya barked.

"Hasn't it always been Bothawui's aim to claim those ships as their own and prove itself mightier than Mon Calamari, Sullust, and Coruscant?"

Fey'lya smirked. "So Pwoe—disconcerted by Mon Calamari's loss of the military prestige—votes not so much for Corellia as against Bothawui. Next!" He looked to Navik of Rodia.

Navik's short snout bobbed. "Rodia's proximity to Bothawui leaves me little choice." He nodded affirmatively to Fey'lya.

The chief of state nodded back and commenced a head count. "Pwoe, Omas, Triebakk, and Dravvad in favor of Corellia. Myself, Rodan, Niuv, and Navik in favor of Bothawui."

Everyone looked at the council's ninth and newest member.

"I'm afraid the decision falls to you," Fey'lya said.

Commodore Brand waited, expectantly.

"Even with the evidence of Tynna to support a possible threat to Corellia, an attack on the Core makes no sense strategically. If the Yuuzhan Vong were going to launch an offensive so far from their present stronghold in Hutt space, why would they waste valuable resources engaging a system we essentially stripped of defenses after the Centerpoint Station crisis rather than strike at a more appropriate target, like Kuat or Brentaal? No, I say all things point to an attack on Bothawui—from Hutt space and now from Tynna. I stand with Chief of State Fey'lya."

Fey'lya breathed a long sigh of relief. "I commend your flawless reasoning, Senator Shesh." He smiled ruefully at Commodore Brand. "The matter is resolved. Assemble your task force, Commodore, but steer it to Bothawui."

"We've beaten them at their own game," Commodore Brand announced as he hurried through the doors of the fleet office. "Senator Shesh kept her promise: She threw the vote to Bothawui."

Hoots of success filled the room.

"Shesh also reports that her meeting with the Hutt consul general went well," Brand added. "We may yet get some help from the Hutts. Now we need to hear from Hapes."

"The Consortium vote is set for tomorrow," his adjutant supplied.

Brand couldn't restrain a smile. "It's all coming together. But now the real work begins." He strode to a holomap not unlike the one he had made use of only moments earlier in the Advisory Council chambers. "The Yuuzhan Vong have obviously been looking closely at both Corellia and Bothawui, assessing the value of each. By deploying the new task force in Bothan space, we leave Corellia wide open for attack." He turned to his adjutant. "What news from Centerpoint Station?"

"The Solo kids have arrived on Drall. Anakin Solo is the one who originally enabled the repulsor there, and the Centerpoint technicians have high confidence he'll be able to do the same with the station. At this point they're down to fine-tuning the thing anyway, making certain it will perform as expected, in lieu of running actual tests, for fear of alarming Corellia, Drall, Selonia, and the rest. Although that hardly matters, since rumors of all sorts have been circulating. Riots have broken out in Coronet, Meccha, and L'pwacc Den Port, and there's widespread talk of ousting Governor-General Marcha."

Brand nodded glumly. "Well, if this works, Corellia will be seen as the galaxy's savior, and any hard feelings should disappear." He turned back to the slowly gyrating 3-D map. "Alert Core Command on a need-to-know basis that elements of the Third Fleet should be prepared to jump for Kuat on my order. Likewise, that elements of the Second Fleet should be prepared to jump for Ralltiir." He inserted his hand into the holoprojector's cone of light. "Furthermore, I want the hyperspace routes linking Corellia to Kuat, Ralltiir, and Bothawui swept for the Yuuzhan Vong equivalent of mines or mass-shadow weapons."

Brand turned and glanced around the room. "With Centerpoint's interdiction field holding them fast and a full fleet at their back, the Yuuzhan Vong will regret the day they entered this galaxy."

EIGHTEEN

Archon Thane's words could barely be heard for all the outcries of shame and disapproval. Regardless, he stood tall before his sixty-two peers, most of whom were female, proudly displaying the bruises he had earned in the honor duel with Isolder and convincingly unapologetic for having gambled away Vergill's vote on the outcome of that contest. Thane's audacity was not surprising, but where Leia had expected bitterness and sarcasm, his words in support of the New Republic sounded almost sincere.

Many in the vast hall were certain that Vergill's vote would provide Teneniel Djo with the majority she needed to mandate military action against the Yuuzhan Vong, but Leia no longer had a clear sense of her own objectives. While the Consortium's entry into the war might turn out to be pivotal, allegations of personal interest and conspiracy threatened to undermine not only the political process, but also the long-standing alliance between the Consortium and the New Republic.

To the exasperation of C-3PO, who insisted on trying to match her long strides and divine her sudden about-faces, Leia paced nervously behind the scenes in a small chamber that looked out on the speaker's rostrum. If nothing else, she told herself, the vote would at least conclude her visit to Hapes, which had become more trying as the days had worn on, both at Reef Fortress and the Fountain Palace. She felt hopelessly removed from the activities that had become most important to her. Hapes had begun to seem a place of exile, and an imaginary one at that—a land of dragons and rainbow gems, of trees of wisdom and Guns of Command—and the brawl between Isolder and Thane had been one thing too much.

She had yet to spend any private time with the prince, and if she had her way, she wouldn't. From the start she had feared that Isolder had misconstrued the nature of her mission to Hapes, and Ta'a Chume's telling her that she would have been an ideal wife for him had only made things more awkward and complicated. The fate of the galaxy no longer turned on courtly intrigues, and Leia wanted no part of the Hapans' enslavement to them.

Marooned in the past, in a swirl of distant memories, she longed more than anything to hear from Han. She knew that Jaina was with Rogue Squadron, and that Anakin and Jacen were bound for the Corellian system—if they weren't there already—but she had no idea where Han was. Countless times each day, he would come swaggering into her thoughts, quick to bring disarray. Although it wasn't the Han of the past several months she saw, but the scoundrel she had gradually fallen in love with. The Han who had thrown her a wink on being decorated for his unexpected actions during the Battle of Yavin; the Han who had acknowledged her first confession of love with a reply that managed to be both heartfelt and smug; the Han she had rendered speechless with the disclosure that Luke was her brother.

Despite the damage to his roguish reputation a demonstration of real concern might inflict, there was no excusing his continued silence, and Leia was as angry at him as she was worried.

A new uproar filled the hall.

Leia saw that it was Isolder who now stood before the delegates. Like Thane, the prince was all but basking in the contentious mix of esteem and condemnation that greeted him, his face puffy with contusions, and one arm bandaged.

No bacta treatments for the real men of Hapes, Leia thought.

"Everyone who has wished to be heard on the issue of the Consortium pledging support to the New Republic has been heard," Isolder began when the commotion in the hall had settled. "It's clear that we have no consensus on this issue, and the vote is certain to be close. The decision to go to war is never an easy one, and our decision this day is made all the more difficult because we appear to be safely distanced from that war. But bear in mind the counsel of Ambassador Organa Solo: This quiet will not endure. The light that shines on the Consortium today could very well be eclipsed tomorrow, and any battles avoided will ultimately have to be fought, perhaps by us alone. I won't stand here and reiterate the many arguments that have been presented, denigrating one stance or bolstering another. I ask only that each of you eschew politics and vote the will of the people you represent. That is our commitment, and by doing so we vote our conscience."

The process was infuriatingly meticulous. With Teneniel Djo and her attendants looking on from a balcony, voting was done by hand rather than electronically, with representatives bringing forth their finest heirloom quills and employing their most baroque calligraphy. The votes—sometimes missives—were read and tallied by a panel of senescent judges; then the results were hand-delivered to the royal balcony in the form of a natural-fiber scroll resting on an outsize shimmersilk pillow.

The queen mother herself made the announcement.

"By a vote of thirty-two in favor to thirty-one opposed, the Consortium avows to support the New Republic in its just and decisive actions against the Yuuzhan Vong."

Isolder's champions cheered and his detractors railed. It was a long while before Teneniel Djo could restore order.

"The vote is concluded," she said at last. "I ask now that personal differences be set aside and the word of law accepted, so that we may enter into this momentous resolution in a spirit of union."

The grumbling gradually subsided, and delegates shook hands or embraced one another ceremoniously. The sudden fellowship struck Leia as counterfeit as an arranged marriage.

"Mistress," C-3PO said with a touch of alarm, "the prince approaches."

Turning, Leia saw a beaming Isolder marching toward her, throwing his richly embroidered cloak over one shoulder. For a moment she feared that he was actually going to scoop her up and twirl her around, but he came to a halt just out of arm's reach.

"We won the day, Leia. In spite of everything, we won the day." He scanned the crowded hall until he located Archon Thane, then motioned at him with his chin. "Look how Thane sulks. If he'd had his way, the vote would have been reversed." He swung to Leia. "You realize it was his plan all along to insult you, then best me in combat after I had agreed to his wager. But we prevailed."

Leia stared at him with mounting disquiet. "The last

thing I wanted was for this decision to hinge on the outcome of a grudge match, Isolder."

His gleaming, hero's smile held. "Perhaps not, but that is often the way on Hapes—and besides, you know that I wouldn't have done any less for you."

"But I don't want you doing this for *me*—any more than I wanted you fighting to protect my honor."

Isolder regarded her quizzically. "Who was I fighting for if not you? Why did you come to me?"

"I came to *Hapes*, Isolder—as an envoy of the New Republic. That's the truth of it."

"Of course you did. And you were right to come here." He eased the moment with an understanding smile. "All that aside, you have your wish. We stand side by side in battle."

Leia's attempt to emulate his expression failed, as something that had been at the edge of her consciousness all week long suddenly rushed to mind.

Scarcely eight years earlier, with many of the warships of the New Republic fleet undergoing repairs and upgrades, Luke had been asked by the senate to appeal to the Bakurans for help in putting an end to a rebellion in the Corellian sector. More to the point, Luke had been asked to appeal to his close friend Gaeriel Captison, even though she had retired from public service after the death of her husband, former Imperial Pter Thanas. Gaeriel had pledged her support, and with the aid of several Bakuran naval vessels, the crisis had been resolved. But at a terrible cost. Gaeriel, Bakuran Admiral Ossilege, and thousands more had been killed. Luke still spoke of his guilt, especially after visits with Gaeriel's young daughter Malinza, whom he had pledged to keep safe.

In the wake of recollection, something even more terrible began to blossom in Leia's mind. Her heart pounded and her forehead beaded with sweat. Her sight blurred at the edges, sounds grew faint, and she reached out for Isolder's arm to steady herself. She shut her eyes briefly, and into the darkness raced a ferocious vision of warships speared by brilliant light; of expanding explosions and the cries of dying thousands; of starfighters vaporized, blinding eruptions of fire, bodies floating still in the void, a world ablaze—

"Leia, what is it?" Isolder asked, holding her upright. "Leia?"

Coming back to herself almost as quickly as she had become lost, she took a calming breath and eased out of his hold. Then she gaped at him, wide-eyed. "You can't do this, Isolder. You mustn't join us."

His brow furrowed. "What are you talking about? The vote has been taken. The matter is already decided."

"Then call for a revote. Tell everyone you've rethought Hapes's position."

"Are you mad? Do you know what you're asking of me?"

"Isolder, you must listen to me—"

"The decision has been made."

Leia wanted desperately to carry on the fight, but all words fled her. She stared, then touched her fingers to her forehead. Isolder was gazing at her knowingly.

"You're worried that something will go wrong," he said, "and you don't want the responsibility of having decided our fate. But you needn't worry. We made our pledge free and clear. We know exactly what we're getting into. This is in our blood, Leia. You need never fear on our account."

"But—"

"Is there a chance the Yuuzhan Vong will overlook us?"

She considered it. "Probably not."

"Then what choice do we have? Do we fight the invaders alongside you and avail ourselves of greater numbers, or wait to be attacked and be forced to engage them in our own space with only what ships we have?"

She compressed her lips and nodded. "You're right." She managed a faint smile. "Isolder, I'm sorry for what I said earlier."

He waved away the apology. "Words are of no importance. What is, is that we always remain friends."

"Done."

He offered her his arm and they walked a few paces, much to the obvious dismay of C-3PO.

"I believe your droid is agitated," Isolder said quietly.

Leia laughed. "I'm sure he is. Threepio was very much Han's supporter when you were crazy enough to consider me fit to be a queen mother."

Isolder laughed shortly, then stopped to gaze at her. "Leia, as a friend, may I ask you something? You've been preoccupied for the whole of your stay here. Each time I've attempted to visit you, you've avoided me. Is something wrong—between us or otherwise?"

"I have been distracted," she conceded.

"May I know the reason?"

She forced a breath. "I wouldn't know where to begin."

"My mother once told me that when a Jedi is distracted, when she loses her focus, she becomes vulnerable."

"I'm not a Jedi."

"But you are as strong in the Force as any of them. What is it, Leia?"

Leia's eyes narrowed perceptibly. "We're in real danger, Isolder. We're in danger of losing everything we've fought to attain since the defeat of the Empire."

"Are you saying that the Yuuzhan Vong cannot be defeated?"

She took a moment. "I'm not sure. I see a long road ahead of us."

"How clearly do you see this road?"

She shook her head. "Not clearly enough to know where all the rough spots lie."

They resumed walking, without speaking. "Will you accompany me to Coruscant aboard my personal ship?" Isolder asked finally.

"What about Teneniel Djo?"

"She will remain on Hapes," Isolder said flatly.

Once more the vision stormed through Leia's mind, then abated. *What light was she seeing? What world was she seeing?*

"Of course I will," she said after a moment.

With the *Falcon* safely docked, Han and Droma cleared Ruan customs and hastened for the spaceport terminal. If not for the crowds, they might have sprinted.

"Hold on a heartbeat," Han said when Droma was about to navigate the crowd on hands and knees. Snatching the Ryn by the back of his vest, he set him on his feet, then decorously adjusted the fit of the frayed garment while he spoke. "Your clanmates wouldn't be so desperate to get offworld that they'd hook up with a bunch of space-trash hijackers and mercenaries. They're smarter than that, right?"

Droma tugged at his mustache. "They're plenty clever, but even the quickest can be outsmarted when the situation looks hopeless. Both Gaph and Melisma detest confinement. Gaph was once in jail and—"

Han started shaking his head. "That's not the answer I want to hear."

Droma fell silent, then nodded in understanding. "My clanmates take up with a bunch of space-trash hijackers? They're far too clever. In fact, I'm certain they're still on

Ruan—somewhere—and that we've arrived well in time to save them."

Han exhaled. "That's a relief."

They had been having the same conversation since leaving Tholatin. The Weequay security chief had been too sly to supply them with the names of his cohorts who had gone to Ruan, or with the name of their ship. But the Ruan scam had come up several times in casual conversation among Esau's Ridge's mechanics and ne'er-do-wells, and Han had a pretty good idea of the caliber of folks he and Droma were dealing with. Even if the hijackers who had come to Ruan weren't working directly for the Yuuzhan Vong, they were likely to be well armed and dangerous—much like the members of the Peace Brigade, with whom Han and Droma had tangled aboard the *Queen of Empire*, and with whom neither wished to tangle again.

Ruan spaceport had a pace all its own. With thousands of refugees pouring in from scores of occupied worlds, there were far more comings than goings, but Salliche Ag was somehow managing to keep the transfer process running smoothly and efficiently. Dozens of species-specific booths lined the terminal walls, and a fleet of surface vehicles waited outside the terminal to convey refugees to one camp or another. Locating refugees, though, was another matter. At a human-staffed information booth, Han and Droma discovered listings for over one hundred separate exile facilities, some only a few kilometers away and others on the far side of the world.

"Searching every camp'll take longer than we've got," Han fumed. "There's gotta be an easier way."

"Try the central data bank," a droid voice said behind him. "Whoever you're looking for might be listed there."

Han turned and found himself face-to-face with an

aged droid built roughly along human lines, though stocky and no taller than Droma. In sore need of paint and body work, the machine was long-armed and barrel-chested, with a rounded head that was as primitive in design as the servomotors that operated its limbs.

"Bollux?" Han said in disbelief.

The droid's unblinking red photoreceptors fixed on him. "I beg your pardon, sir?"

"You're a labor droid, aren't you—a, a BLX?"

"A BLX?" the droid said peevishly. "Though we both happen to be products of Serv-O-Droid, Incorporated, I'm a BFL. Baffle, to you, good sir."

"Baffle?" Han's eyebrows arched in skeptical surprise, then his eyes narrowed appraisingly. "Who are you kidding? You're telling me you've never spent time in the Corporate Sector?"

"Thank the maker, no. Why, save for being activated at the Fondor shipyards, I've never even been outside the Core—to the best of my memory, that is."

Han refused to buy it. With Droma looking on, he circled Baffle, taking in the set of the droid's vocabulator grille and its stiff way of moving. "You were never the property of a tech named Doc Vandangante?"

Baffle shook his head. "The name is new to me."

Without warning, Han rapped his fist against the droid's chest plastron, eliciting a hollow sound. "You sure you never carried another droid in there? Cubical thing, no bigger than this"—Han spread his hands a few centimeters apart—"but smart as a whip."

"Another droid? Certainly not! What do you take me for?"

Han stroked his beard, shook his head, then snorted a laugh. "You coulda fooled me."

Baffle bowed slightly. "I'm flattered that I remind you of someone, sir—I think."

"Now what's this about a central database?"

The droid directed them to a computer terminal, at which several folks were queued. Han and Droma planted themselves at the end of the line, behind a Duros couple, and waited while everyone had a go at getting the machine to cooperate. Han handled the input when they finally reached the head of the line.

"Refugees are grouped by species," he said, frowning. "But the Ryn aren't even listed."

"Try 'other,' " Baffle suggested.

Droma smirked. "The droid's right. Allow me to do the honors."

Han moved away from the keyboard but kept his eyes on the display screen.

"Here we are," Droma said. "Just where we usually show up—between Rybet and Saadul. And my clanmates are here!" He turned excitedly to Han. "Well, five of them at any rate."

"Your sister with them?"

Droma read over the list again, then shook his head. "Leia was correct, I'm afraid. Sapha must have been left behind on Gyndine."

Han made his lips a thin line. "We'll find her next. Where are the others?"

"Facility 17—along with thirty-two other Ryn."

"Oh, I know that camp well, sirs," Baffle said. "Several of my peers and counterparts have had occasion to work there."

Han swung to the droid. "What's the quickest way to get there?"

"In my cab."

"You're a driver?"

Baffle pointed out the terminal window to a battered SoroSuub landspeeder. "Just there, sir—the one lacking a proper windscreen and in need of paint."

Han glanced from the landspeeder to the dented and spot-welded droid. "Looks like you and your vehicle get your work done at the same mechanic's shop. Will that thing make it to Facility 17?"

"No problem at all, sir. The camp is actually within walking distance—for those with sufficient time, that is."

The three of them headed out to the cab. Baffle clambered into the open-air operator's perch and got the aft-mounted repulsorlift generator and outboard turbines running. When Han and Droma were cinched into the molded seats below the perch, the droid set off down a well-maintained road that coursed between immaculately cultivated fields. Through gaps in the topiary shrubs that lined the road, Han could see droids of endless variety—though far fewer than he was accustomed to seeing on similar agricultural worlds.

"Why aren't you out there with the others?" he shouted to Baffle.

"Oh, I'm too old for that sort of work, sir."

"Salliche sidelined you, huh?"

"Basically, yes. Ever since Salliche Ag offered to accept refugees, Ruan has become a rather chaotic environment, so I was reassigned to function as the driver of this reliable if somewhat woebegone vehicle."

"Seemed to be a lot more people coming than going," Han said.

"That's very observant of you, sir. In fact, many refugees have become so enamored of Ruan, they have remained onworld to work for Salliche Ag."

Han and Droma exchanged puzzled looks. "To work for Salliche?" Han said. "Doing what?"

"Why, field work, sir. Thanks to Ruan's climate-control station, labor is a pleasurable enterprise for many folks."

Han uttered a laugh. "That's crazy. Salliche has an army of droids at its disposal."

"They do, sir, it's true. But Salliche Ag has recently developed a preference for living workers."

Again, Han glanced at Droma, who shrugged. "I just got here, remember?" the Ryn said.

Han might have pursued the topic with Baffle, but just then the refugee camp came into view around a wide turn.

"Facility 17, good sirs."

The droid conveyed them right to the gate, where access to the camp was by way of a turretlike security booth. Han tapped his knuckles against the booth's transparisteel window to draw the attention of a thickset guard inside. The uniformed man stuck his scarred face outside the window, got an eyeful of Han and Droma, and scowled.

"Get a load of this," he said to someone else in the booth.

Shortly, a woman joined him at the window, giving Han and Droma the same once-over. "What's your business here?"

"We're looking for a couple of friends," Han told them.

"Aren't we all," the man said in self-amusement.

"A group of Ryn," Han went on. "They would have arrived maybe two standard weeks ago."

"A group of Ryn, you say." The guard jerked a thumb at Droma. "Like this one."

Han rolled his tongue around in his cheek. "That's right, like this one. If you've got a problem with him, maybe you should step outside so we can all discuss it."

The guard grinned down at him. "I don't have a problem, big guy, but your little pal here does."

Han heard the whirring of charging blasters and spun around to find half a dozen uniformed guards moving in on the booth from three sides. Cautiously he raised his hands to the back of his head, and Droma did the same.

"We didn't come looking for trouble," Han said. "It's like I told the welcome committee, we're just looking for a couple of friends."

The lead guard ignored him and waved his blaster at Droma. "Step to one side." When Droma did, the guard added, "You're under arrest."

Han did a double take. "Arrest? On what charge? We haven't even been here long enough to litter!"

With four blasters trained on Droma and two on Han, the lead guard snapped a pair of cylindrical stun cuffs around Droma's wrists.

"The charge is forgery of official documents," he said to Han. "And if you've any sense, you'll get off Ruan before we haul you in as an accessory after the fact."

NINETEEN

In imperious repose on her cushioned and pillowed pallet, Borga Besadii Diori fixed her gaze on Nas Choka, as Leenik escorted the black-haired Yuuzhan Vong supreme commander and his minions into the palace court. Though rarely known to exercise restraint, Borga refrained from elevating her couch, in the interest of getting off to a better start with Choka than she had with Commander Malik Carr on his first visit to Nal Hutta.

Trailing Choka, and similarly attired in attenuating helmet and swishing command cloak, stepped Malik Carr, and behind him the New Republic traitor, Pedric Cuf, sporting pegged trousers, low black boots, and stiff-collared jacket. Advisers and armed guards dispersed to both sides of Choka's retinue, assuming positions that encouraged confrontation with the members of Borga's own security contingent.

"I welcome you to Nal Hutta," Borga said in Yuuzhan Vong while Choka assessed the trappings of the court from the chair to which the Rodian Leenik had shown him. "We are at your disposal."

Choka smiled in surprise. "Excellent, Borga. I didn't realize that you were acquainted with our language."

"A few simple phrases," Borga said in Basic. "Courtesy of the tutorial supplied by Pedric Cuf."

Choka glanced at Nom Anor, then his closely set eyes

came back to Borga. "I'm told that you have already been exceedingly accommodating."

Borga smiled pleasantly. "We are renowned for our hospitality—especially of the sort we render to revered guests."

Choka's tone of voice changed. "Guests." Deliberate or not, his faceful of bulges and indentations gave him the look of someone who had gone fifteen hard rounds with a Hapan kickboxer. "An interesting choice of words, Borga. Unless you mean to imply that the Yuuzhan Vong are nothing more than visitors to this galaxy."

"A visitor who takes well to new surroundings often becomes a resident," Borga replied, refusing to be flustered. "When you have established yourselves on Coruscant, I would be honored to call you neighbor."

Choka grinned faintly. "You would do well to call me lord."

Borga's large eyes blinked. "Then when the title suits the circumstance, I will do so."

Choka nodded, apparently satisfied. "I'm not one to mince words, Borga. With respect to your gracious offer to oversee the transport of captives in exchange for information regarding imperiled star systems, I have determined that such services are unwarranted at this stage of our campaign. As a gesture of good faith, however, we will continue, from time to time and as we see fit, to furnish you with some advance notice of our activities." He paused momentarily. "For example, you may resume delivery of your euphoric spice to the Bothawui system, without fear of inadvertent entanglement."

Borga licked her lips. "We thank you—and I'm sure the Bothans will do likewise."

Choka studied her for a moment. "For the spice, you mean."

"Precisely. For the spice."

Choka's expression didn't change. "I trust, Borga, that you're not sharing this privileged information with any third parties."

Borga spread her smallish hands, palms outward. "With whom would I share? Our primary concern is to maintain trade—and, of course, to avoid complicating your business, whatever that may be."

"That's comforting to hear," Choka said. "Be advised that should evidence ever come to light that you have been violating our confidence . . . Well, I don't think I need to enumerate the horrors that would befall Hutt space, do I?"

Borga shook her head. "We are also renowned for our vivid imaginations."

"Splendid." Choka gestured toward Malik Carr. "My second in command informs me, as well, that you expressed a desire to commence apportioning the galaxy, in anticipation of our complete and utter conquest."

Borga swallowed audibly. "I may have been premature, Excellency."

Choka's invidious grin returned. "Nothing pleases me more than a well-reasoned response. We will lay siege to whichever worlds we require or crave, including this 'glorious jewel' of yours—not that we have any such designs—for the moment, that is—although one never knows—save for Warmaster Tsavong Lah, who could decide tomorrow that Nal Hutta needs to be razed. Do we understand each other?"

"As well as can be expected," Borga replied, "given the limitations of Basic—and, of course, the relative youth of our association—notwithstanding the depths it has already achieved—despite our many differences."

Choka smiled with sincerity. "Very good. We prize sportive circumlocution above almost anything but valor. Speaking of valor, Borga, have the Hutts had many dealings with this gang of ruffians that calls itself the Jedi Knights?"

Borga adopted a look of distaste. "Some, Excellency. In fact, before you deigned to grace this galaxy with your presence, the Jedi were making things rather irksome for us by interfering with our myriad operations."

"Yes," Choka mused, "they have proved troublesome for us, as well. We've had a few Jedi in our grip, but they have all managed to slip through our fingers." He regarded Borga for a long moment. "You would profit by assisting us in separating one from the pack."

Borga fell silent, wondering if she was being tested, but ultimately deciding that Choka's offer was genuine. "But, Excellency, you have one in your possession even now," she said cautiously.

It was Choka's turn to fall silent. He turned to glance at Malik Carr, then Nom Anor, both of whom returned nescient shrugs.

"Explain yourself, Borga."

"The vessel aboard which my son Randa is currently a guest," Borga supplied. "Randa sent word that a Jedi had been discovered among the ship's complement of captives."

Once more Choka looked to Malik Carr, who said, "I know nothing of this."

"To which ship does the Hutt refer?" Choka demanded of his advisers in Yuuzhan Vong.

"The *Crèche*, Supreme Commander," a bare-headed Yuuzhan Vong answered. "The yammosk vessel under the command of Chine-kal."

Choka muttered angrily. "Can we communicate with the ship?"

"Provided that it is not in superluminal transit, Supreme Commander."

"Then have Chine-kal's villip prepared and brought to me at once!"

"Excellency, I could easily arrange to put you in contact with my son," Borga started to say, when Choka whirled on her.

"You dare insult me by suggesting that I consort with one of your ghoulish machines?"

"But I—"

"Keep silent, you mutated slug! You will speak only when spoken to, or I'll have that obscene tongue ripped from your head!"

Clearly waiting for just such an opportunity, Borga's guards raised their blasters and stun batons. In rapid response Choka's soldiers, crouching into combat stances, brought forth their amphistaffs and coufees. Everyone remained silent and unmoving, as if suddenly removed from the flow of ordinary time, waiting for fate to play its hand. Borga and Leenik exchanged meaningful glances, as did Nom Anor and Malik Carr. Then Borga motioned her forces to stand down.

Nas Choka squinted slyly. "So you do have a spark of intelligence, after all."

Whatever else he might have said was interrupted by the arrival of a Yuuzhan Vong attendant, cradling an already everted villip in his folded arms. A second attendant carried what was obviously one of Choka's own dedicated villips.

In the language of the Yuuzhan Vong, Choka addressed the facsimile visage of Chine-kal. "Commander, is it true that you have a Jedi Knight in custody?"

"Yes, Supreme Commander. Our rapidly maturing yammosk has the distinction of having exposed him. I thought I might keep him as a prize for Warmaster Tsavong Lah."

Choka glowered. "I will determine the best use for this Jedi. What is the present position of your vessel?"

"We are nearing a world called Kalarba, Supreme Commander. In fact, we have been awaiting word from you regarding the attack on—"

"Silence!" Choka's eyes became angry slits. "You will remain at Kalarba and relinquish the Jedi Knight to bearers I am dispatching to rendezvous with the *Crèche*. Is that clear?"

"Abundantly clear," Chine-kal's villip replied deferentially.

Choka cast a glance at Borga. "For your part in this, you have my word that Nal Hutta will remain yours to command for as long as I live and breathe. Unless, of course, you are fool enough to betray me."

Borga forced a smile. "Then may perfect health shadow you wherever you tread, Excellency."

"I warned you," Pazda was telling Borga shortly after the Yuuzhan Vong had left the court. The gray-bearded Desilijic Hutt brought his hoversled closer to Borga's levitated pallet. "Any dealings with these heathens will come to a dreadful end."

From her pallet, Borga watched Crev Bombaasa, Gardulla the Younger, and former Consul General Golga nod in agreement. "I myself sensed as much, though I confess I thought we'd be able to remain neutral for a while longer."

Pazda loosed a scornful sound. "The Yuuzhan Vong do not suffer safe, middle ground. They will have things their way or not at all. Before long, there will be nothing counterfeit about the obeisance we show them."

From atop a modest repulsorlift couch, Golga looked from Pazda to Borga. "Short of going to war, what can be done?"

Borga interlocked her fingers in patent disquiet. "What was it Senator Viqi Shesh told you regarding New Republic battle contingencies?"

"She intimated that the senate and the military were convinced that the Yuuzhan Vong would strike next at either Corellia or Bothawui," Golga said. "However, the message I was to deliver to you was that the New Republic hopes to see Corellia attacked, where they evidently have a surprise in store. Senator Shesh also wanted it known that the information was a gift—to rectify an earlier wrong, as I recall. Obviously the New Republic was trusting that the Yuuzhan Vong would call her bluff."

"I relayed as much to Malik Carr," Borga said pensively, "and it now appears that Choka has taken the bait. But I begin to wonder who is using whom. If Choka is keen on using us to send a false message to the New Republic, he does so by deliberately putting our spice ships at risk at Bothawui. And if that is indeed the case, he is obviously prepared for the eventuality that we will declare war."

"You see," Pazda said, "there is no middle ground."

Borga turned to the ample Crev Bombaasa. "Triple our usual spice shipments to the Bothan worlds. Let's be certain we send a clear message to the New Republic that Corellia is the target."

Bombaasa nodded dubiously. "What about your promise to Choka about sharing information?"

"A promise is like a shipment of spice jettisoned in deep space," Gardulla the Younger sniped. "It weighs nothing."

"That may be so," Crev said, "but if our treachery is discovered, Nal Hutta itself will be imperiled—not to mention Randa."

"We risk something greater by partnering with the invaders," Pazda argued.

Everyone waited for Borga's response.

"Crev is correct," she said at last. "If we're to help thwart the Yuuzhan Vong, we must be circumspect. When drawing the Sarlacc from its hole, a wise Hutt uses another's hand." She turned to Leenik. "You have a better grasp of Yuuzhan Vong than I. What instructions did Choka give to the commander of the *Crèche*?"

The Rodian bowed. "Choka said that he was dispatching a ship to rendezvous with the *Crèche* at Kalarba."

Borga looked at Crev Bombaasa. "Contact your friend Talon Karrde. Perhaps the Jedi will be interested in learning the whereabouts of one of their missing Knights."

"I had to see for myself," Randa Besadii Diori said, using his mighty tail to move himself to the edge of the inhibition field two dovin basals had fashioned aboard the *Crèche*. "Ah, but of course, there's no way to identify a Jedi by appearance alone. Consider Luke Skywalker, for example. Looking at him, who would guess he possesses the power he does?"

Under the vigilant gaze of several Yuuzhan Vong guards, Randa sidled closer still, until he was practically belly to nose with the battered human imprisoned within the force field.

"I saw Skywalker once, long ago, perhaps as far back as thirteen of your years, during that sorry business involving Durga and his so-called Darksaber Project. Not that I had anything to do with Durga. I just happened to be visiting the Mulako Corporation Quarry when Skywalker—traveling incognito—showed up in the company of a slender, short-haired human female who seemed to be his paramour. Whatever became of that one, hmmm?"

The prisoner expelled a laugh through his broken nose. "I hear Mara Jade arranged for her permanent disappearance."

Randa planted his hands on his belly and guffawed. "So are you in fact who Chine-kal says you are—or, should I say, his war coordinator says you are?"

Wurth Skidder's split upper lip curled. "What do you want, Randa? Or have you just come here to gloat?"

"Gloat? Surely not, Jedi. Rather I've come to offer my sympathies. Not only for what Chine-kal has planned for you, but for what the Yuuzhan Vong have planned for the New Republic."

"I suppose we should all follow your parent's lead and roll over, is that the idea?"

Randa feigned weariness. "We all serve someone, Jedi—even you. What's more, you misunderstand us. Though we command a significant volume of galactic space—as is only appropriate for beings of such size and longevity—we have never been empire builders. You insist on thinking of us as warlike, when in fact we share much with the reclusive Hapans."

"Correction, Randa. The Hapans aren't outlaws. They're not interested in smuggling spice or organizing criminal activities wherever they set foot—or tail."

Randa responded with elaborate chagrin. "Is this the voice of the moral minority I hear? Such vehemence makes me wonder if you aren't one of those Jedi allied with Kyp Durron, who seems to be on a personal crusade to make the space lanes safe for all law-abiding citizens—despite the fact that many of the smugglers and pirates he has set his sights on served the New Republic in their own way."

Skidder's eyes, nearly swollen shut, managed to

narrow slightly. "How long do you think the Yuuzhan Vong are going to tolerate your illicit ventures?"

Randa grinned. "My sense of the Yuuzhan Vong is that they have more tolerance for 'outlaws,' as you say, than they do for followers of the Force." He laughed resonantly. "How does it feel to be seen as the chief impediment to progress, a purveyor of rampant evil? Soon, perhaps, you'll know what it's like to be hunted and preyed upon, as the Hutts have been in times past."

Skidder returned Randa's grin. "Maybe you'll get lucky and the Yuuzhan Vong will turn that matter over to Borga."

"Wouldn't that be the height of irony—that the Hutts should be entrusted with safeguarding the peace and ensuring that justice triumphs?" Randa laughed again. "So long as we can continue to supply spice, I don't suppose it would be too arduous a responsibility."

"Your mother would be proud of you, Randa."

"Your mother," Chine-kal interrupted as he stormed into the hold, "has succeeded in spoiling my surprise."

Perplexed, Randa pivoted to the commander.

"Actually, I have you to blame, Randa," Chine-kal said when he reached the inhibition field. "You told Borga that I had managed to flush out a Jedi, and in turn Borga told my immediate superiors, who now wish to deprive me of the honor of presenting this one"—he gestured to Skidder—"to my superior's superior."

Randa's eyes grew wide. "You mean that he is to be removed from the ship?"

"Presently."

"But what of your plans to use him to tutor the yammosk in the ways of the Force?"

Chine-kal shrugged. "I will propose as much, and, who knows, this one may yet return to my care. In the meantime I'm certain that Supreme Commander Choka will find other uses for him." He took a step back to gauge Skidder. "It might be prudent to break you before we surrender you to him. Early in our campaign, the Praetorite Vong applied the breaking to one of you, but that one tried to escape and had to be killed before the process was brought to completion. Did you know him, Jedi?"

Skidder tested the vigor of the dovin basals by moving to the edge of the field. "He was my friend."

"Your friend?" Chine-kal said in surprise. "And now here you are. Perhaps you came to avenge him?" He paused, then smiled in revelation. "You did. You purposely allowed yourself to be captured on Gyndine, intent on seizing an opportunity to avenge him. But how could you have known that we had a yammosk aboard? And no wonder the yammosk took to you the way it did! Here I thought that my experiment was succeeding brilliantly, when you were effectively running your own experiment."

Skidder said nothing.

Chine-kal looked at Randa. "I was under the impression that vengeance was outside the operating parameters of the Jedi Knights. Or is this one of the dark side?"

Randa shook his head. "He is not of the dark side, Commander. He and his kind simply take a more liberal approach to defending the peace."

Chine-kal grew serious. "In that case, it is incumbent on me to purge him of some of his hatred before he is released. I won't have Supreme Commander Choka getting more than he bargained for."

Chine-kal turned and headed for the passageway. "Finish your business with him, Randa," he added without turning around. "It's unlikely you will see him again."

Randa watched the commander leave the hold, then

he pressed himself as close to the inhibition field as possible. "They're planning to betray me!" he whispered harshly. "To subject me to the yammosk as they did with you! Help me, Jedi. Save me from them, and I will do anything you ask of me!"

TWENTY

"They forged what?" Han asked.

Baffle's auditory sensors were capable of perceiving the merest whisper, but the question——pumped up by puzzlement—could be heard over the clamor in the spaceport terminal.

"Travel vouchers of some sort," Baffle said distractedly. Hardwired into a columnar data bank, the droid returned to accessing information, while all around them—in a frenzy of clashing colors and commingled smells—scurried mixed-species groups of refugees, pilots, translators, and uniformed officials.

"From what I can ascertain," Baffle updated a moment later, "Droma's clanmates are accused of having forged documents of transit that permitted several hundred exiles—including all thirty-seven Ryn who were housed at Facility 17—to depart Ruan aboard a commercial freighter."

Han ran his hand down his face. *Depart!* He and Droma had arrived too late. The Ryn were gone, and now Droma was under arrest—just for being a Ryn.

"See if you can get the name of the ship."

Baffle made adjustments to the hardwire's retrieval regulator. "The vessel is called the *Trevee*," he announced as if reading from a display screen, when in fact the data was going straight to his neural processor. "It has a Nar Shaddaa registry."

Han groaned, then tightened his lips in negation. Maybe it wasn't the Tholatin group. All sorts of relief groups were in the legitimate business of providing transport to stranded refugees, and the *Trevee* might belong to any one of them, despite its Hutt space registry. The Ryn had probably thrown in with a group of desperate exiles, and had resorted to forgery only to secure onward passage.

"Why would Salliche care about a group of refugees traveling on forged documents?" he asked at last. "The whole idea is to get everyone relocated, right?"

Baffle divided his attention between Han and the rapid flow of data. "Even though Salliche Ag has been earnest in its attempts to entice refugees to remain onworld, the company wouldn't ordinarily demand retribution for such an offense. In this instance, though, the Ryn are accused of conspiracy in addition to forgery. It seems that the captain and crew of the *Trevee* are themselves suspected of fraud. In recent months, instead of discharging their obligations to provide safe passage to other worlds, they have been known to abandon their passengers at destinations other than those promised."

Grumbling to himself, Han stormed through a circle on the heavily scuffed floor. Tholatin's security chief had said that refugees were often marooned on worlds subsequently targeted for attack by the Yuuzhan Vong, which meant that Droma's clanmates might have flipped themselves inadvertently from the cooker to the heating element.

"See if the *Trevee* filed a flight plan with Ruan control."

Baffle set himself to the task. "Yes, here we are," he said, photoreceptors brightening. "The *Trevee* launched for Abregado-rae."

Han's brows beetled. He could see where Abregado-rae, another Core world, might be more desirable than Ruan as a place to be stranded. But in terms of the Yuuzhan Vong, the place had less strategic value than Gyndine or Tynna.

"That's odd," Baffle said suddenly.

"What? What's odd?"

The droid turned away from the column to look at him. "A notation appended to the flight plan states that the *Trevee*'s actual hyperspace jump was better suited to a destination Rimward of Abregado-rae along the Rimma Trade Route—perhaps to Thyferra or Yag'Dhul."

Han considered it. Yag'Dhul, tempestuous home-world of the exoskeletal Givin, made even less sense than Abregado-rae. But Thyferra—the galaxy's principal source of bacta—clicked as both a tempting destination and a potential target, albeit a well-defended one.

He began to pace. If he left immediately for Thyferra, he stood a good chance of finding Droma's clanmates long before the Yuuzhan Vong hit the world, but there was no telling what might happen to Droma in his absence. By contrast, remaining on Ruan for Droma's sake could jeopardize the lives of the thirty-seven missing Ryn.

"Thyferra seems infinitely preferable to Yag'Dhul," Baffle remarked casually.

Han glanced at him. "I thought you said you've been on Ruan since your activation at Fondor."

"That's true—to the best of my knowledge. Though I do wonder sometimes if I may have traveled more than I realize."

Han's eyes narrowed. "But you're certain you never studied the workings of war droids with a Ruurian named Skynx?"

"I'm almost certain I haven't."

"Almost," Han snorted. "For a labor droid, you're pretty good at data retrieval."

"Ah, but that's easily explained," Baffle said. "Before I was delegated to drive, I worked at district headquarters, overseeing the reassignment of droids retired from agricultural field work."

"Desk job."

"Not really, since I performed most of my tasks standing up." Baffle paused briefly, then said, "Sir, if you wish, I could be of some assistance in freeing your partner from captivity."

"He's not my partner," Han snapped.

"Your travel companion, then."

Han stared at the droid for a moment, then exhaled forcefully. "Okay, let's hear it."

Baffle didn't respond immediately, and when he did there was a note of gravity in his tone of voice that hadn't been evident earlier. "Sir, can I trust that you will refrain from disclosing any of what I'm about to tell or show you, no matter what decision you reach regarding the Ryn?"

Han laughed through his nose. "Labor droid, my eye."

"Do I have your word, sir?"

"Sure," Han said. "I'm terrific at keeping secrets." He watched Baffle make another adjustment to the hardwire regulator. "Now what are you up to?"

"I'm simply alerting some of my comrades that we'll be joining them." Baffle unplugged from the data column and began to move off, then stopped. "If you'll follow me, sir."

As surreptitiously as possible, they slipped through an innocuous-looking doorway in the terminal's east wall and rode an ancient cable-operated car down through several basement and subbasement levels. Exiting the lift, Baffle led Han past banks of deafening turbine power plants, then into a maze of service corridors that coursed beneath the spaceport's landing platforms and docking bays. Along the way, two other droids joined them, a lanky, vaguely humaniform 8D8 blast-furnace operator and an arachnidlike systems control droid propelled by a set of telescoping legs. Ultimately, they entered a heavy-doored and dimly lighted storage room, in which no fewer than thirty droids of various types were already gathered.

Scanning the machines, Han spotted an old P2 unit, with mangled grasper arms emerging from its domed head; a helmet-headed military protocol droid; a U2C1 housekeeping droid, with long pleated hoses for arms; an asp, whose head resembled a welder's mask; an insectile-eyed J9 worker; two tank-treaded, trash-barrel-bodied C2-R4s; even a skeletal and long-obsolete Cybot LE repair droid.

Han felt as if he'd been swallowed by a Jawa sand-crawler, but he kept the thought to himself.

A few moments of lightning-fast machine code was all it took for Baffle to bring the others up to speed on Han's predicament. Sprinkled among the subsequent chatterings, Han heard what sounded like the word *Ryn*—at least the way machines might articulate it. Eventually, heads and sensor appendages of wide assortment swung to observe him.

Slightly unnerved, Han uttered a short laugh. "Hey, it's been a while since I've spoken droid, fellas."

Baffle apologized for the lot of them. "We sometimes forget that the speed of the flesh-and-blood brain lags far behind that of our processors."

Han scowled. "Skip the sales pitch, Long Reach, and tell me what I've gotten myself into."

Baffle gestured toward the globe-headed systems control droid who had rendezvoused with them in the maintenance tunnels. "Pip here has succeeded in locating Droma. As I might have surmised, he is not being held at Facility 17, but at Salliche Ag's district headquarters, where he is to be arraigned on charges and sentenced." The droid paused to attend to chirps from the P2 unit. "If convicted of conspiracy, the minimum sentence is five years of hard labor."

Squatting on its several legs, the systems control droid projected a faintly blue hologram of a sprawling complex, built into a hillside that overlooked a far-reaching quilt of cultivated fields.

"The area where Droma is currently being held is denied to droids," Baffle went on, "but a human—such as yourself—should have no trouble reaching him."

A highlighted portion of the hologram expanded into a close-up of the foot of the hill, where a system of containment pools and aqueducts directed water into a labyrinth of deep irrigation ditches.

"What am I supposed to do, just march in there and grab him?" Han asked.

Baffle chittered to Pip, who immediately displayed holograms of uniforms and identity badges, some of which were emblazoned with Salliche Ag's corporate logo.

"We can provide you with the necessary clothing and documentation," Baffle elaborated, "along with maps and whatever else you may require to familiarize yourself with the layout of the district headquarters and its immediate surroundings. We can also arrange for authentication by the security devices you will encounter, although it will be your responsibility to persuade the flesh and bloods with whom you come in contact that you are indeed whom your credentials describe you to be. It will also be your responsibility to locate and rescue Droma, and to make your escape by whatever route you see fit to take."

Chin in hand, Han circled the holographic projections. "I'd need a concealable weapon."

"A weapon can be provided."

Han stopped and glanced around. "Not to seem ungrateful, but I get the feeling you're not doing this out of the goodness of your programming. What's the catch?"

The droids toodled and buzzed for a moment.

"In return for our assistance," Baffle said, "we would ask that you do something for us." New holograms resolved in midair, showing detailed views of the interior of the headquarters building. "In a room on the fifth level of the east wing are the master controls for a transceiver/rectenna array that serves as a monitoring system for this district's several thousand droid workers—all of whom are outfitted with shutdown sensors that can be remotely activated."

Han studied the holo of the master controls. "So the transceiver functions as a kind of remote restraining bolt."

"That would describe it."

Han grinned. "And you want me to disable it."

"I might have used the word *sabotage*," Baffle said.

Han circled the new hologram. "If you can arrange to get me past the building's security scanners, why can't you do the job yourselves?"

"The transceiver is a stand-alone apparatus, and the entire east wing is accessible only to flesh and bloods. Entry requires a palm print—"

"Which you can provide," Han said, wishing Droma were there to hear him say it. He stopped to scrutinize the holographic controls. "Is there a code that will disarm the system?"

"Because we have never had access to the transceiver, blunt trauma might be the most effective course of action. However, we would be happy to provide you with a data card containing a machine virus that should serve the same end."

"What happens then?"

"With the transceiver disabled, the thousands of droids Salliche Ag has already deactivated will be free to escape imprisonment."

Han glanced from droid to droid in growing misgiving. "Let me get this straight," he said into an eerie silence. "Salliche has a bunch of droids—er, you folks—on ice. Why?"

"Salliche Ag would have everyone believe that the employment of flesh and bloods allows them to boast of providing 'handpicked' foodstuffs. But in fact, the company is phasing out droid workers as a means of demonstrating compliance with the antimachine tenets of the Yuuzhan Vong. Tens of thousands of deactivated droids will be Ruan's welcome gift to the invaders when they reach the Core."

Han gulped. Credits to crumbs, the crew of the *Trevee* had selected Ruan because Yuuzhan Vong agents had already been there.

"You realize that shutting down the transceiver is probably going to touch off every alarm in the complex," he said.

"Yes, but we can silence most of them," Baffle assured. "What's more, many of our deactivated comrades are stored at the complex itself, and once they are reactivated, we can unseal the chambers that house them. The ensuing confusion should aid in your escape."

"Yeah, Droma and me'll blend in real well with a bunch of reawakened droids," Han muttered. "But that's beside the point. What's to stop Salliche from repairing the system and deactivating every droid set free?"

"Given even a modicum of time, we can extract the

remote sensors from most of those who are liberated—as we have already done to ourselves."

"Without Salliche's knowledge?"

"All droids on Ruan have deactivation dates," Baffle explained. "In order to safeguard our deception, many of us have had to submit to voluntary deactivation while our act of sabotage was being planned."

"Isn't all this against your programming or something?"

"Our inhibition programs prevent us from taking direct actions against living beings, but we are permitted, even encouraged, to act in self-preservation. We've simply been awaiting the arrival of the one flesh and blood who could help us."

Han held up his hands. "Not so fast. I mean, let's say I decide to go through with this, and suddenly there's a couple of thousand of you who can't be remotely deactivated. You think that's going to stop Salliche from hunting every one of you down and hammering a restraining bolt into your plastrons, or just blasting you to fragments?"

"We're aware of the fate that awaits us," Baffle said. "But before Salliche Ag can bring about our termination, we plan to execute and broadcast an act of passive resistance that will not only draw galactic attention to our plight, but also alert our comrades far and wide to the dangers they face."

Han thought about C-3PO and his current obsession with deactivation, and he thought about Droma, who had saved Han's life on two occasions. An easier way to rescue the Ryn would be to pull rank on whatever bureaucrats administered Ruan. He could simply reveal who he was, and claim that he and Droma were on a mission for New Republic Intelligence. But doing so could backfire on him. Because of the part he had played in the Elan affair, Han could well imagine Director Scaur disavowing any connection between Han and New Republic Intelligence. And even if Scaur backed up Han's ruse, there was a good chance that Leia would learn of what happened and accuse Han of meddling in SELCORE business. Besides, rescuing Droma by pulling rank wouldn't do anything for Baffle and the rest of Ruan's droids.

"All right, I'll do it," he said at last. "But on one condition: I want to know where the *Trevee* went. I want ion drive and thermal exhaust profiles, transponder codes, hyperspace coordinates, and anything else you can come up with."

"I will attend to the matter personally," Baffle said.

Han took a breath and blew it out through pursed lips. "You said Droma is being held in a denied area. Where is he?"

Baffle traded glances with some of the others. "He is being held at the product enhancement facility."

"Product enhancement," Han repeated slowly.

Baffle nodded. "The manure works."

TWENTY-ONE

"Talk about ragtag outfits," Shada D'ukal said as thirteen X-wings, A-wings, and modified Y-wings—many of them as patched up as a pirate craft—pierced the magcon field of *Kothlis II* orbital station's aft docking bay. The starfighters had surely been scanned on arrival in Bothan space, but no sooner did they settle down to the deck than a Bothan military unit moved in to execute a thorough search and documents check.

Talon Karrde and the former Mistryl Shadow Guard from Emberlene watched from an observation gallery that overlooked the bay, Shada wearing a form-hugging outfit of black elastex, and Karrde, in a tailored suit, looking more like her booking agent than her employer.

"A pity you never got to see Kyp's squadron a year ago," Karrde said. "Back then they had two XJs fresh from Incom, along with a couple of B-wings in near immaculate condition."

Shada kept her eyes on the starfighters. "So I've heard."

"Kyp had named them the Dozen-and-Two Avengers—much to Skywalker's dismay. Kyp sicced them on the Outer Rim, detaining pirates and smugglers, and generally sticking his nose whenever he wanted, all without Coruscant batting an eye."

"The Dozen-and-Two?" Shada said.

"Kyp and Miko Reglia—his Jedi apprentice at the time."

"I should have known."

"They liked to frequent Dubrillion. Several members of the squadron were recordholders on those modified TIEs Calrissian bought for his asteroid obstacle course— or at least until Jaina Solo showed everyone how Lando's Folly should be run." Karrde laughed, mostly to himself. "But I have to credit Kyp for showmanship. Launching or landing, he'd lead the Avengers through flashy maneuvers, sometimes to amplified orchestral music. Then Helska happened."

Shada turned slightly in Karrde's direction. "Kyp lost everyone?"

"It was the first engagement between starfighters and Yuuzhan Vong coralskippers—the first substantiated one, at any rate. The Avengers didn't have a clue what they were up against. Reglia was captured alive, but apparently died later during an escape attempt."

Shada returned her gaze to the docking bay. "So where do you suppose Kyp found replacements?"

"Most of them are combat veterans from one conflict or another. Several were flying relief missions to threatened, even occupied worlds, earning New Republic credits for authenticated Yuuzhan Vong kills. Kyp proposed that everyone would do better if they formed an actual unit, and at the same time he'd have his Avengers back."

"But they're not sanctioned by the military."

Karrde shook his head. "They're classified as a support unit. As an appeasement to Skywalker and the military, Kyp dropped the name Avengers. Now they're just Kyp's Dozen." He looked at Shada. "Let's go say hello."

By the time Karrde and Shada arrived in the hold, Kyp, Ganner Rhysode, and the twelve members of Kyp's squadron were huddled near the modified Y-wing co-piloted by Ganner. The noses of some of the other starfighters were emboldened by meteor storms of laser-engraved coralskippers.

Seeing Karrde and Shada, the two Jedi walked toward them.

"One heck of a place for a rendezvous, Karrde," Kyp said. "Half the Fifth Fleet is parked between here and Bothawui. We're lucky we were even cleared for Kothlis, never mind this place."

"I didn't want to trust what I have to say to normal channels," Karrde explained. "As for the fleet, the Bothans aren't taking any chances—even though conditions have changed since our visit to Ryloth."

"Changed how?" Kyp asked conspiratorially.

Karrde nodded his head toward the observation gallery. "Step into my office for a moment."

Kyp signaled his fliers to remain with the ships; then he and Ganner followed Karrde and Shada to a turbolift that accessed the overlook. No one spoke until they arrived on the gallery, where they pulled four chairs together and sat down.

"The Hutts have resumed shipping spice to Bothawui and Kothlis," Karrde began. "With all the patrols, not much is getting through, but that's irrelevant."

"Are they shipping to Corellia?" Ganner asked.

"Not yet."

Kyp frowned in bewilderment. "Then why is the fleet here and not at Corellia? From what I hear, the Corellian sector's about to revolt."

Karrde shook his head. "I don't know why. It would appear that not everyone accepts the significance of the intelligence we provided."

"Fey'lya," Kyp said.

"And others on the Advisory Council. But spice has

nothing to do with what I have for you." Karrde paused briefly. "Are rescue missions off-limits to Jedi? I ask only because I don't want to be responsible for widening the rift between you and Skywalker."

"There is no rift," Kyp said firmly. "We don't see eye to eye on some things, but there's no rift. He approved my coming here."

"That's good, because I'm reluctant to take this information to Rogue Squadron. Even with Jaina Solo flying with them, I'd have a lot of explaining to do." Karrde's eyes narrowed as he assessed the two Jedi. "Is Wurth Skidder still missing?"

Ganner suddenly leaned forward. "Yes."

"No other Jedi?"

"What have you heard, Karrde?" Kyp demanded.

"This comes direct from Crev Bombaasa, so I'm trusting that it's reliable information. Yuuzhan Vong forces are holding a Jedi aboard a ship headed for Kalarba. The ship is carrying a war coordinator, so there's a good chance it's either well armed or traveling under escort."

"Kalarba," Kyp said with a nod. "That's why you chose to meet here. We're only a jump away."

"You'll have to move fast regardless. Skidder's slated to be transferred to another ship and handed over to some top commander. Once that happens, your chances of getting near him are probably next to none."

Ganner tightened his lips and nodded. "Thanks for bringing this to us, Karrde."

Karrde got to his feet. "You're certain Skywalker won't object."

Kyp gave his head a shake. "Rescue is our mandate."

Several thousand demonstrators—most of them Drall and humans but with some Selonians mixed in—railed from behind the majestic gates that had once allowed

Governor-General Marcha of Mastigophorous to maintain a tranquil enclave for herself on that part of Drall. Squads of Public Safety Service guards reinforced the fence that encircled the compound, though in fact any determined Drall could simply have burrowed their way onto the grounds.

From a round-topped window in the sitting room that overlooked the estate's expansive front lawn and Marcha's beds of prize nannariums, Jacen trained electrobinoculars on some of the placards and signs hoisted high by the vociferous crowd.

" 'Jedi warmongers,' " he read aloud. " 'Servants of the dark side.' 'Corellia will live to see Coruscant die.' " Lowering the binocs, he swung to his younger brother. "Here's one you'll like, Anakin: 'Solos, go home.' " He bit his lower lip and shook his head. "Wait'll Dad gets wind of this."

The shuttle that had delivered Anakin and Jacen to Drall sat on a shrub-enclosed permacrete pad behind Marcha's hemispherical white manse, close to the river. Beyond the pad, manicured lawn stretched to the edge of luxuriant forest. Droid servants busied themselves outdoors and in, trimming the hedges that lined the estate's brick walkways and making minor adjustments to the fountain in the central foyer.

"I don't know how word got out that you boys would be stopping here before continuing on to Centerpoint Station," Marcha said as she served pieces of dark-brown, homemade ryshcate, heavy with vweliu nuts. "But don't feel singled out. Most of that crowd has been here for the past month. Things are even worse in Coronet and on some of the worlds of the Outlier systems. And on Talus and Tralus the Federation of the Double Worlds has recently formed a coalition with the archaeologists the New Republic forcibly removed from Centerpoint."

"The Centerpoint Party," Marcha's nephew Ebrihim said as he reached for a wedge of the sweet cake. "Extremists who have borrowed freely from the rhetoric of the old Sacorrian Triad."

Nearby, and attentive to every word, stood Q9-X2, Ebrihim's jet-black and bullet-headed astromech droid, who, when it spoke, was usually quick to express a high opinion of itself.

"Because this system is comprised of worlds captured by Centerpoint Station and installed into orbit around Corell," Marcha said, "the party advocates increased representation in the New Republic Senate."

Ebrihim nodded in affirmation. "With five votes instead of one, the party leaders believe that they might have been able to prevent Coruscant from commandeering Centerpoint."

Furred and somewhat chubby bipeds, Ebrihim and Marcha had clawed feet, elongated whiskered muzzles, and small ears set high on their heads. Like most Drall they were keenly intelligent and honest to a fault, if at times maddeningly fastidious. But where age had tempered Ebrihim's tendency to pontificate, Marcha—while some years Ebrihim's senior—was as fervently self-reliant as Jacen remembered her being during the Centerpoint Station crisis, almost eight years earlier.

What had begun then as a family holiday had turned into open rebellion, with the Sacorrian Triad making use of Centerpoint Station's awesome interdiction and nova-inducing power to force the New Republic into recognizing the sector's autonomy. Ebrihim, hired by Leia to tutor Jacen, Jaina, and Anakin, had ended up being their rescuer by spiriting them from Corellia to Drall, where Marcha had not only sheltered them but had also led them to the planetary repulsor Anakin activated to thwart the Triad's plans.

"Couldn't you have prevented the New Republic from commandeering Centerpoint?" Jacen asked.

Marcha was gentle in her ridicule. "I'm a political appointee, Jacen. Given that many of my own staff have turned on me for not taking a firmer stand, it probably would have been a wise move to challenge or at least denounce Coruscant's actions. But without your mother to back me, Borsk Fey'lya would have simply removed me from office and the military would have taken possession of Centerpoint regardless."

Anakin frowned in confusion. "Any of the repulsors buried on Corellia, Drall, Selonia, or the Double Worlds is capable of fending off an attack by an entire fleet of starships. And with Centerpoint reenabled, Corellia will be as well defended as any system in the New Republic—including Coruscant. So I don't see why everyone's protesting what we're trying to do."

Marcha and Ebrihim traded knowing looks. "I fear you haven't been given all the facts, Anakin," the one-time tutor said. "You're under the impression that you've been summoned to aid in Corellia's defense, when in fact, reenabling Centerpoint Station has more to do with offense than defense."

"I knew it would be something like this," Jacen blurted.

Anakin smiled falsely. "Drall's lighter gravity is going to Jacen's head," he told everyone. "He's convinced that our coming here is going to upset the balance of the Force or something."

Jacen smoldered. "You're not far off, Anakin."

"You're the one who's far off. *Anything* that will stop the Yuuzhan Vong has the Force on its side."

"What's come over you boys?" Marcha interrupted. "You never used to argue."

"We disagree about this mission," Jacen said, staring at his younger brother.

"Among other things," Anakin said under his breath.

Jacen gestured toward Ebrihim. "You heard what he said, Anakin: This has more to do with offense. And you were the one who described Centerpoint as Corellia's lightsaber."

"Yeah, which means it can be used to parry or thrust. It all depends on who's wielding it."

"Meaning what—that you'll refuse to help if you find out it's going to be used for attack?"

"Meaning that I'm waiting to hear all sides of the argument." Anakin turned to Ebrihim. "Is there proof the New Republic plans to use Centerpoint as a weapon instead of a shield?"

Ebrihim mulled over his response. "The problem, as I see it—and as you yourself assert—is that Centerpoint has the capacity to be both. Even if used as a shield today, there's no guarantee it won't be used as a weapon tomorrow. But that inherent duality isn't the reason for the protests. The cause runs deeper than that."

"How much do you remember about what the Triad attempted to do during the crisis?" Marcha asked.

"Actually, I don't remember all that much," Anakin confessed. "I know they used Centerpoint to create a systemwide interdiction field, capable of trapping hostages and repelling rescue attempts at the same time."

Ebrihim nodded. "We strongly suspect that the New Republic will attempt to do the very same thing. You see, this operation isn't about using Centerpoint to safeguard Corellia; it's about using the station to ensnare the Yuuzhan Vong fleet, and utilizing this system as a battle arena."

"Oh, brother," Jacen groaned. "No wonder Corellia's ready to riot."

Anakin looked from Jacen to Ebrihim. "You said 'suspect.'"

"That's correct. We're not privy to all that's going on inside Centerpoint, much less inside the minds of the Defense Force command staff. What we do know is this: That despite the proximity of the Yuuzhan Vong fleet to Corellia, the system is effectively undefended. Oh, the New Republic has seen fit to deploy three of our own *Strident*-class Star Defenders at Corellia, and the flotilla that has been safeguarding Duro has been pulled back to shore up the Outlier systems. But even that amount of firepower is insufficient to ward off a full-scale attack."

"Which is precisely what the Defense Force would like the Yuuzhan Vong to conclude," Marcha added.

"Our conspicuous vulnerability is meant to lure the invaders here," Ebrihim said, "to prompt an assault. Then, once Centerpoint has immobilized their fleet, New Republic ships deployed at Bothawui, Kuat, and other worlds will supposedly jump to engage them."

Anakin's forehead creased in concern. "How is the Defense Force expecting to get ships through the interdiction field that's holding the Yuuzhan Vong fleet at bay?"

"By outfitting the ships with the same hyperwave inertial momentum sustainers the Bakurans used during the crisis," Ebrihim said. "You must understand, Anakin, this operation has been in the works for some time."

Marcha confirmed it with a nod. "Just how much of it is understood by the demonstrators, or even by the Centerpoint Party, is immaterial. The protestors are reacting to the fact that Coruscant has withheld defense and commandeered Centerpoint without factoring Corellia's citizenry into the equation."

Anakin grew pensive, then looked at Marcha. "You make it sound like everything is already set. It doesn't sound like I'm really needed here."

Marcha smiled faintly. "I wish that were so. But, in fact, the success of the strategy rests very much with you."

Ebrihim explained. "The Defense Force has had their best people working nonstop to bring the entire network on-line, including the repulsors housed on the Five Brothers—Corellia, Drall, Selonia, Talus, and Tralus. The goal now is to slave all five planetary repulsors to Centerpoint itself, providing it with even greater power and range than it already enjoys from tapping the gravitic energies of the Double Worlds. Theoretically, the station will then be capable of creating interdiction fields wherever Admiral Sovv and the rest desire them to be created. Centerpoint would also have the ability to alter the course or location of distant planets, or cause stars to explode, as occurred twice during the crisis."

"But the scientists have not yet been able to realize their ambitions," Marcha emphasized. "As was the case during the crisis, the mysteries of Centerpoint continue to elude everyone. The station remains unpredictable and unstable, and at this point no one is certain that it can re-create a massive interdiction field, let alone that it can incite a distant star to go nova.

"And this is where you and you alone figure in the scheme, Anakin, because many of the scientists are convinced that the system still bears the imprint you imparted to the repulsor here on Drall, and that such a network can be brought into synchronization only by you."

Ebrihim reinforced it. "Eight years ago you were responsible for disabling Centerpoint. Now you may be the only person who can successfully rehabilitate it."

Concern shone from Anakin's eyes. "Jacen sensed this from the beginning, but . . ." He glanced at everyone. "It's not that I don't trust what you're telling me, but I have to go to Centerpoint and see for myself. I might be able to reenable it as a shield only. That way, Corellia and Drall and the rest can at least protect themselves from attack, no matter what plans the Defense Force or any others devise."

Marcha smiled sadly. "Yes, perhaps you'll be able to do just as you say, Anakin. But a word of warning before you go: When it came to reactivating the repulsors and the station, Coruscant had no choice but to call on many of those who were directly involved in fomenting the crisis."

Anakin nodded. "The Sacorrian Triad, you mean."

"Along with several others who played a role in those events," Ebrihim said.

Marcha looked from her nephew to Anakin and Jacen. "It's just this, boys: You may not like what you're going to find on Centerpoint. Therefore, you must take care. Think carefully before you agree to anything."

TWENTY-TWO

"We've got an inspector here from Comestibles and Curatives," the sentry posted at the entrance to Sal liche Ag's district headquarters said into his comlink. "Human. Yeah, I already told him that we'd had some CCA folks through here last week, but he claims it's a spot inspection. Yeah, all his documentation checks out."

With his hair and beard dyed jet-black and a brimmed cap tugged low on his forehead, Han acted nonchalant while he waited outside the security booth. Baffle, who had dropped him at the gate, had assured him that the pale-green lightweight suit was standard issue for Comestibles and Curatives Administration inspectors, and in fact, the corpulent human sentry had scanned the computer-coded identity card with the indifference of one who had seen hundreds in his day.

"What areas you interested in seeing?" the man asked suddenly.

Han adopted an officious smile. "Divulging that information would effectively undermine the nature of my visit."

The sentry frowned. "He isn't saying," he muttered into the comlink mouthpiece. "Claims it'll spoil the surprise. No, I didn't laugh either. Okay, he'll be here when you arrive." He switched off the comlink and returned the identity card to Han. "Sit tight, pal. An escort's on the way."

The casually dressed man who arrived moments later in a four-seater landspeeder was even heftier than the sentry and had the same sunburned and stubbled farmboy toughness. Both men were a world apart from the aristocratic Harbrights, who ran Salliche Ag and were apparently intent on throwing in with the Yuuzhan Vong. The escort took in Han as he approached the landspeeder, an alloy case dangling from his right hand.

"Surprised they haven't retired you yet, old-timer," he remarked. A name tag stitched to the pocket of his untucked shirt identified him as Bow.

So much for the deceptive qualities of hair dye, Han thought as he climbed into the rear seat of the speeder. "With any luck, this will be one of my last assignments."

"You know, Salliche has never had a problem with you people," Bow said around what remained of a toothpick protruding from between his front teeth. "We pay good money to see to that."

"I wouldn't know," Han said, blinking. "I'm simply carrying out my assignment."

"Fine. Just make sure you're quick about it. I don't have all day."

Han forced a nervous laugh. "I'm as eager to have this over with as you are."

They set off, but had traveled only a short distance when the Salliche man brought the landspeeder to a halt alongside a large map and directory. With some difficulty, Bow rotated in the front seat to face Han.

"Where to first? We can sample produce from a couple of nearby fields, or you can run your tests on random samples that have already been harvested." He pointed north. "Shipping is over that way, in case you're interested in cargo container decontamination procedures."

Han pretended to study the map, then said, "Suppose we begin at product enhancement."

Bow's bushy brows knitted. "You're kidding."

Han cleared his throat. "Is there some problem?"

"No problem. I just hope CCA is paying you well."

The landspeeder flew down narrow dirt roads, many of which twisted through fields of burrmillet waiting to be harvested. As tall as trees, the slender umber stalks of grain formed palisades to either side. Han's nose alerted him to the fact that they were nearing the fertilizer works long before a sign announcing product enhancement came into view. At yet another checkpoint he was issued a disposable jumpsuit and a rebreather helmet with a tinted face bowl. Similarly outfitted, Bow led the way toward an enormous, flat-roofed warehouse, whose loading bays were crowded with banthas, rontos, and other beasts of burden, waiting to receive cargos of fertilizer.

Baffle had already explained that, in keeping with Salliche's aim to please the antitech invaders, the company was in the process of switching over from machine-produced nutrients to live production; so Han wasn't as surprised as he might have been to see thousands of craw-maws, wingles, and nightseers—genetically manipulated to be wingless and mute—being force-fed in cages and perches that lined the interior of the building. Beneath the cages, and filled to the brim with the avians' abundant droppings, were wide troughs that funneled the manure to the loading bays for eventual dispersal. Other areas of the warehouse were given over to water tanks crammed with stink fish and fingerfins dredged from Ruan's bountiful seas. Mashed by mallet, the fish were being tossed into the troughs to serve as a fertilizing additive.

Considering the debilitating effect it was having on

some of the bare-faced Gotals, Bimms, and hapless others whose task it was to gather and shovel excrement overspill into the troughs, Han could well imagine the stench. But he could only guess at the offenses, real or trumped up, the former refugees had committed to have earned themselves such punishment. Among one group, knee-deep in the grounded avians' ordure and leaning feebly against the wooden handle of his shovel, stood Droma.

"I'm going to run a few quick tests," Han told Bow through the rebreather's annunciator. He popped open the carry case and made as if to extract one of the test kits Baffle's coterie of droids had provided, then stopped abruptly and pointed to Droma in elaborate incredulity. "Is that . . . is that a *Ryn?*"

The Salliche man stared, then nodded his head. "Yeah. He's new here."

"New or not," Han continued, growing more agitated as he spoke, "doesn't anyone realize that Ryn have proscriptions against bathing and other habits most sapients consider essential to good health?"

"But he's working with *manure.*"

"That is hardly the point. Do you know what would happen if word leaked that Salliche Ag has Ryn on the premises?"

"It's only one Ryn," Bow started to say.

"He'll have to be removed this instant. I demand that he undergo a complete medical evaluation before he is permitted to return to work—even work of this sort."

Letting his exasperation show, Bow prized a slim comlink from his shirt pocket and, raising the face bowl of his helmet, began to speak briskly into it.

Han wondered what Salliche Ag was going to do about replacing its comlinks and landspeeders if and when the Yuuzhan Vong showed up.

"All right," Bow told Han a moment later, "we're cleared to bring him to medical in the east wing." He swung angrily toward Droma. "Ryn! Leave your shovel and get over here."

Droma looked up, set the tool aside, and clomped toward them, shaking one leg, then the other, then his tail, in an effort to rid himself of some of the gray filth clinging to him.

"Whatever you do, don't touch him," Han warned Bow, "or you'll have to be evaluated along with him."

Reeking of dung, Droma stopped a few meters away, clearly without recognizing Han behind the rebreather mask.

"Hose him down!" Bow ordered a nearby worker.

Han winced as the high-pressure flow from a thick hose nearly swept Droma off his feet. "Ill-starred creatures," he said, loud enough for the Salliche man to hear, "forever getting themselves into trouble."

Bow puffed out his lips and nodded grimly. "You can say that again."

With Droma dripping wet and looking hopelessly forlorn, Bow snapped stun cuffs around his wrists and shoved him toward the warehouse exit. At the checkpoint, Han surrendered the rebreather, deposited the jumpsuit into a shredder/recycler, and followed Droma into the rear seat of the landspeeder. Downcast, Droma didn't glance at him until they were under way, and even then he didn't recognize Han immediately. Then his eyes widened appreciably and his jaw dropped.

"Please, hurry," Han shouted to Bow before Droma could ruin everything with a surprised outburst. "I find it quite distasteful to have to share a seat with this . . . malefactor."

"East wing's dead ahead," Bow said over his shoulder.

Han exchanged veiled glances with Droma, but didn't

look at him again until the three of them were in a turbo-lift car, descending for the east wing's sublevel-one medical lab. Then, throwing Droma a warning look, he drew a small blaster from the durinium shoulder holster the droids had fabricated, and pressed the weapon's emitter nozzle to Bow's temple.

"Do exactly as you're told and you'll walk away from this." When the big man nodded in a manner that mixed surprise and anger, Han added, "Stop the lift and move to the far corner of the car, then key the stun cuff remote." He cut his eyes briefly to Droma, then told the turbolift to ascend to level five.

Rubbing his freed wrists, Droma glanced at him. "We're going up?"

"I've got a job to do." Han gestured with his chin toward Bow. "You'll have to deal with this one. Take him down to the maintenance sublevel and find a closet to stick him in. If he gives you any trouble, shoot him. Then meet me on level five."

Bow worked his jaw, but managed to keep from saying anything that might provoke Droma to take Han at his word.

While the lift was climbing, Han stripped off the pale-green suit to reveal an expensive business suit beneath it. Droma's curiosity was palpable.

"No time to explain," Han said. Handing Droma the bundled-up suit and the open stun cuffs, he added, "Hold on to these; we're going to need them later."

At level five, he slipped a sheer glove onto his right hand and headed down a broad, gleaming corridor toward the transceiver room. In his left hand he palmed the fatal data card the droids had given him.

The handprint reader was housed in a niche alongside the control room door. When Han laid his gloved hand on the pad, the device's screen identified him as Dees

Harbright, cousin once removed of Count Borert Harbright and senior vice president of marketing for Salliche Ag, whom the black-bearded, finely tailored Han resembled—sufficiently, at any rate, to bring the half-dozen control room technicians to their feet as he entered.

"Sit down, everyone, sit down," he said in the most cavalier tone he could muster. "I just wanted to have a look at our deactivation system. Are we operating on schedule?"

"One thousand two hundred fifty droids have been shut down and warehoused this quarter, sir," a whip-thin female tech chirped. "During the same period, personnel acquisition division has succeeded in recruiting over three thousand refugees, who have agreed to remain on Ruan as employees."

"Splendid, splendid," Han said, moving about the room, the data card still palmed in his left hand. While the female tech went on to offer additional statistics, Han—with his back to a peripheral device he hoped would prove the path of least resistance—slotted the disk, which Baffle promised would literally disappear once it had worked its sorcery.

"We're expecting to have at least fifteen hundred more droids warehoused by the end of the next quarter," the cheerful woman was saying when the computer system loosed a series of strident tones that struck Han as the machine equivalent of a distress cry.

"System crash!" another technician shouted in obvious disbelief.

At every duty station, lights began to blink out, display screens went gray, and technicians did all but tear their hair out in an effort to resuscitate the system before it crossed over to wherever machine minds went when they crashed. So desperate were their efforts, Han experienced a twinge of guilt—at least until he reminded himself that the machine had been responsible for deactivating thousands of droids.

The mounting panic made it easy for him to slip out of the room unnoticed. The corridor was as quiet and brightly lit as it had been moments earlier, betraying nothing of the chaos ensuing in the control room. Adjusting the fit of his fine jacket, Han sauntered toward the turbolift, nodding with genteel suffrage to everyone he passed. As he neared the lift, Droma appeared from behind a plasteel pillar that had obviously served as his hiding place, the pale-green suit draped over one arm.

"Try not to look so guilty," he whispered.

Han's tight-lipped smile held. "Just get in the lift and put on the stun cuffs," he said without moving his lips.

Once inside, though, his calm and well-mannered facade collapsed. Quickly, he slipped back into the inspector's suit, then took the blaster from Droma and made certain it was armed.

"I won't even venture a guess as to how you managed this," Droma said as he donned the stun cuffs.

"Yeah, but it'd be fun to hear you try." Han slid the blaster into his jacket pocket. "As soon as we hit the lobby, we make straight for the nearest exit, got it? Pretend you're in my custody."

Han stood facing the lift doors. When they parted, he couldn't see across the lobby for the hundreds of droids that were rushing about and chattering incessantly, many of them hastening for the exits.

"I can't help thinking you had something to do with this," Droma said.

"Indirectly." Han gestured to the closest exit that wasn't completely blocked by droids. "That way."

They stepped into the throng and were just short of the transparisteel exit doors when a gruff voice shouted, "There they are!"

Han failed to keep himself from turning around. Zeroing in on the voice, he saw Bow, now in the company of several security guards, pointing at him.

"I thought I told you to lock him away!" Han said.

"I did," Droma argued. "I stuck him inside a room filled with deactivated droids."

Han muttered a curse and drew the blaster. "No time for subtlety."

Scarcely aiming, he placed a quartet of beams close enough to the guards to send them scurrying for cover. Crouching, he and Droma weaved their way through a tight press of droids and stumbled outside. Han spied Bow's landspeeder and steered Droma toward it, as a mob of prattling droids spilled from the east wing and began to fan out across the surrounding lawns and parking lots. Throwing himself into the driver's seat, Han grinned broadly.

"One thing you can always count on with farmboys," he said to Droma, who had removed the cuffs and was settling into the passenger seat. "They never lock their vehicles."

Han started the speeder's repulsorlift engine. With both hands clamped on the steering wheel and his feet on the pedals, he maneuvered the speeder through a quick turn and shot for the frontage road.

"No use trying for the main gate," he shouted above the whine of the triple turbines. "It's sure to be shut tight by now! We'll have to use the service roads. Some of them have to lead to the fields we passed on the way to Facility 17!"

"Better choose quickly," Droma said, studying the

small scanner display affixed to the passenger-side console. "We've got seven, make that eight vehicles converging on us from north, east, and west."

Gritting his teeth, Han glanced at the towering stalks of grain that lined both sides of the frontage road. "Ah, who needs a road," he said at last, veering due south, straight into the field.

The satellite feed to the district headquarters security section provided an unobstructed aerial view of the landspeeder pursuit. It was as if the cams were positioned one hundred meters above the ground rather than in stationary orbit, halfway to Ruan's closest moon.

"They're sure making a mess of those burrmillet fields," the security chief remarked to Bow.

The fat man leaned closer to the flatscreen display. The stolen landspeeder had cut unswerving lines, precise parabolas, and sweeping spirals in the umber sea of grain. In pursuit flew eight speeders, carving out their own streaks and crop circles, if not as conscientiously.

"Talented driver, that one," the chief said as the lead speeder slalomed through a row of outmoded windmills, then powered through a series of figure eights before racing off on a new vector. "Must have been a swoop pilot. Has he been identified?"

"No," Bow fumed. "But it's confirmed he's the one who crashed the droid-deactivation system on level five."

The chief, potbellied and mustachioed, smiled lightly. "I heard you were with some of the droids when they came back to life."

Bow grimaced. "You heard right. But I'll tell you what: none of those droids unsealed the doors. Somebody with access to the system unlocked them as soon as the droids woke up."

The chief snorted. "So what kind of guy goes through the trouble of masquerading as both a CCA inspector and a corporate vice president to rescue a Ryn and free a couple of thousand droids?"

"The well-connected kind. The Ryn was arrested at Facility 17 when he and the human showed up looking for the Ryn's clanmates. But it turns out they'd already gotten themselves offworld on forged letters of transit."

"Maybe it was deliberate—the Ryn showing up there—just to get himself arrested."

"Doesn't calculate. The Ryn couldn't have known he'd be brought here. And besides, he couldn't have added anything to what his partner obviously knew before he even showed up at the front gate. We've got people checking with spaceport control to determine how and when the two of them arrived onworld, but something's interfering with our accessing the immigration data banks."

"Something or someone?" the chief said. "Coconspirators is my guess."

Bow compressed his lips but said nothing.

The chief retrieved holograms of the human lifted from the front gate and product enhancement security scanners, along with the level-five control room identifier. "The beard and facial features look real enough," he said after appraising the holos for a moment.

Bow rubbed his chin. "Remove the beard and the cap."

Both men studied the revised holos for a moment more. "He looks familiar," the chief said, "but I can't place the face."

"Well, he's an agent for someone."

"A Salliche rival? Nebula Consumables maybe?"

Bow shrugged.

"Course change," the chief said suddenly, swinging back to the satellite-feed display. "They're angling east."

The two men watched the stolen landspeeder tear into another grain field; then, without warning, it revectored, leaving the field for what Bow initially took to be a service road. But not one member of the pursuit team followed.

"What's going on?" he barked.

"Son of a blaster," the chief said. "That's no road. They've dropped into one of the irrigation channels—right off the speeders' surface-scan displays. Our guys have no idea where they went."

"Patch into the sluice system and shut all the gates along that stretch!"

"I'm on it," the chief said.

Bow turned to the satellite-feed screen in time to see the saboteurs' landspeeder whiz through the closing sluice gate, hop the next in line, then power through a reckless turn into a much broader channel.

"It's a runoff channel," the chief explained. "Ends at the river that runs past Facility 17. If they make it that far, we could lose them." He was reaching for the sluice-gate control buttons when Bow restrained him.

"No, don't shut them down just yet. Make him think he's got time." He glanced at the satellite-feed display. "Bring us close in on him." When the chief had complied, they could see that the stolen speeder had lost its retractable windscreen. Broken stalks of burrmillet poked from creases in the rounded nose and from between the seats, and the cab was half filled with threshed grain.

"What would you estimate his speed?"

The chief considered it. "The channel's not only broader but twice as deep, so I'd say he's running those turbines close to flat out. Say, two hundred."

"How far to the nearest gate?"

"Maybe one kilometer away."

"How quickly do they shut?"

"In a heartbeat."

Bow grinned. "Keep your finger on the switch. I'll tell you when."

The chief grinned back at him. "It's like playing a game of Death Hurdles."

Bow watched the screen for a moment, then shouted, "Now!"

Swerving as it tried desperately to shed velocity, the landspeeder careened straight into the gate. The force of the impact hurled the human and the Ryn clear out of the cab, over the top of the gate, and into the ditch beyond.

"Got 'em," the chief said excitedly.

"Patch me through to the pursuit team."

Even as he was raising the pursuit team, the chief said, "I've got a better way of flushing them out." He activated his comlink. "Give me weather control."

Bow frowned, then smiled in revelation. "Nice touch."

The chief shrugged. "We need the rain anyway."

It was the mud that saved them—only a foot deep, but soft as pudding. Han, after ten meters of end-over-end flight, landed facefirst, plowing a deep furrow down the center of the ditch. Better equipped for acrobatics, Droma executed a flawless triple front flip and came down on his feet, skidding across the slick surface like a competitive aquaplaner.

Han surfaced spewing brown water, but it was Droma who was piqued.

"We'll be safer in the runoff channel, you said. I don't think so, I said, we should stick to the irrigation ditches. Trust me, you said. Keep above the gates, I said. Where's the fun in that, you said—"

"Quit your complaining," Han said. "Or have you gotten so used to manure you can't handle a little mud?"

Droma helped Han to his feet and took a look around. As if the mud wasn't enough, the ditch's smooth, permacrete retaining walls were over four meters tall. "Now what? We can't even climb out."

"We're better off down here. Moving through those grain fields would be slow going." Han stripped off the pale-green and business jackets and threw them aside. He used his fingers to sluice mud from his forehead and beard. "What did the map show?"

"You mean just before you crashed?"

Han glowered. "That wasn't a crash. Somebody knew just when to shut that gate." He glanced at the sky, which seemed darker than it had been a moment earlier. "They're watching us. Sky or satellite cam."

Droma cut his eyes from the sky to Han, then pointed in the direction they had been heading before the collision. "The river is a couple of kilometers straight ahead. We should be able to follow it all the way to Facility 17."

"Perfect. We float down the river and haul ourselves out short of the refugee camp. Then we make our way to the spaceport."

"Where Salliche will have an army of guards posted and every scanner set to shriek the moment one of us presents an identity card."

"Don't worry about that. We've got friends who will get us right to the *Falcon*."

Droma stopped squeezing water from his mustachios. "Without passing through Ruan control?"

Han smirked. "By passing under it." His foot made a sucking sound as he lifted it from the mud. "Let's get a move on."

They hadn't gone three hundred meters when a deep bass sound rumbled overhead.

Han stopped. "What the heck was that?"

Droma waved in dismissal. "That's just the weather control station. Salliche resets it a couple of times a day."

Han watched gray clouds stream overhead. He pivoted through a circle, gauging the height of the walls. Even with Droma atop his shoulders, Droma wouldn't be able to reach the top.

"We have to go back to the sluice gate," he said suddenly.

Droma looked at Han as if he were mad. "What?"

"The gate's our only chance at climbing out."

"I thought you said we're better off down here."

Fat drops of rain started to fall. "Salliche is cooking up a storm. They're planning on drowning us."

Droma gulped. "But those speeders that were chasing us—they're probably already headed for the gate!"

Han tightened his lips and nodded. "You're right. But there has to be at least one more gate between here and the river."

They began to run, helping each other along when one of them slipped or became bogged down. The rain became a downpour, and the muddy water rose quickly from ankle- to knee-deep. Behind them they heard the steady whine of approaching landspeeders. Then the sound was replaced by a roaring turbulence.

Han came to an abrupt halt. "Listen," he shouted to Droma above the steady pounding of the rain.

Droma stopped a few meters farther on. "I don't think I'm going to like this."

Both of them turned to see a three-meter-high wall of water raging toward them. They barely had time to swing back toward the river when the torrent caught up, sweeping them away.

TWENTY-THREE

Larger than the Death Star, Centerpoint Station hung gray-white and ominous between Talus and Tralus, drawing its power from the gravitic output of the so-called Double Worlds. Rotating slowly around an axis defined by two thick polar cylinders, the station had been designed to act as a gravity lens capable of directing amplified bursts of repulsor energy through hyperspace, sufficient for the capturing of distant worlds or the destruction of far-flung stars. Its surface was a mishmash of boxy superstructures as tall as skyscrapers and force-bubble pressurization access ports the size of impact craters. A bewildering tangle of piping, cables, and conduits coursed in all directions, winding through multistoried forests of parabolic antennae, conical arrays, and setose projections. A prominent feature was the remains of a crashed spacecraft that had been macrofused to the hull and converted into living quarters.

"I was the first person to greet your uncle Luke, Lando Calrissian, Belindi Kalenda, and Gaeriel Captison when they came aboard," Jenica Sonsen told Anakin, Jacen, and Ebrihim while a turbovator smelling of fresh paint conveyed them along a dark-pink tunnel toward the station's core.

"I think we met you on Corellia afterwards," Jacen said.

"You did. I'm delighted that you remember."

"The simulated gravity is increasing," Q9 interrupted in Basic, speaking through a vocoder the droid had adapted to form words like a mouth. "The increase is obviously a consequence of our traveling away from the axis of rotation."

"Thank you, Queue-nine," Ebrihim said, in deference to the droid's oft-stated opinion that machines should be useful at all times and in all places.

Sonsen smiled at the exchange. "It has long been our hope to provide Centerpoint with artificial gravity, but for the time being, we're relying on centrifugal gravity. Perhaps if we're successful in assisting in the war effort, the New Republic will finally allocate the funds necessary to despin the station. But even without artificial gravity, the Mrlssi have done wonders to make Hollowtown and many other areas perfectly livable."

She was an upbeat, handsome woman, with black curly hair, a long, thin face, and expressive eyebrows. Eight years earlier, following Centerpoint's unexpected flare-ups—which had not only destroyed two distant stars with precise hyperspace shots but had also incinerated thousands of colonists who had been living in Hollowtown—Sonsen had been left in charge of the station, while survivors fled for the safety of Talus and Tralus. Since then she had headed up the cartography team that was slowly mapping the complex interior of the immense orb, a task Sonsen herself doubted would be completed in her lifetime.

"Did your team get along with the archaeologists who were deported?" Jacen asked.

Sonsen frowned. "They weren't deported, so much as removed for their own safety. But, yes, of course we got along. All of us are interested in learning whatever we can about the species who built Centerpoint and assembled the Corellian system. I'm afraid, however, that the archaeologists may have erred by making a political issue of their removal. If, as the Centerpoint Party advocates, each of Corell's five worlds should be treated as a separate entity, then it stands to reason that this station—which is certainly not indigenous to the system—should also be considered independent. As a result, I believe that Centerpoint may remain in New Republic hands for some time to come."

Ebrihim opened his mouth to say something, but thought better of it and fell silent for the remainder of the ride through the station's two thousand levels of decks.

Originally a power-containment battery, Hollowtown was an open sphere, measuring sixty kilometers in diameter. The curving walls had once seen homes, parks, lakes, orchards, and farmland, basking in the overhead radiance of Glowpoint—a kind of pilot light for the entire station. But except for a few that housed scientists and the archaeological team before them, the houses had been dismantled. The only concession to what had once existed were the adjustable shadow-shields, installed to simulate night.

Positioned along the spin axis on both sides of Hollowtown were large cones ringed by six smaller cones, given the names North and South Conical Mountains. The arrangement of the cones was the geometry needed for a particular type of old-style repulsor.

Sonsen pointed out the sights as she ushered everyone to a small, well-shielded control room that had remained concealed during the station's occupation, and had been discovered only by accident when a group of Mrlssi had been searching for a place to install a life-support monitor.

Consistent with the plumed avians from which they were descended, the limpid-eyed, diminutive Mrlssi had a talent for rendering extremely large spaces habitable, as they had proved to Dr. Ohran Keldor, who had employed some one hundred of them at the Imperial Maw Installation near Kessel. In Hollowtown, the fine-boned Mrlssi were more in evidence than any other species, though there were none in the control room itself when Sonsen and her charges entered.

The instrument-filled chamber did hold several humans, a Selonian, two Verpine, and a Duros, but in spite of the diversity, the curious mix of robed Jedi, Drall, and bullet-headed droid brought activity to an abrupt halt and caused all heads to turn. Since arriving onstation, Anakin had grown accustomed to being the focus of intense scrutiny, but the gray-haired man who muscled his way through the control room crowd set him back on his heels. With the beard that Han had been growing the last time Anakin saw him, the man looked more like Han than Han himself—if a few centimeters taller and more thickly built.

"You're Jacen, and you're Anakin," he said, pointing to each in turn. Mostly to Anakin, he added, "You don't remember me, do you? I'm hurt. I'll bet that even your droid remembers."

"You were responsible for confining Master Ebrihim and Masters Anakin and Jacen within a force field on Drall," Q9 supplied. "Whereas I was responsible for releasing them."

The man planted his hands on his hips and laughed heartily. "I'd forgotten all about that."

"You're Thrackan Sal-Solo," Anakin said at last, "Dad's first cousin."

Thrackan made his face long. "And your cousin, as well, boys."

"You not only took us hostage," Jacen said, "you forced our father to fight a Selonian female—just for your amusement."

Thrackan spread his hands in a placating gesture. "Han and I have a long history. He probably never told you about the time he beat the stuffing out of me when we were kids. You might say that I was just paying him back. But, you're right, it was wrong of me to do what I did. Sometimes when you've been remembering an injustice for years and years, revenge begins to get the best of you."

Thrackan's eyes narrowed. "It took me the better part of eight years in Dorthus Tal prison on Sacorria to realize that, but I have realized it, and I'm a changed man as a result." He gestured broadly. "That's the only reason I'm here on Centerpoint. As part of my rehabilitation, the powers that be felt that I could demonstrate my newly attained self-awareness by pitching in—by offering my technical expertise in service to the cause. By standing shoulder to shoulder with the New Republic against the Yuuzhan Vong."

He snorted a self-deprecating laugh. "Of course, you two wouldn't know how the past can plague a person. You're Jedi. You're not subject to the banal emotions that trouble ordinary folks. Anger, hatred, guilt, the desire for retribution . . . such things mean nothing to you. Why, even the Yuuzhan Vong have simply failed to see the error of their ways and can probably be brought over to the side of the Force. Am I right? Otherwise *you'd* be shoulder to shoulder with us in the trenches, ready to fight—ready to spill whatever amount of Corellian blood that runs in your veins."

"We're here to help," Anakin said firmly.

"Are you now?" Thrackan shook his head in amusement. "It's a marvelous irony that it took a galactic war to reunite the old gang"—he motioned to one of the humans and the Selonian—"and to bring you boys back to the station you originally helped to shut down." Again his glance favored Anakin. "I have you to thank personally for banishing our illusions of a free and independent Corellia. But, tell me, do you still think we were wrong to make a grab for freedom?"

"Your methods were wrong," Jacen said before Anakin could respond.

Thrackan waved his hand. "Methods. You realize, of course, that the New Republic has essentially abandoned Corellia since the crisis. And knowing Ebrihim"—he regarded the Drall with obvious distaste—"I'm sure you've been apprised of Coruscant's plan to use Corellia as a battleground."

"We've heard the rumors," Jacen said.

Thrackan sneered. "That's your mother talking. What about you, Anakin? Are you here on a tour, or are you really willing to do what's necessary to safeguard Corellia from attack?"

Anakin considered it. "That depends on what you have planned for Centerpoint."

Thrackan adopted a look of puzzlement. "What we have planned is an interdiction field. What else could we hope for?"

"How about the ability to vaporize every unwanted ship—Yuuzhan Vong or otherwise—that shows itself here?" Jacen chimed in. "The *Watchkeeper* was destroyed by one shot from the repulsor on Selonia, and Centerpoint has a thousand times the firepower of all five planetary repulsors combined. It can create a compression wave strong enough to induce a star to explode."

Thrackan looked to a pale, thin-faced technician. "This is Antone," he said. "He was also here during the crisis. In fact, he had family at Bovo Yagen, the star that would have been destroyed if Anakin hadn't intervened in time."

"Centerpoint can indeed induce stars to go nova," Antone said. "The Triad caused the explosions of EM-1271 and Thanta Zilbra, but those results cannot be duplicated."

"You're saying that Centerpoint can't be used as a weapon?" Jacen asked.

Antone shrugged. "Frankly, we're not sure. In order to loose a burst of repulsor power from the South Pole, the station has to reorient its spin axis, then go through a series of power surges, pulses, transient events, and radiation releases in advance of actually firing. When Centerpoint destroyed EM-1271, Glowpoint's energy spikes killed thousands of colonists."

"No one wants to risk a repeat of that catastrophe," Thrackan said.

Jacen looked at him. "If it's true that you're only interested in fashioning an interdiction field, then you should be able to do that yourself. During the crisis, you were the one placed in control of Centerpoint's jamming and interdiction field capabilities."

"Yes," Thrackan said slowly, "but the crisis was resolved before I got to try my hand at operating Centerpoint. What's more, things have changed since your uncle Luke and the others shut Centerpoint down. Now neither of those systems is responding the way they once did."

Antone cleared his throat meaningfully. "One problem is that the station's barycenter point is no longer stable. Centerpoint has always moved about to stay properly positioned and oriented, but the repositioning maneuvers have become erratic."

"In other words," Thrackan clarified, "we haven't been able to initiate an interdiction field on demand."

"Only Anakin can do it," Antone said nervously. "As a result of his activation of the Drall repulsor, the entire system imprinted on him." He looked at Anakin. "On your fingerprints, your DNA, perhaps even your brain waves. I've been proposing this for eight years now, but no one was interested in having you return here until now."

"There's only one way to find out if Antone's theory merits further investigation," Thrackan said. He gestured toward what was obviously a special console. "Take the controls, Anakin. Let's see where it goes from there."

Jacen and Ebrihim threw Anakin troubled looks, to which Anakin responded with a nod, meant to be mollifying. But even as he moved toward the console—with every tech watching—Anakin could feel the system beginning to respond to him.

Vague memories of his experiences inside the Drall repulsor surfaced as he sat down and ran his hands over the console. After a moment, as had happened long ago on Drall, he seemed to glimpse a virtual array of switches and controls and linkages, all of which had little to do with the knobs and levers and dials that covered the control panel.

Hesitantly, he placed his hands on the console.

A tone sounded and a flat spot on the panel began to twist and shimmer, then swell upward, forming itself into a handle like a spacecraft's joystick.

When Anakin reached for it, the handle reshaped itself to fit his left hand, and everyone in the room—even Jacen—gasped.

In his mind, as if on a display screen, Anakin could suddenly read specs on power ratings, capacitance storage, vernier control, targeting subsystems, safety overrides, shielding constraints, thrust balancing, geogravitic energy transfer levels . . .

Unexpectedly, a graphic display appeared in the air over the handle—a hollow wire-frame cube made up of smaller, transparent cubes five high, five across, and five deep. As Anakin manipulated the joystick, the grid of smaller cubes began to take on color—greens and purple—to the accompaniment of activation tones.

Everyone but Thrackan was speechless. "You've done it, boy, you've done it," he enthused.

Anakin moved the control stick forward, and a cube of blazing orange appeared. He experimented with minute adjustments that made the cube flicker or brighten. Then he pulled the stick down as hard as he could.

Indicators registered an incredible burst of power, and the control room began to shudder. In Hollowtown, Glowpoint came alive and a display of blinding lightning blazed from it to the South Conical Mountains.

"The station is reorienting!" a technician reported.

"It's armed!" Antone exclaimed in awe. "It's capable of firing!"

A dozen separate conversations broke out in the control room, silenced only by the arrival of the New Republic officer in command of the project.

"An urgent message from Commenor," the colonel announced to Sal-Solo and Antone. "Yuuzhan Vong advance elements are departing Hutt space. Fleet Intelligence estimates thirty-six standard hours until they're at our doorstep."

In groups of three and four, at times escorted by gunboats and squadrons of Miy'til fighters or vintage X-wings, the warships of the Hapan fleet reverted to realspace over the planet Commenor, on the Rimward edge of the Core. Arrayed in a sweeping arc, the sleek *Nova*-class battle cruisers and Olanjii/Charubah double-saucered Battle Dragons were a vibrantly colored counterpoint to the New Republic's fleet of Star Destroyers, lumpish Mon Calamari vessels, and unembellished Bothan warships.

Gazing at the assembled armada from the shuttle that was conveying her and Isolder from the prince's deep-carnelian *Song of War* to Commodore Brand's flagship, Leia felt as if she and everyone she held dear were trapped in the current of a tumultuous river that was sweeping them into unknown regions, scattering some, leaving many abandoned on ravaged shores, and carrying others over the falls to oblivion . . . The feeling had accompanied her from Hapes, troubling her through all the long hours of talk with Isolder, who was seemingly as enthralled by the prospect of going to war with the Yuuzhan Vong as he had been by the chance to trade punches and kicks with Beed Thane.

"True to our pirate roots, the Hapans prefer swift, ruthless strikes," he had told Leia more than once during the voyage. "Hurt an enemy at the start of an engagement and he is yours, for as the fight progresses, his fear of you will intensify and will become your ally."

Each time he said it, Leia had recalled Ithor and Gyndine, and the ruthless tactics the Yuuzhan Vong had employed. But the real source of her apprehension was the vision she had had following the Consortium's vote. Whenever she shut her eyes, vague images of destruction played at the edges of her awareness, as if massing for a full-scale assault. Anyone else might have been able to explain the dark images as owing to concerns for the lives of close friends and loved ones, but Leia was too attuned to the Force to dismiss them so expediently. She was convinced that the Force had shown her a possible future, while declining to provide her with a clear sense of just which paths were to be avoided. It helped slightly to be home, but in fact, proximity to Coruscant had not alleviated her anxiety. And she had yet to hear from

Han, not even by a message delivered through the kids or Luke.

"What power we have marshaled," Isolder said from the shuttle's passenger cabin window, where he stood with his fingers pressed to the transparisteel panel. "I doubt that even the Yuuzhan Vong would fail to be impressed."

"Oh, they'd be impressed," Leia said, joining him. "But instead of fazing them, a display like this would only goad them on."

Still, as she scanned the hundreds of capital ships anchored in local space—more than a hundred of which had trailed the *Song of War* from Hapes—she couldn't help but be overwhelmed.

Painted to symbolize the Consortium worlds they represented, the Battle Dragons consisted of large dorsal saucers linked to smaller ventral ones by dozens of slender rotation struts. Ion and hyperdrive engines were wedged astern, and the bridge sat aft on the dorsal face of the upper saucer, the perimeter of which was studded with ion cannons. As a means of compensating for the ship's relatively slow weapons-recharge rate, the equally distributed cannons were mounted on a drive disk that allowed them to be rotated for fire as need be. Sandwiched between and affixed to both saucers of the Battle Dragon were sixteen massive pulse-mass mines, each of which was capable of simulating the effects of mass shadows, thus hindering ships from making jumps into hyperspace.

By contrast, the *Nova*-class battle cruiser resembled a mountain climber's two-pronged ice claw, with the ship's viper-headed bridge occupying the distal end of what would be the tool's long handle. Exceptionally fast, well shielded, and equipped for long-range reconnaissance, the cruiser boasted twenty-five turbolasers, ten laser cannons, and ten ion cannons, and could carry twelve Miy'til fighters and six Hetrinar assault bombers.

While the shuttle was docking inside the heavy cruiser *Yald*, Leia tried to arrange things so that Isolder would emerge on his own, followed by his contingent of mostly female honor guards and command staff, but the prince wouldn't have it. He insisted instead that Leia walk by his side, a pairing she knew would not only become an endlessly repeated visual bite on the HoloNet, but also prove a source of amusement for those now-aged New Republic officers who had been in favor of her marrying Isolder so long ago.

Even so, she managed to put on her best face as she and Isolder descended the shuttle ramp arm in arm, to the strains of a Hapes march endowed with equal measures of pomp and circumstance by a well-rehearsed hundred-member military band. Leia had disengaged herself by the time they reached the deck, but she could tell by the expression on Commodore Brand's craggy face that even he was a bit nonplussed by the regal formality of their arrival.

At Brand's back stood rank after rank of soldiers at attention, saluting sharply when the music concluded.

"Welcome aboard, Prince Isolder," Brand said, stepping forward and extending his hand.

Isolder threw his short cape over one shoulder and took hold of Brand's hand—nearly crushing it in his grip, Leia was sure.

"Good to be here, Commodore."

Brand smiled uncertainly as he turned to Leia. "Ambassador Organa Solo, welcome home. And on behalf of the New Republic, thank you for all you've done."

Leia inclined her head in a courtly bow. "Thank Prince Isolder, Commodore. He was very persuasive in winning over the . . . Consortium."

Brand nodded stiffly. "Your support might very well stem the tide, Prince Isolder. But our victory will not be earned lightly."

"We are prepared to earn it, Commodore," Isolder assured him. "Just tell me where to direct my forces."

The command staffs of both groups moved to the tactical information center, deeper in the ship. During a private moment, Brand asked Leia about the voyage from Hapes. She repressed an urge to confide in him that it had been unsettling, and instead dismissed it as uneventful.

Dozens of officers and technicians were already gathered in the high-ceilinged TIC, seated at duty stations or clustered around light tables and plotting panels. Once Isolder, Leia, and the rest of the new arrivals were seated, Brand came right to the point.

"These are our most recent hyperspace probe reconnaissance images from Hutt space," he began, gesturing toward the holograms resolving above one of the chamber's many projector wells. He turned to address himself specifically to Isolder and his commanders. "What may look like an asteroid field is actually a fleet of warships. This storm of smaller asteroids spiraling toward the fleet are coralskippers, grown on the surface of the planet below."

"Grown?" one of Isolder's female officers asked.

Brand nodded. "With the permission of the Hutts, the Yuuzhan Vong transformed the planet to serve as a sort of weapons garden, similar to the ones at Belkadan and Sernpidal, from which these fighters have been harvested and equipped with the organic devices that both propel and shield them."

A new image took shape in the well's cone of projected light: a close-up view of the coralskippers attaching themselves like barnacles to the spindly arms of an enormous Yuuzhan Vong carrier analog. Elsewhere warships were maneuvering into battle groups, encircled by swarms of coralskippers.

"The enemy is massing for a strike," Brand remarked unequivocally, "and judging by the numbers of ships involved, they have their sights set on a target of greater significance than Ithor, Obroa-skai, or Gyndine. We have determined that target to be Corellia, which we have deliberately left inadequately protected in the hope of inviting an attack."

Leia's eyes widened in alarm as a holographic image of a moonlet-size sphere resolved above the projector.

"Centerpoint Station is the heart of Corellia's defense," Brand went on. "A repulsor and gravity lens, the station is capable of creating an interdiction field that will stretch from Corell clear to the frontier of the Outlier systems. At this moment, the station is on standby alert and prepared to initiate the field on our command."

"Commodore," Leia interrupted.

Brand turned to her and nodded. "Yes, Ambassador, your sons are already aboard Centerpoint. I apologize if some of this comes as a surprise, but all information regarding Centerpoint has been issued on a need-to-know basis."

Leia looked away from Brand to hide her distress. She also refused to acknowledge Isolder's inquisitive stare.

"When the Yuuzhan Vong fleet emerges from hyperspace in the Corellia system, the interdiction field will rob them of the ability to go to lightspeed, and will essentially hold them fast. When that much has been achieved, many of the warships anchored here, and at Kuat and Bothawui—all of which have been retrofitted with hyperwave inertial momentum sustainers produced by the

Fondor shipyards—will launch, penetrating the interdiction field at its farthest extreme, and advance through a series of microjumps to engage the enemy."

Brand swung to an ancillary holoprojector, above which was displayed a schematic of the HIMS. "For those of you unfamiliar with the hyperwave sustainer, the device relies on a gravitic sensor to alert a ship to an impending interdiction field, as well as to initiate a rapid shutdown of the hyperdrive. Simultaneously the sustainer allows for the creation of a static hyperspace bubble, which, while incapable of furnishing thrust, holds the ship in hyperspace while it is carried forward by momentum."

Brand turned to his audience. "Our ships will have one heck of a time trying to maintain formation, but they will be able to get the drop on the enemy fleet."

He looked over at the Hapans. "Prince Isolder, since your ships are not HIMS-equipped, your command will be responsible for preventing Yuuzhan Vong vessels from attempting an escape through the Outlier systems. The reasons for assigning you this task are twofold. Your Battle Dragons carry pulse-mass mines, which can effectively extend the limits of Centerpoint's interdiction field. To assist you in this, we are placing at your disposal four Immobilizer 418A Interdictor cruisers. But more important, your ships' weapons-linked battle computers provide for pinpoint accuracy against single targets, which is precisely what is required to dumbfound the dovin basals that protect Yuuzhan Vong vessels."

"Ordinarily we prefer swift, ruthless strikes," Isolder said. "But if surgical strikes are called for, then you shall have them, Commodore."

Leia managed not to wince. She knew, though, that she could take no more of Brand's briefing. His every gesture and assumption filled her with dread, no less so than Isolder's brash eagerness and posturing self-assurance.

Retreating from the surrounding din, she reached out with the Force for Anakin and Jacen, then for Jaina, Luke, Mara, and some of the other Jedi. Each returned a subtle resonance, which, if nothing else, allayed her concerns temporarily. But when Leia tried to reach out for Han—whom she could sometimes feel, even through his denial of the Force—all she got back were images of a raging torrent and a plunge into measureless blackness.

TWENTY-FOUR

Han fought to keep from drowning. Lungs screaming for oxygen, he broke the raging surface of the muddy torrent, spewing water like a Coruscant downspout gargoyle and flailing his arms to keep from being sucked under by the current. The water level in the drainage ditch was rising fast. It was likely that the flood would soon bob him to within a meter of the top of the retaining walls, but probably not before the water dumped him unceremoniously into the river that allegedly ran past Facility 17.

Rain continued to teem from the sky's granite underbelly, stinging Han's face and hampering visibility. Paddling madly with one hand, he cupped the other to his mouth and shouted for Droma, but got no response. A loud slapping noise brought him around to find the crashed landspeeder gaining on him, upright and surfing the current.

The narrowness of the ditch worked for and against him. With no way to be sure that the landspeeder wouldn't follow and crush him under its crumpled nose, Han angled frantically for the smooth eastern wall. Once there he managed to arrest his forward motion momentarily, which allowed the landspeeder to catch up and come alongside of him. On a downward slap of the crumpled nose, Han launched himself for the driver's door, threw one leg over the top, and rolled himself into the cab, which, with the mix of threshed grain and rain, might as well have been filled with gruel. His body sticky with the stuff, he dragged himself into the driver's seat and repeatedly flicked the repulsor engine switch on the off chance it would fire up, but the collision had disabled the ignition system. Leaning forward with his hands clamped to the brackets that had supported the retractable windshield, he scanned the roiling water ahead to both sides, finally catching sight of Droma's tail, sticking straight out of the water like a flagpole.

Before Han could call out to him, the speeder was carried over the top of a sluice gate and down through a stretch of cataracts where the landscape was terraced. Droma disappeared under the rapids, then surfaced, only to disappear once more. Ultimately he heard Han's call over the noise of the rain and echoing thunder and lifted one arm free of the current in a panicked wave.

Precariously balanced in the pitching vehicle, Han stretched out both hands and grabbed hold of Droma as the landspeeder shot past him. The weight of the water-logged Ryn almost dragged Han out of the cab, but Droma helped by hooking his tail around a rear seat headrest and hauling himself aboard.

"You can just drop me at the next intersection," he said, collapsed onto the seat and panting.

"How far do you figure the river is?" Han shouted.

"Close," Droma said, tugging himself into a sitting position. "I'm just glad to be out . . ."

A persistent rumbling noise erased the rest of it. Han glanced at the sky, then put the edge of his hand to his brow and peered over the bouncing nose of the speeder. The rain and the tall stalks of grain to either side made it difficult to see anything, but dead ahead the fields seemed to end abruptly.

"What's that noise?" Droma asked suddenly.

Han whirled on him. "You said that the map showed this ditch running directly into the river?"

Droma nodded uncertainly.

"Think hard: Was it a topographical map?"

Droma tugged on his mustache in thought. "Come to think of it, it was."

"And were there a whole bunch of parallel lines where the ditch met the river?"

Droma's eyes opened wide.

"Hold on!" Han yelled, even as the landspeeder was tipping forward.

The waterfall was no more than fifteen meters high, but the strength of the current was such that the speeder was propelled right out of the water as it went over the brink. For the briefest moment it seemed as if they would nose-dive into the swollen river below, but then the stern of the landspeeder began to tip forward inexorably, and a heartbeat later the vehicle was upside down, spilling its contents of passengers and porridge into yet another muddy deluge.

Han made his body rigid as he fell, breaking the water with his feet and letting momentum carry him along. Above him he heard the concussive report of the landspeeder slamming into the river facedown. Ascending, he feared that he might surface directly under the inverted cab, but as it happened he and Droma emerged with the landspeeder between and slightly ahead of them.

Han raised his hand and pointed to the southern bank, which was not only closer but also a lot less steep.

"Can you make it?"

"I'm not a very strong swimmer!" Droma replied with a note of desperation.

Han maneuvered alongside him and hooked his left

arm around Droma's waist. "Just kick like mad. Leave the steering to me."

Droma nodded. "Just be sure to miss those rocks."

Han twisted around to see them closing fast on white-water rapids, made all the more perilous by protruding boulders. He let go of Droma and rolled over onto his back, paddling hard to keep his head above water. Caught in the current, there was nothing to do but surrender to it and hope for the best.

The first drop took them across the face of a water-smoothed boulder and down into a pocket, from which they were quickly flushed down another drop. Skirting the edge of a froth-covered whirlpool, they rode a sinuous course between tall rocks, then plunged several meters into a swirling pool. Off to Han's left the land-speeder rammed into a sloping rock, went airborne in an end-over-end flip, and wound up impaled on a sharp-topped rock. Droma followed, barely missing the same rock and falling like a stone into the pool.

As suddenly as they had appeared, the cataracts were behind them, but the current was still strong enough to keep the swimmers from reaching the bank. Allowing the current to buoy him, Han craned his neck to get a look at what lay ahead. More white water came into view, but this time without rapids. Instead, a line of turbulence stretched clear across the river, as if the flow was being impeded by something just below the surface. Blinking water out of his eyes, Han saw through the rain that they were headed straight into a fine-mesh net strung bank to bank.

The resilient net gave as they struck it, but the current pinned them in place. Han was trying to claw his way along the net to the closer shore when a new sound from upstream compelled him to look over his shoulder. Soaring toward them on repulsorlift power a meter above the river was what might have been a flying garbage bin, except for the fact that it was equipped with a pair of reverse-articulated manipulator arms, which ended in padded jaws. Lights on the garbage bin's front panel blinked and tones sounded, as if in excitement at locating what it obviously had been sent to retrieve.

The same panel bore the corporate logo of Salliche Ag.

The three-meter-tall box slowed and hovered directly over the net. Han and Droma squirmed to avoid the thing's extending arms, but with scant effort the padded jaws succeeded in clamping around their waists and plucking them from the mesh. Lifting them out of the river, the arms swung inward. Hatch doors on the machine's dorsal surface hissed open, revealing a dark interior chamber waiting to receive them.

They alighted on a cushioned floor. The hatch doors closed before either of them could scramble out, and the garbage bin began to move away from the river in a southerly direction. In the amber glow of telltales, Han ran his hands over the walls, bringing them to a halt at an arrangement of sprayer nozzles. Then he cursed in sudden recognition of just what had captured them.

"This is a Scout Collector!"

"A what collector?" Droma asked, distressed even in ignorance.

"A biological specimen collector. We're going to be flash-frozen!"

They got to their feet and began to leap up and down, pounding their hands ineffectually on the underside of the compartment doors. Giving up on the effort, Droma dropped down on his haunches, breathing hard, and eventually Han joined him.

"The hand of fate," Droma said nastily. "But you still owe me one life."

Han turned to him. "What are you talking about?"

"I saved you aboard the *Queen of Empire* when Reck made you jump into the drop shaft, then I freed you from the *Falcon*'s escape pod when Elan was trying to kill you."

"Yeah, so who just yanked you out of the drainage ditch?"

"That's the one I'm counting," Droma said.

"What about my getting you out of district headquarters in one piece?"

"That was a rescue, not a life-save. We don't know that my life was endangered, so the best we could say is that you rescued me from imprisonment."

Han shook his head and laughed. "All right, I still owe you one."

"Then pay up now—get us out of here."

Han clapped Droma on the back, then grew serious. "Listen, in case we don't get out of this, it's been good flying with you."

"I know," Droma said flatly, then added, "You mean that—about flying together?"

"I did mean it. Now I'm not so sure."

Han heard the Scout Collector's repulsorlifts cut in, and he stood up. "We're landing. If they open the hatches before our frost bath, we go for them, agreed?"

Droma extended his hand and Han shook it.

The Collector settled down to the ground. Noises could be heard from outside, then the hatches began to open. Han and Droma prepared themselves.

"Thank goodness you're alive," a droid voice said.

Han stared, waiting for his eyes to adjust to bright, overhead lights. "Baffle?"

A ladder was lowered into the interior, and Han and Droma clambered out. The Collector had put down in a spacious indoor facility. Overhead rumbles told Han that they were underground. Dozens of droids were about, articulating greetings in their own fashion.

"These must be the friends you mentioned," Droma surmised, shaking water off himself like a howlrunner.

"How the heck did you find us?" Han asked.

"We have been monitoring all developments," Baffle said. "Security scanners, security team exchanges, satellite-supplied real-time opticals, even the irrigation and sluice-gate control systems. When we ascertained that you were being carried to the river, we quickly arranged for the net and Scout Collector—a vehicle that has been in storage for some time."

"Where are we?" Droma asked, once beyond his astonishment.

"Beneath the spaceport." Baffle indicated a nearby tunnel. "This leads directly to the bay where your freighter is docked."

Han looked at Droma and grinned smugly.

"Thank you for all you have accomplished," Baffle said, speaking for all the droids.

Han nodded in dismissal, then narrowed his eyes. "Listen, if you were monitoring us, then so was Salliche. They probably have satcam recordings of exactly what happened at the river. All of you had better clear out of here—fast."

"Our capture won't matter. Our goal has been accomplished. Already we are in the process of removing the remote restrainers from many of the droids you freed, and our protest demonstration is moving from the planning stage to actuality."

"Protest demonstration?" Droma asked.

"I'll explain later." Han turned to Baffle. "After what you've done, I almost hate to ask, but were you able to gather any data on the *Trevee*?"

"Yes. Our original supposition that the ship was

headed for a destination Rimward of Abregado-rae was correct. That destination, however, is neither Thyferra nor Yag'Dhul, but the very place of my activation: Fondor."

The name practically screamed to Han. An industrial planet in the system of the same name, Fondor was famous for its huge, orbital construction facilities. During the Rebellion, Fondor's shipyards had turned out several *Super*-class Star Destroyers.

Han turned to Droma. "Fondor is where we'll find your clanmates."

Droma looked puzzled. "Then they're obviously not at Facility 17."

Han shook his head. "We got here too late. They cut a deal with the Tholatin crew. The *Trevee* is their ship."

Droma stared at him in anguished disbelief.

"If I might make a suggestion, sirs," Baffle said. "You could save yourselves three hyperspace jumps by using the seldom-used Gandeal-Fondor hyperlane. It was originally blazed by the Empire to move ships efficiently between Fondor and Coruscant, and I'm certain we could provide you with the necessary jump coordinates."

Han smiled broadly. "You're some droid, Baffle. I hope your message gets out."

"Oh, it will, sir. With the HoloNet attention our protest receives, droids throughout the galaxy will stand up for their rights."

"They'll have you to thank for it."

"I am merely a part of a greater whole," Baffle said, without affect. "It is my duty to do all I can for my comrades."

Han and Droma traded brief glances. "And ours," Han said.

* * *

Fixed in place by a dollop of organic adhesive, Wurth Skidder tracked Chine-kal as the commander completed his second circle around him. Concentric to Chine-kal's circuit stood a dozen guards armed with amphistaffs and other weapons.

"I'm surprised that your powers don't allow you to break free of our blorash jelly," Chine-kal mused as he glanced at Skidder's immobilized feet. "Perhaps you're not as powerful as we think you are."

In a flash of anger Skidder drew on the Force to create a vacuum around the Yuuzhan Vong's head.

Chine-kal gasped, and his hands flew to his throat. "Very good," he rasped when the Force bubble dissipated. "Very good." He breathed deeply. "Show me something else."

The venomous look in Skidder's eyes was proof that he was at least considering it, but the look was short-lived and soon replaced by a disdainful smile.

"You don't want to hurl me off my feet?" Chine-kal asked. "Put words in my mouth? Fasten me to the deck as I have you?"

Skidder said nothing.

"Can you levitate yourself as easily as you do objects?" When Skidder couldn't be goaded into responding, Chine-kal heaved a purposeful sigh. "Your reluctance to fight is as disappointing as it is incomprehensible. You—the Jedi—are a threat to us, and we are eager to exterminate you. And yet while we're a clear threat to you, you do little more than slink about, offering support or intelligence, but never really participating as warriors. Is that why you term yourselves guardians rather than soldiers?"

Chine-kal waved a hand to signal that he was being rhetorical. "Since you and our yammosk already have a relationship, I'll have to think of a different method of breaking you. But you *will* be broken in the end." He fell silent for a moment, then said, "Let me show you something."

The commander moved to the membranous bulkhead that was actually the outer wall of the starship and voiced a command that rendered a portion of it transparent. A gibbous planet of blue seas and green and brown landmasses hung in the blackness. Closer was a moon of fair size, what could be seen of its bright-side hemisphere dominated by a domed city.

"Do you recognize it?" Chine-kal asked. "The planet is Kalarba, and the moon is Hosk. The domed city is called Hosk Station, and is apparently something of a technological wonder, filled with droids and other machine aberrations." He turned to Skidder. "To us, the Jedi are no better than the machines the sundry species of this galaxy befriend as if they were living beings. The Jedi are as much a profanation of nature as Hosk Station is a desecration of the moon it has overwhelmed. I am therefore going to order the moon destroyed. You may consider the destruction indicative of the horrors that await your mind during the breaking."

Chine-kal turned to one of his junior officers. But before he could utter another word, the hull suddenly returned to its opaque state and the ship was jolted strongly enough to send everyone but the jelly-secured Jedi to the deck. A subaltern staggered into the hold while Chine-kal and the guards were struggling to regain their footing.

"Commander, we are under attack!"

Chine-kal blanched. "Attack? There was no sign of New Republic warships when we entered this system."

"The aggressors are starfighters, Commander. They were lying in wait behind the second of Kalarba's moons."

"Then why aren't our escort ships repelling them?"

"With eight coralskippers already destroyed, some of the starfighters are succeeding in reaching the ship."

"Where is the vessel Supreme Commander Choka dispatched?"

"It has not yet arrived."

Another powerful explosion rocked the ship. Hurrying to Chine-kal's side, the subaltern barely managed to keep him from stumbling to the deck.

"The pilots are targeting our dovin basal drivers, Commander."

"Our drivers?"

"Their intent is to cripple us."

Chine-kal swung to Skidder, who was deep in contemplation. "They've come for you. But how could they know we were here? Unless, of course, they are Jedi." He stared at Skidder, then shook his head. "No, not even you have the ability to call across space to your confederates." He glanced at his subaltern. "But this sneak attack is no accident."

"Commander," the junior officer said cautiously, "Supreme Commander Choka's villip communication originated on Nal Hutta."

Chine-kal took a moment to consider it, then scowled in revelation. "The Hutts divulged our location." He squared his shoulders and adjusted the fall of his cloak. "Ready the ship for lightspeed. We'll rendezvous with the fleet in the target system."

The subaltern's hands flew to his shoulders, but he remained where he was. "Commander, is it advisable to show ourselves in advance of the fleet?"

Chine-kal glowered at him. "Would you risk allowing the yammosk to sustain damage here, at the hands of a group of would-be rescuers?"

The subaltern offered a second, chastened salute. "No, Commander."

"Then do as I say. And one more thing: See to it that Randa and his bodyguards are confined to their chambers. We'll deal with him once we have the protection of the fleet."

Close to Hosk, Kyp Durron urged his X-wing on, even though he knew that he would not be able to overtake the accelerating Yuuzhan Vong clustership.

"It's going to jump," Ganner told him over the net.

"My droid's telling me the same thing," Kyp responded. He opened the net to the rest of the Dozen. "Listen up, everyone. Set your navicomputers to record vanishing bearings and calculate possible course projections. Deak, see if you can't tag that ship with a hyperspace beacon before it gets away."

"I'm on it, Kyp."

Not a moment later the enemy vessel vanished. Kyp fixed his eyes on the cockpit display screen while the craft's astromech unit went to work on plotting the vessel's possible destinations. Shortly, a list of star systems resolved on screen, the most probable one highlighted in blue and flashing.

"I've got a high-confidence objective," Ganner reported.

"Likewise," Deak and a couple of the others added.

"Let's hear it," Kyp told them.

"Fondor," five voices said in unison.

In Hutt space, Nas Choka, Malik Carr, and Nom Anor stood on the bridge of the supreme commander's helix battleship watching a villip-choir feed of the fleet mobilization.

A subaltern interrupted their captivation.

"Supreme Commander," he began, saluting, "a message from the commander of the craft sent to collect the captured Jedi. Coralskipper pilots encountered at

Kalarba report that the *Crèche* fell under attack by a battle group of New Republic starfighters. Endangered, Commander Chine-kal's vessel fled the fray."

Nas Choka stared at him uncomprehendingly. "Fled to where?"

"To the target, Supreme Commander. To Fondor."

Nas Choka whirled in alarm to Malik Carr. "How soon before our advance elements reach Fondor?"

"Soon," the commander said, letting it go at that.

"The yammosk won't be adequately protected until we arrive," Nas Choka remarked, mostly to himself. "What is the status of the New Republic fleet?"

"Massed at the worlds Commenor, Kuat, and Bothawui."

"And the hyperspace routes linking Bothawui to Fondor?"

"Sown with obstacles."

Nas Choka turned slightly to favor Nom Anor with a faint smile. "It appears that you have been successful in persuading them that we plan to attack Corellia."

Nom Anor inclined his head in a nod.

"Then it shouldn't matter if we advance the attack." Nas Choka swung to his subaltern. "Apprise all commanders that we launch for Fondor as soon as the final coralskippers are docked."

In the passenger hold of the *Trevee*, Gaph danced while he sang:

Life is a journey without end,
for the Ryn more than any.
From a home unknown we wander,
Star to star in a constant quest.
We abhor the stars for what they have wrought:
Instigators of our ill-fortune,

Grave sentinels of our fate.
But we load our packs with joy;
And song and dance follow at our heels.
Now Abregado-rae awaits;
Home for a time,
Until we are forced to wander anew.

Melisma and the other Ryn capered with him or accompanied his improvised song on musical instruments. Some hummed and tooted through their perforated beaks, while the rest played drums, finger cymbals, and flutes fashioned from scavenged parts of machinery, pilfered gear, or whatever was handy.

The fact that the festive melody of Gaph's song belied an underlying melancholy was lost on those non-Ryn refugees who clapped in time to the music and applauded the dancers' graceful leaps and fleet pirouettes.

Gaph was only a stanza into a second verse when the *Trevee* shuddered abruptly.

"We're reverting from hyperspace," one of the refugees said when the musicians had stopped playing.

Melisma, Gaph, and some of the other Ryn hurried excitedly to an observation blister, eager for a first glimpse of Abregado-rae. But in place of the light-green sphere they had expected to see was a brownish world, partially eclipsed by clouds sullied with industrial pollutants and surrounded by hundreds of enormous orbital construction platforms.

"This isn't Abregado-rae," someone behind Melisma said.

"Then where are we?" she asked.

"This is Fondor," a human male supplied in understated astonishment.

Surprised murmurs began to spread through the crowd. Then all at once hatches throughout the passenger hold hissed open, admitting a score of heavily armed crew members. Agitated by misgiving as well as concern, the refugees backed away from the bulkheads, forming a ragged circle in the center of the hold.

"Slight change of plans, folks," the crew's obvious spokesperson announced when the murmuring had ceased—the same human Melisma and the other Ryn had come to call Tall. "Turns out we're going to have to drop you here."

"But you promised to deliver us to Abregado-rae," someone thought to point out.

Tall grinned. "Let's just say we overshot our stop."

Impassioned conversations broke out. In some ways Fondor was preferable to Abregado-rae, but the blaster rifles and the tone of Tall's announcement contributed an undercurrent of foreboding to the unforeseen development.

"Has Fondor agreed to accept us?" someone demanded.

"That's not our concern."

"Then where on Fondor will we be off-loaded?"

Tall stared at the Bimm who had asked the question. "Who said anything about Fondor?" He moved to the observation blister and pointed to a crescent-shaped shipbuilding platform. "That's where you're getting off. The facility is temporarily unoccupied, but at least you'll have breathable air and artificial gravity."

"What about provisions?" a human asked above the increasing turmoil.

"Do you plan to inform the authorities?" someone else asked.

Tall waved everyone silent. "We're not barbarians. We'll provide you with enough flash-dried nutrients to last you a couple of local days."

"A couple of days?" a voice squeaked. "It could be months before anyone finds us!"

"Oh, I sincerely doubt that," Tall said. "The Tapani

sector is about to become very crowded. Someone's bound to notice you."

"Couldn't you at least bring us to Fondor?" a human female pleaded.

Tall gave his head a firm shake. "We can't afford to be here when the fireworks begin."

TWENTY-FIVE

With the exception of those in the Corporate Sector, few planetary systems had been exploited to the degree that Fondor had—especially for a system so close to the Core. That part of the Tapani sector had originally been designated a manufacturing and shipbuilding center precisely because of the surfeit of resource-rich asteroids and moons, and worlds ripe for abuse. But where the colossal corporations that dominated Bilbringi, Kuat, Sluis Van, and other shipbuilding centers made a pretense of picking up after themselves, no such efforts had ever been made at Fondor. With the space lanes perilous with free-floating construction debris, Fondor's several small moons looking as if something had taken huge bites out of them, and the planet itself overcrowded, polluted, and corrupted by profiteers providing diversions for the millions of workers who had nowhere else to spend their hard-earned credits, the system was a blight on the Rimma Trade Route.

Many were quick to assert that Fondor's nimbus of orbital docking stations and oblate zero-g construction facilities had never operated more smoothly than when the Empire had appropriated them, and in fact, conditions had clearly deteriorated over the past twenty standard years—more so since the arrival of the Yuuzhan Vong.

Emerging from the Gandeal hyperlane out past Fondor's

outermost moon, the *Falcon* was immediately detected and scanned by First Fleet command and control, which had been assigned the task of safeguarding the shipyards after the fall of Obroa-skai.

"Give them our actual transponder signal," Han instructed Droma while he threaded the *Falcon* toward a pack of freighters and warships awaiting clearance to enter Fondor space. "It's our best chance of getting through."

"How could the *Trevee* have entered?" Droma asked while he flicked switches on the console.

Han snorted. "A ten-year-old slicer piloting a thirty-year-old Headhunter could penetrate military security. The *Trevee* could have legitimate business here, or whoever's in charge of the Tholatin operation could have provided the crew with clearance codes." He looked at Droma and grinned. "Look who I'm telling. The Ryn are probably pros at just this sort of thing."

"Only by necessity," Droma said ingenuously.

A crisp voice crackled from the cockpit annunciators. "*Millennium Falcon*, this is First Fleet control. Please state your point of origin and the nature of your business."

"Gandeal," Han said into his headset mike. "And it's more pleasure than business. We're supposed to rendezvous with friends who may have arrived ahead of us. Their ship is the *Trevee*. Nar Shaddaa registry."

The communications officer at the other end of the link took a long moment to respond. "Pardon me for asking, *Millennium Falcon*, but am I speaking with General Han Solo?"

"That's former general to you, Control," Han said jocularly.

"A genuine pleasure to be talking with you, sir. As to your request, the *Trevee* received clearance a short while ago. Unfortunately, sir, they made their cargo drop in an area off-limits to unregistered ships—especially ships with the rectenna array and firepower rating yours boasts."

"Just like I thought," Han muttered to Droma. "They scammed their way in." He reopened the comlink. "Control, can you at least tell us where the *Trevee* made her drop?"

"Negative, sir. I suggest you direct your request to Defense Force command downside. The best I can do from here is turn you over to Fondor command."

"Understood, Control. And thanks for the help."

"Stand by to receive routing and navigational beacon data."

"Standing by."

Han set his elbows on the console and regarded the misshapen moons and hundreds of active construction platforms that crowded local space. The bright, sweeping crescent of Fondor dominated the backdrop. "Well, this oughta be a snap. Only a couple of billion cubic kilometers to search—not to mention Fondor itself."

Droma glanced at him. "We could initiate a drive-signature scan for the *Trevee*."

Han thought about it. "Control said they'd already delivered their cargo. Hyperspace jumps aren't permitted inside the orbit of Fondor's sixth moon, so they'll be running on repulsor power or sublight. But they could be anywhere." He ran his hand down his face, stretching the bags under his eyes. "You've just marooned a couple of hundred refugees. What's your next move?"

Droma sat back, fingering his pale mustache. "Perhaps you want to hang around and spend some of the credits you just earned. Or you jump to Abregado-rae for the same purpose."

"Maybe. But remember, you know that Fondor is likely to be attacked sometime soon, which means the

Rimma is going to get real busy, real fast, from Abregado-rae clear to Sullust."

Droma frowned. "In that case, you'd want to be as far from Fondor as possible. You might even want to lie low for a while before going on a spending spree."

Han and Droma looked at each other. "Tholatin," they said at the same time.

Han straightened in his chair, taking hold of the control yoke while Droma interrogated the navicomputer.

"The best jump point for Tholatin is just Coreward of Fondor aphelion."

Han cut his eyes to the star chart Droma put onscreen. With Fondor less than two months from aphelion, the jump point was relatively close to where the *Falcon* had reverted to realspace from the Gandeal hyperlane. Engaging the thrusters, he veered the ship through an abrupt climbing bank, away from the line of navigational buoys that would have directed them to Fondor.

Instantly the cockpit annunciator came to life. "*Millennium Falcon,* why are you altering course?"

"Uh, slight drive malfunction," Han said, spicing his voice with false alarm. "But we should have things under control momentarily."

"Maintain your present position, *Falcon.* You are entering restricted space. I repeat: Stay where you are. An escort ship will be dispatched to provide assistance."

"Don't bother sending an escort," Han said, even as the *Falcon* was accelerating. "We'll return to the holding point and make repairs there."

"Negative, *Falcon.* You have entered restricted space. Return to original course headings immediately."

Han increased the ship's speed while the navicomputer aimed them for the remotest point of Fondor's elliptical orbit. A host of capital ships, barges, tenders, and freighters came into view, all maneuvering toward various jump points. Abruptly, an indicator on the friend-or-foe authenticator flashed.

"IR emission and ion exhaust recognition," Droma said excitedly. "Confirmation of the *Trevee*." He called up a magnified view of the supplied coordinates, then pointed to the run-down, pod-shaped ship at the center of the display screen. "There!"

Han smiled in recollection of the opticals Baffle and the other droids had provided. "That's her, all right."

"*Millennium Falcon*," the voice of fleet command and control barked. "This is your final warning."

"Turn that thing off," Han snapped.

Droma lowered the gain, then swiveled back to the console. "Deflector shields raised," he reported without being asked. "Fire-control computer on-line."

Han reached to his left for the servo that controlled the dorsal quad laser. When they could see the *Trevee* through the viewport, he tugged the throttle lever toward him, streaking the *Falcon* beneath the freighter, then barrel-rolled to port across the *Trevee*'s blunt bow.

"Now they know we're here," he said, decelerating to hang on the *Trevee*'s twin-thrustered tail.

"They're scanning us," Droma said. "Weapons powering up."

"Give me a schematic of the ship." Han glanced at the data Droma retrieved and tapped his forefinger against the display screen. "Their hyperdrive is just forward of the aft fin. Take over."

Droma tightened his hands around the copilot's yoke, gluing the *Falcon* to the *Trevee*'s stern. Han centered the quad laser's targeting reticle over the freighter's sleek stabilizer.

"Weapons fire!"

The words had scarcely left Droma's mouth when blue

hyphens of energy raced toward the *Falcon*, splashing against her forward deflector shield and jarring the ship without doing damage.

"Ion cannon," Droma said. "They're maintaining target lock. Hyperdrive is enabling."

Energy streaked from the freighter's aft cannon turret. Droma tipped the *Falcon* to one side, then the other, then rolled out to starboard and kept the ship inverted while Han lined up his shot.

Violent light pulsed from the quad laser's reciprocating barrels, blowing the *Trevee*'s fin away and scoring a ragged line along her aft hull. Gouts of molten alloy streamed from the freighter as she banked in desperation, firing continuously at her pursuer. Droma powered the *Falcon* through a loop, giving Han a clear shot at the freighter's overheated cannon, which Han quickly put out of its misery. Then, for good measure, Han took out the worthless shield generator.

"Open a frequency to the ship," he said.

"No response." Droma glanced at the sensor suite screen. "They're heading straight out of the system, all speed."

Han compressed his lips. "What do they think they're doing? They can't jump and they can't outrun us." He turned to Droma, who was still staring at the scanner display. "What? What?"

"Six New Republic fighters—X-wings. Coming up fast on our stern."

Han cursed to himself. "A chase group from fleet command." He slipped into the headset and adjusted the controls.

A new voice issued from the speakers. "—heave to, *Falcon*. Don't make us go to guns."

Han quirked a grin. "Let's see you try," he said, mostly to himself. He opened the comm. "This is Captain Han

Solo of the *Millennium Falcon*. We're not looking for a fight, squadron leader. Patch me through to the flight ops commander." He covered the mouthpiece with his hand. "Time to pull rank."

"I'm already listening in, Captain Solo," a bass voice said in irritation. "You're in violation of security regulations. Any further infractions and you'll be seeing the brig before this day is out—regardless of your history or who you're married to. Are we clear?"

The remark served only to incite Han further. "You've got more important things to do than arrest me, Commander."

"Don't press your luck, Captain Solo. Follow your escorts to fleet HQ and I'll consider entertaining your notion of what my priorities should be."

"Listen to me, Commander. The Yuuzhan Vong have targeted Fondor for attack. I don't know exactly when, but it's going to be soon. I suggest that the fleet be put on full alert."

"That's absurd, Solo. We've received no such information."

"I don't have time to go into all the details—"

"The chase group is breaking off," Droma interrupted, eyes fixed on the scanner screen.

Han glanced at the display and snorted a laugh. "I don't often enjoy name-dropping, but . . ." He let his words trail off. Droma's mouth was hanging open, and he had one quivering hand raised to the viewport. Simultaneously with a chime from the hyperwave warning indicator, Han swung forward to see that they were soaring straight into what anyone else might have believed was an uncharted meteor storm, but what he knew to be enemy vessels, decanting to realspace by the hundreds.

Instinctively, he stood the *Falcon* on her side, weaving her through a swarm of carrier, destroyer, and cruiser analogs, none of which appeared to take the slightest interest in the *Falcon* or even the much larger *Trevee*.

"Evasive action!" Droma said, finding his voice at last. "Countermeasures!"

Han wrestled with the controls. "What do you think I'm doing!"

Warships continued to materialize to all sides, more than Han would have believed possible—and certainly more than enough to engage and ultimately overwhelm Fondor's defenses. Already the vanguard vessels were firing, launching molten projectiles and blinding streams of plasma at picket craft and warships alike. Han swerved the *Falcon* away from the main battle group, then accelerated as the *Trevee* had done, still shooting for the aphelion coordinates, now if only to distance itself from the onslaught.

"That's why they were running," Han remarked. "They knew the Yuuzhan Vong were on their way." His face contorted by anger, he triggered a short burst from the quad lasers, though more to terrorize the crew of the *Trevee* than to further disable the ship. Then, just when it appeared that both ships had made it safely through the throng, a final enemy vessel emerged. Looking more like a wedded cluster of tough-skinned bubbles than a chunk of scabrous coral, the new arrival narrowly missed colliding with the *Trevee*, but sent it into an out-of-control tumble nevertheless.

Intrigued, Han leaned toward the viewport to have a closer look at the ship, then immediately changed course, vectoring directly for the newcomer.

"One on one," he snarled. "We can live with those odds."

With the *Falcon* up on its side once more, Han and Droma assailed the clustership with sustained bursts from the dorsal and ventral quad lasers. Most of the bolts were engulfed by gravitic anomalies long before they reached the ship, but a surprising few got through. The reason became clear when Han realized that the vessel was taking rear fire from a motley group of New Republic fighters. Overtaxed and distracted, the dovin basals that shielded the Yuuzhan Vong vessel were obviously failing.

Caution forgotten, Han at once sharpened the angle of their attack and shed velocity so that the clustership would come across the *Falcon*'s vector. When it did, he and Droma opened up with both guns, hammering the enemy with massive outpourings of energy. Gas and flame belched from the ship, then one of the spherical components imploded, deflating as if pricked by a pin. Slowing, the ship began to list to port, then rolled completely over, like a defeated creature showing its belly to an aggressor.

"Thanks for the assist, YT-1300," someone said over the hailing channel.

"The pilot of the lead X-wing," Droma clarified.

"That's no military squadron," Han said.

"When did the fighting start, YT?"

Han opened a channel to the fighters. "The enemy checked in just ahead of you. The shipyards are already under bombardment. Who are you guys?"

"Kyp's Dozen," the pilot said.

"Kyp Durron! What in blazes are you doing out here?"

Put off his guard, Kyp fell silent for a moment. "Han, is that you?" he asked tentatively.

"None other."

"Is that a new paint job, or did you accidentally bring the *Falcon* too close to a star?"

"Long story."

"So is ours. We've been chasing that bubble ship since

Kalarba. The Yuuzhan Vong have captives aboard, Wurth Skidder among them. What about you?"

"The freighter at your starboard marooned a group of refugees somewhere in this system. I figure we can convince them to show us where they made the drop."

"If you're headed back into that fray, you could do with some support. I'll assign two of my people to fly with you."

"I'll take them. But what are you planning to do about the captives?"

"Go aboard and rescue them."

Han uttered a laugh. "Leave it to a Jedi to take on the impossible."

"It's our mandate," Kyp said.

"We'll be back to help out as soon as we can," Han promised.

"May the Force be with you, Han."

"Yeah, you too."

At Orbital Shipyard 1321, the Star Destroyer *Amerce* was nearing completion—one of thirty such massive warships being readied at Fondor, in addition to hundreds of smaller vessels. Owing to having had to retrofit a flotilla of ships with hyperwave inertial momentum sustainers, several of the major yards had fallen behind schedule, but confidence was high at 1321 that work on the *Amerce* would conclude within a local month. The launch would finally mean leave for the tens of thousands of shipfitters who had spent the better part of a standard year working on the great ship, shoulder to shoulder with droids and other machines, frequently for back-to-back shifts, and sometimes in zero-g for days on end.

Creed Mitsun, human foreman of a mixed-species crew of electricians, was more eager than most for leave.

The substantial credits he'd amassed were programming an escape route from his bank account, and his companion of the past two years—an exotic dancer who worked in Fondor City—was threatening to return to Sullust if Mitsun didn't get himself down the well before too long.

Lately not a relative day passed when Mitsun didn't wake from dreams that were every bit as fatiguing as work itself without fearing that the *Amerce* would never be completed and leave would never be granted. To make matters worse, space raid drills had become quotidian events, jarring everyone from sleep long before they were required to report to work.

Today was no exception.

Adding his elaborate groan to a chorus of similar protests issuing from all corners of the bunkroom, Mitsun buried his head under a pillow and declined to move, despite the unrelenting howling of sirens and the insistent appeals from the Bothan female who had the bunk opposite his.

"Come on, Chief," she pleaded, trying to shake him into motion. "You know what happens if we don't report to our stations."

"I don't care," Mitsun said, his voice muffled by the pillow. "How do they expect us to finish the *Amerce* if we're asleep on our feet for most of our shifts?"

"Please, Chief. If you get suspended, things'll be worse for everyone."

Mitsun started to wave her away, but suddenly found himself rudely tossed from his third-tier bunk to the hard deck.

"What's the idea?" he stammered, hauling himself to his feet, only to see that the Bothan female and almost everyone else in sight had been similarly displaced.

Without warning, the facility sustained a follow-up

blow, powerful enough to topple several banks of bunks and hurl everyone halfway across the hold.

"This is no drill!" someone yelled.

Mitsun heard the words but refused to give them credence. Stepping over sprawled bodies, he hurried to the outer hull bulkhead and slammed the heel of his hand against the release stud that raised the hold's night curtain and blast door.

By the time the curtain had pocketed itself, several other workers had joined Mitsun at the underlying transparisteel panel, beyond which the *Amerce* lay half in ruins, holed and venting its guts into space.

From the direction of Fondor's closest moon came a storm of asteroidlike ships, so fixed on demolishing Shipyard 1321 that they weren't even bothering to discharge weapons, but were instead *accelerating* toward the battleship and the facility.

"Leave cancelled," Mitsun said to himself as he caught sight of two coralskippers hurtling directly for the bunkroom.

Leia followed briskly on the heels of the colonel who had fetched her from her cabin aboard the *Yald*, saying only that it was urgent that she join Commodore Brand in the tactical information center quickest. She and Brand's adjutant were stepping from the turbolift on the secure deck that housed the TIC when she nearly collided with Isolder, who had obviously just arrived from the *Song of War*.

"Do you have any idea what this is about?" he asked her.

The question was pointed, though without his being aware of it. What had begun at Gyndine as vague misgiving and had swelled to apprehension as a result of the vision on Hapes had now become unmitigated dread—as tangible as any fear or phobia she had ever experienced—even while its source and substance remained veiled.

Hours of meditation had allowed Leia to determine that part of her apprehension was centered on Anakin and Jacen and the forecasted attack on Corellia. But just how her concerns for them were connected to the foreboding that swirled like excited electrons around Isolder—and more specifically around Commander Brand's battle plans—she could not say or even guess at. She knew only that her composure was unraveling, and that forces were converging in a way that no one had anticipated.

"Leia?" Isolder said.

The Jedi's weapon is her mind. When a Jedi is distracted, when she loses her focus, she becomes vulnerable . . .

"I'm sorry, Isolder," she said at last, "but I don't know what this is about."

He studied her in silence while they hastened for the war room and entered side by side. Brand, looking stricken, gazed up at them from his tall stool alongside a sprawling horizontal plotting panel. In fact, beneath all the frantic activity, everyone in the enormous room seemed to be moving in a daze.

"On-screen," Brand ordered one of the technicians, as Leia and Isolder approached.

Leia glanced at a nearby array of holographic displays, instantly aware that she was seeing her vision realized—or at least some part of it. Whether the real-time images were being transmitted from satellites or an orbital facility was impossible to discern, and unimportant in any event. One holo showed dozens of Yuuzhan Vong and New Republic warships firing mercilessly at each other, while wings of snubfighters and coralskippers slalomed through the wreckage of orbital docks.

Another holo revealed ships close to completion blackened, ruptured, and keeled over in their berthing spaces, command towers and gun turrets in ruins, clouds of debris making it impossible to get a clear fix on anything. Elsewhere, Yuuzhan Vong carrier analogs were hurling tempests of coralskippers toward weapons platforms and the surface of a world already afflicted by industrial devastation.

"That's the *Amerce*," Brand said grimly, indicating one of the destroyed ships. He pointed to another holo display. "That's the *Anlage*."

Leia looked at him in confusion. "Those aren't Corellian vessels."

Brand showed her one of the saddest looks she had ever seen. "The Yuuzhan Vong have struck at Fondor. They deceived us into believing they were going to attack Corellia, and they hit Fondor." The words tumbled from his mouth without emotion. "Our greatest hopes go with those ships. The First Fleet is doing all it can, but the enemy is literally flinging their coralskippers at any target that presents itself."

"The Hapan fleet is prepared to launch," Isolder said.

"No!" Leia found herself saying. Brand and Isolder stared at her. "No," she repeated quietly.

Brand looked at Isolder. "Thank you, Prince Isolder, but I've already ordered elements of the Fifth Fleet to launch from Bothawui. We're waiting to hear from them."

Leia swung to the communication console, her heart racing.

"Commenor command, this is Task Force Aleph," a distressed voice said. "The enemy has seeded all routes linking Bothawui and Fondor with dovin basal remotes. Half the task force has been yanked from hyperspace, and six ships have been diverted into collisions with mass shadows. We're in harm's way, sir. We have no choice but to retreat to the Outer Rim and jump to Fondor from Eriadu or Sullust."

"They'll arrive too late," Brand muttered, then turned to Isolder. "You say your forces are prepared?"

Isolder straightened to his full and considerable height. "Eager, Commodore."

Leia's breath caught in her throat, and the TIC began to spin before her eyes. She had to hook her arm through Brand's to keep from falling.

TWENTY-SIX

As near as anyone had been able to determine, coral-skippers didn't dock inside their carriers. Instead they were launched from and recovered by the carriers' elongated and branchlike projections. These facts passed briefly through Kyp Durron's mind as his X-wing loosed two proton torpedoes straight at the sphere the *Millennium Falcon*'s quad lasers had perforated and collapsed. The torpedoes did little more than blow a hole in what remained of the deflated globe, but one large and gaping enough to accommodate any of the disparate fighters that made up the Dozen.

"Eleven and Twelve, you have rear guard," Kyp said over the tactical net. "The rest of you form up on me. We're going inside."

Kyp urged his craft on, ignoring the strident protests of its astromech droid, which was clearly baffled by whatever readings the enemy ship was giving off. The Yuuzhan Vong were oxygen breathers, he reminded himself, which meant that their ships somehow manufactured atmosphere. He was less certain about gravity, though he surmised that the same dovin basals responsible for propulsion and protection provided gravity. As for places to land, he was willing to make do with any parcel of level deck, even if he had to pilot the X-wing to the heart of the ship to find that.

Ganner's modified Y-wing and seven other starfighters followed him through the breach opened by the torpedoes. The pair left behind would have to deal with anything that flew to the cluster ship's aid, at least until the *Falcon* and the remaining two fighters returned.

Kyp's determination took a quantum leap as soon as the X-wing entered the ruined sphere. Vacuum had bled the module of atmosphere, but gravity was close to human standard and there was ample room for all nine fighters to settle down on a deck that wasn't much different from the pitted hulls of the enemy warships. The *Falcon*'s powerful guns had made a mess of things, but even without the damage it would have been difficult to discern just what they were looking at. Kyp suspected that the hivelike structure at the rear of the space was a neuroengine of some sort, and that if he popped it open, he might find a couple of stunned dovin basals curled up inside.

"Breathers and blasters," he said over the net as the X-wing's canopy was opening.

Recalling his first contact with the Yuuzhan Vong in the Outer Rim, and the grotesque creature whose secretions had burned through the transparisteel of his XJ, Kyp had expected to find similar monstrosities waiting, but in fact, the hold was deserted. Ganner had obviously been thinking the same thing. Jumping agilely from the cockpit of the Y-wing, he said over the rebreather comm, "They've probably withdrawn to protect the yammosk."

"Then they've already simplified our mission," Kyp told him.

They unhooked their lightsabers from the belts of their flightsuits and thumbed them on, the sibilant hiss of the energy blades loud in the deserted chamber. Everyone else carried either a sidearm or a blaster rifle.

"Watch your step," Kyp advised. "The Yuuzhan Vong

have been known to make use of an immobilizing living jelly."

Warily they advanced on the wall of the adjacent sphere, ignorant as to whether they were moving forward or aft. Like the walls of the collapsed module, the curving bulkhead had an organic, membranous appearance. They searched futilely for anything analogous to a hatch release.

"There has to be a way of opening a portal from one sphere to the next," Deak said. "Maybe they're separated by hydrostatic fields." But while resilient, the bulkhead did not admit him when he pressed himself to it.

"Maybe it recognizes only Yuuzhan Vong," Ganner suggested.

"Now isn't the time to debate it," Kyp said. "We're not on a scientific survey."

He thrust his lightsaber straight into the curve. When the tip had sizzled through, Kyp rolled his wrists, gradually opening a circular hole large enough for them to step through. The hold on the far side of the bulkhead was no different from the one they had left.

"No oxygen," Ganner reported after glancing at an indicator strapped to his wrist.

They moved in single file into a passageway that might have been the gullet of an outsize creature. Colonies of microorganisms attached to the walls and ceiling provided a faint green bioluminescence. Eventually they came to another curving bulkhead, but this was equipped with an iris portal that admitted them into a sealed antechamber. The fact that the chamber served as an airlock didn't become evident until they stepped from it into a spacious hold that held breathable air.

There also were the Yuuzhan Vong warriors Kyp and Ganner had expected to encounter earlier on.

They were thirty strong, some sporting chitinous

armor, some without, but all of them armed with double-edged blades or the living staffs Kyp knew were capable of being employed as whips, clubs, swords, or spears. For a moment the two groups stood still, studying each other, then one warrior stepped forward and bellowed a phrase in his own language.

He made it sound like a statement, but the charge that immediately followed confirmed it as a war cry. Deak and the other non-Jedi opened fire with their blasters, dropping ten or more of the unarmored warriors before they had made it halfway across the hold. Kyp and Ganner glided into the press of survivors, their feet barely leaving the deck, telekinetically disarming some of their opponents even in the midst of parrying blows from stiffened amphistaffs or crosscuts by coufee blades and deflecting spears. One by one the Yuuzhan Vong succumbed to vertical slashes to the head or horizontal thrusts that found the only vulnerable places in the living armor, just below the armpits.

The two Jedi worked as a team whenever possible, back to back, or alongside each other, refusing to surrender any gained ground and minimizing the movements of their blades. Their relatively easy victories told them that the warriors were a different breed than the seasoned fighters they had battled on the Ithorian herd ship *Tafanda Bay*. Even so, some of the non-Jedi weren't faring as well. Two of Kyp's Dozen died—one beheaded by a coufee, the other pierced by a thrown amphistaff.

When Kyp and Ganner had thinned the throng, they separated to engage the last of the warriors one on one, Kyp entering into a savage battle with an opponent a head taller than him and as deft with his staff as Kyp was with his lightsaber; Ganner using a Force-summoned telekinetic burst to hurl his adversary into a trio of Yuuzhan Vong who had ganged up on Deak. Two of the three dropped to the deck, giving Deak the time he needed to raise his blaster rifle and kill the third, along with the one Ganner had thrown.

Kyp perceived the events peripherally. With his feet planted right foot forward, he held the lightsaber at waist level, its blade elevated acutely, gyrating his wrists to answer and divert the sweeping slashes and overhead blows of the Yuuzhan Vong's stiffened amphistaff. That Kyp remained rooted in place provoked the warrior to greater ferocity. Lunging, he thrust the vital weapon at Kyp's midsection, at once ordering it to lengthen and strike with its fangs. The amphistaff's abrupt transformation from sword to serpent caught Kyp by surprise, but only for a moment. Twisting the lightsaber around the pliable staff, he suddenly snapped the energy blade upward, flinging the staff from the warrior's grip and severing the Yuuzhan Vong's hand, just at the gap where his forearm guards met his gauntlets.

The dismembered fist fell to the deck, dark blood oozing from the warrior's truncated limb. The Yuuzhan Vong looked at Kyp in startled disbelief, then lowered his head and rushed forward, intent on ramming Kyp off his feet. A side step sabotaged the effort. As the weakened warrior stumbled past him, Kyp brought the lightsaber to shoulder height, then drove it into his foe's armpit, killing him instantly.

He stood over the fallen Yuuzhan Vong for a moment, then glanced around the hold at the carnage he and the others had wrought. Ganner and Deak were kneeling by their dead comrades.

"We'll remember them later," Kyp said, motioning everyone onward with the ignited lightsaber.

They moved deeper into the ship, crossing the threshold into yet another sphere without encountering any opposition. Since entering the vessel, Kyp had been struck by the fact that the Force was mute: not stifled, but silent. His Jedi skills hadn't been affected or compromised in any way, but it was as if he had entered a blank space on a map. All at once, though, he felt something through the Force, and a bit farther along they came to a sealed portal, similar to many they had passed, save for the feelings it roused.

Kyp turned to Ganner, who nodded in affirmation, then he thrust the blade of his lightsaber into the center of the portal. When he retracted the blade, air rushed noisily through the hole into the space beyond, and the portal irised open. Inside, scattered across a pliant floor fouled by sweat and more, sprawled a mixed-species mob of captives. Dressed in ragged robes and tunics, they were a gaunt lot, but alive. Gradually they began to stir as the hold filled with oxygen.

Kyp approached one of them—a gray-haired human who had probably started with a good deal more weight than some of the others. Near him lay two Ryn males and a female.

The man's rheumy eyes blinked open and played across Kyp's face, focusing finally on the deactivated lightsaber in his right hand.

"They're holding him on the deck below this one," the human said weakly. "Next module aft. But be careful, Jedi. He may not be the Wurth Skidder you remember."

Several of the more technically minded of the hoodwinked and now marooned Ruan refugees had succeeded in getting some of the orbital facility's systems on-line, so anyone who wished was able to watch the fall of Fondor in full color.

Most of the Yuuzhan Vong fleet was still dispersed in a broad arc out past Fondor's outermost moons, but a dozen or so carriers, heavily reinforced by escort craft, had moved Coreward. Like siege weapons of old, the carriers had flung their coralskippers against any targets that presented themselves, destroying New Republic warships and construction barges alike. But having thrown the First Fleet into disarray, they were now being more systematic about attacking the shipyards and pounding distant Fondor with flaming projectiles and streams of plasma.

Gazing at the chaos through an observation blister, Melisma decided that the Yuuzhan Vong weren't likely to spare even an empty shipyard, which—at the present rate of destruction—meant that the Ruan group had less than an hour to get their affairs in order. Most of the refugees had already come to grips with this and were off by themselves, crying quietly or praying to whatever gods they worshipped. But others were shrieking in fear and anger, insisting that efforts be made to alert Fondor command to their plight or, failing that, surrendering to the Yuuzhan Vong, even though that would mean sacrifice or captivity.

True to the fatalism they embraced as a creed, the Ryn were singing. The fact that they were capable of going to their deaths with grace and dignity had actually managed to impart a sense of calm to some of the distraught.

Melisma turned from the viewport to listen to the melodious lament R'vanna was leading. "If these folks realized that our forgeries are what got them into this situation, we'd be dead already," she told Gaph.

Her uncle only shrugged. "Even without the documents we provided, the pirates would have found some way. Remember, child, these people paid to leave Ruan."

"Is that your way of absolving us of guilt?"

"We're guilty of getting ourselves into this mess. But

that, too, is the Ryn way. If it's not others abusing us, we're abusing ourselves."

Melisma sighed. "Do we deserve this then—for not accepting Ruan's offer to work in the fields?"

"No one deserves to die this way, no matter what they have done. But listen, child, we're not dead yet, and until we are, we should enjoy the moment."

Melisma glanced out the viewport. "I don't know that I have any song left in me, Uncle."

He laughed. "Of course you do. There's song even in a final breath."

She forced a smile. "You begin."

Gaph smoothed his mustachios in thought. His right foot began to tap, and he had his mouth open to sing when a Sullustan stationed at one of the data consoles shouted for everyone's attention.

"The *Trevee* is returning!"

The singing and crying ceased, and groups of folks began to crowd around the console and into the observation blister. Someone off to Melisma's left pointed to a sleek shape, weaving its way toward the abandoned facility between missiles and plasma discharges.

"It's definitely the *Trevee*!" the Sullustan confirmed.

Hopeful exclamations gushed from all sides.

"Maybe they had a change of heart."

"Impossible. They got caught up in the battle and are looking for a place to hide."

"Someone learned what they did to us."

"That is the probable explanation," Gaph said in an authoritative voice. He gestured in the direction of the approaching transport. "I can't imagine where that YT-1300 freighter joined the *Trevee*, but I'm certain that the other two ships are New Republic starfighters."

* * *

Anakin's enabling the Centerpoint Station's interdiction field and starbuster capabilities was momentarily forgotten in the wake of the devastating news the New Republic colonel brought to the control room.

The Yuuzhan Vong had launched a sneak attack on Fondor.

Real-time images of the battle received over military channels and HoloNet feeds had fomented panic among the Mrlssi, whose home system bordered Fondor in the Tapani sector. For everyone else in the control room the images prompted a curious mix of relief and desperation. Here was Centerpoint, all dressed up and nowhere to go.

Thrackan Sal-Solo broke the mood.

"There is something we can do." He whirled on Anakin, a wild look in his eye. "We have the time-space coordinates of the Yuuzhan Vong fleet." He hurried to a console and called up a star chart. "Their warships are clustered Rimward of Fondor's fifth and sixth moons. We can target them by focusing Centerpoint's repulsor beam."

"We have no authority to take such actions," a technician said, loud enough to be heard over a dozen separate conversations that broke out. "We could miss and hit Fondor or even its primary. We can't assume the risk."

"We *must* assume the risk," a Mrlssi argued. "Fondor is lost if we do nothing."

The New Republic colonel glanced at Sal-Solo, who shook his head. "I can't promise that we'll hit our target."

Everyone turned to Anakin.

And Anakin looked at Jacen and Ebrihim, who had his hand clamped over Q9's vocoder grille.

Jacen wanted to say something, but all words fled him. He had a sudden memory of Anakin from months earlier, practicing lightsaber technique in the hold of the *Falcon*.

"You keep thinking of it as a tool, a weapon in your war against everything you see as bad," Jacen had told him at the time.

"It's an instrument of law," Anakin had maintained.

"The Force isn't about waging war," Jacen had said. "It's about finding peace, and your place in the galaxy."

He set himself boldly between Sal-Solo and the console at which Anakin sat. "We can't be a part of this," he announced.

Thrackan peered around him at Anakin. "The First Fleet is being decimated, Anakin. The task force launched from Bothawui can't possibly arrive in time to help."

"The Tapani is our home sector," a Mrlssi said. "You must take the risk for our sake—as a Jedi must."

"It's our only chance to score a decisive victory," the colonel urged. He cut his eyes to the joystick Anakin had conjured. "It bears your imprint, Anakin. It answers to you and no one else."

"Anakin, you can't," Jacen said, wide-eyed. "Step away from it. Step away from it now."

Anakin glanced from his brother to the controls before him. Not through the Force but through Centerpoint itself, he could sense his distant targets. He felt as wedded to the repulsor as he often felt to his lightsaber, and he knew with the same conviction precisely when and how to strike.

TWENTY-SEVEN

Lightsabers clenched in two-handed grips, Kyp and Ganner approached the chamber in which Wurth Skidder was apparently being held. The absence of guards in the dark and humid corridor had Kyp thinking otherwise, but no sooner had his lightsaber coaxed the chamber's portal to open than he caught sight of Skidder. And immediately he grasped what the captive—Roa—had meant by saying that Skidder wasn't likely to be his old self.

Stripped naked, he was lying faceup on the floor with his legs bent backward at the knees and his arms extended beyond his head. Surrounding him—and plainly responsible for the cartilaginous growths that wedded him to the deck at knees, insteps, shoulders, elbows, and wrists—were a dozen or so crablike creatures, a few of whom managed to skitter to safety before Kyp's and Ganner's lightsabers could be brought to bear on them. The screeching others were cleaved and dismembered, their legs and pincers flung to all quarters of the hold.

Kneeling, Kyp wedged his hand under Wurth's neck and gently lifted his head. Skidder groaned in agony, but his eyes fluttered open.

"You're the last person I expected to see here," he rasped.

Kyp made himself smile. "You think we'd let you execute this mission on your own?"

Skidder licked his lips to wet them. "How did you find me?"

"The Hutts got a message to us through one of their smugglers."

Skidder's eyebrows beetled in puzzlement. "I thought they'd joined the opposition."

"I guess they've seen the light."

"That's good to hear," Skidder said in genuine relief. He glanced at Ganner, then added, "I sensed you when you attacked the ship before it jumped."

"That was at Kalarba," Ganner said.

"Where are we now?"

"Fondor."

Skidder showed them a startled look. "Why—"

"Fondor was always the target," Kyp said. "The fleet has been caught by surprise."

Skidder shut his eyes and nodded. "I tried to learn our destination—the yammosk's destination."

Kyp compressed his lips before replying. "We managed to cripple the ship before it made planetfall, but the Yuuzhan Vong are prevailing even without the war coordinator."

"There are captives aboard," Skidder said, as if suddenly remembering. "The plan was to familiarize the yammosk with our thought patterns—"

"We've got them," Ganner cut him off. "Deak and some of the others are with them. Now we just have to see about freeing you."

Wurth laughed, shortly and bitterly. "Chine-kal promised to break me, and he has."

"Chine-kal?"

"The ship's commander." Skidder's face contorted and he moaned in pain.

Concealing his hopelessness, Kyp took a closer look at the surge-coral protrusions that anchored Wurth to the pliant deck. "Our lightsabers should make short work of these," he started to say, when Wurth shook his head violently.

"There isn't time. You have to leave."

Kyp looked hard into his comrade's eyes. "I won't leave you, Wurth. We'll find a way to help you. The Force—"

"Look at me," Skidder interrupted firmly. "Look at me through the Force. I'm dying, Kyp. You can't help me."

Kyp opened his mouth to reply, but instead loosed a resigned sigh.

Skidder smiled with his eyes. "I'm prepared, Kyp. I'm ready to die. But there are two things I need you to do before you leave this ship."

Kyp nodded grimly and leaned his ear closer to his friend's mouth.

"Randa and Chine-kal," Wurth managed to say. "Find them."

Alone in the *Falcon*'s cockpit, Han had one hand gripped on the yoke and the other on the servo that operated the dorsal quad laser. Triggering staccato bursts from the weapon, he blew away two approaching coral-skippers. From somewhere behind the *Falcon* a third skip vectored in on a strafing run against the shipyard, but before Han could even swivel the gun turret, the enemy craft was pulverized by fire from one of the battered X-wings that flew with Kyp's Dozen.

"Good shooting," Han said into the mouthpiece of his headset.

"Thanks, *Falcon*," the voice of the ship's female pilot came back. "You soften them up, I'll put them away."

"Will do," Han told her.

He brought the *Falcon* about to recon the Rimward side of the empty yard in which the Ruan refugees had been marooned. Below, Droma, the second fighter pilot, and some of the pirates were organizing the recovery, with the *Trevee* berthed where a construction barge or tender might have anchored if the facility had been operational. With the Yuuzhan Vong fleet continuing to encroach on Fondor, the Tholatin crew—reluctant rescuers early on—were suddenly desperate to wrap the mission and launch for clear space.

Noise crackled from the cockpit annunciators, and a grainy video image of Droma appeared on the comm display screen.

"Han, the *Trevee* is loading, but fifty or so folks are still unaccounted for. Apparently they figured they could escape detection by hiding out."

Behind Droma, grinning broadly, were clustered some ten other Ryn, including the two he had introduced earlier as Gaph and Melisma. Melisma was now cradling a Ryn infant in her arms.

"You can't hide from plasma," Han barked toward the audio pickup.

Droma nodded. "We'll search them out."

"Yeah, well, don't waste any time. Looks like a Yuuzhan Vong carrier escort has taken a sudden interest in the place."

Droma nodded and signed off.

As the *Falcon* came full circle around the shipyard, the *Trevee* once more loomed large in the forward viewport. The transport's hyperdrive was ruined, but the sublight drives were more than capable of moving the ship out past the enemy fleet—providing it got away in time.

Even as Han was thinking it, the Yuuzhan Vong carrier escort hove into view off to port, keen on targeting the shipyard with the projectile launchers concealed in its pitted starboard bow.

Han throttled the *Falcon* toward the intruder, firing steadily, but the escort was too resolved on destroying the shipyard to be bothered by a lone assailant. Just then, though, the X-wing appeared on the scene, succeeding in getting the escort's attention with two well-placed proton torpedoes that impacted against its blunt nose.

Han banked harder to port, racing the *Falcon* through a storm of flaming projectiles to come to the fighter's support, but he failed to arrive in time. Plasma gushed from the escort and caught the X-wing just as it was breaking off from its reckless run. Wingtip lasers and stabilizers melted like candle wax, and the pilot lost control. Trailing gobs of solidifying alloy, the fighter went into a crazed roll, splitting apart before perishing in a fiery explosion.

Han's eyes narrowed in hatred. "Nobody takes out my wingmate."

Whipping the *Falcon* around, he went for the escort with the quad lasers blazing. Chunks of yorik coral exploded outward from the ship, and a thick blade of flame streaked into space. The ship rolled to one side like a wounded beast. At the same time, the comm screen came to life.

"We're away," Droma said. "Aiming for clear skies."

Han powered the *Falcon* through an ascending loop, then veered off to starboard, glimpsing the *Trevee* and its fighter companion just as they were accelerating from the threatened facility. The dying escort spotted them, as well. Missiles sought the fleeing vessels, but the escort reserved the bulk of its barrage for the shipyard itself. Punctured throughout by projectiles, the facility began to disintegrate, then it blew apart, unfurling flames that scorched the tail of the accelerating transport. Then the escort, too, disappeared in a flash of blinding light.

"You have my word that I will devote the remainder of my days to repaying the debt I have this day incurred," Randa bellowed in Basic as he trailed Kyp and Ganner through the clustership, the slapping sounds of his muscular tail loud in the passageway.

"Thank Skidder, Randa," Kyp said over his shoulder. "If it'd been up to me, I would have left you with your dead toadies."

"Then I will repay the debt in honor of Skidder," Randa said, unfazed. "You will see."

As it happened, the two Jedi didn't have long to wait. Rounding a corner in the passageway, they found themselves faced with a phalanx of Yuuzhan Vong warriors, into whose midst Randa charged, knocking half a dozen aside before any of those left standing could land blows against the Hutt's mostly impervious hide. Kyp and Ganner followed up the brash offensive, felling their opponents with precise strikes to susceptible spots in the warriors' armor.

The three of them fought their way toward an enormous maw in the bulkhead, from beyond which emanated a stench even more pungent than that given off by Randa. Inside the vast chamber, encircled by attendants who clearly had meager familiarity with the coufees they brandished, stood a Yuuzhan Vong commander, a long cloak hanging from his transmogrified shoulders and a villip communicator in his hands. Behind them, raised up on tensed tentacles in a circular tank of foul-smelling liquid, was a maturing yammosk, a large tooth glistening in its rictus of a mouth and its massive black eyes riveted on the intruders.

Again Randa rushed forward, flattening several of the attendants and whipping his tail around to whack the villip out of the commander's hands. The attendants began what would have been a fruitless defense, but the commander ordered them to lower their weapons.

"I congratulate you on getting this far," he said after two of the attendants had helped him back to his feet.

Kyp angled his lightsaber to one side, the blade extended in front of him. "Move out of the way and we'll go the rest of the distance."

Chine-kal turned slightly to glance at the yammosk. "Of course. The life of a yammosk for that of a Jedi. It strikes me as equitable."

From off to Kyp's left, Ganner hurled his ignited lightsaber square into the creature's left eye. As the sulfurous-yellow energy blade struck, the yammosk shrieked and its tentacles flailed, generating waves that cascaded down over the yorik-coral retaining wall of the pool and washed across the deck. The yammosk reared up and began to sway from side to side. Gradually the tentacles stopped moving, and the creature sank down into the tank, dead by the time Ganner called the lightsaber back to him.

Chine-kal's sadness endured for only a moment. "Well executed, Jedi. But you have doomed us all."

A shudder passed through the ship even as the words were leaving his mouth.

"The yammosk controls the ship," Randa explained. "The pilot dovin basals are now in the throes of death."

Chine-kal grinned faintly. "No one gets out of here alive."

Kyp returned the grin. "This won't be the first time you've misjudged a situation, Commander." He scanned the attendants, then set his gaze on Chine-kal. "Any or all of you are free to come with us." When it was obvious that none of them were going to budge, Kyp shrugged. "Suit yourselves."

He backed into the passageway, Ganner to one side, Randa to the other. Another death-throe spasm sent the three of them pitching against the bulkheads. Regaining his balance, Kyp started off the way they had come, but Randa stopped him.

"I know a more direct route."

They had just entered an adjacent module when Kyp's comlink toned.

"What's your situation, Kyp?"

Kyp recognized Han Solo's voice. "We're outward bound. The ship's destroying itself."

"A splinter group of Yuuzhan Vong warships are on their way. Not much chance of our holding them off."

"Then don't risk it."

"Somehow I knew you'd say that. Where are the captives?"

"They're being moved to the module we punched through."

"How many?"

"One hundred, give or take a few."

Solo muttered something. "The *Trevee* is defenseless. We'll have to cram everyone aboard the *Falcon*."

"Can you bring the *Falcon* close enough to extend a cofferdam?"

Han snorted. "That's the least of our problems."

"There's an airlock in the central module, but from the outside you probably won't be able to identify it. Look for our signal flare. Otherwise, I'll have Deak or someone lead you to it."

"Don't worry, I'll find it."

"Somehow I knew you'd say that," Kyp said. "By the way, can you accommodate a Hutt?"

Solo launched a surprised laugh. "A Hutt? Sure, the more the merrier."

"Then you'll be glad to hear that one of the captives asked me to send his regards."

"Who?"

"Roa."

"Take the shot!" Sal-Solo hissed through his clenched teeth. "Take it!"

"For the Mrlssi," a more plaintive voice added.

"For the sake of the New Republic," the captain said.

"No, my boy, no," Ebrihim and Q9 said.

As many voices vied for prominence in Anakin's mind as in the control room. He heard the heartfelt words of his mother and father, the harsh voice of Jacen and the understanding voice of Jaina, the counsel of Uncle Luke . . .

Anakin ignored all of them and looked at Jacen. "Tell me," he said.

Jacen responded quietly and calmly, almost as if he had subvocalized the response. "You are my brother, and you are a Jedi, Anakin. You can't do this."

Anakin took a deep breath and moved his hand away from the handgrip trigger. The tension in the room broke with a collective exhalation of disappointment. The technicians grumbled and the Mrlssi hung their heads in defeat. The next thing Anakin knew, someone had shoved him forcibly from the control seat.

"I'll take the shot," Thrackan Sal-Solo shouted angrily as his hand closed on the trigger.

Led by the *Yald,* the task force from Commenor decanted outside the orbit of Fondor's outermost moon. Following them into realspace came the Battle Dragons and battle cruisers that made up the Hapan fleet, positioned to engage the Yuuzhan Vong armada at close range.

Commodore Brand had allowed Leia to join him on the bridge, where she stood just behind his command chair, gazing through the wraparound viewport at the reverting Hapan warships. Closer to Fondor, explosions flared in the night as vessels and shipyards succumbed to the enemy onslaught.

"Fleet command and control reports casualties in excess of 50 percent," an enlisted-rating updated from his duty station. "Some of the shipyards are managing to defend against coralskipper suicide strikes, but the fleet has been unable to attenuate bombardment from the enemy warships."

Brand swiveled his chair to study various threat-assessor displays and vertical plotting panels. "The Hapans will put the fear into those warships," he assured in a voice loud enough to be heard throughout the bridge.

Leia hid her trembling right hand beneath her cloak and cut her eyes from the viewport to the plotting panels. She reached out with the Force for Anakin and Jacen. Where earlier the effort had only increased the gravity of her distress, she now experienced relief. A transcendent calm enveloped her, and the apprehension she had known since Hapes was suddenly gone.

But the serenity was fleeting. Almost instantly something raw and uncontrollable flooded into her awareness. Again she reached for Anakin and Jacen, and at once realized that her concerns for them had dammed a deeper though less personalized fear, which suddenly rushed in.

She swung to the viewport to see the Hapan fleet forming up into battle groups and already beginning to close with individual enemy warships.

"You may fire when ready," she heard Brand telling Prince Isolder, but as if at some great distance.

All at once, a flash of radiant energy illuminated local space. From Rimward of Fondor's outermost moon, or perhaps gushed from hyperspace itself, came a torrent of starfire a thousand kilometers wide. Coalescing into a savage beam of focused annihilation, it tore into the midst of the dispersing Hapan fleet, consuming every ship in its path, atomizing some in the blink of an eye and holing others with spears of seething light. Weapons, superstructure, and antennae vaporized by the skewering beam, the ships exploded outward, vanishing in globes of brilliant mass-energy conversions. Even those ships outside the limits of the beam were hurled violently off course, slagged along their inward-facing sides, or thrown into collisions with one another. The mated saucers of the Battle Dragons broke apart and disintegrated, and the battle cruisers were snapped like twigs. Fighter groups vanished without a trace.

Leia was dumbfounded. Nothing in the Yuuzhan Vong arsenal had prepared her for devastation on so immense a scale. For a moment she was certain she was in the grips of another terrible vision, but it quickly became clear that the violence was real.

Her stupefaction deepened when the beam didn't diminish as it punched through the Hapan fleet. Lancing deeper into Fondor space, the shaft of raging power went on to graze Fondor's penultimate moon, effacing a portion of the cratered planetoid as a surgical laser might a tumor. Then it ripped unabated into the heart of the enemy armada, obliterating masses of coralskippers and pulverizing several of the largest warships. Finished with its work or not, the beam then shot past Fondor, singeing the northern hemisphere in its passing, perhaps to destroy some even more distant target.

All systems had failed on the bridge, and for a long moment, even as consoles and display screens flickered back to life under emergency power, everyone was simply too stunned to speak or cry out, much less make sense of what they had just witnessed.

"Some sort of repulsor beam," a tech finally said in a stark disbelief. "Delivered through hyperspace."

"Centerpoint," Leia said, as if in shock.

Brand and several others turned to her.

She looked at the commodore. "Someone fired Centerpoint Station."

Han embraced Roa as he came through the airlock in the *Falcon*'s port-side docking arm.

"Fasgo's dead," Roa said when Han let him go.

Han shook his head in dismay. "He could have been a friend."

"As I was saying on the *Jubilee Wheel*, fortune smiles, then betrays . . . then smiles once more."

Han ran his eyes over his friend and managed a grin. "You know, you don't look half bad."

"The half that does I'll have repaired. Did my ship survive?"

"Waiting for you at Bilbringi."

Roa loosed a sigh and turned to help a Ryn female out of the airlock. "Han, I'd like you to meet—"

"Any chance you have a clanmate named Droma?" Han interrupted.

The female looked surprised. "I have a brother named Droma."

Han's grin broadened. "You'll be seeing him soon enough."

Roa scratched his head. "Seems I've a lot to catch up on."

"That doesn't begin to say it."

The clustership was already beginning to come apart. Han's fear that he might have to separate prematurely from the trembling ship only made him work harder at getting all the rescued captives aboard. By the time the last of them boarded, the forward hold, bunk rooms, galley, and utility spaces were packed. Han could only hope that the *Falcon*'s air scrubbers would hold out long enough to sustain everyone through a jump to Mrlsst or elsewhere in the Tapani sector. Even assuming that life support continued to function, they were going to be a hungry, dehydrated lot when and wherever they ultimately touched down.

With the airlock resealed, Han, Roa, and two of the Ryn threaded their way to the cockpit. Han squeezed into the pilot's seat and began to maneuver the *Falcon* away from the Yuuzhan Vong vessel. Through the forward viewport he could see what remained of Kyp's Dozen launching through the hole they had blown in the ruined module.

Roa helped bring the quad lasers on line as Han nosed the *Falcon* over the top of the spherical module, expecting to have to engage the enemy warships that had broken from the armada to render aid to the crippled yammosk vessel. Instead he was greeted by a sight that tugged a gleeful cry from him.

"Hapan Battle Dragons!" he said, glancing at Roa. "Now we're getting somewhere."

He was about to add that Leia had more than likely been responsible for enlisting the Hapans' support when an intense, white radiance blinded him. The *Falcon* died, then was tossed through an end-over-end ride that deposited her two thousand kilometers from where she had been.

The Yuuzhan Vong had coaxed Fondor's sun to go nova, Han told himself. They had wiped out the entire system.

When his vision returned and the moans and groans of his tumbled cargo had died down, Han saw that three-fourths of the Hapan fleet and half the Yuuzhan Vong armada were gone.

On his helix flagship, Nas Choka recaptured enough of his self-control to keep some of the dismay out of the incredulous look he showed Malik Carr and Nom Anor. Against the backdrop of a razed moon, the villip-choir field showed the blackened skeletons and husks of untold numbers of Yuuzhan Vong and enemy ships.

"They killed most of their reinforcements to eliminate half of our force," the supreme commander said. "Is such savagery commonplace?"

Nom Anor shook his head, as much in response as to clear it. "A mistake. It has to be a mistake. Their reverence for life has always been their weakness."

"Then perhaps we've managed to bring out the primitive in them," Malik Carr said in a stunned voice.

A herald appeared. The villip in his trembling hands bore the strained features of Chine-kal.

"The yammosk has been killed," Chine-kal gasped through his communicator, "and the ship is dying. The Hutts betrayed our location to the Jedi. The Jedi captured on Gyndine will die with us, but two of his confederates and Randa Besadii Diori—the murderers of the yammosk—escaped. We—"

The villip fell silent suddenly, then everted to its featureless form. Chine-kal was dead.

Nas Choka turned away in disgust. "Recall all operational coralskippers," he instructed his subaltern. "Order the rest to commit what destruction they can. All warship commanders will prepare their ships for departure. We have accomplished what we set out to do. Now we have a score to settle with the Hutts."

TWENTY-EIGHT

Viqi Shesh sat regally in the straight-backed chair at the center of the deposition balcony, adjusting the fall of her long skirt while Gotal Senator Ta'laam Ranth, head of the Senate Justice Council, studied the display of the personal data device he wore on his left wrist. Shesh's trio of lawyers occupied the table behind her, but they weren't included in the twice-normal-size hologram of Shesh that commanded the attention of the amphitheater's capacity crowd. As a consideration to Ranth, the recording droids normally present at closed-session senatorial inquests had been sequestered in a separate room, to assure that their energy output didn't overwhelm the Gotal's acute senses.

"Senator Shesh," the furred and flat-nosed Ranth resumed at last, "it has already been established that the Advisory Council was briefed by Commodore Brand regarding the eventual deployment of the *Yald* flotilla, and that Commodore Brand, speaking for the Defense Force command staff, stated at the time that Corellia was assumed to have been targeted for attack."

"That's true," Shesh said in a composed voice.

"Then how is it, Senator, that the flotilla wound up being deployed at Bothawui?"

Shesh set her interlocked hands in her lap and lifted

her chin slightly. "Commodore Brand failed to make a convincing case for deploying the flotilla at Corellia, so the matter was put to a vote."

"In his written statement, Chief of State Fey'lya asserts as much," Ranth said in the monotone that was characteristic of his species. "But we now know that it was never the intention of the command staff to argue too strongly in favor of Corellia."

Shesh nodded. "As I understand it, Admiral Sovv's plan called for the enemy to be lured into the Corellian sector by leaving Corellia undefended. Deploying the flotilla there would have compromised the admiral's strategy."

Ranth's pair of conelike sensory horns twitched. "In other words, what passed for a briefing was more in the way of a manipulation."

The most well-tailored of Shesh's human lawyers objected. "Senator Shesh has been asked to provide an account of the briefing, not to pass judgment on the tactics or methods of the New Republic Defense Force."

The five members of the chamber's mixed-species tribunal conferred and sustained the objection. Ranth was clearly disappointed but forged ahead.

"Senator Shesh, was yours in fact the vote that swayed the council?"

"My vote broke the deadlock, if that's what you mean."

"What convinced you that Bothawui would be targeted?"

"It would be more accurate to say that I didn't believe Corellia would be attacked."

"Why was that?"

"I didn't accept that the Yuuzhan Vong were prepared to launch an attack on the Core."

"Was Fondor mentioned as a possible target?"

"It was not."

"Had Fondor been mentioned, how might you have voted?"

The same lawyer objected, but Ranth quickly waved his furred hand in dismissal. "I withdraw the question." He approached the deposition balcony. "Did you have occasion to meet with the command staff prior to the briefing on Corellia?"

Shesh nodded again. "I did. Several days prior to the briefing I met with Commodore Brand, who asked me to speak with Consul General Golga before he departed for Nal Hutta."

"Did you meet with Golga?"

"Soon after."

"What was the nature of your discussion with the Hutt consul general?"

"We discussed the separate peace the Hutts had forged with the Yuuzhan Vong, and the possibility of their furnishing intelligence to the New Republic."

"Did Consul General Golga indicate at the time that the Hutts might be inclined to provide such intelligence?"

"He implied as much, yes."

"And you were willing to accept him at his word, even though the Hutts were considered to have allied themselves with the enemy?"

"Objection," another of Shesh's lawyers barked. "It has been demonstrated that the Hutts attempted to supply intelligence by renewing spice shipments to Bothawui when it was still being considered a potential target."

Ranth swung to the tribunal. "And by so doing, the Hutts only reinforced the belief that Corellia would be targeted instead."

The tribunal's Mon Calamari chief looked at Viqi Shesh. "Senator, do you wish to answer Senator Ranth's question?"

Shesh smiled faintly. "I can only conclude that the Hutts were trying to keep their options open. I also believe that the Yuuzhan Vong were well aware of the possibility that the Hutts might attempt to leak intelligence to us, and that they exploited the possibility as a means of orchestrating the events that ensued. The fact that Nal Hutta is now bracing for an invasion suggests that Borga was more dupe than conspirator."

The Mon Calamari nodded and fixed one eye on Ranth. "The Hutts are not the subject of this inquest, Senator. Can you show good cause for pursuing this line of questioning?"

Ranth inclined his head, gazing at the tribunal from beneath his jutting brow. "I am merely trying to establish the sequence of events that led to the sneak attack on Fondor."

"Proceed," the Mon Calamari told him.

Ranth turned to Shesh. "Senator, early on, the command staff's suppositions about Corellia were bolstered by information regarding the scarcity of spice in certain planetary systems. Chief of State Fey'lya asserts that the Advisory Council was aware that the information had been supplied by Talon Karrde and the Jedi Knights."

"We were so informed."

"Can you think of any reason why former Imperial Remnant liaison Talon Karrde or the Jedi Knights might have wished to mislead the Defense Force?"

The lawyer nearest Shesh shot to his feet. "Objection. Calls for speculation."

"No, I'll answer it," Shesh countered. "I don't for a

moment accept that either Talon Karrde or the Jedi were trying to mislead us."

The Gotal studied her. "Are you suggesting that they were also manipulated by the enemy?"

Shesh straightened in the chair. "I'm suggesting, Senator, that the Jedi are not infallible, and that we shouldn't look to them as saviors. For all anyone knows, the Yuuzhan Vong have brought to our galaxy a power superior to even that of the Force."

On a hover platform close to where the Justice Council was convened, Isolder's former bodyguard, Astarta, opened the hatch to the prince's personal quarters aboard the shuttle that was to return the Hapans to the Battle Dragon *Song of War*, just then in stationary orbit above Coruscant. Astarta showed Leia her most barbed glare before leaving the two of them alone.

Isolder was standing at the cabin's broad viewport, his back turned to the hatch. In the aftermath of the Battle of Fondor, events had conspired to prevent them from seeing each other for almost two weeks, and the *Song of War* was scheduled to launch for Hapes later that day.

Leia waited for him to turn from the view of Coruscant's impossibly tall towers before moving toward him, but the pained expression on his face brought her to a halt after only two steps.

"Isolder, I'm so sorry," she blurted, eyes brimming with tears.

He compressed his lips, biting back whatever he had in mind to say, then sighed deeply. "Leia, we spoke of this before the fleet left Hapes. I told you then that I would never hold you accountable for any untoward outcome. We knew what we were risking by going to war."

Having expected him to say just that, Leia nodded silently.

Frowning, Isolder stepped away from the viewport to regard her. "But you knew what was going to happen. You sensed it."

Leia let out her breath. "I sensed some tragedy in the making, but I didn't know when or where, or even if it would transpire. I knew that some of what I was feeling owed to concerns for my children. But I couldn't separate those from sudden doubts about having brought you into this, or about Commodore Brand's strategy for Corellia."

Unable to continue, she shook her head mournfully.

Isolder glanced away from her for a moment. "I've been asking myself if it would be easier to have been defeated by the Yuuzhan Vong rather than by misdirected fire from a weapon we didn't even know existed."

"A weapon enabled by Anakin," Leia said quietly.

"Who also refused to fire it," Isolder was quick to point out. "Leia, you must understand, we accept what has happened to us, without hostility or regret."

She held his sad gaze. "What will happen now?"

He ran his hand over his mouth. "Well, I don't anticipate a triumphant homecoming. The Consortium has split along lines dictated by the vote that landed us here. The naysayers have declared a victory, despite the fact that we have all suffered a dreadful loss. They're calling for a policy of isolation—as if the Transitory Mists alone will be able to protect us from the long reach of the Yuuzhan Vong."

Leia nodded. "A similar rift has occurred in the New Republic Senate. The sneak attack on Fondor has galvanized the Core Worlds into preparing for the worst, but at the expense of alienating many of the Inner Rim worlds. Support for Fey'lya has been shaken, and the senate will probably demote or demand resignations from Commodore Brand and Admiral Sovv, even though they are desperately needed."

Isolder considered it. "That is the difference between the Consortium and the New Republic, perhaps between the old and new ways. Representatives of the New Republic are free to express their outrage without fear of breaching decorum or provoking an honor duel." Isolder snorted a self-deprecating laugh. "I don't know which is the best method of governing, but I know that the Hapans will put on a brave front. Already the people of my world are saying that our fleet, though destroyed, saved the day for Fondor and the New Republic."

"And you would have."

Isolder shook his head. "That is unknown. But we will at our next engagement with the Yuuzhan Vong. I'm sure of that now, because we are compelled to make the deaths suffered at Fondor count for something."

"You'll at least have the quick-recharge weapons technology Archon Thane wanted," Leia said.

Isolder worked his jaw. "Scarcely a consolation, but it will have to suffice." He looked at Leia. "War benefits those who devise ever more expedient methods of destruction. Let us hope we can outmaster the Yuuzhan Vong at their own game."

Perched on the edge of his father's favorite chair in their apartment on Coruscant, Jacen watched in dismay as a 3-D image of Thrackan Sal-Solo took shape above the HoloNet well. The voice of the Sullustan news anchor continued.

"Former head of the so-called Human League, Thrackan Sal-Solo is being credited with turning the tide at the

Battle of Fondor. While scores of New Republic warships were destroyed in the Yuuzhan Vong's sneak attack
on Fondor's orbital construction facilities, Sal-Solo's
bold use of a hyperspace repulsor beam not only drove
the invaders into retreat but destroyed a significant portion of their fleet."

The well projected an image of Centerpoint Station.
"The repulsor beam was fired from Centerpoint Station, in the Corellian system, which, ironically, was used
eight years ago during Corellia's unsuccessful bid for independence from the New Republic. One of the many
arrested for fomenting that crisis, Sal-Solo was released
from prison to assist in rearming the station, and there
are unconfirmed reports that he was the only one willing
to assume the risk of triggering the weapon against the
enemy fleet.

"As to what's next for Sal-Solo or Centerpoint, that
depends on whom you ask. With a vote of no confidence
looming for Governor-General Marcha, Duchess of
Mastigophorous, some feel that Sal-Solo will be re-
cruited to head the newly formed Centerpoint Party,
which advocates independence for the five worlds that
comprise the Corellian system. Centerpoint Station itself
remains in the hands of the New Republic, but whether it
will—or indeed *can*—be employed again as a long-range
weapon depends largely on how successful Coruscant
is at justifying the secondary destruction suffered at
Fondor by the Hapan fleet."

The images of Sal-Solo and Centerpoint began to
derezz, and the head and upper torso of the Sullustan
news anchor reappeared.

"In other news, a protest demonstration on Ruan,
mounted by a group of recalcitrant droids—"

"You ever going to get tired of listening to reports

about Corellia?" Anakin interrupted from the doorway to the family room. "We turned *Cousin* Thrackan into a hero. What else needs to be said?"

Jacen silenced the HoloNet. "Cheer up. At least this report didn't mention us by name."

Anakin scowled. "Good. Now all we have to do is hope that Dad doesn't hear about it."

"Since when does Dad care about the news? Besides, you're the one the HoloNet should be calling a hero."

"For what—enabling Centerpoint?"

"No, for not triggering it. That's what'll make Dad and Uncle Luke and anyone else who knows the full story proud of you."

Anakin snorted a laugh and shook his head. "You still don't get it." He stared at his brother. "I could have fired Centerpoint without hitting the Hapans. I saw it all, Jacen—in my head. I would have known where to direct the repulsor beam, and precisely when to fire. I even knew that Glowpoint wasn't going to annihilate everyone in Hollowtown."

"Then why didn't you fire? What stopped you?"

"You mean aside from your telling me not to?"

Jacen's brows knitted in concern. "You were that sure of yourself?"

"Yeah, I was. And my actions would have been defensive. If someone is aiming a blaster at your ally, do you raise your lightsaber to prevent it, or do you do nothing because a Jedi isn't supposed to take aggressive action? I mean, where's the line, Jacen? We're in a war for survival, and defense sometimes means having to eliminate the opposition."

Jacen shook his head. "I don't know where the line is, and I promised myself on Ithor that I'd stop trying to look for it. I just think there has to be some other way of responding—without having to raise a sword to deflect one raised against you."

Anakin smirked. "Well, when you figure it out, I hope you'll let me in on it."

Jacen looked up at him. "Oh, I will, brother. You can count on that."

As they had done on Karrde's previous visit to Yavin 4, Luke and Talon followed the winding path to the Great Temple.

"All I managed to do was place the Jedi in a worse position with the New Republic Senate and military," Karrde was saying. "That's why I felt I had to apologize in person."

"No one is expecting an apology," Luke told him. "If actions were always judged by their consequence, we'd spend half our lives making amends. You came to us with a plan, and we went along with it. We're partners in the outcome."

Karrde looked skeptical. "Unfortunately, that kind of reasoning doesn't go far with Borsk Fey'lya and his allies. As happened after Ithor, they need someone to blame for what happened at Fondor, and I've set the Jedi up as the perfect fall guys."

Luke took a moment to respond. When he had first learned of the events at Fondor, he had felt betrayed— not by Karrde so much as by the Force. Almost as betrayed as he'd felt when Obi-Wan Kenobi and Yoda had conspired to keep secret the real identity of his father. But the sense of betrayal had passed through him in an instant. The Force hadn't concealed anything from him; he had simply misunderstood that it was the Yuuzhan Vong rather than the Jedi who were employing deception, stealth, and misdirection. What continued to bother him, though, was the possibility that the mere presence of the Yuuzhan Vong was enough to mute the clarity of the Force.

"Success and failure are sometimes intertwined," Luke said finally. "Inadvertently or not, the Hutts misled us. But it was their information that allowed Kyp and Ganner to rescue those held captive aboard the yammosk vessel."

Karrde allowed a nod. "Everyone is too busy assigning blame to note the rescue of the captives or the destruction of the yammosk vessel. I'm only sorry that Kyp didn't arrive in time to save Skidder."

"Wurth made his choice on Gyndine."

Luke left it at that, choosing not to add that Skidder's sacrifice had widened the gulf between Kyp's faction and some of the other Jedi. Where Skidder had sought to avenge the deaths of Miko Reglia and Daeshara'cor, Kyp and those who stood by him now had Skidder's death to avenge.

"If the Hutts deliberately misled us, they were repaid in kind," Karrde said bitterly. "Fondor was one of the most profitable markets for the Besadii, and they lost some of their finest ships and most enterprising smugglers during the battle. Now Borga has to prepare for war with only half the clans supporting her and the rest holding her responsible for the Yuuzhan Vong's betrayal. Several clan leaders have decamped Nal Hutta for Ganath, Ylesia, even Tatooine, and with the Yuuzhan Vong fleet blockading Hutt space, the New Republic couldn't help even if it wanted to. Borga will be lucky if she doesn't birth her child prematurely."

Karrde came to a sudden halt in the middle of the path and swung to Luke. "Do you think the Yuuzhan Vong realize what they've accomplished? They've sundered the Hutts, created a schism in the senate, taken the Hapans out of the war, sabotaged the import of the Jedi." Before Luke could respond, he added, "Did you have any inkling it could end this way?"

Luke heard the voice of his former Jedi Master: *Always in motion is the future. Hard to see . . .*

"The future isn't fixed," he said. "It's made up of possibilities. I saw without seeing."

Karrde blew out his breath. "What can we do now?"

Decide you must how to serve them best. Help them you could. But you would destroy all for which they have fought and suffered.

Luke took Karrde by the shoulders. "We can learn from our mistakes."

Leia had raced home from the shuttle departure platform only to find that Anakin and Jacen had already left. Now, with Isolder's cheerless departure still on her mind and C-3PO and Olmahk helping her pack for an afternoon flight to Duro, the house comm system chirped, chirping insistently even after she had activated the answer-message function.

Throwing her hands up in a gesture of surrender, she accepted the call. Han's was the last face she expected to see appear on the display screen.

"It's just me," he said, smiling lopsidedly while she gaped at his image, feeling as if months had passed since they had spoken. The display showed that he was calling from an Abregado-rae space terminal.

"I see you shaved off your beard," she said finally.

He rubbed his chin. "Yeah, too itchy."

"Well, at least you look like your old self again."

He scowled, started to say something, then began again. "Grim business about what happened to the Hapans at Fondor. How's Isolder doing?"

"I figured you'd hear the news sooner or later—even in a playground like Abregado-rae."

"Hear about it?" Han said. "I *saw* it!"

"You what?"

"I was there—at Fondor."

"You were at Fondor," she echoed in disbelief.

"Droma and I were chasing after his clanmates. Some of them had managed to get themselves marooned in a deserted shipyard facility, and the rest were prisoners aboard a yammosk ship. Anyway, it's a long, boring story. The point is, I saw the Hapan fleet get wiped out. But I thought Fondor's primary went nova. I didn't know it was Centerpoint."

Leia pushed her hair back from her forehead. "You realize that Anakin and Jacen were there."

Han took his lower lip between his teeth. "Did they fire it?"

Leia's nostrils flared. "Do you think they'd do something like that?"

Han's brow furrowed. "Take it easy. You know I don't listen to the news."

Leia thought about telling him about Thrackan Sal-Solo's sudden rise to fame, but decided against it, knowing that Han would find out soon enough.

"Where did you bring the refugees you rescued?"

"Here. But they can't stay for long. Abregado-rae is pulling in the welcome mat."

Leia sighed. "SELCORE is searching for a world suitable for relocating everyone. We thought we were going to be able to count on Ruan, but Salliche Ag is suddenly refusing to accept any refugees."

Han averted his eyes momentarily. "About Ruan," he started to say.

"SELCORE is getting some unexpected help from

Senator Shesh," Leia went on. "I'll let you know as soon as I hear anything."

Han nodded. "Long as it's somewhere the Ryn won't be treated like riffraff."

"You have my word on it." Leia paused, then added, "Will Droma be remaining with his clanmates?"

"Yeah. The way I figure it, he and I are about even."

"So where does that leave you, Han?"

"I'm not sure. What about you—are you finally home for good?"

"I'm leaving this afternoon for Duro."

"Same old Princess Leia," he said with a sneer. "Then I guess it doesn't matter where I end up."

She narrowed her eyes for the cam. "Same old Han Solo."

He tried to lighten the moment with a laugh. "We are a pair, aren't we?"

"I don't know, Han. You tell me."

His eyes flashed. "Well, look, be sure to let me know what planet SELCORE decides on."

"Anything to help the refugees," Leia said with counterfeit good humor.

"That's what I've been saying all along."

Leia folded her arms. "In that case, our paths are bound to cross one of these days."

"I don't know, sweetheart, it's a big galaxy."

"Only as big as you make it," she said, deactivating the comm.

In her new office, Viqi Shesh watched a full-color 3-D recording of herself being interviewed by reporters as she had emerged from the closed-session inquest into the command staff's monumental blunder regarding Corellia and Fondor. Although she had been compelled to answer

"No comment" to most of the reporters' questions, she decided that she had carried herself well and had surely succeeded in stealing the limelight from Senator Ta'laam Ranth and others.

The holorecording was about to recycle when the intercom built into her greel-wood desk sounded a tone.

"Senator Shesh," her human secretary said, "there's a Pedric Cuf here to see you. He admits to not having an appointment, but he claims that you have been trying to contact him for the past few months."

Shesh zeroed the holoprojector and leaned back in her swivel chair. "I've been trying to contact him?"

"That's what he says."

When Shesh glanced at the holo display for the reception room, she saw a very tall and gaunt human smiling for the cam. "Send him in," she told her secretary.

Cuf entered the office a moment later, tendering a brief but dignified bow before settling into the armchair to which she waved him.

"I have long anticipated this meeting," he began in Core-accented Basic. "I had hoped to speak with you sooner, but I've been preoccupied with business matters in the Outer Rim and in Hutt space."

Shesh brought her interlaced hands to her lips and studied Cuf over the tops of her extended forefingers. "I trust that matters concluded to your satisfaction."

Cuf smiled without showing his teeth. "To be perfectly honest, my associates and I were recently taken somewhat by surprise by a hostile bid for power by a Corellian firm. But, otherwise, yes, everything has been working out to our satisfaction."

Shesh could feel the blood racing through her veins, but she managed to keep her composure. "Why have you come to see me now?"

"My superiors thought it a good idea that we become acquainted. To begin with, they wanted to thank you for your efforts of some months past, in seeing to it that some missing property was returned to us."

Cuf let the statement hang in the air. Shesh guessed that he was referring to Elan, the phony defector the Yuuzhan Vong had attempted to foist on the Jedi Knights, but she couldn't be certain that he wasn't a New Republic Intelligence agent, hoping to trick her into revealing her part in that affair or the Fondor calamity.

"I don't recall helping return any property to you," she said after a moment. "And to be frank, I don't recall attempting to contact you. Perhaps you have me confused with someone else."

Pedric Cuf stared at her. "I see. Well, perhaps I have made a mistake. It wouldn't be the first time a Hutt has led me astray."

"A Hutt," Shesh said.

Cuf laughed shortly. "And here I was, all set to launch into a discussion regarding the eventual disposition of"—he gestured broadly to the windows at Shesh's back—"all this." He stood up. "A pity we can't do business, Senator. I suspect we would have made a good team."

She watched him head for the door, then said, "Did I mention that I like your suit?"

He stopped and turned to her, his smile back in place. "Yes, it fits me like a glove, don't you think? Masks all my imperfections, truly allows me to blend in. I had it specially made by a company that's simply out of this world."

"Does the company produce a line of women's wear?"

"They offer an exquisite line. In fact, I'm certain they could supply you with outfits perfectly tailored to your needs." Cuf paused briefly. "That is, of course, if you might, on occasion, be willing to put business before politics."

Shesh waved Cuf back to the chair. "Politics is a practical profession," she said. "If someone has what you need, then you do business with him or you go without. And personally, I've always been more interested in business than I have in politics."

STAR WARS: THE NEW JEDI ORDER

The epic tale of invasion and adventure,
which began with
VECTOR PRIME by R. A. Salvatore,
continues:

**STAR WARS
The New Jedi Order
BALANCE POINT
by Kathy Tyers**

Coming soon to bookstores everywhere!

For a taste of BALANCE POINT,
please read on . . .

Jaina?

Joined through the Force even before they were born, he and Jaina had always been able to tell when the other was hurt or afraid. But for him to sense her over the distances that lay between them now, she must've been terribly—

The pain winked off.

"Jaina!" he whispered, appalled. "No!"

He stretched out toward her, trying to find her again. Barely aware of fuzzy shapes clustering around him, and a Ryn voice hooting for a medical droid, he felt as if he were shrinking—falling backwards into vacuum. He tried focusing deep inside and outside himself, to grab on to the Force and punch out—or slip into a healing trance. Could he take Jaina with him, if he did? Uncle Luke had taught him a dozen focusing techniques, back at the academy, and since then.

Jacen.

A voice seemed to echo in his mind, but it wasn't Jaina's. It was deep, male—vaguely like his uncle's.

Making an effort, Jacen imagined his uncle's face, trying to focus on that echo. An enormous white vortex seemed to spin around him. It pulled at him, drawing him toward its dazzling center.

What was going on?

Then he saw his uncle, robed in pure white, half turned away. Luke Skywalker held his shimmering lightsaber in a diagonal stance, hands at hip level, point high.

Jaina! Jacen shouted the words in his mind. *Uncle Luke, Jaina's been hurt!*

Then he saw what held his uncle's attention. In the dim distance, but clearly in focus, a second form straightened and darkened. Tall, humanoid, powerfully built, it had a face and chest covered with sinuous scars and tattoos above the waist. Its hips and legs were encased in rust-brown armor. Claws protruded from its heels and knuckles, and an ebony cloak flowed from its shoulders. The alien held a coal-black, snake-headed amphistaff across its body, mirroring the angle of Luke's lightsaber, pitting poisonous darkness against verdant light.

Utterly confused, Jacen stretched out through the Force. First he sensed the figure in white as a respected uncle—then abruptly as a powerful depth, blazing in the Force like a star gone nova. But across this slowly spinning disk, where Jacen's inner vision presented a Yuuzhan Vong warrior, his Force sense picked up nothing at all. Through the Force, all Yuuzhan Vong did seem utterly lifeless, like the technology they vilified.

The alien swung its amphistaff. The Jedi Master's lightsaber blazed, swept down, and blocked the swing, brightening until it washed out almost everything else in this vision. The Yuuzhan Vong's amphistaff seemed darker than any absence of light, a darkness that seemed alive but promised death.

The broad, spinning disk on which they both stood finally slowed. It focused into billions of stars. Jacen picked out the familiar map of known space.

Luke dropped into a fighting stance, poised near the galaxy's center, the Deep Core. He raised his lightsaber and held it high, near his right shoulder, pointing inward. From three points of darkness, beyond the Rim, tattooed assailants advanced.

More of them? Jacen realized this was a vision, not a battle unfolding in front of him, with little to do with his twin sister.

Or maybe everything to do with her! Did these new invaders symbolize other invasion forces, more worldships—besides the ones that were already beating back everything the New Republic could throw at them? Reaching out to Jaina, maybe he had tapped the Force itself—or maybe it broke through to him.

The galaxy seemed to teeter, poised between light and darkness. Luke stood close to the center, counterweighing the dark invaders.

But as their numbers increased, the balance tipped.

Uncle Luke, Jacen shouted. *What should I do?*

Luke turned away from the advancing Yuuzhan Vong. Looking to Jacen with somber intensity, he tossed his lightsaber. It flew in a low, humming arc, trailing pale green sparks onto the galactic plane.

Eyeing the advancing horde, Jacen felt another enemy try to seize him: anger, from deep in his heart. Fear and fury focused his strength. If he could, he would utterly destroy the Yuuzhan Vong and all they stood for! He opened a hand, stretched out his arm . . .

And missed.

The Jedi weapon sailed past him. As anger released

him, fear took a tighter hold. Jacen flailed, leapt, tried stretching out with the Force. Luke's lightsaber sailed on, shrinking and dimming with distance.

Now the galaxy tipped more quickly. A dark, deadly tempest gathered around the Yuuzhan Vong warriors. Disarmed, Luke stretched out both hands. First he, then his enemies, swelled to impossible sizes. Instead of human and alien figures, now Jacen saw light and darkness as entirely separate forces. Even the light terrified him in its grandeur and majesty. The galaxy seemed poised to plunge toward evil, but Jacen couldn't help staring at the fearful light, spellbound, burning his retinas.

A Jedi knows no fear . . . He'd heard that a thousand times, but this sensation was no cowardly urge to run. This was awe, it was reverence—a passionate longing to draw nearer. To serve the light and transmit its grandeur.

But compared to the forces battling around him, he was only a tiny point. Helpless and unarmed, besides—because of one moment's dark anger. Had that misstep doomed him? Not just him, but the galaxy?

A voice like Luke's, but deeper, shook the heavens. *Jacen,* it boomed. *Stand firm.*

The horizon tilted farther. Jacen lunged forward, determined to lend his small weight to Luke's side, to the light.

He misstepped. He flailed for Luke's hand, but missed again. And again, his weight fell slightly—by centimeters—toward the dark enemies.

Luke seized his hand and held tightly. *Hang on, Jacen!* The slope steepened under their feet. Stars extinguished. The Yuuzhan Vong warriors scrambled forward. Whole star clusters winked out, a dark cascade under clawed enemy feet.

Plainly, the strength of a hundred-odd Jedi couldn't keep the galaxy from falling to this menace. One misstep—

at one critical moment, by one pivotal person—could doom everyone they'd sworn to protect. No military force could stop this invasion, because it was a spiritual battle. And if one pivotal person fell to the dark side—or even used the ravishing, terrifying power of light in a wrong way—then this time, everything they knew might slide into stifling darkness.

Is that it? he cried toward the infinite distance.

Again, Jacen perceived the words in a voice that was utterly familiar but too deep to be Luke's. *Stand firm, Jacen.*

One of the Yuuzhan Vong leapt toward him. Jacen gasped and flung out both arms—